Angela Thirkell

Angela Thirkell, granddaughter of Edward Burne-Jones, was born in London in 1890. At the age of twenty-eight she moved to Melbourne, Australia where she became involved in broadcasting and was a frequent contributor to British periodicals. Mrs. Thirkell did not begin writing novels until her return to Britain in 1930; then, for the rest of her life, she produced a new book almost every year. Her stylish prose and deft portrayal of the human comedy in the imaginary county of Barsetshire have amused readers for decades. She died in 1961, just before her seventy-first birthday.

"A novel of wit and style in which at least three delightful heroines struggle separately through the wilderness to the promised land of marriage with a nice, solid man."

—*The New Yorker*

"The simple happenings in Barsetshire will go on indefinitely and somehow one just does not tire of the delightful life within the wall."

—*Library Journal*

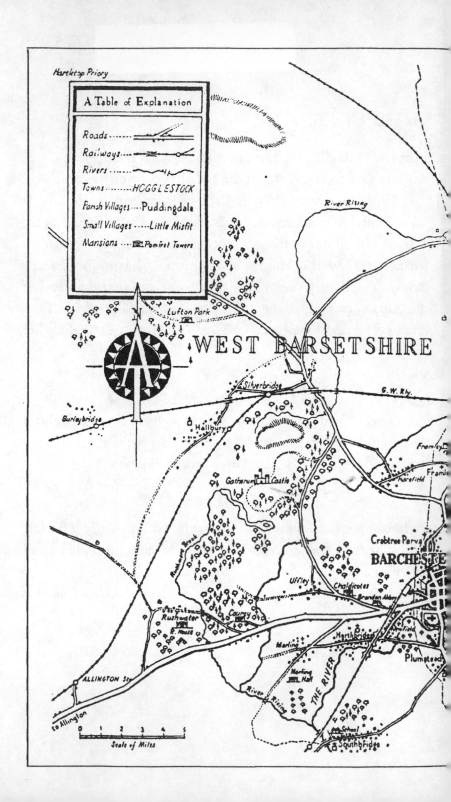

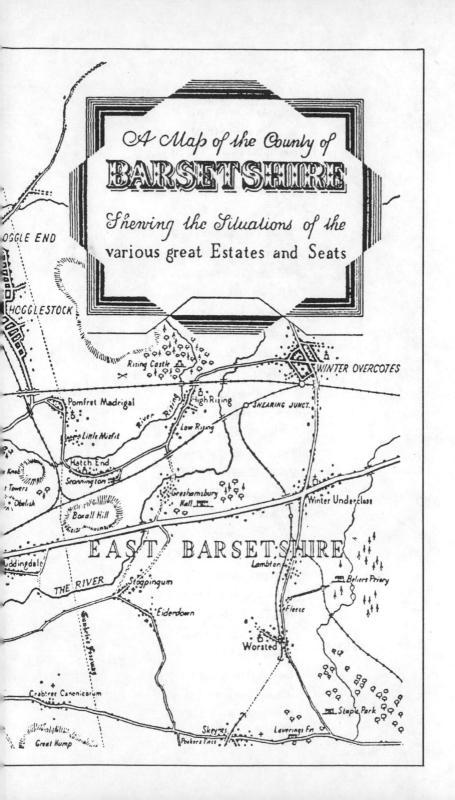

COUNTY
CHRONICLE

A Novel by

Angela Thirkell

MOYER BELL

Wakefield, Rhode Island & London

Published by Moyer Bell
This Edition 1998

Copyright © 1950 by Angela Thirkell
Published by arrangement with Hamish Hamilton, Ltd.

**LIBRARY OF CONGRESS
CATALOGING-IN-PUBLICATION DATA**

Thirkell, Angela Mackail, 1890–1961.
 County chronicle : a novel by
 Angela Thirkell. — 1st ed.
  p. cm.
 ISBN 1-55921-213-6
 I. Title.
 PR6039.H43C68   1998
 823'.912—dc21   97-31905
                         CIP

Cover illustration: Detail from *A Summer Afternoon*
by Frank Walton
Chapter illustrations from *Great Magazine Covers of the World*
by Patrick Frantz Kery

Printed in the United States of America
Distributed in North America by Publishers Group West, P.O. Box 8843,
Emeryville CA 94662, 800-788-3123 (in California 510-658-3453).

CHAPTER I

Miss Lucy Marling, as we all know, had a great deal of courage and a dogged perseverance that had helped her through many difficulties connected with the market gardening and farming ventures of her present employer and future husband, Mr. Adams. She was also the possessor of a hearty bellow which had so far never failed to penetrate her father's deafness whether natural (as indeed it was and not improving with age) or assumed, as his family had often known far too well and much to their annoyance. It was on Saturday evening in early autumn after a happy day of clearing out Mr. Adams's well that the rich ironmaster had asked her to be his wife. All that night she had slept heavily and dreamlessly. All through Sunday she moved in a kind of trance of quiet happiness, only disturbed by the thought that her parents must be told, for so far her happiness was so unexpected and overpowering that she did not know how to speak of it. She had not telephoned to Mr. Adams, nor expected him to telephone to her, but her parents must be told now lest the news might reach them from some other source. She reflected that it would be just like father to be at his most deliberately deaf when she had such important news to tell him and in spite of her courage it was not without a certain sinking of what is usually described as the heart but feels much more like the stomach that she zipped herself into a four year old house-coat, hit her face very ineffectively with a powder-puff (though it was alas! not a proper swansdown puff as They do not like us to have them but a nasty pad of orange-pink plush), scraped her hair with a comb and went into the dining-room prepared for battle. Her parents were not yet down. Lucy went to the window and looked over the lawn away to the farm and wondered if it was wicked to leave one's parents to whom one was so useful as to be almost a necessity. Horrid doubts assailed her, as indeed we believe they assail every nice young woman however deeply in love when the thought first strikes her that she is deserting for ever the roof and the elders who have fed and sheltered and cherished her, transferring her heart and her allegiance to strange gods. Thoughts of the garden and the farm, now for some years almost entirely under her capable and masterful rule, rose accusingly against her, making her feel hollow and causing her eyes to prick uncomfortably. What would her parents do without her? How would her father ever carry on with the farm? Vain fears, but Lucy though no child in years was very young in many ways and had not yet learnt the useful, comforting, though it must be confessed slightly mortifying lesson that no single one of us is indispensable. Then she thought of Mr. Adams; the smell of his country tweeds, her assurance of his devotion, his utter dependability, the bliss it had been when the foolish insignificant cloud between them had melted under his honesty and his affection; and she shook herself angrily and turned as her mother came into the room.

"Did Percy Bodger get the well done?" said Mrs. Marling.

"Yes, he made a good job of it," said Lucy, and Mrs. Marling, though she could not see her daughter's face against the westering light, wondered what had happened. The child—she might be nearly thirty but one's child is always a child to one—had not seemed happy of late. Mrs. Marling had said nothing, had not asked questions, but she saw her Lucy working fiercely and defiantly, early and late, and stood waiting to help if Lucy would allow her. "I'll tell you what though," Lucy continued, wearing a brave front in spite of a general sensation of being in an earthquake. "Mr. Adams said would I marry him. So I said Yes."

If there had been a garden path Mrs. Marling would undoubtedly have sat flat down in it; but being the dining-room she kept her feet and only said, "Oh, darling."

"And I hope you and father won't mind," said Lucy, almost nervously, "because I don't."

"My darling," said her mother again and having no other words at the moment she gave her daughter a very loving hug.

"Thanks most awfully," said Lucy, returning the hug with such vigour that her mother was nearly suffocated. "I knew you'd be pleased. He's really an angel."

As to this, Mrs. Marling felt she was not in a position to judge. She liked and respected the self-made ironmaster who had helped her husband by buying land and given her younger daughter a chance to see her undoubted gift for organising food production on a large scale, but to be asked so suddenly to accept him as a son-in-law was not easy. Then she remembered that there is one thing one can always do for one's children. One can stand by them whatever happens: whether your son marries a duke's daughter with a hundred thousand pounds or forges a cheque, whether your daughter remains at home working for everyone or suddenly elects to marry right outside her class a man whom one has grown to like and respect but never—let us be frank—considered as one of one's own kind.

Her hesitation was over almost at once and whether Lucy noticed it we cannot say.

"If you love him, I shall love him too," said Mrs. Marling firmly and so dazed was Lucy by the strange turn in her affairs that she gratefully accepted her mother's assurance and they had another very happy, slightly tearful hug.

"I knew you'd be pleased, mother," said Lucy. "I'll have to tell father, I suppose. Ought I to tell him now, do you think, or after dinner?"

"Your father did say something about having a bottle of port up this evening," said Mrs. Marling. "I shall have half a glass to please him."

Lucy said she wouldn't touch port to please anyone, horrible stuff, but it might make things easier with father and then in came Mr. Marling, holding a letter in his hand.

"What does your employer want to see me for?" said Mr. Marling to his daughter. "You been givin' trouble, Lucy?" at which words Lucy, bewildered, looked to her mother for help and not in vain.

"What is it, Will?" she said. "Can I see the letter?"

"Yes, my dear," said Mr. Marling, sitting down heavily. "You won't be any the wiser though. Feller brought it in a car, kind of office boy or something, said a verbal answer would do. Verbal answer," Mr. Marling repeated with some scorn. "Why couldn't Adams telephone? Anyway he's coming over after dinner so it's just as well I've got the port up. What's this soup?"

"TOMATO," said his wife and daughter in one breath and that a fairly loud one.

"All right, all right," said Mr. Marling. "Not out of one of those damned tins that feller Cripps makes us buy?"

"OUR OWN TOMATOES AND OUR OWN MILK, FATHER," said Lucy and then remained self-convicted of impatience and almost rudeness.

"I'll tell you what the feller said in his letter," said Mr. Marling, who was getting into great difficulties with eyeglasses on a black cord to which he had taken lately on the grounds that (a) he was always losing his spectacles and (b) he had always dealt with the same oculist and would pay his way as he always had and no jumped-up Welshman was to think he could tell him where to get glasses for nothing at his age: which fine but muddled piece of thinking will, we hope, be clear to all our readers. "He says—now wait a minute, that's not his letter— here we are. He says can he come over and see me this evening on a matter of some importance. Feller must have known I was opening a bottle of Uncle Fitzherbert's port," said Mr. Marling. "Well, Lucy, what have you been doing?"

"I was over at Edgefield yesterday helping Percy Bodger to clean Mr. Adams's well," said Lucy, loudly and clearly. "There was an awful lot of muck but Percy got everything cleared."

"Ah well," said Mr. Marling, "when Bodger's dead there won't be a man left in the county that understands wells. High time *I* was dead," with which comforting words he went on with his dinner while his wife and daughter talked about the approaching visit of the elder son Bill, a professional soldier, with his nice dull wife and their four children, and of the elder daughter Lettice, now Mrs. Barclay, with her four children of her two marriages, and how nice it would be to have the whole family together for once. Especially, said Lucy, if Oliver could get down, for her brother Oliver, as yet unmarried, was her particular friend and confidant, or had been up to the present. Lucy knew how long and hopelessly he had loved the enchanting actress Jessica Dean and though she thought rather poorly of going on being in love with someone who had turned you down again and again, not to speak of being now respectably married to the well-known author-actor-manager Aubrey Clover, she always listened most kindly and seriously to his complaints. But rarely, and even more rarely in the last year, had she told him any of her own troubles, partly from a strong and quite unrancorous feeling that her affairs would not interest him, partly because of late she had found a curious and unsurmountable difficulty in mentioning Mr. Adams's name.

"Not bad, this port," said Mr. Marling who, rather meanly we think, was sampling it before his guest arrived. "Last bottle of the lot old Uncle Fitzherbert left me. I remember we drank two bottles the Christmas Lettice got engaged to Barclay when that feller Harvey and his sister, good-looking woman like a rocking-horse, were here. Pity it's the last. Still even port won't keep for ever."

"And it won't keep at all if you drink it before Mr. Adams

comes," said his undutiful daughter under her breath, at which moment the gardener's wife who waited in an obliging though sketchy way at dinner came in to say it was Mr. Adams please. Mrs. Marling was going to get up and leave the men together, but as Mr. Adams, rightly distrusting the gardener's wife as an ambassador, had followed her into the dining-room she felt it would be only courteous to stay for a few moments. Mr. Adams shook hands with his hostess and his host, smiled towards Lucy and took the seat Mr. Marling offered him.

"Glass of port, Adams?" said Mr. Marling. "You won't get one like it now. Last of what my old Uncle Fitzherbert Marling left me. He was a good preacher. Never made his sermon more than twelve minutes. Ferguson's '66, that's what this is; the last we'll ever see," at which point he checked himself rather suddenly and Lucy knew that only his sense of duty as a host had stopped him saying "and probably the first you've ever tasted."

"Very good port indeed, Squire," said Mr. Adams, "but I believe I can set you right on one point. It's not the last. I got a dozen the other day."

Mr. Marling stared with such disbelief written on his face that Mr. Adams, apparently amused but not in the least offended, added, "From Hepplethwaite and Crowther."

At this name of power, wine merchants of old and untarnished fame to whom dukes could cringe in vain if not personally introduced by two customers of old standing; who were known to have refused the patronage of Mr. Gladstone in his youth because he was in favour of slave emancipation, accepted it in 1860 because his budget contained a proposal to reduce wine-duties and shut the door on him again in 1886 on the Home Rule question; at this name, we repeat, having nearly lost the thread of our argument, Mr. Marling stared in a perfectly apoplectic way.

"I know what you want to say, sir," said Mr. Adams, throwing an amusedly conspiratorial look at Lucy. "If Mrs. Marling weren't present you would say 'And how on earth did *you* get in with Hepplethwaite and Crowther?' It's quite simple. I was able to oblige them in a business way. I've got a few shares in the firm and they tell me what wine I ought to buy. I bought some wine from Miss Sowerby too when I took the Old Bank House. Her father had laid it down and there's a claret I'd like you to try if you will do me the honour of coming over some time."

"Claret, eh?" said Mr. Marling. "I remember my old governor talkin' about Sowerby's claret. I'd like to try it. Now, Adams, what's all this about important business at this time of night?"

"Perhaps Mrs. Marling and Miss Marling would rather not listen to a business talk," said Mr. Adams, but Mrs. Marling, who was deeply interested in the impending discussion, said even if she and Lucy couldn't take part they could listen and as she had, against her usual custom, taken half a glass of Uncle Fitzherbert's port, she proposed to drink it slowly, like a gentleman.

"Well, my dear, just as you like," said Mr. Marling. "My wife's as good a man of business as I am, Adams, and as for my girl Lucy, you know what she's like. Carry on."

There was a short silence during which Mr. Marling drank some of his port in a very knowing way while his wife and his younger daughter sat silent. Mrs. Marling was amused and interested in her usual detached way but Lucy, to her great mortification, found her heart beating so hard and fast that she felt almost giddy.

"I have," said Mr. Adams, looking abstractedly at his wine as he held the glass between him and the last evening light and watched the translucent ruby glow, "something to tell you, sir. Miss Marling would like you to know, but I feel that it's my duty to be the first to speak about it. Miss Marling and I have been working together for quite a time and a better business partner I've never had. But I want to make it more permanent. And I want to make it so that whatever happens to me, she won't be the loser. I've seen too much of a woman being put upon when I was a kid and my old dad spent every penny of his wages on beer except what my mother took out of his trouser pockets when he was too drunk to notice. Not that it happened often," continued Mr. Adams, apparently rather enjoying the emotion recollected in tranquillity, "because my old dad was a man of principle and his principle was, Don't leave the pub till there's nothing in your trouser pockets, or the wife will get it. I've done all sorts of queer odd jobs for my mother when I was a kid. I've begged sometimes, though I wasn't much of a hand at it; more like a highwayman I was, with Your money or your life. Well, Dad got rolling drunk once too often and was run over and not missed, unless it was the chaps that he used to stand drinks to, and I worked hard for my mother and though we were poor—really poor, not what men nowadays call poor with high wages and shirking all they can, while their wives never stop working—mother could sleep at nights without waking up in a fright thinking the master was coming home drunk again. Well, that's old history and neither here nor there. But the world isn't so easy for the good, hard-working, honest women and I don't like to think that Miss Marling might—for nothing's sure nowadays—be in a position where she couldn't run things her own way."

He paused and looked at his wine. Then he looked at Lucy, but dusk had fallen, the room was almost dark and her face invisible. Mr. Marling, perplexed and perhaps a little apprehensive of something unknown, gave a kind of grunt which was no help at all. Mrs. Marling wondered why men could never come to the point, but held her peace.

"So," said Mr. Adams, "and this is why I came over, I have asked Miss Marling to do me the honour to marry me and she has said she will. I have my daughter to consider, but her and me have talked it over and I should like my lawyer to get in touch with yours about a settlement, so that if I happen to die the day after the wedding she will have a home and be independent. Not that I mean to die," said Mr. Adams, "but Timon Tide waits for no man and you never know your luck. Well, Squire, that's what

I had to say and I shall be honoured if you will give me your permission to marry Miss Marling, but if you don't feel like it there will be no ill-feeling and we'll get married just the same."

By this time Mrs. Marling was quite certain that her husband would have a fit. There was complete silence in the now almost dark room. Lucy, strangely moved and almost frightened by feelings she could not understand, moved her chair cautiously a little nearer to Mr. Adams and laid her hand on his coat sleeve. A large, powerful hand quietly enveloped hers and the silence grew till Mr. Marling drank the last of his port, put his glass down and said, "It's for Lucy to say, Adams. She's a good girl. And you've proved a good friend. Well, Lucy?"

"But I *have* said," said Lucy. "When Mr. Adams asked me to marry him I said I would so long as Mrs. Adams wouldn't mind and he said she wouldn't. So I hope you won't mind. Mother didn't."

"Mrs. Adams? What the dickens do you mean?" said her father, justly puzzled and irritated.

"It was your girlie's kind thought of my wife, Heth's mother that was," said Mr. Adams, "though come to that I suppose she's still her mother, poor soul. Now, Squire, is it yes or no? If it's yes, well and good. If it's no, well not so good. Miss Marling and I are getting married whatever happens and if your lawyers won't act I'll get another firm to act for her. This is remarkably good port but they say a blind man can't appreciate wine, and it's too dark to see, and consequently to taste."

"Put the lights on, Lucy dear," said Mrs. Marling and as Lucy switched on the light in the old carved and gilded chandelier the sky outside was suddenly dark and the long windows onto the lawn became mirrors of the lighted room within.

Mr. Marling pushed his chair back and got up.

"Lucy's a good girl," he said. "It's not what I expected, but be good to her, Adams, and you're a lucky man to get her. I'll tell my lawyer to get in touch with yours. I've done my best, but all these

changes are too much for me. I'm goin' to my room. Letters to
write," and he moved heavily towards the door.

"Father!" said Lucy.

"All right, all right, my girl," said Mr. Marling, taking Lucy in
his arms and patting her back. "It's all in the Bible. Leave your
old father and go off with some young feller, it says. You're a
good girl, Lucy. Bless you, my dear."

He kissed her affectionately and went slowly out of the room.

"Gosh. I feel perfectly *ghastly*," said Lucy.

"That's all right," said her accepted suitor calmly. "Your
father's taken a bit of a knock, same like as I did when Heth got
engaged to Ted Pilward. But I had you, Miss Marling, and the
Squire has got your mother. Now, don't you worry, girlie. That's
right, isn't it?" he added to his future mother-in-law.

"Perfectly right," said Mrs. Marling. "I have some letters to
write, Mr. Adams, so I will leave you with Lucy. I am glad to
welcome you as a son-in-law. We will talk about a date for your
marriage later."

"No hurry," said Mr. Adams, but not ungallantly. "Lawyers
are as slow as a go-easy strike and one can't do a bit of business
like this in a day. My Heth's being married this autumn and I've
a good lot of business on my hands one way and another. We'll
take our time. And as for being a son-in-law, well, I may say
there's not a lady in Barsetshire that I'd be prouder to have as a
mother-in-law unless it was Mrs. Belton, but as she only has the
one daughter and that daughter's married to an Admiral, the
question doesn't arise. My girl here can't give up all her jobs in a
hurry. Say sometime next spring."

Mrs. Marling who had assisted at her elder son's marriage and
the two marriages of her elder daughter knew quite well that it is
usually the bride's parents who fix the date of the wedding, and
when her elder son's in-laws had arranged for their daughter to
marry him in the middle of her most important week of county
work she had quietly delegated everything, told herself that she
was not really necessary (which indeed is true of all of us) and

appeared at Camberley as a lady of perfect leisure. It was for her and her husband to say when their younger daughter should marry and no business of Mr. Adams's at all. But with great good sense she resigned herself to what was obviously inevitable and said again that they would talk about it later.

"Well, that's that," said Mr. Adams when he was alone with his future bride. "Your father and mother are a fine old couple, Miss Marling. I suppose I'll have to kiss your mother after the wedding. Well, it can't be helped."

"I'll tell you what," said Lucy, who during the last few minutes had been applying her powerful mind to things in general. "If we're going to get married you can't go on calling me Miss Marling. And I suppose you ought to kiss me; though it seems a bit awkward."

"That's right," said Mr. Adams, comfortably. "I remember in the first war when I was quite a kid people used to say the first seven years of a war were the worst. Things shake down of themselves if you give them time. But one thing I shall do and that is to give you an engagement ring. And when I say that, I mean it, and Sam Adams's word is as good as his bond."

"All right," said Lucy, somehow pleased at her lover's peculiar methods. "But I'll tell you what, you oughtn't to say your word's as good as your bond all the time. Everyone knows it is."

"Right, my girl," said Mr. Adams. "I'm not too old to learn. And I may add that if you say 'I'll tell you what' again I'll get a special license and marry you out of hand and lock you up till you've learnt sense. You may know a lot of things I don't know, but I know a lot that you don't. Give and take, live and let live, that's what my poor old mother said and what I say. You can't teach an old dog new tricks and I'm an oldish dog by now. And if you knew how much I love you, you'd be surprised," said Mr. Adams reflectively.

There was a moment's silence till Lucy, going very red in the face, said, "But I do know. Because you'd be just as surprised about me."

Never in his long, adventurous, slightly piratical life had Mr. Adams been so surprised. And even greater was his surprise when his bluff, highly reliable farm manager looked at him through eyes brimming with tears, held out her hands in a helpless gesture and coming up to him laid her head on his shoulder and began to sob. For a few seconds he was entirely taken aback, then his powerful commonsense asserted itself and he took Lucy in his arms and held her kindly and firmly till she had recovered her self-control, which did not take long. It was perhaps inevitable that the gardener's wife, impatient to clear away and get the washing up done, should choose this moment to come in.

"Ow, I'm sorry, I'm sure," said the gardener's wife, seeing Miss Lucy in Mr. Adams's embrace.

"That's all right, Mrs. Pardon," said Mr. Adams cheerfully. "Miss Marling and I are engaged to be married and it's always a bit upsetting for a young lady."

"Well, I'm sure I wish you both joy," said Mrs. Pardon, who was already mentally composing the account she would give in the kitchen at Marling Hall and later to all her friends in the village of this interesting episode. "I felt just the same when Pardon spoke for me. Cried like as if I'd been peeling onions, I did, and created in the coach-house till Dad threw a jug of water over me. And when's the wedding to be, sir?"

"Next spring," said Mr. Adams, pressing a large white handkerchief into Lucy's hand. "You can clear away now."

"Oh, not just this minute, sir," said Mrs. Pardon, shocked. "I'll come in later on," and before he could remonstrate she had left the room to tell the kitchen all about it.

Lucy, having gratefully wiped her eyes and blown her nose on Mr. Adams's handkerchief was now more or less herself again, though with a new look in her eyes which touched Mr. Adams to the quick, a look of such adoration as he had never thought nor hoped to see.

"Thanks most *awfully*," said Lucy. "I suppose Mrs. Pardon has gone to tell everyone."

"Not only that," said Mr. Adams, "but she wanted to know when the wedding would be, so I said next Spring. Is that all right, Lucy?"

His future bride stared at him.

"Anything wrong?" asked Mr. Adams.

"No," said she. "Only you called me Lucy. You never did before. It's rather nice."

"And you will have to get used to calling me Sam," said Mr. Adams, but his Lucy was not listening.

"Gosh!" she said in a reverent voice. "I've just thought of something. I'll tell you what, I shall be a stepmother," at which thought she laughed with such real amusement that Mr. Adams couldn't help laughing too and quite forgot his threat about the special licence.

"Well, it's heaven," said Lucy. "I'll talk to the Dean about us getting married. It would be rather nice if it could be just quietly at Marling, but there'll be heaps of people that want to come. I expect it had better be the cathedral. If the Palace send me a wedding present I'll have to ask them, but I expect they won't. Anyway Heather's wedding comes first and that's the most important thing. You don't think she'll mind, do you?"

"Bless my soul, no," said Mr. Adams. "She'd have made me propose to you even if I hadn't wanted to. You see she didn't like to think of her old dad alone."

"I wish Heather could have been a bridesmaid," said Lucy, "but now she can't. And anyway," she added thoughtfully, "being married in September she mightn't feel like being a bridesmaid next spring."

"We'll cross that bridge when we come to it," said Mr. Adams. "I must go now. See you tomorrow as usual—thank God," he added.

A new Lucy, but yet most clearly the old Lucy, kissed him as if she had always done it and he drove away. Lucy said good-night to her father and mother and went to bed, feeling unaccountably tired, a physical sensation to which she was almost a stranger. As she got into bed, she thought of Oliver and wondered if he would be pleased. But within five minutes she was asleep.

After this emotional evening Lucy's life ran in its accustomed groove till the following weekend when her brother Bill, now Colonel of his regiment, his nice dull wife, Mrs. Bill, whom we must call by that name as no one ever called her anything else, and their four nice dull children arrived from Camberley. They were shortly followed by her sister Lettice Barclay with her husband Captain Barclay (now out of the army and farming in Yorkshire) her two Watson girls and her two little Barclay boys. By a miracle of management Mrs. Marling had provided not only rooms—for there were plenty of empty rooms in Marling Hall—but quite sufficient domestic help from the village who made up in zeal what they lacked in experience, had elevenses in the kitchen all day long, and treated their employers very well.

In the first flush of welcomes, of comparing the rival heights and ages of the children, of settling so far as such things can be settled the rival claims of Mrs. Bill's Nana and Lettice Barclay's Nurse (for of Mrs. Bill's under nurse we need not speak as she was called Everleen and came from an orphanage) no private conversation was possible. Dearly would Lucy have liked to have a good talk with her sister Lettice, but she was busy all day over the new cowsheds at the Adamsfield Market Garden and as soon as she got home was seized by Diana and Clare Watson who insisted on describing in detail life at the select preparatory boarding school where, so their Aunt Lucy considered, they were learning nothing except to be rather bores. But she was a good kind aunt and took them to see the new separator in the dairy and gave them each a ride on the old pony by which time only five minutes were left to dress for dinner, or rather to change her skirt and breeches for an old flowered dress with a broken zip. In the drawing-room there was a moment when she could say to her sister Lettice "I've something *frightfully* important to tell you. It's about——" and she was going to say "about Mr. Adams and me" when her brother Oliver came in, fresh from town, and there was such a bustle of greetings that she held her tongue. For many reasons she wanted to tell Oliver herself. She had not written, or rather she had written and torn up three times, because it looked so silly on paper, hoping to catch him as soon as he came back from town. Tears of disappointment sprang to her eyes as the opportunity vanished. Still a quarter of an hour till dinner and no chance of getting her dear Oliver to herself. The more she thought of telling him the more her confidence oozed away. Not in her decision, not in Mr. Adams, nor in herself, but in Oliver on whom, much as she loved him, she could never quite count. Sometimes she wondered if he were a little selfish and then she repented and thought of all the selfish things she had done herself. Under cover of Mrs. Bill's jolly voice telling the Pater, a form of address that Mr. Marling particularly disliked, about the regimental point-to-point and how Bill's mare had cast a shoe but came in a good second, she slipped out into the hall, lifted the receiver, replaced it, lifted it again and asked the exchange for a London number. After not too long a wait she heard the bell ring and almost at once the lovely voice of Jessica Dean asked who it was.

"I say, Jessica," said Lucy. "I'm Lucy Marling. Are you frightfully busy?"

"Not for the next five minutes," said Jessica's voice. "If it's Oliver you want he isn't here."

"I know. He's here," said Lucy. "It's you I want, Jessica. I say, please listen. I've got engaged to Mr. Adams."

"My precious lamb, how absolutely IT," said Jessica's voice. "Can I be a bridesmaid? I *adore* Mr. Adams. So does Aubrey. Do let me be a bridesmaid. I'll dress as an ingénue and nobody will know me. Aubrey! Lucy's going to marry Mr. Adams. Darling, Aubrey is *enchanted*. He wants to give you away and be Old

Fashioned Father, and then he can kiss me and the other bridesmaids."

"Jessica, *please*," said Lucy. "I don't know about bridesmaids, but *please* are you really glad. I am. In fact I'm almost bursting with gladness and Mother and Father are being as good as gold. But I wondered——"

"Of course I'm glad, my poppet," said Jessica. "Are you expecting trouble with your brother Oliver?"

Lucy paused and then said Yes.

"I thought so," said Jessica. "Seldom have I met anyone so selfish and self-indulgent. Of course I adore him, but he's getting a bit above himself with seeing so much of Aubrey and me. It doesn't seem to occur to him that Aubrey and I don't *always* want company. Listen, my lamb. If Oliver gives any trouble, ring me up and I'll come and settle his hash. And I don't think I'll be a bridesmaid. Kiss Mr. Adams for me. Have you kissed him yet?"

"Of course," said Lucy with some dignity.

Miss Jessica Dean's famous laugh was heard, but a kindly laugh, and the telephone clicked and went dead so Lucy, strangely comforted, joined the rest of the party who were going into the dining-room where it was impossible for her to sit next to Oliver, and exerted herself to entertain her brother Bill and Lettice's husband Tom Barclay. It was strange to think how during the war—seven years ago it must be—Tom had come to Marling Hall and she had cared for him a great deal. Not enough to break her heart when he married the lovely widowed Lettice, but enough to be silently unhappy for quite a long time. She still liked him very much, but how could she ever have thought of Tom Barclay when Mr. Adams was in the world? Well, all that was long ago. Lettice looked young and happy and beautiful and had two sturdy Barclay children as well as her two Watson girls, and she, Lucy, was going to marry a man whom she loved and whom she could rely on at any moment in peace or storm. It was all heaven and Captain Barclay said to himself that he would never have thought that Lucy would turn out so handsome and pleasant, while Lucy smiled and talked and knew that below her words there lay infinite peaceful happiness, when to her horror her father, raising his voice, said,

"Well, now we're all here, I'll tell you the news. Fill your glasses everyone. It's good French white wine and there's not a headache in a bottle of it, but if it stays in the cellar much longer it'll be vinegar."

"Oh father! *please,*" said Lucy, but her father didn't or wouldn't hear. She saw her mother making what they used to call when they were children a "No-face," but Mr. Marling was well away.

"Come on, pater," said Mrs. Bill.

"You know Lucy's engaged," said Mr. Marling, putting the cart before the horse as his wife and younger daughter at once realized. "She's been a long time about it. Why, bless me, my mother was engaged when she was nineteen and had six children before she was thirty and they're all dead except me."

As he paused for applause Bill said to his sister Lettice that Father was running true to form. Lettice agreed, but rather absent-mindedly, for she had seen Lucy's face and wondered what was wrong.

"He's a bit older than she is, but one of the finest men I know," said Mr. Marling. "In fact if he hadn't bought that bit of land of mine I don't know where I'd be now," which remark entirely flummoxed those of his family who had thought he was going to say Sir Edmund Pridham. "Well, no good beating about the bush. It's Adams. Lucy's a good girl, and deserves her luck. Bless you, my dear."

The devastating effect of his speech can best be realized when we say that Mrs. Bill's voice remarking that They said Mr. Adams was simply rolling, was for the moment the only sound to be heard. But the others quickly recovered themselves and expressed very loving and genuine joy at her engagement, tempered in the case of Mrs. Bill by never having seen the bridegroom and in the case of Captain Barclay of his never in his remote, self-contained Yorkshire fastnesses having even heard of him. Mrs. Marling quickly brought him up to date and he said it seemed a very sensible arrangement and he was delighted with Lucy's good luck, so that what with Mr. Adams being a M.P. and well off and also much liked in the county, all her family felt that she had done very well and on the whole brought glory upon them. It was known that Mr. Adams was very rich and that people like Lord Pomfret and the Dean and Sir Edmund Pridham thought well of him as a citizen, and though he had regrettably (though perhaps understandably in view of his origin) stood for Parliament as a Labour man it was a matter of common knowledge that he was, as Professor Macphairson Clonglocketty Angus M'Clan, son of an elderly labouring man and Scottish Home Rule member for Aberdeathly had so wittily said, "ane sair member for the Labour whips," though why the English papers who had never heard of David I. found the words so entertaining will never be known.

Mr. Marling, pleased with his success, now gave the toast of Lucy's happiness which was lovingly honoured by the company. We wish we could say by all the company, but Lucy to her frozen dismay saw her brother Oliver sitting moodily, fingering his glass but not raising it. She looked across at him appealingly but he was carefully observing the movements of a small spider who had escaped from a glass bowl of flowers on the table and was lost in the damask wilderness.

"You *are* a prize wool-gatherer, Oliver," said Mrs. Bill in her cheeriest regimental voice. "It's Lucy's health we're drinking. Come on; the pater's waiting for you."

Feeling himself unable to argue with Mrs. Bill, who had the perfect self-confidence of a happy and not very intellectual wife and mother, Oliver lifted his glass, sipped from it and set it down.

"Corked?" said his brother Bill sympathetically.

Oliver said no, it wasn't corked. And seeing his mother's

impartial but piercing eye fixed on him he drank the rest of his wine and relapsed into rather ostentatious gloom which no one but his mother and Lucy noticed. Mrs. Bill then told what she said were some screamingly funny stories about her children at which the company, who were one by one realizing that Oliver was in what Mrs. Bill called "in one of his moods," laughed in a very flattering way and so the incident was glossed over for most of them. But not for Lucy and her mother who were deeply distressed; Mrs. Marling for Lucy's pleasure marred and Lucy because she could not bear her dear Oliver not to share her joy.

The evening had somehow to be pulled together. Mrs. Marling took Mrs. Bill aside and said being engaged was always a trying time and it would be nice for Lucy if they all played some amusing game. Something easy she said, as Lettice's two girls were to stay up for a special treat.

"I couldn't agree more, mater," said Mrs. Bill who had a gift amounting to genius for picking up the cheaper catchwords of the moment. "When I was engaged to Bill I was perfectly *ghastly* at home and the tempers I used to get into were just nobody's business. I know an awfully good game. It's called Hunt the Cripps and the dealer auctions the cards and has to tell the most awful lies to make people buy them. We always have shrieks of laughter when we play it. The fun is seeing what the other players lose on their cards of course. We play a penny a hundred. Oliver will simply love it. I mean he's so brainy he'll get it at once."

Mrs. Marling, with private reservations as to the complete horribleness of the game, found some packs and asked Mrs. Bill to take charge as she and her husband wouldn't play. This Mrs. Bill who was very goodnatured willingly did, calling Oliver to sit next to her and she would teach him.

"I don't think I will, Mrs. Bill," said Oliver. "My eyes are rather bad. I'll just read in a corner."

"You read too much," said his sister-in-law, with the complete candour of the happily married wife of an elder brother speaking to a bachelor younger brother. "Come by me and I'll play your hand for the first round. I've read a book you'd love. It's called *Hamlet's Mother* and its the love-life of Anne Hathaway because she had a son called Hamlet which seems funny when there's a play with the same name, only she was really in love with Ben Jonson or someone. It makes one absolutely *feel* the days of good Queen Bess. Well, we may have a Queen Bess again one day, though not for years and years one hopes. They say history repeats itself and it certainly would. Oh Lord! I've dealt all wrong. I'll do it again. I'm simply longing to meet Mr. Adams. He sounds a perfect pet. Now how many are we? Us two, Lettice two, her girls two, you and Lucy two."

"I really can't," said Oliver, to which his sister-in-law who was famed for her good nature answered Rubbish and not to be a spoil sport, after which he resigned himself in a not very gracious way to do as he was told. The game if played in the right spirit was full of noise and laughter and Lucy forgot her depression while Mrs. Bill and Captain Barclay made the most outrageous valuations of their cards and Lettice's girls showed themselves worthy pupils. Presently Oliver went away with a mumbled excuse.

"Ringing up Jessica I suppose," said Bill Marling, for Oliver's passion for that seductive charmer was common property. "Why don't I look pea-green and miserable so that stars fall in love with me?"

"Because I wouldn't let you," said his wife. "I say, mater, when are you going to put Lucy's thing in *The Times*?

"Not just yet, I think," said Mrs. Marling. "They don't mean to get married till next spring. Mr. Adams's daughter is getting married this autumn and apparently lawyers take a long time over settlements when one is as rich as he is."

"Well, it's your funeral, mater, not mine," said Mrs. Bill. "I must say if it were me I'd put it in soon. 'A marriage has been arranged and will take place early next year' sort of thing. It gives people something to talk about and really with one thing and another they need it."

Lettice and her husband supported the idea as did Bill, so Mrs. Marling said if her husband agreed she would do as they suggested, while Lucy listened with interest but made no comment, for such things as newspaper announcements did not seem to her to touch her new-found happiness in any way. Then Oliver came back, very much improved in spirits, and said Jessica and Aubrey were going to her people next day (which they often did, as the Cockspur Theatre was closed on Mondays, which it could well afford to do) and would look in on their way, probably before lunch. Mr. Marling was then begged to draw up an announcement for insertion in *The Times*, subject always to Mr. Adams's approval.

"Don't know what *The Times* is comin' to," said Mr. Marling, flattered by the request. "All this damn nonsense—beg your pardon, Mrs. Bill—about to so-and-so and so-and-so the gift of a brother for Jeremy. Bah!" he said, greatly impressing his hearers. "'The lady of John Bull Esq. of a son'; that's what they used to say."

Everyone then gave hideous examples of what they had read in those august columns, Lettice being adjudged winner with a notice which had said, "To Cedric and Rosemary ('Chuckles') Bloggs a fourth daughter (Mabelle)—but dearly loved," and when Mrs. Bill had tried to tell fortunes with cards and signally failed by saying that Oliver had a fair woman coming into his life, they began to go to bed. On the way up Lucy got Oliver to herself for a moment.

"I say, Oliver, you *are* pleased, aren't you?" said Lucy. "Jessica was most *awfully* pleased."

But though Oliver was almost himself again and unusually affectionate to his dear Lucy, he felt obliged (quite unnecessarily) to point out that Lucy was honouring Mr. Adams by accepting him.

"I'm not," said Lucy. "It's absolutely equal."

"And who will keep an eye on the parents?" said Oliver, at which Lucy, who had turned down the offer of excellent positions during the war and the peace because of her father and mother, said "Anyway I know who won't" and then stopped, horrified at her own thoughts.

"You're quite right," said Oliver. "I haven't. I'm sorry, old thing."

But it was too late, the harm was done, and though the generous Lucy had repented her words even as she spoke them, true though they were, there remained between Oliver and herself a shadow which had never before visited them and neither had a very good night.

As the Barclays had come laden with butter and bacon from their Yorkshire farm and Mrs. Bill had done some good work on the side with her husband's ex-batman who had a licence to keep pigs and the Marling fowls happened to be laying, a proper Sunday breakfast was provided and Mrs. Bill and Lettice reported that even the two nannies had expressed satisfaction. Mrs. Marling asked who was coming to church, adding that Bishop Joram was taking the service.

The ex-bishop of Mngangaland, now a canon of Barchester with one of the beautiful houses in the Close, was universally liked and even Mrs. Bill whose idea of Sunday morning was to put on trousers and give her husband's horses severe exercise and an extra grooming said if it was that old pet she would hold the fort with anyone and would bring the two elder children. Lettice also wanted to come with Diana and Clare and it was agreed that her Barclay children and the younger Bill Marlings should go with the perambulator contingent and visit Mrs. Cox who kept lodgings, sometimes obliged as cook at the Hall, and always had peppermints in a glass bottle owing to being a cousin of the postmistress who kept the Shop.

"And what about Oliver Cromwell?" said Mrs. Bill, whose keen sense of humour had caused her to choose this pet name for her brother-in-law.

"I think not," said Oliver, rather weakening his case by saying that his eyes were worrying him.

"Now that's naughty," said Mrs. Bill. "I suppose you know the service by heart and if you don't you ought to. That's what it's there for."

Mr. Marling asked in a loud voice, of no one in particular, what the doose Mrs. Bill meant.

"The pater does love teasing," said Mrs. Bill. "You know quite well what I mean, pater. If you take children while they're young they get it all by heart, I mean the ordinary service not the collects and all those bits and pieces, and then there they are. I can say right through the morning and evening service without a book. The words are just *in* you. Turn the tap and out they all come, and one doesn't need to even *think*. Of course when the government go altering everything it's more difficult."

Mrs. Marling said she much disliked being fair to the present government, but it was no use pretending that they had revised or deposited the Prayer Book, and just as well, for the people who had done it, though it had upset everything, were at least gentlemen.

"I expect you're right, mater," said Mrs. Bill good-humouredly. "But really the way they've vetted the marriage service gets me down. Give me the good old marriage service. It makes sense and if anyone thinks a girl is likely to be upset by the prayers, take it from me you could say nursery rhymes and most of them wouldn't know the difference. You really feel quite *dotty* while you're being married. I know I did and I'm sure the girls will, not but what they know of course what marriage *means*, brought up with animals as they've been but as I say, take it from me a few good old English prayers aren't going to put them off their stride. Am I talking too much?"

"Yes," said her husband. "I'm coming to church and then I'm going round the place with father before lunch. You coming, Barclay? That's right. And you, Oliver?"

"I don't know," said Oliver, stammering slightly as he often did when thinking of Jessica. "Jessica and Aubrey are coming before lunch and I must be here when they come."

"If little Jessica's comin' I'm not going round the place," said Mr. Marling. "You young fellers can go," on which Bill Marling and Tom Barclay expressed an equal determination to sacrifice all to Jessica Dean.

Oliver looked black, but said nothing.

"Lucy," said her father. "What's Adams?"

Lucy who by long practice usually knew what her father meant, explained in a loud but kind voice that he used to be chapel but owing to the insistence of the Reverend Enoch Arden on the equality of all men, a thing which Mr. Adams said was impossible, he had for some years been a staunch supporter of the Church of England, at which her father grunted a kind of approval and said he must go and look at the lessons for the day, a task which he had for many years punctiliously fulfilled ever since the dreadful day when the gilding on the pages of a new Bible that he had presented to the church made two pages stick together and he had read straight on for several verses before he discovered his mistake.

"That's all right," said her father. "Thought he might be a Dissenter." He moved ponderously out of the room and the rest of the party went about their various jobs till a little before eleven when most of them walked down to the church.

Marling church was not very old, not very interesting, but several generations of Marlings had been married in it and buried in the churchyard, and they were all calmly attached to it and usually liked the vicar. As the present incumbent was on holiday Bishop Joram was taking the service for him which he did very well though, as he afterwards said, he still had nostalgic longings for the black worshippers in his sub-Equatorial diocese and the active absence of Good Form with which they flashed their white teeth, filed to a point, at the more exhilarating passages of the services and rhythmically beat the war-drum (consecrated by his predecessor) to support the harmonium.

The children behaved very well. Mr. Marling grappled satisfactorily with Ezekiel 3, v. 15 and I Corinthians 9, v. 4, though Lucy afterwards told Mr. Adams that she had distinctly heard him add to the words "Have we not power to eat and drink," the gloss, "Not under this Government." By twenty minutes past twelve they were all out in the churchyard and shaking hands with Bishop Joram.

"I have a piece of news for you, Bishop," said Mrs. Marling, for his friends called him Bishop and Canon indifferently, having become used to him under his former title. "My younger daughter Lucy is engaged to Mr. Adams, the M.P. for Barchester. They have known one another for a long time and my husband and I are delighted."

"My warmest congratulations," said the Bishop, wringing Lucy's hand with a vigour equal to her own. He then picked a daisy from the grass, dug his heel into the path, dropped the daisy into the hole and trod it well into the gravel, the whole with a slightly furtive air.

"A relic of the old man in me, I fear," he said, as Mrs. Marling and Lucy looked at his work. "In Mngangaland no sooner is a betrothal announced than a number of cattle, varying of course with the position and wealth of the bride's father, are slaughtered and burnt. This custom was deprecated by my predecessor and finally put down during my episcopate, but I always allowed them to perform what I may call a token sacrifice with fruit or vegetables. When I heard your splendid news, Miss Marling, I felt I must follow the example of my black friends, though more in remembrance of their delightful ways than in any heathen spirit of propitiation. You will not think me unduly familiar, I hope," he added anxiously.

As Lucy was obviously burning to ask the Bishop more about the engagement and marriage rites of his dusky flock, her mother changed the subject by asking him to lunch, an invitation that he accepted enthusiastically.

"Not but what I should be honoured to come in any case," said

Bishop Joram, "but today your kind invitation is as it were a raven in the wilderness, for I must either go back to Barchester and have whatever fare my housekeeper who has gone out for the day has seen fit to leave, or I must accept the invitation of a lady, a widow, who lives in the village and whose hospitality I rashly accepted last Sunday. I am not, I hope, a conceited man," said the Bishop, "but I believe she meant to marry me."

"Joyce!" said Mrs. Marling.

"Mrs. Smith!" said Lucy, and with one accord they looked towards the vestry from which came a very thin elderly woman with fine eyes, dressed in what could only be half mourning so were black and purple scarves intertwined about her, carrying a large bunch of flowers which Lucy had no difficulty in recognising as the Michaelmas daisies that she had taken up to the church the previous evening.

"Just the widow's mite," said the newcomer. "As our dear Bishop is not giving us a second service today I thought my little good deed should be to take the lovely flowers back to my wee temporary home. They die so soon without water, you know. And may I offer you a little refreshment, Bishop? Only the widow's cruise, you know; just going round the larder seeing what there is on the shelves with a willing spirit which is after all half the battle," said Mrs. Smith, evidently taking the word in question as meaning a roving quest for food rather than a pot or jar. "When Mr. Smith was here, before he passed over I mean, he would often come in quite tired and out of sorts after an evening with his gentlemen business friends and I used to take quite a pleasure in knocking him up a little something."

Bill Marling said to his wife in a too audible aside that Mr. Smith's complaint had been D.T. and cirrhosis of the liver and if any knocking up had been done it was old Smith that did it.

"It's very nice of you, Joyce," said Mrs. Marling, "but Bishop Joram is an old friend and he is coming to lunch at the Hall. Are your tenants behaving well?"

"Very pleasant people," said Mrs. Smith. "A Mr. and Mrs.

Bissell. He is Headmaster of a London school. They go walking a good deal and while they are out I just nip into my little home to see that all is well and take away any little treasure that has beautiful associations for me."

Mrs. Marling firmly said good-bye to Mrs. Smith.

"A good woman but very tiresome," she said to Bishop Joram. "She was the infant school teacher here before the war and married a man who had some kind of business; coals, I think. He drank himself into D.T. and luckily to death. She's all right, but she has a passion for unconsidered trifles and snaps them up like anything. We must consult you about Lucy's wedding. It won't be till next year, sometime before Easter. Mr. Adams has no special preference and our church is too small, so we thought the cathedral, if the Dean approves."

The Bishop said it would be most appropriate, as Mr. Adams was the Member for Barsetshire, and within the cathedral walls politics would fade away. And then they got to Marling Hall where, under the shade of a large tulip tree, Oliver was entertaining Mr. and Mrs. Aubrey Clover.

At the sight of the returning churchgoers Jessica opened her lovely eyes to their full extent and in one graceful movement got up from the chaise longue on which she had been reclining and speeding fleet-foot towards the Bishop flung her arms round his neck.

"I run, I run, I am gathered to thy heart," said Oliver, half aloud.

"Yes, but it doesn't mean anything," said Aubrey Clover. "You know Jessica."

"Hokey-pokey!" said Jessica rapturously and then turning to her audience, for so any people who gathered together in one place always became at her approach, added,

"Colin Keith brought Bishop Joram to see me after the play last year and I simply *adored* him and we danced a cancan, didn't we, my sweet?"

"We did," said the Canon of Barchester, whose variety of

religious experiences had made him very wide-minded. "It was
an old song my father used to know in his young days in some
musical play, and I always found it had a strong appeal to my
friends in Mngangaland. 'Hokey, pokey, winky, wum,' I think it
ran."

"'Pitty-bo-peepy, ibly cum,'" said Jessica.

"'Tonkery, wonkery, winkery, wum,
    The King of the Cannibal Islands!'"

sang both together, with some slight but neat footwork, after
which Jessica laughed her infectious laugh and with her husband's able assistance sank back gracefully onto her chair.

"Lady Hamilton," said Aubrey Clover, looking with detached
interest at his wife.

"Don't glower, Oliver darling," said Jessica. "I adore Hokey-
Pokey, but he alas adores Lady Graham and Mrs. Brandon and
all the middle-aged women with poise and distinction. We must
be going, Aubrey, or Mother will have gone to sleep once too
often and we shan't be able to wake her. Lucy, my lamb, I have
brought you a *heavenly* present. I hope it is the first. Just a small
rubbish with my love. Where is it, Aubrey?"

From under her chair Aubrey Clover drew a white cardboard
box with a well-known name on it.

"Ought I to open it now?" said Lucy.

"Of course, my lamb," said Jessica. "I want to see your reactions."

From clouds of tissue-paper Lucy drew a Spanish shawl of
deepest orange silk with a deep knotted fringe of the same
shade, embroidered with flowers and birds in brilliant colours.

"OH!" said Lucy, while the female relations' eyes nearly came
out of their heads and they all wondered, we regret to say, how
much it had cost.

"Oh! *Jessica!*" said Lucy.

"I thought you'd like it," said Jessica. "I brought two back
from New York, never ask me how, one for me and one for the
first friend who needed a present. You can wear it any way you

like. All slim like this," and Jessica was swathed in its clinging folds from head to foot like a lovely Tanagra statuette, "or all majestuous like this," and she became a heavy peasant woman wearing the silk with a kind of ponderous majesty. "We all wear our rue with a difference," said Jessica with a mocking inflection that made Oliver uneasy, though why he could not tell, "and I hope you will too, my precious good girl. Now we must *fly*."

"Oh, Jessica, *couldn't* you be a bridesmaid?" said Lucy, kissing the actress fondly. "You look *exactly* like one."

"Oh, I'm a chameleon," said Jessica. "I mayn't look like this when you are married. When is it to be?"

Mrs. Marling said next spring.

"Then I certainly shan't," said Jessica. "From gold to gold of my girdle, there'll be an inch between by then. And probably a good deal more."

Only Mrs. Marling saw Oliver's face, suddenly stricken to grey stone. Mrs. Bill, whose total indifference to the finer shades was sometimes rather restful, suddenly shrieked, "Oh, Jessica! You're not going to have a baby! Cheers!"

"I thought I'd feel an awful fool if I didn't," said Jessica who was obviously bursting with pride.

"So did I!" said Aubrey Clover. "I mean for myself as well as Jessica. So it's to be a girl and we shall call her Sarah Siddons Clover and bring her up in the coulisses, whatever they are."

"Wait a minute, wait a minute," said Mr. Marling, who had been a puzzled spectator of the foregoing scene. "What's all this? Little Jessica goin' to have a baby?"

"Yes, if you please, sir," said Jessica, dropping a curtsey.

"You're a young baggage," said Mr. Marling. "Bill! get some champagne. You know where the key is. We've got a few bottles left. Well, Clover, congratulations. I didn't think you had it in you," at which unintentional brick the younger members of the party giggled most undutifully and Lucy wondered if Oliver was going to be sick, but somehow didn't care. She did not wish to explain her feelings to herself, nor do we think she could have done so if she tried, being quite unselfanalytical. But if we may attempt to explain them for her, we think that she felt her ship had been launched on thrilling uncharted seas and that Jessica Dean, Jessica whom they admired as an actress and thought of as a child, Jessica whom Oliver had loved so foolishly and so long and, one might add, so selfishly and exhaustingly for everyone else, Jessica who was Aubrey Clover's wife, had embarked with banners flying and trumpets sounding upon the same voyage that Lucy Marling had promised to make. In neither of these voyages would her dear Oliver, though she would always love him and help him, have much share. Too long had his little bark attendant sailed. He must try now to find some other star by which to set his course, and high time too. Nothing would change Lucy's affection for Oliver, but she suddenly saw him as a great many other people had been seeing him and felt slightly ashamed; not of him, but for him.

While Jessica practised her arts on the company, holding Lettice by one hand and Mrs. Bill by the other, ogling Captain Barclay very prettily, promising the elder children a box for Aubrey's play in the Christmas holidays in which (she said) she would be acting the part of an elephant, flirting simultaneously and disgracefully with the Bishop and Mr. Marling, Bill had brought out two large bottles of champagne with glasses, not forgetting the champagne nippers, and everyone including the older grandchildren drank to the health of Jessica and Sarah Siddons Clover and then, because Jessica said No Heeltaps, to Lucy, or Aunt Lucy, as the case might be, and Mr. Adams.

"I say, Mrs. Clover," said Mrs. Bill.

"No; please not," said Jessica. "Say Jessica."

"Well then Jessica," said Mrs. Bill, "and my name's Deirdre but it's so ghastly nobody says it, let's drink Lucy's health and Mr. Adams's. We did last night, but it wasn't champagne," at which betrayal Jessica favoured Mr. Marling with Mrs. Carvel's

famous wink and the health was drunk. Jessica kissed all those
present and Aubrey Clover gave all the children his autograph,
said farewell to Mrs. Marling and Lettice with respectful chiv-
alry, to Mrs. Bill with a kiss which made her bridle and shriek, to
Lucy with real avuncular affection and to all the men with a
charming, manly, yet slightly deprecatory handshake which
seemed to say, "I know you are better stuff than I am, but I do
my best and God bless you."

Oliver was not visible. But as Aubrey shut the door of his
huge road-eating car, a face which felt haggard but was to the
outward eye distinctly peevish looked in at the window and said
"Good-bye."

"Good-bye," said Mr. and Mrs. Aubrey Clover with one
breath and that a breath of relief, and before Oliver could annoy
them any more Aubrey had sounded his siren (specially attached
by him to his car to show his American friends what the war was
like), the car had apparently leapt six feet into the air and twenty
feet forward and they had vanished down the drive.

It will not surprise our readers to hear that for the rest of the
day the conversation at Marling Hall was almost exclusively
about Jessica Dean and Aubrey Clover. In fact, of all those who
had been present, Mr. and Mrs. Clover if we may so call them
were the only people unaffected by their own personalities. They
lunched peacefully at Winter Overcotes with Jessica's father and
mother, had tea peacefully at Beliers Priory with the Warings
(where Jessica insisted on entering her as yet highly problemati-
cal child for Philip Winter's prep. school), ran over to Skeynes to
see Mrs. Middleton and get the latest news of her nephew by
marriage Denis Stonor who had promised to do some music for
Aubrey Clover's next production as soon as he had finished his
contract with Nat Blumenfelt in New York, and so back to
London; a day which would have wrecked most ordinary people,
but left Aubrey and Jessica, those strange children of the theatre
whose life was most real when it was unreal, no more than

pleasantly fatigued and quite ready to go to bed at ten o'clock or to dine late and dance late at the Wigwam. On this particular evening early bed seemed the more agreeable prospect, and so they had a late supper and gossiped about their day. And if any reader is captious enough to ask how they got a late supper, we will explain to such an one that both Jessica and her husband had a genius for getting people to work for them and that Miss Mowbray, mostly known as Miss M., the daughter of a doctor in the East Riding, asked no more of life than to stand between Jessica and the world in every possible way, not to speak of being a first-class cook. As for Aubrey Clover, she tolerated him as the man who wrote (and rehearsed and produced and acted in) the plays that made Miss Jessica Dean the idol of the whole female theatre-going population as well as a large proportion of that much weaker body, the male theatre-goers.

"A pleasant day, I hope," said Miss M. materialising as soon as Jessica appeared. "And how were the Marlings?"

"Hullo, Miss M., do you know them?" said Aubrey Clover.

"Oh no," said Miss Mowbray, "but I have so often seen Mr. Oliver Marling here that I feel they are quite old friends."

"Be an angel and take up my things," said Jessica, dropping bag, gloves, coat and various scarves on the table. "We had a heavenly time. Oliver's father made us drink Sarah Siddons's health in champagne and Oliver looked too too dim and vengeful, poor lamb."

"Did he now?" said Miss M., who had always greatly disapproved Oliver's frequent visits to her flat. "And why, may I ask?"

"I think he has rather a refined mind," said Jessica sadly, "and we can't live up to it."

"Are you crying, my sweet?" said Aubrey Clover.

Jessica was heard to say, indistinctly, that it was soda water bubbles flying up her nose.

"Well, if you ask me, which you don't and of course it is no business of mine," said Miss M., "it's high time Mr. Marling got

married. Hanging round married women is no life for a man. If
you want anything else, just call. I shan't be going to bed for an
hour or so," and she went away.

"Bless her heart," said Aubrey Clover. "And yours and Sarah
Siddons's. Miss M. is quite right. It's time Oliver stopped
hanging round. He's too good for that."

"I'm afraid it's a bit my fault," said Jessica. "He looked so
miserable always and I had to give him a crumb. He looks like an
owl that's got its feathers wet, poor sweet."

"Yes, it was your fault," said Aubrey Clover. "Condoned by
your husband, I admit. And as the very thought of Sarah
Siddons has scared him, we can go on from there. Was it really
soda water?"

"Of course it was," said Jessica. "Do you think I'd cry for
Oliver, poor pet? I'll be all right for acting for quite some time,
thank goodness. I suppose Sarah and I will have to go into
retirement about February. It all depends on her view of life and
the public's view of me. There's only one thing that worries me."

"Tell me," said Aubrey Clover. "It shan't worry you, not if I
have to act in films with Glamora Tudor to support you."

"What worries me and Sarah Siddons," said Jessica, "is how
on earth you can get anyone as good as us to act with you."

"Of all the conceit!" said Aubrey Clover. "I had a kind of mad
idea of a two-man show with Denis Stonor. He'll be over here in
the winter and what with my brains and his piano we might
make rather a hit."

At this point both parties began to talk at once, Jessica taking,
or rather creating, a very unfair advantage by saying that she was
speaking for Sarah Siddons as well as herself. So much noise did
they make that Miss M. in a dark red dressing-gown with a net
over her hair-curlers, opened the door and said, "Now that's
enough, Mr. Clover. We must consider ourselves and we need all
the sleep we can get. I shall take all the telephone calls till I hear
your bell. Good-night."

*   *   *

The news of Lucy's engagement soon became known to her friends but the formal announcement was postponed by consent of everyone concerned till after Heather Adams's wedding.

"I see it this way, Heth," said her father when discussing the matter with her. "You and Ted are going to be married among our own people at Hogglestock and there'll only be our friends and the people from the works and very nice too and Mother would have been pleased. It's all in the family as you might say and there's no one coming that isn't well known to us except that aunt of Ted's who is a sour-faced cat if ever I saw one."

"She did give me a present, Dad," said Heather, whose happiness made her feel in charity even with aunts-in-law.

"Handkerchief sachet," said Mr. Adams scornfully, "and bought at a Charity Bazaar I'll be bound."

"No it wasn't," said Heather, "because she told Ted she'd had it by her for a long time and thought she'd never get rid of it, and anyway she's only an aunt by marriage. But you're right, Dad. When Ted and I are back from our honeymoon would be a good time."

"Right, girlie," said her father, "and it's as well you're going to see a bit of a world, as this lot," by which we fear that Mr. Adams meant his own Party, "aren't going to make travelling any too easy in the future. I wish I'd seen a bit of Europe myself but when I was young I hadn't the cash and now I'm old I don't feel much like it. If I want to know anything about business in France or Belgium or anywhere, well I can pay the right man to go and so can old Pilward. I daresay you and Ted will find yourselves spending a couple of years on the continent one of these days. I'll tell you what, girlie——"

"Now, dad, I won't have you saying it too," said Heather. "You've caught it from Lucy."

"So I have," said Mr. Adams. "She told me off for saying my word was as good as my bond and I told her off for telling everybody what. Well, we're both old dogs to unlearn old tricks and Lucy is one of the very best."

As we all know, Mr. Adams's progress from what we can only call an outsider in a teddy-bear coat and bright yellow driving gauntlets and a violent check suit with cap to match to the not undistinguished-looking man he had become, was a good deal due to Mrs. Belton of Harefield whose kindness to a very sullen, spotty, conceited Heather had won his heart. Under her unobtrusive tuition he had learnt to dress, to speak with assurance among her friends many of whom had become his friends, and through her quiet and excellent taste he had furnished his house at Edgewood in a way that money alone could not have done. Heather, though younger and less set in her ways than her father, had also benefited in many ways and was devoted to Mrs. Belton but, luckily for her, her taste had remained very conventional and her refurnishing of the house in Hogglestock was much approved by her future parents-in-law, and if it was not interesting it kept a decent man between fumed oak with green hearts inlaid in it and the functional furniture which Mr. Adams privately considered only fit for a board-room, if that.

A few weeks before Heather's marriage Mr. Adams had asked Mrs. Belton to lunch with him at the County Club, choosing a day when he knew she would be in Barchester for a committee.

"Now, Mrs. Belton," he said when they were seated at lunch. "I have a great favour to ask you."

"You have already earned it by choosing what we are to eat," said Mrs. Belton, "not to speak of drink, which is a treat for me. You can't think how little a housekeeper wants to decide about her meals when she is taken out for a treat. What is it?"

"Well, it's Heth's wedding," said Mr. Adams. "The Pilwards have a lot of friends hereabouts and we've asked them all. Heth and I have some very good friends too, but we haven't a family. Ted will have his father and mother and two brothers and three sisters and the Lord knows how many cousins and uncles and aunts. I am giving my Heth away, and I suppose I'll have to arm old Mother Pilward down the aisle afterwards, but I'll be all alone. I haven't a single relation I know of in the world unless it may be a cousin of my old Dad's who went to New Zealand and was never heard of again."

He paused, perhaps to take breath, perhaps as a tribute to his cousin.

"I think," said Mrs. Belton, "that I have known you long enough to be allowed to make a suggestion. If you are asking us to the wedding and I know it is to be only personal friends of the bride's and bridegroom's families, may I have the pleasure of acting as friend—I won't say as mother—for Heather?"

Mr. Adams took out a large white handkerchief, finer so Mrs. Belton noticed with slight envy than any her husband now possessed, and blew his nose.

"Thank you, Mrs. Belton," he said. "You've been everything kind to me and my Heth ever since she fell into the lake and I accept your offer on behalf of my little Heth—I don't know what to say."

"Don't say anything," said Mrs. Belton. "It is all settled and I shall make it a pretext to buy a new hat. And now, though I believe it is quite against etiquette to do so before the announcement, I want to tell you how very happy we all are about Lucy's engagement. Amabel Marling told me and she says Lucy is radiantly happy. My love and every good wish to you both, dear Sam."

She raised her glass and drank.

It was the first time that anyone among his new friends had called the wealthy ironmaster anything but Mr. Adams and he reddened as he tried to thank Mrs. Belton. Part of him was deeply flattered and pleased: another part, a part which appeared to him to move and think independently of its owner, had a sneaking feeling that to be called by his Christian name did indeed set the seal of the county's approval on him, but on the other hand was almost a badge of servitude. And we think he was right. A man may be young, handsome, wealthy, cultivated, charming as Mr. Smith; but from the first moment of his engagement to be married, even if to a duke's daughter with American dollars in her heritage, he has shown that he is but mortal. The ladies who would have fought, delicately, for his presence in their drawing-rooms, feel without realising it that being the prey of Venus has somehow dimmed his lustre and may even speak when he is not present of "poor dear Charles." And if the preceding remarks seem slightly out of date, reflection will show that there is still something in them. The rest of the meal passed in talk about the market garden and the doings of Mrs. Belton's children and grandchildren.

"I must go now, Mr. Adams," said Mrs. Belton, looking at the clock on the mantelpiece which represented in bronze an elephant carrying a howdah, the nearer side of which was a dial, presented by a remote ancestor of Mr. Belton's known as the Nabob, who had managed to dissipate most of the considerable fortune he had amassed in India by keeping (in open sin) a very expensive Parisian lady who ran away with the French architect who was building a rococo Chinese pavilion in the grounds, taking with her all the cash and jewels she could lay her hands on. "I really must, or I shall keep our chairman Lady Pomfret waiting. We will meet at the wedding, and I will bring my daughter-in-law if I may."

"Bring anyone you like," said Mr. Adams, much relieved that his Christian name had been quietly dropped, "and thank you again for my Heth and me. Before you go, I'd like to show you the ring I got for Lucy."

He pulled a small box from his pocket and showed Mrs. Belton a very fine pale sapphire in an open claw setting.

"I had it set that way so that it's easy to clean," said Mr. Adams. "If I know Lucy she'll cart muck or dig a drain in it. A nice wrought iron ring would have been more practical but not quite the thing for a bride."

Mrs. Belton quite truthfully admired the ring, which seemed

to her to have the blue of Lucy's candid eyes, and told Mr. Adams so.

"Just what I thought when I saw it," said Mr. Adams with pleasure. "I never saw eyes as straight as Lucy's. Not in the nature of squinting I don't mean; I mean that girl couldn't tell a lie if she tried."

Mrs. Belton said (quite truthfully) that she was sure of it and hurried off to her committee.

We shall not go into any details about Heather Adams's wedding. Firstly because we hardly know her husband (a very nice, intelligent young man with a good Army record) or his family, and secondly because we do not think Mr. Adams would like it. For the better we have got to know him over the last five or six years the more we have come to respect his fundamental integrity and his power of keeping his own personality, whether in annoying his own party in the House of Commons, defeating business rivals, or keeping his head, his heart and his place among his newer county friends. Suffice it to say that when Heather and Ted Pilward were married the church at Hogglestock had never seen a costlier wedding, and, as Mr. Adams had previously foretold, half the works didn't turn up on time next day owing to pledging the happy pair at Mr. Adams's expense too deeply and too often.

"Which," said Mr. Adams to his housekeeper Miss Hoggett, "didn't surprise me, because with the stuff my Party gives us under the name of beer, you'll be sick long before you're sorry. And that," said Mr. Adams reflectively, "is what most of them were. And now, Miss Hoggett, I've a piece of news for you, at least I don't suppose it will be news, knowing the way things get about, but I should like to tell you myself before it's in the papers."

"It's very kind of you, I'm sure, sir," said Miss Hoggett, "and if it's about Miss Marling I'm sure we've all been saying for a long time that it really seemed as if it was meant, Miss Marling being your fiancée, now Miss Heather is getting married. May I offer congratulations, sir, for me and Annie and Eileen."

"Oh, you all knew it, did you?" said Mr. Adams, who had not realised the interest his domestic staff took in his concerns.

"Oh yes, sir," said Miss Hoggett pityingly. "They say the lookers on see the most of the game and we'd all like to send our respectful good wishes to Miss Marling. When is it to be, sir?"

Mr. Adams said in the spring and it would be in *The Times* next week.

"Well now, isn't that nice, sir," said Miss Hoggett. "This house does need a lady, if you'll excuse my saying so, sir."

A less sensible man might have seen in this remark some slight upon Heather, but Mr. Adams was in most things eminently sensible and remembering Miss Sowerby's parting words about the Old Bank House needing a mistress he felt that he had more than done his duty by it.

Accordingly the Wednesday issue of next week's *Times* (and why Wednesday we do not know) contained under "Forthcoming Marriages" the news that a marriage had been arranged and would take place in the early spring between Samuel Adams, M.P. of The Old Bank House, Edgewood, and Lucy Emily, younger daughter of Mr. and the Hon. Mrs. William Marling of Marling Hall, West Barsetshire.

As may be imagined, the county, more especially the western half, was in a perfect uproar of telephonings and rushing into teashops for a good talk, and incidentally wondering (a) what on earth possessed Lucy Marling to marry a man like Mr. Adams and (b) how on earth a man like Mr. Adams came to think of a girl like Lucy Marling. Mr. Adams, with sound business acumen, had transferred himself for the time being to his flat in London where he was attending to his Parliamentary duties, and his competent and reliable secretary Miss Pickthorn was enjoying herself rapturously as call after call came through on the office telephone; some from friends sincerely "wanting to know," though more benevolently than Miss Rosa Dartle; some from people who felt that their position made it reasonable, nay necessary, for them to be impertinent. Among the latter our readers will be glad to hear was the Dowager Lady Norton, well known to all her acquaintances as The Dreadful Dowager.

"The Hogglestock Iron Works speaking," said Miss Pickthorn. "Victoria, Lady Norton? Yes, Lady Norton, it is Mr. Adam's secretary speaking."

"I want Mr. Adams himself," said the voice of Lady Norton.

"Mr. Adams is in London. Can I take a message?" said Miss Pickthorn who then put her hand over the mouthpiece and said to Miss Cowshay, formerly the cash desk at Pilchard's Stores, then in charge of the teleprinter in the Regional Commissioner's Office in Barchester and now second-in-command of the works costing department, that if she listened in on the extension she'd hear something.

"No," said her ladyship. "I must speak to Mr. Adams myself."

"I'm sorry, Lady Norton, but Mr. Adams is in London," said Miss Pickthorn. "I could take a message for him."

"You can give me his London number," said Lady Norton. "I do not at all understand this engagement and wish to speak to Mr. Adams myself."

"I'm sorry we are not allowed to give his London number," said Miss Pickthorn.

The silence which followed was extremely enjoyable not only to the two ladies but to Mr. Evans the production manager who had come in, he said, to get that file.

"I don't know who it is speaking to me," said Lady Norton's voice. "I wish to speak personally to Mr. Adams. I cannot understand this engagement at all. It is outrageous."

"It is Mr. Adam's secretary speaking," said Miss Pickthorn, who was always admirably unmoved by rudeness on the telephone, and just as well.

"I do not care who it is," said Lady Norton. "Whoever you are I shall report you for insolence."

"It is Mr. Adams's secretary," said Miss Pickthorn, on the verge of the giggles.

The audience held its breath in joyful expectation of Lady Norton's rejoinder, when the words, "You can't talk like that to people, Moggs. Give me the thing for a minute," were heard, followed by a kind of scuffle, after which another woman's voice said, "Sorry, but my mother-in-law's a terror on the telephone. What does she want? Well, of course if you aren't allowed to give it, you can't. I'll tell her to write to him at the House of Commons. Good-bye."

The idea of the Dreadful Dowager's pet name being Moggs made everyone laugh so much that Mr. Evans forgot what he had come for and was just going away when he stopped and said, "Oh, that file."

"Which is it, Mr. Evans?" said Miss Cowshay. "The York and Ripon Ecclesiastical Metal Works, or Amalgamated Vedge about those mechanical bean-slicers?"

"No, no," said Mr. Evans impatiently. "*My* file."

"Ow, if I hadn't forgotten all about it," said Miss Cowshay, at the same time turning the contents of her handbag out onto the table. "Mr. Evans lent it me because there's a screw loose on the lock of the stationery cupboard. Here you are, Mr. Evans. I managed ever so well."

"I am thinking," said Mr. Evans, "—pardon me, ladies, but it's a split finger-nail and really the agony if it catches in anything is what they call ex*qui*site—of writing a little handy volume on "Things you can use as other things." There's quite a lot of things like that."

"That's right," said Miss Cowshay. "If my brother's beaten my young nephew once for using his chisel as a screw-driver, he's beaten him fifty times. 'It's no good, Bob,' I said to my brother, 'your beating that child. You wouldn't check him when he was a kid and now you're getting what you asked for and that lad will never make a good tradesman. A government office is all he's fit for,' I said, at which interesting anecdote her audience, who were well educated and gave the word tradesman its right value, expressed their applause.

"No, what I was thinking of," said Mr. Evans, putting the nail file back in his waistcoat pocket, "was things like using a safety-pin when you haven't got a bodkin, or one of those book straps that the more you pull them back on the buckle the tighter they hold———"

Miss Pickthorn said did he mean one of those ones made of a sort of browny-orangy-reddy stuff rather like very weak braces, only the worst of them was you couldn't make a handle and had to dangle the libery books or carry them under your arm, in which case string would have done as well.

"—the tighter they hold," repeated Mr. Evans in an almost savage way, "or for a belt, if you happen not to be wearing braces and haven't got such a thing as a belt about you."

Ignoring this indelicate subject Miss Pickthorn said they must get up a subscription for Mr. Adams's wedding and it had better be done soon, because if past experience was anything to go by they'd have spent everything they'd got by Christmas Eve, not to speak of all these National Health contributions and what not. All present agreed and the party broke up. And we may say that although at least seven minutes had been spent in conversation all three, being heads in their own particular branch, remained in the office till everything was done.

From now onwards presents and congratulations began to pour in at Marling Hall. Lucy, who was always busy out of doors from dawn to dusk, began to feel almost afraid of the accumulating pile of correspondence and at last confessed this to her mother. Mrs. Marling, who had not for years attempted in any way to control her masterful daughter, was touched by her child's appeal and gave her very sensible mind to the question. What was needed was a temporary secretary, someone who could (if anyone could) stop Lucy tearing open her parcels and overlooking or mislaying the contents, keep an eye on letters

containing cheques two of which had after an hour's very
unpleasant search been rescued from the paper dump which the
West Barsetshire County Council collected every week, docket
the congratulations and perhaps take over some of the secretarial
part of Mrs. Marling's county work so that she might have time
to thrust the question of a trousseau upon her unwilling daughter. On this difficulty she decided to open her heart to her cousin
Lady Graham who had come over from Little Misfit to have tea
and a gossip.

"Darling Amabel," said Lady Graham, "I can't tell you how
happy Robert is about the news. He has never really met Mr.
Adams, but he has several friends in Parliament who know him
and speak very highly of him. He sends you his love and simply
longs to come to the wedding, but you know how difficult it is for
him to get away." To which Mrs. Marling with a sense of
humour that she rarely showed replied that it was not yet settled
and would probably not be till the early spring.

"Robert says," said Agnes Graham, whose sentences were
very apt to begin with these words, "that he would like to give
Lucy a pig for a wedding present if she is going to have them
when she is married."

There was a small pause while Mrs. Marling considered the
offer and Agnes too appeared to do a little thinking, for she
added, "Of course Robert's Holdings Goliath did only get
second prize at the Barchester Agricultural, and William's pig
was first, but our cowman Goble says our sows are wonderful
breeders, and Robert has a fine young one."

These words from Lady Graham, who always looked and
mostly spoke as if her mind could not entertain anything heavier
than swansdown or caramel soufflé, might have surprised her
many admirers, including Bishop Joram, but as Mr. Marling had
said, more than once, Agnes might look like a Pompadour but
she had uncommon good horsesense. And though the comparison was a poor one he was quite right in his recognition of the
sound bottom of common sense in her.

"It is extremely generous of Robert," said Mrs. Marling, for to offer a sire (we speak in a general way) may be generous, but to offer a dam (or in this case a sow) is princely. Even as the Arabs jealously guarded their mares, mares about whom noble poetry has been written, so do pig-breeders guard their sows, and this offer of Sir Robert Graham's was flattering, for not only did it show his good will to his wife's young cousin, but also his appreciation of Mr. Adams as a citizen, for as a private individual he had barely met him. "It is really *most* kind of him, Agnes. I will ask Lucy what her pig plans are, but it is really difficult to get a moment alone with her. She insists on going on with her work for Mr. Adams and she works very hard here and really I sometimes wonder how she will find time to get married. Come and look in the old drawing-room, Agnes."

She took Lady Graham to the large drawing-room with its handsome cornice and panelling, its long line of French windows on three sides, which had not been used since 1945. The family had taken over a large bedroom as their living-room and a very pleasant room it made, and the drawing-room had been used for Red Cross Stores and was still stacked with hospital supplies. One end of the room had been cleared and here, on the old dining-room table with all its leaves in it, were Lucy's wedding presents in most unadmired disorder.

"You see, Agnes," said Mrs. Marling.

"Oh, dear," said Agnes in her soft voice. "How very upsetting. You must feel quite worried."

"I do," said Mrs. Marling. "If I knew a nice woman who would come here and help with letters and telephoning and keeping things tidy, I would be thankful. Really I could do with a secretary for several months, as I *must* take Lucy to London for clothes whether she likes it or not, and I can't do the wedding single-handed. We are thinking of the cathedral as our church is so tiny. Only then I don't know what to do about the reception. Lady Fielding was lucky when Anne was married because she lives in the Close and people could walk across. You are so practical, Agnes. Do think of something."

Although practical was the last word anyone would have thought of applying to Lady Graham, those who really knew her and they were not very many although her admirers and acquaintances were legion, would have heartily concurred in it. Her appealing charm covered a good deal of the Pomfret masterfulness and the Leslie commonsense, she was an excellent judge of people, could manage servants and children and never appeared ruffled whatever happened. Her husband consulted her about most things and as often as not followed her advice, although we sometimes wonder if he was conscious of it.

"Darling Amabel, it is quite *dreadful*," said Agnes, her dove's eyes darkening with distressed sympathy. "How I wish I could think of someone. Someone like Merry," said Lady Graham, alluding to the invaluable Miss Merriman who had been secretary to old Lady Pomfret and then guide, philosopher and friend to Lady Emily in her last years, "but she promised to go to Sally Pomfret after mamma died."

Mrs. Marling's heart, which had risen a little, sank back with a dull thud.

"Have you heard about Sally?" said Agnes.

Mrs. Marling said not in particular. What was it, she asked.

"You know poor Gillie is never very well and he will overwork himself in the Lords, besides killing himself in the county," said Agnes. "So Sally got the bit between her teeth and she is taking the whole family to the villa at Cap Ferrat for the winter, and Merry is to go with them. We all think it an excellent plan. Sally had been most sensible and if Mellings doesn't go to his prep school till Easter it doesn't matter at his age. He is one mass of nerves, poor darling, but Sally says he has been much better since she found he was frightened of riding, thanks to Eleanor Grantly that nice girl who was her secretary at the Hospital Libraries. And that," said Agnes, her gentle voice becoming almost animated, "reminds me."

"What of?" said Mrs. Marling, as Agnes appeared to have got to the end of her sentence.

"I don't want to raise your hopes," said Agnes, "but there have been some disagreeable differences at the Hospital Libraries and Sally is resigning for six months at any rate and I hope for ever, and that nice girl Isabel Dale who was in the secretary's office, is resigning too. I wonder."

"Who is taking over then?" said Mrs. Marling, more interested for the moment in the St. John and Red Cross Hospital Libraries' difficulties than in her own.

"Eleanor Norton," said Agnes. "She will do very well I think. Robert says that anyone who can call old Lady Norton Moggs and alter the drawing-room furniture at Norton Hall can run the Libraries with one finger. Sally told me that Eleanor Norton had a talk with Isabel Dale and they agreed in quite a nice way that they would both rather work with someone else. Would you like me to find out? I wish darling Clarissa could help you, but she is at college which is too too sad and will be there for two more years. But luckily they have very long holidays and perhaps she will grow out of it," said her ladyship, who appeared to think of a university education as a form of measles, catching but not dangerous.

Mrs. Marling sympathised about Clarissa and asked Agnes to find out more about Isabel Dale and then Agnes went away.

CHAPTER 3

It was one of Lady Graham's many charming ways that as well as being gentle and lovely and extremely capable she had never been known to forget a promise, even if she could not fulfill it at once. Time passed and just as Mrs. Marling was beginning to wish (though not really) that Lucy could be married out of hand and all this fuss over, Agnes rang up to say that young Lady Norton was taking over the Hospital Libraries and Isabel Dale was leaving her job by friendly and mutual agreement. Eleanor Grantly, she said, who was not being married till after Christmas (or to put it more truthfully till after the Michaelmas Law Sitting ended and Colin Keith was free) was going to stay on and get the new secretary into the ways of the office.

"So if you would like to see Isabel, will you ring her up?" said Agnes. "I would love to ask you both to tea at Holdings, but Robert thinks the Women's County Club would be better. Besides it gets dark so early now, and we shall be back in Ordinary Time soon, which is so bad."

Mrs. Marling agreed.

"Darling mamma never liked Summer Time," said Agnes, evoking by her sweet melancholy voice a vision of Lady Emily fading in the glare of late summer afternoons, "but as she did not particularly notice which kind of time it was unless we told her, it was really all quite nice," upon which remark her ladyship went away leaving her cousin Amabel to reflect that David

Leslie was not far wrong when he spoke of his sister Agnes as a divine idiot.

With great courage Mrs. Marling mentioned Agnes's plan to Lucy who, much mellowed by love and a long hard day with Mr. Spadger about the new cowsheds, kissed her mother in a manly way and said a very good idea to have someone nice to help with letters and presents and things, all of which she appeared to look upon as natural phenomena in no way connected with herself, and Isabel Dale's uncle Christopher Dale over at Allington had grown that new Canadian wheat better than anyone in the county, emboldened by which remark her mother did not ring up, for it was to her slightly undignified to begin an acquaintance by telephone, but wrote to Miss Dale. Within two days she had an answer from Miss Dale and went into Barchester to meet her at the Women's County Club. As she entered the dark strangers' room a figure rose and came towards her.

"Mrs. Marling?" said a pleasant voice, "I am Isabel Dale. It was very kind of you to ask me to lunch."

Mrs. Marling made a suitable reply and took her guest up to the dining-room where she had reserved a table for two. Here, when the not very interesting meal had been ordered, she was able to see Miss Dale more clearly. She was a not quite young woman, probably about Lucy's age, she thought, which was nearer thirty than twenty, tall, good-looking, fair and blue-eyed with the oval face that is today very rare. Her clothes Mrs. Marling appraised in her brief glance as very good and very suitable and she was pleased to observe that though her lips were slightly reddened her nails were not.

"I suppose," said Mrs. Marling, "that Lady Graham told you more or less what I wanted, though it is difficult to say exactly what I *do* want."

"I think I understand," said Miss Dale. "A kind of extra daughter who isn't a daughter plus a secretary who isn't a secretary. If you were different I would say someone you can be just as nice or as rude to as you would be to your own family, only I'm perfectly sure none of you are ever rude. I can do shorthand and typing and housekeeping and gardening and hens, but I don't know cows or pigs. I was with the Red Cross through the war and then lately at the Hospital Library in Barchester, living at home, and I have a general feeling that if I live with my mother much longer we might annoy each other. Nothing against her, nor against me, but it doesn't work and she has two old servants and a lot of friends at Allington. I shall have some money when she dies, I believe, but I like to earn as well, as you can't trust Them for a moment when it's a question of invest-ments. I am never ill and I have quite a good temper, except when mother says how sad it is that girls don't want to stay at home now, or that girls don't seem to marry now. I think that's all."

Mrs. Marling had been thinking hard while Miss Dale was speaking, and if anyone says you can't listen and think simulta-neously they are wrong: and a good many people can not only listen and think but talk as well. And how one's mind does it we cannot say, for the human mind is a queer place and much of it unexplored and likely to remain so. She had liked her guest's voice and much approved her allusion to Them.

"Thank you, Miss Dale," she said. "It all sounds quite reason-able. As Lady Graham will have told you, my elder children are married. My younger son Oliver lives in London and usually comes down for weekends and holidays and my younger daugh-ter Lucy, who is a farmer, is engaged to Mr. Adams, our M.P. I have a good deal of county work and so has my husband. I must tell you at once that he is always rather deaf and becomes stone deaf if he doesn't like people. Do you feel that you could fit happily into our busy life, beginning by getting Lucy's wedding presents into some sort of order?"

"I think I could," said Miss Dale. "If you would like to try me I suggest a month on trial on both sides so that I could see about the presents and get the hang of things and you could see if I give satisfaction. I am twenty-nine, though I don't look it because

I'm fair, and am not engaged or likely to be so. He was killed in Italy. Lady Pomfret will give me a character and I can shout at deaf people quite quietly. John's father was rather deaf and I used to talk a lot with him. He died of a broken heart I think in the end. I didn't, so here I am."

Mrs. Marling had a curious feeling that Miss Dale was interviewing her rather than being interviewed, but her whole impression of her was favourable and it was arranged that Miss Dale should come to Marling Hall on the following Saturday and start work on the Monday.

Accordingly late on Saturday afternoon Miss Dale arrived at Melicent Halt, the little station which served Marling. While she was getting her suit-cases down from the rack a porter came up.

"Are you Miss Dale, miss?" he said, taking her luggage firmly under his protection. "Miss Lucy's outside in the van. She said to bring you out, miss, because she's got a pig inside."

Miss Dale, a countrywoman born and bred, liked this beginning to her adventure and followed the porter to the gate. In the little station yard was a Ford van from which came gruntings and squealings and by it stood a handsome weather-beaten young woman of about her own age.

"Hullo, are you Miss Dale?" said the young woman. "I'm Lucy Marling. I say, I hope you don't mind pigs. I had to bring this one over from Barchester. He's spending the night here and tomorrow I'm taking him over to Adamsfield. Stick the suit-cases under the seat, Bill. Come on."

Thus summoned Miss Dale got into the van beside Lucy and they drove through the pretty village of Marling Melicent and up the drive to Marling Hall. The journey did not take more then ten minutes but during that time the two young women were able to take stock of each other and found it satisfactory. Lucy stopped at the back door, for the front door had hardly ever been used since 1939 except for Red Cross parties, took a suit-case in each hand and saying "Come on" led Miss Dale up what were obviously back stairs, though very nice ones, to the second floor.

"Here's your room," said Lucy, hitting a door open with her knee and banging the suit-cases onto the floor. "The bathroom's through that door and I'm on the other side of it. Mother and father sleep on the first floor but they aren't below us so it doesn't matter if you make a bit of noise. I put a writing table for you and there are plenty of cupboards and things and I know the bed's all right because I sleep in it sometimes if I want to get up very early so that mother and father won't hear the alarm clock. If you'd like to unpack I'll go and see about the pig and come back to you."

Hardly waiting for an answer she went loudly downstairs.

Miss Dale left to herself began to unpack, putting her clothes neatly and methodically into drawers and cupboards. She liked her room which faced west and was drenched in warm sunlight. The old-fashioned wallpaper of large pink roses and trailing leaves was faded where the sun had lain on it, the good walnut furniture bore signs of family use. The carpet had once, she thought, been an Aubusson, but was now little more than a pinkish string floor-cover though very clean. Some engravings of family portraits hung on the walls and there was a bookcase containing a number of Miss Charlotte Yonge's novels, a Bible, two volumes of Good Words for the Young, a very old edition of the Encyclopaedia Britannica and a medley of Victorian yellow-backs which Miss Dale looked forward to exploring. An em-broidered bell-pull hung by the fireplace and on the marble mantelpiece were two money boxes, one of Anne Hathaway's cottage and one of Burn's cottage, two china statuettes of very curly white French poodles and a dirty penwiper.

When Miss Dale had put her things away and stacked her suit-cases on a high shelf in the cupboard, she stood up, stretched herself, went to the window and looked out over the garden to the farm lands and the meadows, where the winding course of the river was marked by alders and rushes, to the distant downs.

"It's a good view, isn't it?" said Lucy coming back. "I say, I've parked the pig. What would you like to do? Mother and father are out but they'll be back before dinner and my brother Oliver is coming down from London. He works there. We might walk down to meet him. I suppose you wouldn't like to see the presents, would you?" said Lucy, faintly embarrassed. "It's awfully good of people to send one so many presents but it's pretty awful remembering which is which. I mean the cards mostly seem to get lost or something. Is your room all right? Don't ring the bell because it doesn't work and it usually comes down with a bang. That's how Anne Hathaway's chimney got broken. We're pretty shabby, but we've still got some nice linen, only I'm not much good at mending."

Miss Dale said, quite truthfully, that she loved the room, and began to examine the sheets and pillowcases and towels.

"You *have* got some lovely linen," she said. "Perhaps your mother wouldn't mind my doing some mending when I've finished my other work. I would love it."

Lucy, though surprised by this peculiar form of pleasure, said she was sure her mother would be very grateful for help and then took Miss Dale down to the drawing-room where, as we know, the wedding presents were beginning to accumulate in horrid confusion.

"It's enough to make one wish one weren't going to be married," said Lucy despondently.

Miss Dale said there was something to be said for cheques, because then you could buy what you wanted.

"The trouble is we really don't need them," said Lucy. "Mr. Adams is very rich and I've got two hundred a year of my own and he is going to make a settlement or something. I don't know. I say, do look at old Lady Norton's present."

Miss Dale gazed with horrified respect at a small bronze statuette of gorilla carrying off—doubtless with the best intentions—a naked female in whose hand had a branch with an electric light at the end of it.

"Lord!" she said.

"I know," said Lucy. "And I ought to have thanked her a week ago, but it's so ghastly I don't know what to say. I say, Miss Dale, do you really know what one ought to say about presents one doesn't like?"

Miss Dale suddenly felt very sorry for her hostess. She was not going to run her head into the noose of friendship without looking, but she felt a kind of compassion for Lucy Marling so ignorant of the most ordinary rules of society, so entirely unspoiled by the prospect of riches, so capable, so bewildered. Her own life had stopped, or the core of it had, long ago. To help Lucy Marling would at least give one the illusion of being useful.

"It is certainly difficult to feel grateful for the gorilla," said Miss Dale, "but I'm sure we can invent something."

"It would be most awfully useful if you could," said Lucy. "I'm frightfully busy with the market garden just now, and mother keeps on wanting me to think about clothes but I simply haven't time. I say, it's awfully good of you to come. It's rather ghastly here sometimes. I mean father and mother are angels but—oh well, I don't know. Sorry," and she looked with dislike at her wedding presents and then away into the garden.

Miss Dale said nothing and went on inspecting the presents, a great many of which were very good ones, generously and affectionately given. As one's own life was finished and one's heart desolate, one could at least try not to intrude one's loss; one could possibly make things easier for people like Lucy who were ignorant of so much in spite of intelligence, energy and goodwill.

"At any rate," she said, "we can make a shot at it. And to begin with, please call me Isabel. My people call me Bell, after an old aunt of father's, but I like my real name."

Lucy said she would love to and how lucky it was that there

wasn't a short for Lucy, as nobody could be called Looce, and it was time they went down to meet Oliver.

When the train stopped at Melicent Halt, Miss Dale saw a tall thin man get out, upon whom Lucy flung herself with abandon.

"Here's Oliver," she said, as proudly as a dog who has found a ball thrown by its master. "This is Isabel Dale. She's come to stay to help mother and me with those ghastly wedding presents and all that rot."

Miss Dale observed on a closer view that Mr. Oliver Marling had rather long hair which she disliked, but brushed well back which was better; that he wore very large horn spectacles and his eyes looked tired; that his town clothes were well cut and well kept and that he gave the impression that country clothes would not suit him so well; that like his sister Lucy he had long hands and feet, but while her hands were browned and battered and capable, his hands looked singularly useless. But all this took place in a second and when she said How do you do to Oliver Marling no one could have guessed all she had seen and thought. Their walk back to Marling Hall was enlivened by Lucy's artless dissertation on the market garden, pigs, drains and other useful subjects which made general conversation almost impossible and then dinner was ready.

During the war and the first years of so-called peace the Marling family had to some degree kept up the appearance of dressing for dinner, but gradually as servants melted away and clothes wore out and heating became more and more difficult they had given up the unequal struggle. Lucy was naturally the first to succumb, for her farm work kept her out till all hours and when Summer Time kept the world light till far into the evening it seemed unreasonable to make oneself clean only to get dirty again. Her parents had at one time shown a slightly rebellious spirit about breeches at the dinner table, but had finally given in.

Oliver had also tried to keep up some kind of standard, but as his evening clothes wore out and could only be replaced at great expense of money and coupons by vastly inferior ones he too had resigned himself. Coupons were now not needed, but the poor quality and terrifying price of clothes did not improve. So except in winter when Mrs. Marling and Lucy wore woollen house-coats against the winter's flaw, everyone dined in much the same clothes they had been wearing all day: as did the greater part of the world. There were indeed rumours from people who had been to London that the young girls were again wearing pretty frocks and the young men dinner jackets and even tails at dances, but to Barsetshire these things were small and undistinguishable, like far-off mountains turned into clouds; and they remained as they were.

"This is Miss Dale, William," said Mrs. Marling to her husband who had just come in with a very good imitation of a man stiff from a day's hunting, though he had hardly been on a horse for the last two years. "She is going to help me and Lucy with the presents and Lucy's clothes. You know——"

"Now, wait a minute," said Mr. Marling, shaking hands with Miss Dale and letting himself down into his chair. "Dale. Now your people are over Allington way, young lady."

From some this might have appeared to be in the nature of a query, but so doggedly nay threateningly did Mr. Marling say it that Miss Dale felt almost guilty.

"Now don't tell me," said Mr. Marling. "Your father's a grandson of the Dale who married the girl with money, patent medicines or something. Used to see him on the Bench some-times. Shot with him once in '13, or was it '14. What's he doin' now?"

Mrs. Marling and Oliver looked quickly and agonisedly at each other. Of course Papa would put his foot in it and would probably put it in a good deal further before he had done. Miss Dale who had very good manners and disliked seeing people embarrassed said, quite truthfully, "I don't exactly know, Mr.

Marling. You see he died ten years ago," but her words were overpowered by Lucy who, prefacing her words by a sotto voce "Isn't father ghastly" to Miss Dale, said in her most powerful voice, "He's DEAD, father. You went to the funeral and got an awful cold."

"Funeral?" said Mr. Marling, "whose funeral? Oh, I see. Beg your pardon, Miss Dale. I'm gettin' an old fool and my memory's not what it was. I know now. Shockin' weather it was. Coldest I've ever known. Pomfret wouldn't come into the church; said he was sure your father would understand if he sat in his car while the service was goin' on. Took his hat off, of course. And he's gone too. Well, I'm sorry, my dear. I'm not much longer for this world and I shan't be sorry to go."

Miss Dale was, or appeared to be, suitably impressed, yet managing to convey at the same time to Oliver and Lucy that she didn't believe in their father's intimations of mortality any more than they did, and the rest of the meal passed without any particular incident. After dinner Oliver and Lucy took Miss Dale round the garden in the warm autumn dusk and they talked about country and county matters and got on very well, and Lucy told Miss Dale about Heather Adams's wedding and showed her the pale sapphire which, just as her betrothed had foretold, she wore day and night, whether working with her hands or telling other people who were working with their hands what.

"Aren't you afraid of losing the stone?" said Miss Dale.

"It's awfully safe with these claws, and if it did fall out we'd buy another," said Lucy simply, and Oliver marvelled at the way she took her future wealth for granted. Then she went to have a last look at the pig and Oliver brought chairs onto the stone walk up against the warm west side of the house and he and Miss Dale sat there talking.

"You know Jessica Dean, don't you?" she said presently.

As happened whenever that enchantress's name was mentioned a thousand little shafts of flame were shivered in Oliver's bony frame (and we fear that on the whole he enjoyed this peculiar experience) and he said he did.

"We hear about them from Mrs. Lover," said Miss Dale. "Her husband was the Bank Manager where my mother's family lived in Loamshire."

Oliver said politely that he was afraid he didn't know Mrs. Lover.

"Aubrey's mother," said Miss Dale. "Aubrey's real name, but of course you must know this, is Caleb Lover and he used to sign his letters C. Lover, because Caleb is such a dreadful name, and he writes so badly that it always looked like Clover. So then he needed a Christian name and chose Aubrey, because his mother's name is Audrey."

Most of this interesting story Oliver had heard, vaguely, at some time or another, but he had never heard the bit about Mrs. Lover's name being Audrey and expressed an interest which, he hoped, entirely hid his complete want of it.

"Did you know they are going to have a baby?" said Miss Dale. Did Oliver know? Had his soul not been seared by the news. Had he not, on his midnight pallet lying (which was an uncommonly comfortable spring mattress) been smitten to the core by the thought, going so far in mortification and abnegation of self as to consider offering to be a godfather.

"Yes, isn't it delightful?" he said. "Jessica says they are going to call it Sarah Siddons."

Miss Dale said what would they call it if it was a boy, which inspired them both to such foolish suggestions as Harry Tate and David Garrick, and then it was cold, so they went in.

During the next weeks Miss Lucy Marling had occasion to tell her betrothed more than once that she wished they could go to a registrar's office and get it over, so boring to her were the discussions about the when and the where of the wedding, but Mr. Adams with his usual good sense reminded her that the wedding was entirely to please her parents and the numerous friends of both contracting parties. Mrs. Marling was also exercised about Mr. Adams's business friends to whom she wished to be polite and friendly while feeling in the depths of her heart that they had nothing in common whatsoever. Since Miss Dale had come to Marling Hall she had proved herself daily more sensible, intelligent and useful and at last Mrs. Marling, choosing an evening when Mr. Marling had gone to dine at the County Club with Mr. Adams to talk over the lawyers' proposals, opened her mind to Miss Dale and asked her advice.

"We would like our own church," said Mrs. Marling, "only it's so small. And the Dean, who has very nicely said he wants to marry Lucy himself—I mean do the marrying himself, I mean marrying Lucy——" and here she stopped, overcome by the difficulties of the English language.

"Yes?" said Miss Dale, in so understanding a way that Mrs. Marling plucked up courage and went on, "Of course it would be delightful if the Dean did it in the Cathedral, but it would mean borrowing a house in the Close for the reception as people could never get out here. And then I know Bishop Joram would like to help, only again we don't want to offend the Vicar."

She was silent, contemplating the difficulties of life.

"But, Mrs. Marling, surely they could *all* marry Lucy," said Miss Dale. "Then we could get the *Barchester Chronicle* to put The ceremony was performed by the Dean of Barchester assisted by Canon Joram and the Vicar of Marling Melicent. Of course we'd have to get all the Reverends and things right, but your Vicar would know about that. And then you could have the wedding and the reception here. We could make the drawing-room perfectly lovely."

Mrs. Marling after a few minutes' consideration said it seemed a very good plan and if her husband and Mr. Adams approved she would fix a date with the ecclesiastical gentlemen concerned.

"Then that's all right," said Miss Dale. "You will ask Mr. Marling of course. What about Mr. Adams?"

"Well, someone has got to do it," said Mrs. Marling wearily, for she was beginning to agree with her daughter Lucy that the sooner the better. "I can't give up my committees and the County work for three or four months just for a wedding. At least I really mean I don't want to," she added, overcome by an attack of honesty.

"But, Mrs. Marling," said Miss Dean. "You did engage me to help you. All you really need to do is to tell the Dean and Bishop Joram and the Vicar yourself, and then I can do the rest. And I know Miss Pickthorn, Mr. Adams's secretary, because her sister was in the Red Cross with me in the war."

Mrs. Marling was interested and grateful but not convinced, and her husband coming in at that moment she put her difficulties before him.

"Most sensible thing I've heard yet," said Mr. Marling. "No good keeping a dog and barking yourself, my dear. You've quite enough to do and here's Miss Dale ready to help. Much better to have the wedding here. Pity my old uncle Fitzherbert Marling isn't alive. The Archdeacon," he added in an aside to Miss Dale. "*He'd* have married them. He laid a wager with old Belton, Belton's father over at Harefield, that he'd ride five miles and drink a quart of claret and marry a couple within an hour, and he did it too."

Miss Dale said it was a pity they couldn't get the bishop to make a bet like that as it would be such fun to see him lose it and burst all the buttons off his gaiters, at which Mr. Marling laughed so heartily that his wife felt she had done a very good deed in asking Miss Dale to spend the winter with them, for she had not seen her husband so well amused for a long time

"Good girl," said Mr. Marling approvingly. "I didn't like to mention the bishop before. You might have been one of the Palace lot and I wouldn't like to hurt your feelings."

"We all Hate and Despise the Bishop at Allington," said Miss Dale with surprising energy, "that is when we think of him which is practically never. My father was at college with him and they used to call him Old Gasbags."

So delighted was Mr. Marling by this intelligence that his wife was quite prepared for him to kiss Miss Dale by way of cementing this common dislike of the Bishop.

When once Mrs. Marling had made a decision she was prompt in action. She had a word with the Vicar who was delighted that the wedding was to be at Marling Melicent and perfectly agreeable to the Dean and Bishop Joram officiating. She then made her husband write to the Dean himself, the letter being drafted by Miss Dale. His ready consent being obtained she then rang up Bishop Joram and, with Miss Dale prompting her, secured his enthusiastic collaboration. As for Mr. Adams, Miss Dale and Miss Pickthorn arranged a meeting between him and Mr. Marling during which both gentlemen were stricken with sudden self-consciousness, a state of mind foreign and disturbing to them, and showed every symptom of shying off the subject altogether. On the evening of the day on which this inconclusive talk had taken place, Miss Pickthorn and Miss Dale decided on the Thursday before Holy Week and on the following day each gentleman was complimented by his secretary, or guest, on his choice of day. Lucy rather grudgingly said in public that she supposed Thursday would be all right, but went so far as to tell her affianced that it was the most heavenly day in the world, at which he was deeply moved.

The months moved on in their usual way. All the presents were acknowledged. After Christmas Jessica Dean asked Lucy to spend a fortnight with her in London, as she was shortly retiring into private life for what she called The Last Days of Sarah Siddons, and worked even harder at taking Lucy to dressmakers and tailors and every kind of shop than she worked at the Cockspur. In vain did Lucy make her usual plea of Rot. It was impossible to contradict Jessica, especially at a moment when any contretemps might, so Lucy thought, produce a baby marked with some fatal sign that its mother had been thwarted.

"Bless you, my lamb," said Jessica. "Do you think Sarah Siddons might have twelve toes because you don't want to go to Madame Martha and have your face made over? You don't know Sarah."

"Nor do you, my love," said Aubrey Clover. "She may have twenty toes and probably has by the look of her," to which Jessica replied, "La, Clover, you are indeed a Horrid Coarse Wretch and before Miss, too," and Lucy began to realise that interesting as were cows and pigs and other domestic animals, people in general and babies in particular might be just as interesting; and if Jessica could find a baby even more enthralling than the Cockspur, there must be something in them.

Oliver dined with them during her visit and could not but admire Jessica's influence on his sister Lucy, who was vastly improved by Jessica's bullying care and rather touchingly pleased by finding that one could take pains about one's appearance without anyone thinking the worse of one.

On her last evening Oliver, who though he had renounced Jessica found it necessary to visit his sister Lucy at the Clovers' flat, found Jessica and Aubrey alone.

"Lucy has gone to a film with one of the twins," said Jessica, whose flat was always open to any of her family who had to be in London. "She won't be long. Oh, here's Miss Barchester. You don't know her, do you? She is the Barchester Beauty Queen for this year and Aubrey is thinking of giving her a part in his new play," and in came a tall handsome girl with slightly waved hair, wearing a very good tailor-made suit, who looked as if she had just come back from warm beaches in the South.

"Hold it, darling," said Aubrey, as Oliver rose to be introduced. "Twenty-eight, twenty-nine, thirty. I've won."

Oliver looked; and then felt and indeed appeared rather mad.

"It was only a joke," said Miss Barchester, giving Oliver a bear-like hug which none but his sister Lucy could have given. "Aubrey betted me I could take you in for thirty seconds and I said I couldn't possibly. Do you like it?" she asked anxiously.

"Of course I do," said Oliver. "But what have you done?"

"Nothing, my sweet," said Jessica, "except do what I told her. A bit of hair-do; a spot of face-do; a good belt, and I've told Miss M. to give the old one to the Cats' Home; and an expensive but *most* repaying visit to a few good houses."

"She doesn't mean *people's* houses," said Lucy kindly to her brother. "She means dressmakers."

"Not that word, my pet," said Jessica shuddering. "And I'm coming to the wedding if it's in a bath-chair and if you don't do *everything* I told you, I shall forbid the banns. By the way, Oliver, I told a lie about the twin. Lucy was having tea with her ironmaster. What did my charming Adams say to you, darling?"

"Oh, just rot about me looking nice," said Lucy, sitting down. Jessica screamed.

"NOT in that suit, my lamb," she said, sinking back in a stage faint. "Go and change it at once."

Lucy got up obediently and went out. Miss M. looked in and said Was Mr. Marling staying to dinner.

"Is he?" said Jessica.

"I'd love to," said Oliver, "but I'm afraid I can't."

Jessica looked at Aubrey Clover with a face of amused simulation of self-pity and held out a hand for Oliver to kiss.

"But why?" she asked.

"Isabel Dale is in town for the night," said Oliver, "and I think she expects me to take her out."

"Be an angel, Miss M. and ring her up and ask her to dinner," said Jessica. "Mr. Marling will give you her number. I must go and tidy myself, for it's no good calling it dressing for dinner with Sarah Siddons about."

Oliver tried to protest, but Jessica had left the room, Lucy was not back and Aubrey Clover was typing suddenly and violently in a corner. So presently Miss Dale came, delighted to see such famous people at close quarters and full of admiration for Jessica's work on Lucy, and Oliver had the pleasure of watching his goddess and the girl, who though no goddess seemed to him more sympathetic than other girls, making great friends, while Aubrey Clover plied Lucy with flattery which, though she was not deceived by it, amused and pleased her.

"Well, my pretty one," said Jessica when her guests had gone. "A penny for your thoughts."

"I thought how kind you and Aubrey were and how I'd tell Mr. Adams all about it," said Lucy.

CHAPTER 4

As we know (or should know considering the number of times the present writer has mentioned it), Marling Melicent was a very small village and marriages were not very frequent. No marriage from The Hall had taken place since Mr. Marling's Aunt Lucy had married the Duke of Omnium's youngest son, and as they had both been drowned in the *Titanic* and had no children, Lucy said it didn't count. The Vicar, who was a very nice worthy man but so dull that we shall not trouble to invent a name for him, was naturally enchanted by the luck that had befallen him and was even suspected of having given advance news of the wedding to the young man from the *Barchester Chronicle*.

Lucy had at first stood out manfully against what she called all that bridesmaid rot, but when she found that her cousins Emmy and Clarissa Graham had been counting on it, her kind heart was moved and she gave in. Mrs. Marling had gone through some private anxiety about her future son-in-law's best man. It certainly was, putting Mr. Adams's essential uprightness and niceness aside, an awkward position. If he chose one of his tried business associates one quite frankly didn't feel it would fit, though of course it might and one didn't in the least wish to be snobbish. If he asked one of his newer friends, who was there who would suit? If Mr. Belton could have supported him to the altar it would have been perfect, but it was unusual to have an elderly married man as groomsman and the last thing Mrs. Marling (or Mr. Adams either for that matter) wanted was to be in any way conspicuous. As usually occurred when Mr. Adams's plans were in question, that gentleman thought it out for himself and all Mrs. Marling's fears were vain.

When, after a tiring morning broken by perpetual telephone calls, Miss Dale again answered the nagging bell which none of us have the courage (or perhaps want of curiosity) to ignore a voice announced itself as Miss Pickthorn and said Mr. Adams would like to speak to Mrs. Marling if convenient.

"It's Mr. Adams, Mrs. Marling," said Miss Dale with her hand on the mouthpiece. "For you."

Mrs. Marling took the receiver, almost ready to snap off Miss Pickthorn's head for bothering her, but Mr. Adams with the innate courtesy that so often surprised his acquaintances was already at the telephone with the awning spread and the red carpet on the ground as it were.

"Good morning, Mrs. Marling," said Mr. Adams. "I wouldn't have rung you up as I know what the telephone can be when you're busy, but I thought I would have the pleasure of telling you myself that Mr. Gresham has kindly consented to be my best man. It's just as well we're being married while Parliament is up," said Mr. Adams, to whom it did not appear to have occurred that his Lucy's family would have considered this point, "or he couldn't have come. No more couldn't I, for that matter," he added reflectively. "Well, that's all, Mrs. Marling, and I'd be glad if you could tell me what the bridesmaids would like. No sense in giving girls something they don't like. What they want is something that everyone else is wearing, whether it's a necklace or a brooch or a wrist-watch. Miss Emmy Graham is a fine hand with cows and Clarissa is as pretty as they make them, but that's no help."

Mrs. Marling expressed approval of Mr. Gresham, promised to find out what the bridesmaids wanted, and came back to her writing-table.

"If only Mr. Adams didn't have to talk so much he would be perfect," she said.

"I expect it's because he is used to doing all his thinking aloud," said Miss Dale. "Uneducated people usually do. If *we* think aloud it usually means we are gently going mad. But I can't help feeling that practically everything Mr. Adams does is right because it is all so like Mr. Adams. What had he to say?"

"Mr. Gresham is going to be his best man," said Mrs. Marling, in whose voice her secretary could hear relief and approval. "And he wanted to know about the bridesmaids' presents."

Miss Dale made no answer and there was silence for a moment while each lady reflected upon the excellence of Mr. Adams's choice. The Conservative Member for East Barsetshire, a middle-aged bachelor of old county stock; the seal of the County's acceptance of the rich self-made ironmaster. And possibly, though neither lady was going to say so aloud, an adumbration of Mr. Adams's future political views? But this did not really matter at present. Mr. Gresham was an old and valued acquaintance, liked and respected by everyone, with such trifling exceptions as the Reverend Enoch Arden who had a cure of souls in a small red-brick edifice with Anglo-Saxon dog-tooth moulding in yellow brick round the top of its front door, called Ebenezer, in Hallbury New Town; and the headmaster of the secondary school at Silverbridge who appeared to be under the impression that Mr. Gresham exercised in fang and out fang and was in the habit of cutting off the bow fingers of his tenantry and the claws of their dogs, besides keeping his servants in a kind of Little-Ease and living on untaxed dividends of at least two hundred per cent. It would be very agreeable to the Marlings that he should stand by Mr. Adams in his hour of danger: and also very nice to have a talk with him afterwards, as owing to petrol and other troubles they rarely met.

Well, that was settled and the bridesmaids' dresses were settled though that had been difficult as Emmy was large and fair and blue-eyed and sunburnt and Clarissa was like her mother with dark cloudy hair, dark eyes and a skin of exquisite fairness, rose-flushed, with a pretty figure and small elegant bones. It was their mother who had finally settled the question by taking both girls to London and showing them to her own dressmaker.

"You see, Madame Sartoria," said Agnes, looking with slightly despondent affection at her offspring.

"I see," said Madame Sartoria. "Cheval de charrue et cheval pur sang. Pour le morale, je ne dis pas, mais pour la taille— Enfin———." with which discouraging words, at least as far as Emmy was concerned, she summoned assistants from the vastly deep and caused fabrics from France to be draped on chairs, while Agnes looked on in her usual state of placid want of interest.

"NON," said Madame Sartoria, "enlevez-moi tout ça. Il faut que je réfléchisse."

"They must be Ascot frocks," said Agnes, speaking out of a kind of Pythoness's trance. "I don't think anything else would suit them both. Only *summer* Ascot of course," upon which Madame Sartoria called on her creator to bear witness that she had been struck with exactly the same thought and made her head assistant bring printed silks patterned with leaves and flowers, such as England had not seen for many years. Measurements were taken, and Madame Sartoria promised to find or make coronals of leaves as it was obviously impossible to put Emmy into a hat. The total cost, which no one thought of mentioning, would be about seventy-five pounds for the two of them, but Agnes for all her silly sweetness understood money and knew that such dresses, from Madame Sartoria, would see both girls through all the festivities there were likely to be for the spring and summer, including the Garden Party if Their Majesties gave one.

When she got home she rang up Mrs. Marling and told her about the dresses.

"I think you have saved my life, Agnes," said Mrs. Marling.

"Mr. Adams was asking me what to give the bridesmaids. You haven't mentioned bags."

Agnes admitted that she had not considered them. "They will be a perfect present," she said. "I will send you a snippet of the silk, Amabel, so that Mr. Adams can see the kind of colour. I would love to see them in long wrinkled suède gloves but we really can't."

Mrs. Marling said the price of good gloves was appalling.

"I didn't mean that," said Agnes. "I was thinking of Emmy's hands. Robert's pigskin gloves are just the right size for her. I shall have to put them into net gloves. It can't be helped. But darling Clarissa would wear wrinkled long gloves so nicely. Mamma had pairs and pairs of long suède gloves, some with twenty tiny buttons. I am keeping them for Clarissa, if ever she wants them. One wonders."

Mrs. Marling then asked Miss Dale to ring Mr. Adams up and tell him that bags would be the most desired present for the bridesmaids and to send the snippets of silk to Miss Pickthorn, and a few days later there came two bags of the finest petit point with garlands of tiny flowers and leaves and exquisitely wrought gilt clasps set with lovely pretence jewels.

"Aren't they lovely?" said Mrs. Marling to Lucy. "How very clever of Mr. Adams to find them."

"Mrs. Belton found them," said Lucy, and Mrs. Marling remembered that Mrs. Belton had been responsible for a good deal of the furnishing in the Old Bank House. "What's really clever is Mr. Adams getting Mrs. Belton to do it. He's awfully good at picking the right person for the job." And in these unromantic words her voice melted to a restrained tenderness new to her mother's ear.

Everything was now in train. Invitations had been accepted and noted by Miss Dale. Messrs. Scatcherd and Tozer the well-known Barchester caterers had been commissioned to supply the food and the champagne for the reception. The estate carpenter with the help of Ed Pollitt the handy man had moved furniture in the great drawing-room and put up the heavy silk curtains, stored all through the war and the far worse peace. Casual labour from the village had polished the floor to the accompaniment of tea enough to float the Great Harry, almost depleting Mrs. Morland's hoarded American gifts. It was hoped that the weather would be fine, but if it was not there would be room for the guests in the drawing-room and the large hall. Clarissa had come over the day before and with Miss Dale's help had stripped the garden of such flowers as were out and made swags of fresh green foliage to hang between the tall windows. Emmy came over to dinner, as both bridesmaids were to spend the night at Marling.

Mrs. Marling had rather dreaded the last evening with the thought of Lucy leaving them next day, but she found her fears had not been necessary, as indeed few of our fears are, though this does not prevent our having them. Oliver exerted himself and talked. Miss Dale had a pleasant turn of wit and kept Mr. Marling amused till Emmy got him away onto cows, bellowing at him almost as loudly as a Rushwater bull. Mr. and Mrs. Bill, Lettice Barclay and her husband, all helped, as did Bishop Joram and Charles Belton who were spending the night, and the Vicar who had only been asked (though he did not know it) to make even numbers.

"I say, Bishop," said Lucy, "have you brought your things with you? I mean your surplices and things?"

Bishop Joram said he had.

"I wondered," said Lucy, "because I thought perhaps you had a special kind of suitcase for vestments if that's the right name and when I took your luggage up it was only two ordinary suitcases."

"My *dear* Miss Marling," said the Bishop, much shocked, "was it you who took my bags up? I am horrified. I shall never forgive myself. And on the eve of your wedding too."

Emmy whose attention had been caught by their talk threw a look of scorn in Bishop Joram's direction and was so obviously about to say that if it had been several months after the wedding instead of the evening before there might have been more reasonable cause for anxiety, that Miss Dale quickly asked her who was looking after the Rushwater cows during her absence.

"Oh Herdman's doing them," said Emmy. "He's first rate with cows, but he hasn't much sense about bulls, but he has been better since Rushwater Churchill chased him round his stall," and so returned to Mr. Marling.

Everyone breathed again except Mrs. Bill who had been telling Oliver about one of her husband's horses which had pulled a shoe off on a wire fence but was luckily none the worse, and so missed his excursion.

"I was over at Pomfret Madrigal last Sunday," said Bishop Joram to Mrs. Marling, "doing locum for Mr. Miller. I was rather distressed about Mrs. Brandon."

Mrs. Marling, who liked Mrs. Brandon though she did not know her very well, asked is she had been ill.

"I don't think so," said the Bishop. "At least she didn't say anything about it. She looked rather thin and worried. Charming, of course, as she always is, but not her usual self. If it had been in Mngangaland I should have at once suspected witchcraft of course."

"How absolutely priceless," said Mrs. Bill, deserting Oliver for the Bishop.

"I am very sorry," said Mrs. Marling. "I didn't know anything was wrong. She has accepted for herself and for her son and his wife."

"She mentioned that," said Bishop Joram. "She said she was looking forward very much to the wedding."

"She sent me an awfully nice looking-glass," said Lucy, appearing to think that this was sufficient proof of Mrs. Brandon's good health. "I say, ought we really to call you Bishop or Canon? It's a bit confusing."

"Once a bishop always a bishop, I believe," said Bishop Joram. "I left my diocese a good many years ago now. But I hear from my successor who is doing splendid work there, that my friends still speak affectionately of Mngjoram Mngbngkngl."

He smiled and appeared to be lost in a Sub-equatorial reverie.

"Is that Manganese?" said Mrs. Bill, which witticism produced a great deal of laughter from a company who were feeling slightly emotional.

"It is," said the Bishop, "or more correctly Mngangamngese. It means Joram who rides a bicycle. There is no sibilant in the language so bicycle become mngbngkngl."

Most of those present made not very successful efforts to say the word and a good deal of laughing went on between Mrs. Bill and the younger members of the party.

"But, if I may, I will tell you something which gives me great pleasure," said Bishop Joram to Mrs. Marling, "and which may perhaps solve Miss Marling's difficulty as to my correct title. The Archbishop has, in recognition of what he kindly calls my valuable work in Mngangaland though to me it was absolutely *nothing*, a pure labour of love, most generously conferred a Lambeth degree upon me, so I am entitled to be called Doctor Joram. And what makes it the more delightful is that His Grace is an Oxford man and I shall therefore be entitled to wear the Oxford D.D. hood. Had he been a Cambridge man I should have been equally sensible of the honour, but worn the outward signs with less joy. This is, as it were, in confidence for a few days, but I felt I must let you know as you have been kind enough to let me take part in tomorrow's ceremony."

Mrs. Marling was of course delighted to hear the news and said so, though she secretly felt that Dr. seemed rather a come- down after Bishop, and then her thoughts went back to their earlier conversation and she asked him again about Mrs. Brandon.

"Why did you say it made you think of witchcraft?" she asked.

"I exaggerated, as indeed I so often do," said Dr. Joram as we may now call him. "It is a fault against which I struggle when I remember, but I usually remember too late."

Mrs. Marling said she had exactly the same experience about her own shortcomings, for which Dr. Joram seemed grateful. But could he, she said, explain what he meant about Mrs. Brandon.

"I can't," said he. "But she looked a little afraid. It sounds ridiculous and doubtless is. I felt as if someone might have been not quite kind to her. Ridiculous, of course, because there she is with her son and his delightful wife and their charming children. I ought not to have spoken."

"Francis and his wife have been at Stories quite a long time now," said Mrs. Marling. "They were married in the autumn of '46. Getting on for three years. She may find it a little too much. Still, the winter is always trying, and probably she will be all right now the weather is getting warmer. And it is a delightfully warm spring this year."

And then they talked about other things and the incident passed from her mind. As on a previous occasion Mrs. Bill was a great help, forcing most of them to play what she called cheery games after dinner. Dr. Joram and Charles Belton particularly distinguished themselves at the cheating card game "Hunt the Cripps," while Miss Dale and Oliver, to everyone's surprise came out as first-class charade players, under Mrs. Bill's management, so that Emmy said it was just like Christmas. At eleven o'clock Mrs. Marling collected the ladies and the Vicar took his leave at the same time in view, he said, of the happy day which was dawning on them next day, a day which he felt sure they would all look back upon as a day which stood out from other days. The rest of the men stayed on to smoke and talk, while Mrs. Marling shepherded her ladies towards the stairs. She had watched this moment approach with a slight feeling of apprehension because she felt it her duty to have a few last words with her younger daughter, but did not know what the words were and felt rather sick at the thought of saying them. As they crossed the wide landing one of the village women who helped in the kitchen on occasions like this came up to her and said,

"Please Mrs. Marling, Ed Pollitt's downstairs and says could he speak to you."

"I really don't know," said Mrs. Marling. "It's very late. Is it very important?"

"He says it's the goats," said the woman.

"Goats?" said Mrs. Marling.

"You know, mother," said Lucy coming forward. "Ed and Millie are keeping goats. Millie says the milk's good for the children. I'd as soon drink that ghastly pasteurised stuff the Government makes the cows give us as goats' milk. I had it when I was with Jessica and it was awful. Those poor children in London don't know what real milk tastes like. It's all horrible and when it turns it turns in a beastly sort of way and no good for cream cheeses. I'll go and see about Ed."

She ran downstairs and was back in a few minutes.

"It's a nanny," she said. "Trouble with the kids. She wasn't due to kid or whatever it is till next week and Millie's gone to her mother for the night and Ed doesn't know what to do, and two of the children have whooping-cough."

"It can't be any worse than cows," said Emmy, the light of fanaticism in her eye, "and cows are no trouble. Shall I come?"

"Rather," said Lucy. "Did you bring your breeches? If not I'll give you Oliver's old slacks. Come on. We'll be down in a second, Ed," she shouted over the banisters.

"But, Lucy," said her mother and then, suddenly seeing the ridiculous side of trying to catch her daughter for a last word from a mother who didn't know what she ought to say and was pretty sure Lucy wouldn't want to hear it, began to laugh and was joined by Mrs. Bill who said she didn't know what it was all about but it was a frightful rag, as good as when Bill won the regimental cup for jumping and they all went to the Bag O' Tricks Caboose and drank cider and champagne mixed and danced till daylight.

"Lucy," said her mother again as the bride came downstairs in her farming outfit accompanied by her cousin Emmy who was obviously going to split Oliver's old flannel trousers before the night was out.

"Good-night, mother," said Lucy, kissing her affectionately. "I expect I'll be late. I'll leave the scullery window open. Come on, Emmy."

Mrs. Marling saw the rest of the ladies to their rooms and then came back to the sitting-room to tell her husband that Lucy and Emmy had gone to look at Ed Pollitt's goat, to which Mr. Marling quite reasonably replied that he would back Lucy against any goat.

"But it's after eleven," said Mrs. Marling, "and she ought to be in bed, and so ought Emmy."

"Nonsense, my dear," said Mr. Marling. "Those girls can look after themselves. What's wrong with the goat?"

"It's a nanny," said Mrs. Marling, "and she seems to be having trouble with kids."

"She'll be all right with Lucy and Emmy," said her husband. "You go to bed, my dear. We'll hear the girls come back."

Peace gradually fell upon the upper part of the house. Lettice before she went to bed came and sat for a while in her mother's room and they talked of Lucy and her future happiness, of which they felt as certain as one can be about other people's lives. Mrs. Bill did her exercises, brushed her hair with fifty strokes, and went to bed where she read a few pages of a very nice book she found in her room called *The Thirty-Nine Steps* and went to sleep with the light on. Clarissa showed her dress and her wreath and her bag to Miss Dale who was most sympathetic and then they said good-night and went to bed. In the sitting-room the men talked about politics rather ignorantly but with a praiseworthy distrust of the present government and Dr. Joram gave a very interesting account of how his late flock elected their representatives for the local parliament, the form of election being to see who best survived a bowl of very hot, nauseous, and intoxicating liquid, which caused Bill Marling to say he wished

Sir Stafford Cripps' supporters would do the same, after which he relapsed into a conversation with Oliver about their old preparatory school. Mr. Marling sat bolt upright in his high-backed chair, looking very distinguished, and occasionally woke himself by nearly falling forwards onto the carpet, while Captain Barclay and Charles did *The Times* Crossword Puzzle, refusing all offers of help but not making much progress.

"By jove," said Bill Marling, "it's half-past twelve. What *are* those girls doing."

From the quiet spring night was heard the noise of a car coming up the drive at a considerable speed. It stopped at the front door and there was a sound from the landing of excited voices, trying to hush themselves but not making much success of it.

"What the dickens is that noise?" said Mr. Marling, suddenly waking up.

Oliver suddenly felt quite sick. He had renounced Jessica for ever since she had so far forgotten herself and lost all claim on his affection by her coarse and frequent references to Sarah Siddons, but her voice disturbed him, pierced him to the quick. A conspiratorial scuffling was heard outside and in came Lucy and Emmy, hot and dirty, followed by Jessica Dean and Aubrey Clover.

"Dearest Mr. Marling," cried Jessica, but in a muted cry not to disturb the people who had gone to bed, "and my darling Oliver, and Brother Bill how nice, and Tom Barclay my pet, and Charles who adores me, and Bishop Joram whom I adore. What heaven. Listen, my sweets. This is *not* a formal call, but we thought we'd run down after Aubrey's show and spend the night at Winter Overcotes to show my father and mother how well I am and then I had a brain wave because I *knew* Lucy can't do her hair, so I made my dresser come with me who is an *angel* with hair and I shall send her over tomorrow to see to your hair, my sweet, which is divine when properly done but too too quite disintegrating at the moment. Well, bless you all. I shall be at

the church with Aubrey tomorrow. Aubrey is frightfully good at
being the bride's father or brother or best man, or anything. And
he can play the organ and read the lessons divinely if necessary.
Just let him know. He only has to turn his hat inside out and put
on a false moustache."

She kissed everyone lightly and Lucy with real affection.
Aubrey Clover, now the devoted husband solicitous for his
wife's well-being, gave her his arm and led her away.

"Upon my soul," said Mr. Marling. "Well, Lucy, how's the
goat?"

"Oh, she's all right," said Lucy. "Emmy was splendid. She——"

"That's all from you tonight," said her brother Bill, not
unkindly. "Bed for you girls at once."

As Emmy was giving the most soul-cracking yawns this
seemed good advice. Lucy saw a light under her mother's door
and hesitated. Then her natural kindness and her sense of duty
triumphed over the thought of tip-toeing to bed. She opened
the door quietly and went in. Her mother was reading in bed.

"Oh, the nanny had three kids and we had a heavenly time,"
said Lucy, "and Ed gave us parsnip wine. Oh, and thank you
frightfully for *everything*, mother, and I'm going to bed."

She kissed her mother with quick yet clinging affection, shut
the door quietly and went away.

Although but early April the day was as warm and bright as
only an England spring can be. Lucy had plans for cleaning the
gardener's tool shed as a last tribute to her home, but Mrs.
Marling had told Miss Dale that they must stop her at all costs,
in the first place because it was unsuitable and she would never
get the dirt off her hands and in the second place because the
gardener would undoubtedly give notice and although he was
old and lazy he knew the garden and they would never get
another one if he left. Miss Dale had asked Mrs. Marling not to
worry, and by now she trusted Miss Dale so much that she really
hardly worried at all. Emmy and Clarissa were then detailed to

keep Lucy at bay, which they did so well that at twelve o'clock she was only half dressed and was with difficulty prevented from giving the nylon stockings that David Leslie had sent her from America to her cousin Clarissa, on the grounds that Clarissa had such nice legs and that once this rot was over she, Lucy, wasn't ever going to wear nylons again, because one only laddered them.

"Rubbish, my dear," said Clarissa in her grown-up way. "You'll have to go to dinner-parties with Mr. Adams, and America and all sorts of things. You can't let him down."

"Give them to me," said Emmy, who was packing Lucy's going-away luggage, and she wrapped them in tissue paper and put them into a corner that needed filling.

Lucy stood up and shook herself. There had been a heated argument with her cousins about the new belt, but as Jessica's Miss M. had given the old one to a Jumble Sale and her other and less constricting belt was packed, there had been nothing for it but to cram herself in, and very handsomely did it become her figure. A knock was heard.

"You can't come in," said Emmy, who appeared to be under the impression that some kind of ritual attempt to carry off the bride was about to be made by Mr. Gresham and an armed band, and was prepared to be Katherine Barlass in Lucy's defence.

Miss Dale's voice said it was Mrs. Trapes, Jessica's dresser.

"Oh, hullo, Mrs. Trapes," said Emmy, throwing open the door, "come in. Lucy and I had a marvellous time last night with Ed's nanny. She had three kids."

To an outsider it might have appeared that somebody's nurse had given birth to triplets, but Mrs. Trapes seemed to know all about it, and said goats were nasty dirty things and Miss Marling looked nice in the new belt and she hoped Miss Marling wouldn't forget to *roll* it off very carefully, not *pull* it, and remember to wear it alternately with her other belt.

"I haven't got another one," said Lucy rebelliously. "At least only a comfortable one. I'll tell you what, Mrs. Trapes, I *know* my hair will come down if you do it that way you said."

Mrs. Trapes, paying no attention whatever to Lucy's plea, took off her hat and coat, put on a white overall, opened a box of toilet articles, and asked Lucy to sit in a comfortable chair opposite the mirror. She then put a white cape on her victim and began to brush and comb her thick brown hair, while her cousins watched, Clarissa with frank interest, Emmy much as a good low churchman might observe High Mass at St. Peter's, with a mixture of fear, scorn and unwilling admiration.

"Miss Dean sent her love, Miss Marling," said Mrs. Trapes, "and you are to have a glass of champagne with your lunch and not so much as stir a finger after I've dressed you. You know, miss, Mr. Clover's fixed up with Mr. Stoner for the rest of the season, till Miss Dean can act again. It's to be a musical act with two pianos and some comedy scenes just for the two of them. Mr. Clover's accompanist was quite annoyed about it. Quite strong language he used, because when Mr. Clover doesn't play himself he always plays for him. I really thought the flat would fall in, such really violent language he used. Now, a little colour for the face."

"I say, I can't," said Lucy. "I'll look an awful fool going to church with stuff on my face."

"You'll look too too dim if you don't," said Clarissa, who was re-arranging the flowers she and Emmy were to carry. "Mr. Adams might thing you were ill," on hearing which Lucy, though not altogether convinced, held her peace, while Mrs. Trapes rouged and powdered with confident delicate fingers and to Lucy's horror put a little blue on her eyelids and painted a faint becoming colour on her lips.

"Really, Miss Marling, a young lady with a skin like yours hardly needs more than a touch of colour," said Mrs. Trapes. "Give me a thick skin every time, I say. So much easier to clean and they don't go all hard and flaky. There, Miss Marling. And when you've had your lunch I'll see to the dress and the wreath."

"I do feel AWFUL," said Lucy, after a prolonged inspection of her face. "Like a cow at a cattle show with ribbons on her," to which Mrs. Trapes replied that Miss Marling would have a first class if prizes were being given and went downstairs to have her lunch with Mrs. Marling's old cook and Mr. Tozer of Scatcherd and Tozer the Barchester caterers and Mrs. Simnet the old housekeeper from Rushwater.

Miss Dale then summoned Emmy and together they brought up a tray of lunch for the girls and Miss Dale went back to help Mrs. Marling who was entertaining the Dean and Dr. Joram.

"This is champagne," said Clarissa who had been examining the tray. "But no nippers. Too, too discouraging, my dears. Shall I go down and ask for some?"

"I've always wanted to knock the head off a bottle," said Emmy and before the two other girls could stop her she had hit the head with undeserved dexterity against the top bar of the old-fashioned grate and caught every bubble of foam, every drop of the wine, in one of the large goblets, so that Clarissa, who was apt to undervalue her elder sister for doing things she herself neither could nor wished to do, was reduced to admiring silence.

"Here, you must have a dressing-gown," said Emmy to Lucy. "You can't have lunch in a silk slip. You'll catch cold. Where's yours?"

"Packed," said Lucy. "At least the old one's somewhere."

"Here you are," said Emmy, shoving her cousin into a manly bath robe. "Now drink your champagne."

"It ought to be a peignoir," said Clarissa sadly.

At half-past one Mrs. Trapes came back and dismissed the bridesmaids to their own toilets, saying she would like to have a look at them when they were ready. She then carefully dressed Lucy in her white gown, arranged the wreath and veil upon her strangely neat and shining hair, and suddenly opening the bedroom door nearly knocked over a small party of helpers.

"I knew it," said Mrs. Trapes. "Time and time again in plays you open a door and there's someone behind it. You can have a look. And now get along downstairs. If anyone was to come into Miss Dean's room while I'm dressing her, I'd let them know it. Miss Marling is quite ready, madam."

And Mrs. Marling came in, holding a faded blue velvet case.

"My mother's pearls, darling," she said. "Lettice has your other grandmother's jewels, so you must have my mother's. Will you fasten it, Mrs. Trapes."

With deep approval of this dramatic scene Mrs. Trapes put the single string of fine pearls round Lucy's neck and clasped it.

"If it was a mannequin show and Miss Marling was modelling the bride she couldn't look better, madam," said Mrs. Trapes. "Should we be coming down now?"

"Yes, I am going now," said Mrs. Marling. "Mr. Marling is ready downstairs and so are the bridesmaids. Don't move, Lucy. You will spoil the veil. Lucy, my darling, my darling. Look after her, Mrs. Trapes."

She went away and Mrs. Trapes extracting from Lucy's last minute suit-case a handkerchief which Lucy had scornfully said would come to bits the first time you wanted to tie up a cut with it, very gently wiped from Lucy's eyes the two large tears that were trembling there.

"That's all right, Miss Marling," she said. "You won't do it again. Now, do just as you're told, and it will be over before you know it's begun. Take your train like this."

She laid the train over Lucy's arm, preceded her downstairs and delivered her to her father, who was looking so handsome in his grey suit and grey top hat with a deep red carnation in his buttonhole that Mrs. Trapes said to the cook, as the bride drove away with her father, that they made as handsome a couple as you'd wish to see, and Mr. Adams would never be like Mr. Marling if he lived a hundred years, thus profoundly shocking the cook who was a chapel-goer and said husbands were one thing and fathers were another and the Bible said you was to leave your father and cleave to your husband.

"That's no argument," said Mrs. Trapes. "Husbands and

fathers may be two different things today, but if you read your Bible regularly, Mrs. Cook, you might have noticed Genesis, Chapter Nineteen, verses thirty to thirty-eight. My father made us girls read a chapter aloud every night till we was old enough to go our own way. My sisters all went to the bad and they've done nicely out of it, but I married Trapes, in the profession he was, and a good husband according to his lights and as he was lit as often as not you may judge for yourself, and here I am, dresser to Miss Dean. And here I stand gabbling when there's the room to tidy."

"Aren't you going to the wedding, miss?" said the cook, dazzled by Mrs. Trapes's sophistication and as she had not understood anything that lady had said, bearing no ill-will.

But Mrs. Trapes did not deign to reply, contenting herself with saying in a loud voice to an unseen audience as she went upstairs that she had never set foot on the stage after the curtain went up and never intended to.

All weddings are much alike except that some are better stage-managed than others. Not even those high authorities Miss Jessica Dean and Mr. Aubrey Clover could have found any fault with the production, though neither of them was in a mood to criticise, for Miss Dean was crying in a most becoming way from start to finish and Mr. Clover was becoming each actor in turn from the Heavy Father in the shape of Mr. Marling, dignified in spite of being deeply moved, to the second soubrette Miss Clarissa Graham who was thinking how she would manage her own wedding, though the bridegroom had no identity and was merely a foil for the bride. The Vicar, Dr. Joram and the Dean did their part faultlessly. The small choir who had been lent by the Dean and the Precentor sang very well and everyone thought, as people always do, what little pets the choirboys looked. Mr. Adams in strictly conventional and very well-made clothes showed no outward signs of nervousness, though when he had put the ring on Lucy's hand and she raised her serious loving eyes to his face he felt as if the biggest casting the works had ever produced was thundering over him.

A suitable party made an excursion to the vestry, a good many people kissed other people whom they had never kissed before and were never going to kiss again, and Mr. and Mrs. Adams came down the aisle, got into Mr. Adams's car and were driven back to Marling Hall.

At this point the principal actors in the foregoing scene felt that nothing was real and that at any moment they might find themselves back in their mud hovel. But each one behaved excellently and said the right things so perhaps it did not much matter. Apart from the bride and bridegroom the chief attraction was of course Miss Jessica Dean who, exquisite in a cloud of black lace with a twenty-five guinea piece of nonsense on her head that no one else could have worn, languished in an interesting condition on a small settee and completely turned the heads of all susceptible gentlemen, married or single. It must however be said of Miss Jessica Dean that she had no special preference for men, having always found women very good company, so that her settee became as it were a kind of meeting place from which couples who were interested in each other could pair off. So had Clarissa hung herself upon Charles Belton's arm. So had Emmy got into a corner with Sir Edmund Pridham to discuss drains. So had Heather Pilward carried off Mr. Belton who had always liked her. From this mart did Mrs. Crofts, wife of the Vicar of Southbridge emerge with the Noel Mertons' agent Mr. Wickham to settle the matter of a Lesser Halfwit which she had observed nesting in the Vicarage Garden three weeks before its usual time. From here did Mr. Birkett and Everard Carter, the past and present Headmaster of Southbridge School, withdraw to a window with Philip Winter, the owner of the very thriving prep. school at Beliers Priory, to talk shop. Here did Miss Pemberton from Northbridge, in a dress of striped peasant weave with a large raffia hat and bag stand guard over her sensitive and scholarly boarder Mr. Downing while he talked to Mrs. Sydney Carton, the ex-Headmistress of the Hosiers' Girls' Foundation School, about a newly discovered manuscript of Fluvius Minucius, the fourth-century poet whose works Mr. Carton had edited.

And so the county roundabout turned, with Jessica Dean always as the hub, while Aubrey Clover made himself useful to dowagers as a respectful nephew, to younger ladies as an indulgent uncle, to the older men as a respectful and intelligent young man and to the girls as himself, that is as their matinée idol. Presently his wanderings brought him to what he recognised as the back of his friend Mrs. Francis Brandon, formerly Mrs. Arbuthnot, with whom he had given a performance in aid of the Red Cross a few years ago.

"Well, Peggy dear, how are you?" he said. "As pretty as ever I see. Or perhaps not?"

"It is all very well for you," said Mrs. Francis, as most people called her, "but you haven't any children."

"My dear girl," said Aubrey Clover, "you only have to look at Jessica to see that I have triplets."

"Don't be silly," said Mrs. Francis, with a petulance that was not so wholly charming as, Aubrey reflected, it used to be. "One baby is fun. Twins on the top of it is not quite such fun. And it's rather a squash. I suppose it's having lived in India, but I do hate squashes and people thick on the ground."

"Be reasonable, my sweet," said Aubrey, now the elderly friend, possibly a widower, who from the depths of his experience helps the young wife in her difficulties. "You have, I imagine, board and lodging free at Stories. You have a resident grandmamma to help with the children and a resident and most capable nurse. And, I believe, Cook and Rose and a good deal of odd help."

"I wish you wouldn't be so *sensible*, Aubrey," said Mrs. Francis, almost peevishly. "It's all very well saying things aren't as bad as they might be. It's not what things *might* be that matters, it's what they are."

Aubrey inquired about the children, to whom Mrs. Francis was genuinely attached.

"You'll only use it for copy if I tell you," said Mrs. Francis. "Effie is an angel and the twins are devils. Or quite often it's the other way round. I can't think where they get their tempers from."

"From Francis, of course," said Aubrey Clover. "Think of old Miss Brandon who killed all her companions and lay in bed frightening people. Not from your mother-in-law certainly."

"Oh no, Granny is always *most* kind," said Mrs. Francis, and Aubrey Clover's practised ear felt that something here rang false. However it did not interest him, so he slipped away to get a drink and at the buffet found Francis Brandon.

"I am drowning sorrow," said Francis, handing Aubrey Clover a glass of champagne as he spoke. "I think Mr. Gresham is going to propose the young couple's health. I must say they look very nice. Lucy is a lucky girl."

"So is Adams," said Aubrey, "if you get my meaning. Anything wrong with Peggy? She didn't seem pleased."

"Nothing," said Francis. "We're all a bit thick on the ground at Stories and it does get on one's nerves sometimes. If my mamma weren't dead set on having us, we'd like to be on our own for some things. Of course it's her house and it's angelic of her to have us and it's the perfect position, easy for Barchester and easy for Gatherum, but the servants are a bit of a bore. Old servants always are. And Nurse—you know, our old Nurse— has a way of getting across our Nanny. The ways of bringing children up have altered since Delia and I were little. Now Gresham is going to speak."

Mr. Gresham, whose speaking was well thought of in the House by such members as had any power of independent thinking, said in a few words what everyone felt about the bride and bridegroom and proposed their health, then Mr. Adams thanked everyone and drank to his new father and mother-in-law, a toast which evoked much feeling among the guests, and then Lucy slipped away to change into her travelling clothes.

"Where are you going, Adam?" said Mr. Belton.

"Only as far as Edgewood tonight," said Mr. Adams. "Lucy and I have a fancy to spend a night or two in our own house. Then we are going to Paris and shall see a bit of the country and be back of course before the House is sitting."

"A very good plan," said Mrs. Belton. "There is nothing like being at home."

"You're right there," said Mr. Adams, "and I owe my home to you, Mrs. Belton. If you hadn't borne with me ever since my Heth fell into the lake by her own silly fault, and showed me all the things I couldn't learn by myself, I'd never have found my Lucy. I don't forget that and I don't intend to," to which Mrs. Belton, much moved, could only reply "Bless you both" and then Lucy came down and hugged her father and mother and the rest of the family with tears in her eyes.

"I've nothing to say and no words to say it with," said Mr. Adams, holding Mrs. Marling's hand. "Lucy and I expect you both to dinner on Saturday. Don't worry. I'll take care of your girl through thick and thin. Come along, Mrs. Adams."

Lucy looked round questioningly.

"Oh, *me!*" she said, and took her husband's arm. Her family stood on the steps to see her drive away and the wedding was over. The guests began to disperse and Dr. Joram was at last able to get near Mrs. Brandon.

"How nice to see you," she said. "It is always so terribly flat when a wedding is over. I wish we could have them in the evening. They are allowing people to be married later and later, so perhaps we will. Are you ready to go, Francis?"

"I'll find Peggy," said her son. "Oh, mamma, would you mind if we went round by Gatherum Castle? There's a talk of some amateur theatricals for the Conservative Association and Lady Cora wants Peggy to act with them."

"I didn't know," said Mrs. Brandon. "Of course, darling. Where is Peggy?"

Francis said he would find her and went away.

"I must tell you, Dr. Joram, *how* much I loved the service," said Mrs. Brandon, "and your part of it *specially* if it isn't irreligious to say so."

Dr. Joram was flattered, but deprecated such an honour for himself, saying that he was but one participant and that an unworthy one in one of the most beautiful of our services.

"I do so agree," said Mrs. Brandon, looking up at him with her fine eyes, which he thought looked more tired than he liked. "Especially when they use the *proper* words. Why "With my body I thee honour" should be more respectable than "worship" I really do not see. And really the hallowing of natural instincts is much more embarrassing than the bit about procreation, because one doesn't quite know if one wants to know what it means. Mr. Miller is *splendid* about having the proper words."

Seldom had Dr. Joram, a churchman of the old school as far as the Prayer Book goes, though with a mind greatly broadened by the need to encourage his black flock in their devotions, been so struck by the beauty of a really intellectual conversation on the higher plane as he was while Mrs. Brandon spoke her mind about the Marriage Service. She had flushed becomingly in her zeal and her eyes were as lovely as ever, but all the same he felt a vague unease. Brightness had fallen from the air.

"Francis is a long time," he said. "And you must be feeling the fatigue of today's celebration. Would it be presumptuous if I offered to drive you home? It is a long way round by Gatherum and you ought to be resting. My car is here."

"How *very* kind of you," said Mrs. Brandon. "I think I shall die if we go to Gatherum. It is a long way and I don't know how long Peggy may be kept and I don't really know the Gatherum people. I must let Francis or Peggy know."

"You are too tired," said Dr. Joram firmly. "I will get my friend the Vicar to tell Francis and then I will drive you straight home."

"That will be Heaven," said Mrs. Brandon, sinking onto a chair in her relief, "though I suppose I oughtn't to put it like that to *you*. And you must have some tea at Stories if you aren't having a service or anything."

Dr. Joram went on his mission. He was soon back and then drove Mrs. Brandon quietly to Stories where they had tea in her little sitting-room.

"I have given Francis and Peggy the drawing-room," she said, "so that they can have friends or dance if they like. Oh, Nurse, here is Bishop Joram. He drove me home, because the children wanted to go to Gatherum first."

"I'm sorry, madam," said Nurse, bestowing upon Dr. Joram a gracious look which he afterwards said reminded him of Kitchener's order to the first hundred thousand, "Be courteous to women, but no more." "From what Rose's cousin says it's not the sort of house it used to be. Foreigners in the kitchen, like those Mixo-Lydians we had in the war and the family taking up with all sorts of people. What I really wanted to say to you, madam, was that if Mrs. Francis's nurse is to have cook send her up butter for breakfast when others I could mention are having margarine, it will cause a great deal of unpleasantness. I'm never one to complain, madam, and I'd eat margarine for ever if it would make for peace, but there's times when we really must speak out."

Mrs. Brandon said she would certainly enquire about it.

"Milk and sugar?" she said to the Bishop, and her hand shook a little and the milk slopped over into the saucer. She set the milk jug down, put her handkerchief quickly to her eyes, and as quickly replaced it in her bag.

"You must see my grandchildren after tea," she said. "They are angels and it is delightful to have them here and then Peggy can go out much more. She and Francis are acting again a great deal. They are both so clever."

"I beg your pardon," said Dr. Joram. "I wasn't listening to what you were saying."

"One mostly doesn't," said Mrs. Brandon. "One is too tired. Tell me about your new house."

"Won't you come and see it?" said Dr. Joram. "It is worth a visit and I should be extremely honoured. Next week perhaps?"

"I would *love* to," said Mrs. Brandon. "Next week is Holy Week, but I don't suppose it would matter Thursday being Maundy Thursday unless you have something very special to keep you busy."

Dr. Joram said tea on Thursday would be delightful and unless she wished it he would not ask anyone else.

"That is *most* understanding," said Mrs. Brandon, looking up at him from under her long lashes. "Must you go? Thank you again for that *wonderful* service."

"It is indeed a beautiful form of prayer," said Dr. Joram, "and it is always a privilege to speak those words. But not everyone recognizes these things as you do."

When he had gone Nurse came in.

"I have put a hot bottle on the sofa in your room, madam," she said. "Mr. Francis phoned up to say they would be late for supper, so Cook is going to put you something nice on a tray, and Rose or me will bring it up."

"Thank you, Nurse. I *do* feel tired," said Mrs. Brandon and went slowly upstairs to the nursery, where the children were being bathed and put to bed.

"Here's Granny," said Francis's nurse brightly. "Tell Granny we're just going to bed and mustn't be excited."

Mrs. Brandon kissed her soft delightful grand-babies and went slowly back to her own room, feeling old. Nurse brought up a very nice supper tray, followed by Rose with a half bottle of white wine, which made Mrs. Brandon wonder if the Millennium had come.

"Just wore out, madam is," said Rose when they returned to the kitchen, "and no wonder. Mrs. Francis's Nanny won't so much as let her look at the children, her own grandchildren too. Sweet little things they are too."

"Madam needs a real change," said Nurse. "There was this talk of Mr. Francis finding a house, but we haven't heard any more of it. If Mr. Brandon had been alive madam wouldn't be put upon the way she is."

"Ah," said the Cook, which, regarded as a tribute to the late Mr. Brandon who had been uncommonly dull while alive and had died some thirty odd years ago leaving his widow very well off, seems adequate.

And then Mrs. Francis's Nanny came down for her supper and an atmosphere of armed truce settled upon the kitchen.

Meanwhile at Marling the family were dining quietly on the remains of the wedding food except Oliver, who in honour bound as a kind of groomsman had gone with Emmy and Clarissa and Charles Belton to the Barchester Odeon. The only incident worth recording was the appearance of a peculiarly revolting pudding which made Mr. Marling swear, a thing he rarely did before his wife.

"What the devil has Cook given us, Amabel?" he enquired. "Filthy mess. Whoever made it deserves hangin'."

"I'm afraid I know what it is," said Miss Dale. "You know about Ed's nanny. The first milk is supposed to be particularly rich and good and Ed brought it up to the Hall as a thank-offering to Emmy. The country people in the North make a kind of pudding with it very like this. They call it beastings."

"And a damned good name too, sorry, mother," said Bill with much feeling.

CHAPTER 5

Having safely married Lucy Marling to Mr. Adams, the county simmered down again into its usual routine. The warm early spring quickly flowered into an early summer such as had not been seen for many years, as beautiful as the summer after Dunkirk, even hotter and more determined to keep it up, making Mrs. Morland say that Todger's could do it when it chose, a remark that went down very well at the Deanery where she was having tea in the garden with Mrs. Crawley. The one drawback to the Deanery, as Mrs. Crawley sometimes said, was that it faced east and only got the morning light in the best rooms and she sometimes envied Sir Robert and Lady Fielding at Number Seventeen on the far side whose beautiful rooms were flooded with light all through the long days of summer. On the other hand the large Deanery garden, sloping down to the river, was protected to the east by the house and to the north by a very high wall of mellow Barsetshire stone, which had been raised to its present height by Dean Arabin. All along its length a stone terrace had been laid so that the ladies of the Deanery could take the air dryshod in damp weather and sit in shelter through most of the year. A large lime tree at one end gave shade when shade was required, but Mrs. Crawley and Mrs. Morland, both sun-worshippers, were sitting basking like lizards. Mrs. Crawley's herbaceous border, the pride and envy of the Close, was bright with colour. Bees were noisily and industriously at

work among the scented lime-blossoms. At the far end of the
long lawn various young grandchildren were sitting on a low
brick wall watching the other older grandchildren mucking
about with boats, as old Tomkins the sexton put it. Old
Tomkins was mowing the lawn with his scythe, not holding, he
said, with those motor lawn-mowers as tears the guts out of the
ground. Now a nice big lawn-mower with a pony, well it stood
to reason that was all right, and there was the pony's dung as well,
and when he was a lad and used to help his father, his father he
made him collect the muck in a bucket and take it home and his
father won the first prizes for garden produce every year at the
Barchester Town Gardeners Show, he did. Ar, he said, pausing
in front of the ladies, muck wasn't what it was in his young days.
All along of this Government it was, grudging the food as made
proper muck. When he were a lad, he said, there was a lot of talk
about Home Rule and all that, and he never paid no attention to
it, he didn't, for it stood to reason if you could give your horses
a good feed of corn, you'd get it all back, Home Rule or no
Home Rule. This lot, he said by which he was understood to
mean His Majesty's present government, didn't know what
muck was, and it would do them a sight of good to do a good
day's work for once in their lives. He'd show them what muck
was, he said. A man as had plenty of good muck needn't fear
God or the Devil.

"Good hay, sweet hay, hath no fellow," said Mrs. Morland,
who was enjoying it all very much, but Mrs. Crawley, alarmed
lest Tomkins should begin on hay, said she was sure the kitchen
tea was ready, upon which old Tomkins straightened himself
and slowly wiped his gleaming blade.

"I'm a-going to put her away," he said. "*And* lock her up. I'm
not going to have none of them young ladies and gentlemen
mucking with *my* scythe. Might take a nick out of it they might,"
and he talked himself away towards the tool-shed.

"How nice of you to send me your new book, Laura," said

Mrs. Crawley. "I really don't know why you go on putting me on your free list."

"I like you to have them," said Mrs. Morland, "and I make Adrian Coates give me ten copies instead of six, so I can play about with them."

Mrs. Crawley asked How, exactly.

"Well," said Mrs. Morland, pushing some hair away behind one ear, "you see first there are the duty people. There are the four boys, and my aunt Edith, and George Knox because he always sends me his, and they *must* have copies. So then I have one for myself and three to play with and I sometimes get quite wild and distracted choosing whom I want to give one to. I thought of you, because I know how *awful* it is when you meet someone who has written a book and you haven't read it, especially if they mind."

"You don't mind, Laura, bless you," said Mrs. Crawley.

"Of course not," said Mrs. Morland, surprised that anyone should take her novels seriously. "You see the *great* thing," said Mrs. Morland earnestly, "is to please the people that read one's books, not one's friends."

"Mrs. Rivers would say My Public," said Mrs. Crawley, who in common with most of Barsetshire had no particular love for Mrs. Rivers or her books.

"One must be fair," said Mrs. Morland judicially, "and Mrs. Rivers really has a Public. At least she gets millions of letters, because she always tells one about them. But I can't write books about the Love Life of Middle-Aged Women."

"That is the first unkind thing I have ever heard you say, Laura," said Mrs. Crawley.

"No, not unkind," said Mrs. Morland. "I just can't. I can only write the sort of books that I *can* write."

Mrs. Crawley said she expected Mrs. Rivers was in much the same predicament and did Mrs. Morland know that the Dreadful Dowager had wanted to bring a libel action against Mrs. Rivers for having a character called Lady Norton in a book.

"What happened?" said Mrs. Morland.

"Nothing," said Mrs. Crawley. "Her son and his wife told her she would only look silly if it got into court as she might have to prove that she wasn't like the one in the book and didn't have very pure affairs with young men, and once you prove you *aren't* something, people always say you are."

"*I* nearly had a libel action," said Mrs. Morland proudly.

"Laura!" said her friend. "But how? All your people are so unreal if you don't mind my saying so."

"Of course they are," said Mrs. Morland proudly. "That is My Art. If they seemed real nobody would be interested in them. Adrian Coates wanted me to take it into court but all that sort of thing repugnates me as that dreadful Madame Brownscu, the Mixo-Lydian refugee whom you must remember, used to say. And I knew that if I had to stand in the dock I should go MAD," said Mrs. Morland, pulling her hat well down onto her head as she spoke, the better to emphasize her point.

Here her story appeared to end.

"So what *did* you do?" said Mrs. Crawley.

"Well the lawyers said an apology would do," said Mrs. Morland.

"How could you, Laura?" said Mrs. Crawley. "It must have been so mortifying to apologise to the Dowager."

"Not at all," said Mrs. Morland. "I thought of Dr. Jowett."

"Really, Laura, I wish you would be less allusive," said Mrs. Crawley. "What on earth do you mean? Josiah," she said to her husband who had taken a chair beside them, "do make Laura talk sense."

"I believe our dear Laura *is* talking sense," said the Dean. "As far as I remember, but the story is an old one, when Jowett was offered the Mastership of Balliol they asked him if he could subscribe to the Thirty-Nine Articles and tradition has it that his answer was 'Give me a pen.'"

Mrs. Morland looked gratified and then the talk, as it was still apt to do, got round to Mrs. and Mrs. Adams who were back from their honeymoon and settled at Edgewood, from which quarter Mrs. Adams was riding the whirlwind and directing the storm in her usual downright way.

"A most unexpected marriage," said the Dean, "but apparently a most successful one."

His wife said not to be pompous.

"If to state two facts in plain English is pompous," said the Dean, "doubtless you are right. I was speaking as all men speak."

And as his grandfather must have spoken, to judge by his *Life and Letters* privately printed and just as well as no one would have bought it, said Mrs. Crawley rebelliously.

"Peace, woman," said Dr. Crawley, an old family joke for his grandfather was reputed to have used these words to Mrs. Proudie, the disliked wife of the colourless bishop of those days. "What I am really thinking of is the wish, expressed by Adams some years ago, to give a window to the cathedral in memory of his late wife. We managed to scotch it then, but have lived in fear of his repeating the kind offer. Now, I think we are safe."

"You know," said Mrs. Morland, "that I earn my living by writing books and it does make one notice *words*."

"Both premises are granted," said the Dean. "What next?"

"You know," said Mrs. Morland reproachfully, "how *impossible* it is to express what one means." She paused.

"I have often experienced the sensation when trying to write my sermons," said Dr. Crawley. "But do not at the moment see its application."

"Well, what I *want* to say," said Mrs. Morland, generously ignoring the Dean's remark, "is that you all call him Adams now. It would have been 'that man Adams,' or even Mr. Adams, a year or two ago."

The Dean said that the creature had glimmerings of reason in her, which Mrs. Morland good-naturedly took as a compliment.

"And now," said Mrs. Morland, "what I want to know is, will they be the Adamses, or the Samuel Adamses, or even the Sam

Adamses? I can't decide which would be best, but I hope the Adamses."

"My dear Laura, your silliness really passes all bounds some-times," said the Dean. "I admit that he used to speak of himself as Sam Adams, in the third person and far too often, but I think Mrs. Belton who has really a genius for tact cured him, and Lucy will be a great help. They will be the Adamses," to which Mrs. Morland replied meekly that he ought to know because he married them.

The fascinating topic of the Adamses having been intro-duced, they might have gone on talking till sunset but that the parlourmaid appeared, escorting Lady Fielding.

"I had to come," said Lady Fielding, who appeared strangely disordered, her hat crooked, her usual reserve and self-possession obviously leaking at every seam.

"Come and sit down," said Mrs. Crawley. "There's nothing wrong, I hope," for it was a matter of common knowledge that her only child Anne, the wife of Robin Dale a housemaster at Southbridge, might have a baby at any moment.

"Twins!" said Lady Fielding, letting herself drop in a quite exhausted way into a chair. "Robin rang up to tell me and Robert is away and I felt so peculiar that I *had* to come over and tell you before I burst. Two little girls, doing excellently, and Anne had a very good time. Oh dear, I am going to cry."

"Don't," said the Dean, though kindly.

"Do," said Mrs. Crawley, who as the mother of a large family all happily married and part-time owner of a great many grand-children of all ages, could speak with authority.

"I can't get over it," said Lady Fielding in a very gulping kind of voice. "Anne! It is all so extraordinary."

"You must pull yourself together, Dora. After all, she has been married nearly two years," said Mrs. Crawley. "And it isn't as if it came as a surprise. I mean one can't help *seeing*."

"Though I must say, you were marvellous before Octavia was

born," said Mrs. Morland. "No one would have guessed till about two months before. Still being winter was a great help."

"I don't know," said Mrs. Crawley thoughtfully. "A fur coat on top of a baby is a good size."

"It reminds me of a little family joke we had," said Dr. Crawley. "We had decided that an eighth child should be called Octavius, or if a girl Octavia, and I remember saying to my wife, as a joke, that I would not be surprised if she had eight children at once."

So enthralled were the Crawleys and Mrs. Morland by these scenes from clerical life that Lady Fielding began, quite justly, to feel neglected, and drying her eyes resumed her position as wife of the Chancellor of the Diocese a position which, in her own private opinion though she never expressed it aloud, was superior to that of the Bishop's wife; in which opinion the whole of well-thinking Barsetshire would have concurred.

"Of course they will be christened in the School Chapel," said Lady Fielding, already planning ahead.

"Do let Josiah know if he can help you," said Mrs. Crawley. "He has a wonderful way with babies. It is very sad that Robin's father can't be there."

As old Dr. Dale had died two years previously there did not seem to be any reasonable comment to make. And then yet another visitor was seen coming down the garden and it was Miss Dale, who had been in Barchester to do some odd jobs for Mrs. Marling and was delighted by the news and pleased to see Mrs. Morland whom she knew.

"I was at the wedding," she said. "Anne looked so lovely."

"We enjoyed it too," said Lady Fielding. "Robin is your cousin, isn't he?"

Miss Dale said he was and that they had tried to work it out more than once and always gone mad.

"I think the families split quite a long time ago," she said. "My people had what was left of the Dunstable money and Robin's were cousins of theirs."

"But didn't Dr. Dale marry a wife with money—I mean in the *nice* sense," said Mrs. Morland, in case anyone should suspect her of hinting that Dr. Dale married for money and poisoned his wife.

Miss Dale, who seemed to know all about it, said that was quite true, and Robin had inherited his mother's fortune, or what the Government if they called themselves that thought fit to let him have, and Mrs. Morland suddenly felt a little out of it.

"Nothing wrong, Laura?" said the Dean, who had a particular liking for Mrs. Morland as a person and was known to have read all her books.

"Only I sometimes wish I *belonged*," said Mrs. Morland. "Everyone else is Barsetshire and I'm an outsider. And it's all very well for you to talk, but that's true."

"I didn't know I was talking," said Dean, "at least not in that sense. Don't be foolish, Laura. How many people do you think there are who would give *anything* to write books that people enjoy reading? Dozens of people in the county would give their eyes to be able to get a book published, if they could write it. Some even pay. Look at Lady Norton and her dreadful garden anthology, *Herbs of Grace*. Her son told me she had to pay a hundred pounds to get it published, while you and George Knox have publishers tumbling over themselves to get you."

"But what an *extraordinary* idea to pay for one's own books," said Mrs. Morland. "If Adrian Coates had ever suggested anything of the sort to me I should have said No. But then of course Lady Norton doesn't have to earn her living."

"She couldn't if she tried," said the Dean, "unless she went to Madame Tussaud and posed as a waxwork."

"Well, I do apologise," said Lady Fielding, who was now again her tireless, competent self, ready to tackle any number of committees. "I must go back."

"What is Anne going to call the babies?" said Miss Dale.

"I don't suppose she knows yet," said Lady Fielding. "But she always said if she had a girl she would give it Maud for a second name, after her old governess, Miss Bunting."

"I remember her the summer she was with Anne at Hallbury," said Mrs. Morland. "She used to be with the Leslies, usen't she?"

"With the Leslies and the Marlings and the Marquess of Bolton and all sorts of people," said Lady Fielding. "She was a remarkable woman and brought Anne on in a most remarkable way." Then she took her leave and Mrs. Crawley and Miss Dale had a comfortable talk about people, for both, as Mrs. Morland had said, belonged, and could unravel families with skill and certainty, while Mrs. Morland sat back and let her writing self listen idly, for she could trust it to snap up trifles and make use of them later. And then the Cathedral bell began to sound for the evening service, so they all went across to the cathedral and as always Mrs. Morland was overcome by the beauty of the great white nave drenched in afternoon sunlight, with the darker chancel beyond it, and candles burning before the choir stalls in the dim dusty air; a chill air, despite the sunlight, as the air of a church always is. Even if close and incense-laden it does not warm the worshipper and Mrs. Morland first wished she had borrowed a coat from Mrs. Crawley and then blamed herself for mundane thoughts, but went on thinking them all the same, for the flesh is quite remarkably stronger than the spirit in the matter of chill draughts.

"Out of God's blessing into the warm sun!" said Mrs. Morland triumphantly as the Deanery party emerged from the cathedral.

The Dean, who was still feeling professional, said this was not the moment for such words, and what did Laura mean.

"It is Shakespeare," said Mrs. Morland with great dignity. "And if it isn't, it's somebody else. Oh, Dr. Joram," she said to the Canon, who had just joined them, "perhaps you would know. After all it must have happened all the time in Mngangaland."

Dr. Joram, slightly perplexed by Mrs. Morland's snipe-flight,

as indeed that worthy creature's friends often were, asked to
have the position explained to him. He could not help, but
suggested that they should all come across to his house and have
a glass of sherry and he would look it up in a dictionary of
quotations. The invitation was gladly accepted by everyone. By
the Dean because Dr. Joram's sherry was excellent, by Mrs.
Crawley because she liked him and by Mrs. Morland and Miss
Dale because they had not yet seen his house and wanted to
know what it was like.

The house, known as the Vinery, had belonged to old Canon
Thorne, who had been an unusually unconscionable time a-dying
and during the last years of his life had refused to see any visitors.
Except when engaged in his cathedral duties he shut himself up
in his study in a kind of entrenchment or fortress of books,
writing a commentary on the Pastoral Charges of Hippocam-
pus, Bishop of Rhinoceros in Cappadocia in the sixth century
A.D. an ardent supporter of the Nestorian heresy. Here, like a
malignant tortoise, he had lived in his shell, occasionally poking
an angry wrinkled face on a long wrinkled neck into cathedral
affairs and as angrily retiring to his fastness. At his death, some
time before this story begins, there had been considerable rivalry
and scheming, both open and subterranean for the reversion of
his house, but a powerful party headed by the Dean and the
Precentor had tanked (if we may be excused the neologism) over
all the pretenders and offered it to Bishop Joram, who had
joyfully accepted at once.

There had been wagers to, we regret to say, quite a considerable amount among the Chapter and most of the laymen connected with the cathedral as to whether the house, old Canon
Thorne's books having been removed, would at once collapse
like the House of Usher. Great support was given to the pro-
moters of this theory by Mr. Fanshawe, Dean of Paul's College
at Oxford and closely connected through his wife with Barsetshire, who said it was well known that the Old Bodleian was
only held together by its books and that if they were at any time

removed to that revolting Block, offensive alike to eye and
taste, a hideous example of what They wished to foist upon us
in the name of progress, a shape he greatly feared of things to
come when Oxford had been depressed and Nuffielded into
nothingness—he supposed, he said, that his hearers knew their
Yorick—that if, he repeated, the books were at any time removed, the building itself would collapse as, so he understood
from those who cultivated the baser sciences, an empty tin
biscuit box hermetically sealed would collapse if placed in a
vacuum. He craved his hearers' pardon if he had trespassed in
ignorance upon *terrae incognitae* which, as far as he was concerned, might as well have remained undiscovered for all the
good they had done anyone. But his words were not unfruitful
and wagers were even laid, not exceeding half-a-crown, upon
the probable disintegration of Canon Thorne's house.

To the barely veiled disappointment of all concerned the
house did not collapse. However it was found to be in so bad a
state that considerable repairs had to be made and Dr. Joram,
who had learned in his sub-equatorial diocese how to deal with
most kinds of difficulties, so cajoled, bullied and bribed the
cathedral authorities, the government officials and the workmen that repairs went on apace and he was able to contrive an
excellent system of central heating, have the old basement
turned into a flat, and install a compact modern kitchen on the
ground floor behind the dining-room. And when we say bribed,
we do not mean that money passed, but Dr. Joram had learnt in
sunny Africa what the ten-year sufferer first under The War and
later under Them had learnt here, that three things will ease
one's path and provide service; first cigarettes, then unlimited
cups of tea and finally to listen with an air of intense sympathy to
everything other people say. And so well did Dr. Joram combine
these that everyone concerned agreed, in their various spheres
and manner of speech that Joram would Do, that that there new
one wasn't half bad, and that we really *must* get our new Canon
to show us what he has done to Dr. Thorne's house, my dear.

"Why The Vinery, I don't quite know," said Dr. Joram opening his elegant front door and standing aside for his guests to enter. "There *is* a glass house in the garden but no sign of anything but tomatoes in it, and there *is* a passion-flower on the south wall of the house; but otherwise nothing. Come in."

They found themselves in a square hall, small but of good proportions. A not inelegant staircase went up three of its walls to the first floor; on the fourth wall was the door to the dining-room and at the back a door to the Canon's study. On the three walls of the staircase were wall-paintings of imaginary landscapes, framed in painted columns, and on the ceiling a few quite modest gods and goddesses on clouds.

"My dear Joram!" exclaimed the Dean, "what a revelation! One never saw these in Thorne's time."

"He had canvas stretched over most of them," said Dr. Joram, "and the rest were very dirty. I had a man down from London to restore them; Lord Pomfret told me about him. I thought it better to have a good man."

"But it must have cost a *great* deal," said Mrs. Morland, who living much of her life alone was apt to express her thoughts aloud.

Some of those present may have felt faintly shocked but it was evident that Dr. Joram did not, for he obligingly told Mrs. Morland exactly how much he had paid, a sum which impressed the whole party a good deal.

Mrs. Crawley, seeing that her friend Laura was about to ask Dr. Joram as a mother might ask a son except that no mother could afford so to risk her position, whether he could really afford it, was about to interfere when the Canon obligingly saved her the trouble.

"It seems a large sum," he said, finding as most people did that Mrs. Morland was very easy to talk to because she was so genuinely interested in what people said and never put them into a book, chiefly because, as she had once told Lord Stoke, any book into which he might be put would fall dead of its own weight. "But I lived entirely on my salary while I was in Mnganga-land. One's wants are so small there. A pot of boiling water and a handful of Mngogo-gogo. I have often bicycled thirty and forty miles a day on it. So when I got back, early in '41, I found a very substantial sum in my bank. And then an aunt died, so," said Dr. Joram simply, "I can afford to be extravagant. And not having a wife, I think this house is worth being extravagant about."

Mrs. Morland heartily agreed. The rest of the party, feeling a certain delicacy about listening to the Canon's general financial confession, had moved into the dining-room and were examining its dignified white panelling and the good, old-fashioned furniture, but when Dr. Joram and Mrs. Morland joined them they were very ready to see the rest of the house, which was indeed as pleasant a residence as one would wish to see, in good if not exciting taste.

"It is rather large for me," said Dr. Joram, when he had showed them the third floor with what had once been servants' bedrooms commanding a view over the river and away beyond the water-meadows to the downs, "after living for so long in my Mngpalagn; but I can shut up some of the rooms and I also hope to have old Oxford friends to stay with me."

Mrs. Crawley asked what his—she was sorry she could not pronounce the word—was.

"Oh, the Palace," said Dr. Joram. "It was a large, really a *very* large hut built of mud and straw, which when well mixed, cut into squares and baked in the sun make excellent bricks, and a roof thatched with reeds. The Mnganga language has, you know, no sibilant, so Palace became Palagn. There was a large brick bungalow provided for me, but I could not feel it fitting to live in luxury, so we used it as a guest house. And now, I hope you will try my sherry."

Accordingly he took them down again to the drawing-room which, like that of Lady Fielding and of most of the other residents on that side of the Close, was on the first floor and drenched in the western light.

"You had remarkably good sherry last time I was here, Joram," said the Dean, who was considered to know more about wine than anyone in the Close. "May I ask where you get it?"

"I don't know much about it," said Dr. Joram with the utmost candour. "My man appears to know everything, so I leave it to him. I'll ask him," with which words he rang the bell.

At this the company's eyes nearly jumped out of their heads, and Miss Dale, when telling Mrs. Marling about it later, said that she to her certain knowledge and the same was probably true of the rest of the company, had not seen or heard a bell rung in a private house since the London schools were evacuated in 1939.

"You rang, sir," said a voice, which had come upstairs and into the room without being heard.

Dr. Joram was about to answer when he saw the Dean looking as if he had seen a ghost.

"It's not you, Simnet?" said Dr. Crawley.

"Pardon *me*, sir, but it is," said the butler. "I hope I see you well, sir, and Mrs. Crawley and Mrs. Morland whom I had the pleasure of waiting on when you were at the School in the autumn of '39, madam, and your youngest son whom I well remember as a youth in Mr. Carter's house. I do not think that I have had the pleasure of seeing you, sir, since Miss Anne Fielding's I should say Mrs. Robin Dale's wedding when I obliged at Number Seventeen."

"So you did," said the Dean. "And Mrs. Robin has twins now."

"These things are bound to occur, sir," said Simnet.

"I didn't know you had left Southbridge," said the Dean, an inveterate and sometimes rather inconsiderate county gossip.

"I had no intention of doing so, sir," said Simnet, "and I may add that it came equally as a surprise to Mr. Carter and myself.

The fact is, sir—well, you may remember Eileen at the Red lion, sir?"

"The blonde with the red finger nails?" said Mrs. Morland, bursting into the conversation. "I remember what a *wonderful* help she was when we had the Christmas party for the evacuated London schoolchildren in 1939. When I think of it I sometimes wish the war had gone on for ever. We *were* so happy with Mr. Churchill and Lord Woolton."

Dr. Crawley who though without much real hope sometimes felt it was his duty to keep his old friend Mrs. Morland from making a fool of herself in public was about to expostulate, but Simnet spoke first.

"Yes, madam," he said. "I was passing the same remark to Mr. Tomkins only last week. It is not for Us, living in the Close as We do, Tomkins, I said, to say anything against this government as they call themselves, but we'd all be a deal happier, I said, if we was back when there was a War On."

"Oh, *how* right you are," said Mrs. Morland, and was about to pursue this fruitful subject when the Dean, considering that Mrs. Morland had quite enough rope, cut across any further speech and asked Simnet about his having left Southbridge.

"As I was endeavoring to state, sir," said Simnet, speaking to the Dean as man to man, though with proper reverence for the Dean's position, "myself and Eileen had been keeping company for several years, and it really began to seem time to take Steps but Eileen said I had missed the bus and she was now walking out regular with the Reverend Crofts's man, but, she said to me, why not my sister Florrie, Mr. Simnet. She is a nice girl, she said, and has been cook-housekeeper for the Honourable Mr. Nutfield and knows what gentlemen like. So Florrie changed her day off to suit mine and we agreed to fix things up as soon as I could get Mr. Carter suited. Edward the odd man whom you may remember, sir, came into Mr. Carter's house Under Me and when I spoke to Mr. Carter about the possibility of a Change in my circumstances, I took the liberty of recommending Edward to him. Edward came for a fortnight on trial while I was on holiday and when I returned I found that he had on the whole given satisfaction, which enabled me with a clear conscience to give in my Notice. So me and Florrie," said Simnet, suddenly descending from his oratorical peaks and becoming human, "was married in the School Chapel. Florrie, I regret to say, sir, was a Baptist and wished for a chapel wedding, but when I had pointed out to her that by being married as I had arranged the ceremony would be taking place in a Chapel just the same, she was quite reasonable. It was a very successful Affair, sir. Matron gave Florrie away and Mr. Dale kindly lent the dining-room in his House for the reception. I could wish I had had the super-vision of the reception myself," said Simnet wistfully, for his handling of large parties was famed throughout the county, "but it was not quite in keeping with my position as bridegroom. And as his reverence," said Simnet, who obviously only restrained himself with great difficulty from saying His Lordship, "was enquiring for a Couple, we was able to oblige."

"Sherry, please, Simnet," said Dr. Joram.

Simnet, evidently appreciative of his employer's lordly ways, made a slight bow to the company, went onto the landing and returned with a tray of bottles and glasses which he placed on a table with quiet triumph as one who would not be caught napping.

"I expect you would like to see Mrs. Simnet before you go, Crawley," said Dr. Joram. "Tell Mrs. Simnet the Dean will visit the housekeeper's room before he goes. That is all."

"Thank *you*, sir," said Simnet retiring.

"My dear Bishop," said Mrs. Crawley, for his old friends still often used his African title, "how on *earth* do you do it?"

"Do what?" said Dr. Joram, offering sherry to his guests.

"Bully your servants," said Mrs. Crawley. "It does my heart good to hear you stand up to Simnet who has terrorised South-bridge School ever since I remember him."

"I don't know about bullying," said Dr. Joram. "You see in

Mngangaland I had thirty or forty servants one way or another and one has to exercise a certain amount of authority. I never had them flogged, for which I sometimes blame myself," said the Colonial Bishop wistfully, "for it would have given them a good deal of pleasure, but I knew if I did it would make things difficult for my successor, who would possibly not understand them as I did. So I refrained. But if they were insubordinate I used to get the local witch-doctor on to them, and he frightened them into fits. Life there was, if it is not irreverent to say so, an Earthly Paradise."

The Dean wondered vaguely if he ought to make a formal protest against this doctrine, but reflecting that a man who gave his guest real Spanish sherry of just the right dryness ought to be encouraged, he refrained. The two men then of course fell into cathedral gossip, while the ladies sat by one of the large sash windows looking over the Close and presently Miss Dale asked Mrs. Morland if she minded being told how much people liked her books.

"I simply love it," said the talented authoress, who was now going through a kind of winding-up process with her back hair which always reminded her more educated friends of Miss Pleasant Riderhood. "And at least I am sure none of my books can do you any harm."

"Do you always have to say that, Laura?" said Mrs. Crawley.

Mrs. Morland looked guilty.

"Well, I invented it once," she said, "and it seemed quite a good thing to say, so I go on saying it. And after all, no one can say my books do do any harm and anyway they are all exactly alike."

Dr. Crawley, deserting the subject of the Close, said kindly that logic was not our dear Laura's strong point and he must be getting back, but he had absent-mindedly allowed Dr. Joram to refill his glass so they lingered for a few more moments and Mrs. Morland asked Mrs. Crawley if she could give her a few names for her library list.

"It is really hopeless at Gaiters," she said. "You give them a list a mile long and everything is out, or they haven't got it yet. You always know the latest thrillers."

Mrs. Crawley said there was another Miss Silver one and another Mrs. Bradley one and she couldn't remember the names but they would know at Gaiters'; and why didn't Mrs. Morland make a list out of the newspapers. She herself, she said, always meant to every week, but somehow she didn't.

"I know," said Mrs. Morland sympathetically. "Or people tell you a book at a party and you write the name on an envelope or something and then you lose it, or else you put it in your engagement book and either you can't read it or you can't think what it means. My book is absolutely *full* of things that mean nothing at all to me, though they must have meant something when I put them down. I'll show you what I mean," she continued, and rummaging in her bag took out a small pocket diary. "Now here is January the eighteenth and I have 'Little Prince, age 10 size 12.' And suddenly on March the third 'Mr. Macdowell.' And on April 7 '53 tram from Vic.' And what any of them mean I have not the faintest idea."

" 'Ogygia—seen—Philip—but wasn't,' " said Dr. Crawley and Mrs. Morland looked at him with gratitude, for it is not everyone who knows his *Happy Thoughts* as he should.

"Oh, that reminds me about God's blessing," said Mrs. Morland, rather to the Dean's alarm. "You said you had a dictionary of quotations, Dr. Joram."

"I am so sorry," said her host. "Here I have the Oxford Dictionary of quotations, though I much prefer my old friend Bartlett. Let us look!" He took it down and ran through the index.

" 'God's blessing, out of,' pages seventeen and nine hundred and seventy one," he said. "Dear me. First it is Heywood with references to Lyly and Shakespeare, and then Cervantes."

"But it can't be. Cervantes wasn't English,' said Mrs. Morland, "and it is an *English* quotation. I shall go on thinking of it as Shakespeare."

"If we are to visit Mrs. Simnet, we really must go, Joram," said the Dean, rather cross with his old friend Laura Morland for wasting time and stupidity. So they went down to the hall and then down again by a back stair to the basement which was really only one by courtesy, as the ground floor was eight steps above the level of the garden. Here Mrs. Simnet received the visitors in a very friendly way and exchanged with Mrs. Morland reminiscences of the early days of the war when the Hosiers' Boys' Foundation School from the East of London had to be billeted within twenty-four hours and the happy days when England stood alone within her seas, with her Great Pilot at the helm.

"Come along now, Laura," said Mrs. Crawley, but Mrs. Morland lingered for a moment to say how nice the flat was.

"It's lovely," said Mrs. Simnet. "And Dr. Joram, well he's a lovely man and it's a pleasure to work for him, but it's a shame he isn't married. When I go up for my orders in the morning he'll say, Oh I'm out to lunch, Mrs. Simnet and anything will do for dinner. Well, Mrs. Morland that's not right. A gentleman like him, well he ought to look after himself with all those services in the cathedral and no heating. When he has one of the other gentlemen from the Close to dinner I see to it that they get a real good meal, chicken or something, for as for the meat we get on the ration now it's not hardly fit for soup, and not enough of it to put in a hollow tooth as the saying is. He ought to be married, Mrs. Morland. You may wonder at me saying so, but it's too much responsibility and Simnet says so too. Now a nice wife, his own age, perhaps a lady who's lost her husband and understands how to make a gentleman comfortable, whether he likes it or not, that's what he needs. Me and Simnet's very comfortable in our flat and there's plenty of room on the top floor if Dr. Joram did set up housekeeping with a lady. It's a bit lonely in the Close, and I'd like some company at nights when Simnet's out at his clubs and things, or obliging in the Close. A nice woman, not too young, like Jessie at Mr. Carter's house at Southbridge at least it's Mr. Dale now but we always call it Carter's."

Mrs. Morland had no particular opinion of herself, but she could not help feeling that Mrs. Simnet's remarks were directed more or less at her and was thankful to escape and rejoin the rest of the party. Farewells were said and Mrs. Morland walked with Miss Dale to the end of Barley Street where all the motor-buses congregated.

"Oh," said Miss Dale, as they parted, the one towards the High Rising bus the other towards the station to take the local train to Melicent Halt. "I thought of a book you might like for your library list. Have you read Lisa Bedale's last thriller, *Aconite at Night*?"

"Oh, but what fun," said Mrs. Morland. "I didn't know it was out. I hope Gerry Marston is the detective?"

"He always is," said Miss Dale, "and the villain is called Frank Mulliner this time. When is your next Madame Koska thriller coming out?"

"About October as usual," said Mrs. Morland. "The villain this time is a professional Government snooper who gets a job in the stock-room to try to prove that Madame Koska is evading income tax. I'll put the name down because I forget everything owing to this Government," and Mrs. Morland got out her engagement book and pencil.

"I'll put it on Christmas Day," she said, "then I'm sure to remember what it is," with which triumph of hope over experience she boarded her bus and Miss Dale went on towards the station. On the platform she found Oliver Marling who had come down from London for the week-end and was waiting for the local train.

"Well?" said Oliver, putting down a suit-case and a large important-looking brief-case, or whatever name one likes to give to those accordion-like receptacles with a brass lock, the better to greet Miss Dale.

"Quite well, if that is the right answer," said she. "I have shopped for your mother and had tea at the Deanery and sherry with Dr. Joram, and Anne Dale has twins."

"What kind?" said Oliver, but just then the local came in with as much noise and importance and letting-off of steam as if it were the express. Miss Dale's mouth worked but no sound was audible and they had to wait till they were in the carriage and out of the noisy station.

"Girls," said Miss Dale when she could make herself heard. "And Lady Fielding said that one of them would be called Maud as a second name after Anne's old governess."

"Good lord, that's Miss Bunting," said Oliver. "Good old Bunny. She governessed my uncles and hundreds of other people and when they were evacuating London mother asked her down here. Then she went to Hallbury and governessed Anne who was a bit invalidish then. She was the only person my cousin David was ever afraid of. Any other news?"

"Only that Dr. Joram has a very beautiful house," said Miss Dale, "and the kind of furniture that has no particular period but fits in comfortably. And the most beautiful painted stair-case. He is an extraordinarily nice person, with less egoism or egotism whichever you say than anyone I know. And what sort of a week have *you* had," said Miss Dale who had discovered before she had been at Marling Hall very long that Oliver, though very pleasant, was like most men entirely interested in his own affairs and would gently evaporate as it were if one ever introduced any affairs of one's own. Very few men did feel any interest in their female friends' affairs she thought. When she was younger she had believed that one might have a friend who without being in the least in love would be a kind of protector in an honourable sense; someone to whom one could tell one's ordinary troubles, without of course inflicting upon him the more elusive troubles of one's own heart or mind. But as she grew older, and she had waited for John for three years because her mother needed her and John was away, and then John had been killed in the landing in Italy and as she grew older she realised what many of us never learn, that a man who can be a helping friend is the rarest thing in the world. He may be delightful, intelligent, kind, but never try to tell him your heart's troubles; he will much prefer to tell you his. Do not consult him about business, about leases, about any personal difficulties; he will at once counter with his own which are of course to him, and you must pretend they are to you, much greater than your own; and he will feel obscurely that his liberty is threatened. Not that you wish to marry him and indeed he does not suspect you of that, but he does not wish to take any responsibility or have to think of you except at such moments as he wishes to think of you, and you must do your best to wear the mask that he prefers. John was not like that, but he was himself and so different from other men. And he had been dead a long time now.

"A penny for your thoughts," said Oliver.

"Wool gathering, not worth a penny," said Miss Dale. "Tell me, is there any news from Adrian Coates?" for this very rising, or indeed risen publisher, whose success had been considerably helped by Mrs. Morland whose Madame Koska books he had published steadily for a great many years, had been persuaded by that worthy creature to look at a book which Oliver Marling had been writing off and on for some time. It was a Life and Works of the Reverend Thomas Bohun, M.A., Canon of Barchester from 1657 to 1665 when he rashly made a journey to London to observe the effect of the Plague upon human bodies (hoping also to find some trace of the Soul) and never returned. A memorial tablet had been put up in the cloisters a couple of years earlier, owing to the misguided zeal of the Friends of Barchester Cathedral who had a larger balance than usual. But it was on the whole considered a victory by all right-minded people, as the Palace had done its best to get other people to subscribe for a chapel and if, the Dean had said, the fact of Bohun having written a number of very erotic poems was a suitable reason for erecting at considerable expense a chapel to his memory, then doubtless the Bishop knew best.

"Not yet," said Oliver. "I had lunch with him on Thursday and he said he liked my stuff immensely, but he wants two of his readers to see it before he can decide."

Miss Dale said she was sure Mr. Coates would not pass it on to his readers unless he felt pretty sure about it, for she noticed that he usually backed his own taste in the end.

"Do you know him then?" said Oliver.

Miss Dale said he had known Mrs. Morland for quite a long time and had met Mr. Coates there, and also Mr. Johns, who was a very good publisher too.

"I am only wondering," said Oliver, in what Miss Dale secretly described to herself as a silly, grown-up, pretentious voice, "whether my chapter on his Rosicrucian studies may not be a little stiff for the ordinary reader."

Now was the moment when his dear sister Lucy was badly needed, to say "Rot" in no uncertain tones, but Lucy was at that moment in her garden at Edgewood, practically standing on her head in the herbaceous border under the direction of old Miss Sowerby. For Miss Sowerby, as Lucy freely admitted, knew far more about flowers than she, Mrs. Adams, could ever learn, and as long as Miss Sowerby felt well enough to come over from her widowed sister's house at Worthing in Mr. Adams's car, so long would Lucy gladly and patiently learn all that she could from her.

"Perhaps," said Miss Dale, "some of your readers will be glad to hear about Bombast Paracelsus and Read what Fludd the Seeker tells us, Of the Dominant that runs Through the Cycle of the Suns," and that, she said to herself, will show you.

"Good lord! Do you read the mystics?" said Oliver.

"Oh no. Only Kipling," said Miss Dale. "You will find the poem in *Plain Tales from the Hills*. Is there anything in the evening paper?"

Oliver said there wasn't, as one always does, but had to hand his newspaper to Miss Dale who read it with much interest till they reached Marling Halt.

"I do miss Lucy when I come back," said Miss Dale, who had now forgiven Oliver for his showing off; and as a gentleman cannot or ought not to sulk, Oliver made an effort and recovering from his sulks made himself perfectly pleasant as they walked up to the Hall, where Miss Dale went to find Mrs. Marling and account for various commissions her employer had given her. She also told her about Anne Dale's babies and the beauty of Dr. Joram's house, which last item made Mrs. Marling think how nice it would be if he fell in love with Miss Dale, only the Hall would seem rather lonely without her.

"I don't think you have heard anything I have been saying for the last five minutes," said Miss Dale, but in a friendly and most unspiky way.

"I haven't," said Mrs. Marling, almost mechanically. "I *beg* your pardon, my dear," she added. "The fact is I was thinking.

"About——?" said her guest.

"Chiefly about how much I shall miss you when you have to go," said Mrs. Marling.

"I rather wanted to talk to you about that myself," said Miss Dale. "Have you a moment to spare?"

"Twenty," said Mrs. Marling. "We don't dine till a quarter to eight tonight as my husband has been kept by some district council business."

"Will you talk first, or shall I?"

"You, my dear," said Mrs. Marling.

Miss Dale looking at her hostess and employer saw the woman she had grown to respect, to like and almost to love; the elderly woman carrying her years well, with the good looks that come of breeding and an intelligent unselfish mind, rather than any real beauty.

"Just as you like," she said. "I think I have done the job you engaged me for and I hope I have been able to help. If there isn't any more work for me, I expect you would like me to go fairly soon. We only meant this to be temporary and it has somehow gone on. But if I *can* help, I would like to help. Of course if mother were ill again I would have to go, but while she is well we are really better apart."

"Thank you, my dear," said Mrs. Marling, "that is just what I wanted to know. Now I will tell you my side of it. My husband and I are most grateful for all you have done, including a great deal that wasn't in the bargain. We miss Lucy—that goes without saying—and we are in a way rather crippled without her. You have been extraordinarily good to William. If you think you could be happy here, we should like you to think of this as your other home for the present at any rate. I may say that Lucy feels the same. Will you think it over?"

Miss Dale was silent for a moment and then said, "But I don't think I need to, Mrs. Marling. This is more like a home than my mother's house. I am sorry, but it is. May I stay? If you find it doesn't work, let me know. If I may take some time every day for my own, for letters and business and things, the rest of the time I will do all I can. Would it suit you if we said a month's notice on either side? And of course if mother is really ill, I'll have to go," to which Mrs. Marling saw no objection.

"Then that is settled," said Mrs. Marling, too proud to show the relief she felt, "and we needn't talk about it again," but Miss Dale came up and kissed her and they both felt that anyone else might have cried, but they wouldn't.

"So Amabel tells me you're staying with us, my dear," said Mr. Marling at dinner. "A very good thing too. I miss Lucy. I don't get about as well as I used. And I may say that your help with my girl's wedding and your being here have made all the difference to my wife and myself. You'll be marrying too, one of these days."

Miss Dale said perhaps she would. Or perhaps she wouldn't. Mrs. Marling looked at her husband with such meaning that he suddenly realised how unfortunate his remark had been. But this was not the moment to apologise, so he talked of what had been said and done at the council meeting and Mrs. Marling mentally sank back in her seat with a sigh of relief. She knew her husband would be pleased and she knew how pleased he was, for he had talked as only he, she thought, could talk, dropping what his irreverent children called his Olde Englishe Squire mannerisms and showing his real self. It ought to be a peaceful happy summer for William, if all went well, and heaven knew he deserved it. Lucy was happy. She herself, having got over the wrench of Lucy's marriage, felt there was much to be thankful for. Her elder son and her elder daughter were leading their own lives successfully. Only her difficult Oliver, her ugly duckling, seemed ever dissatisfied in spite of the work that he liked, his London interests, his excursions into mild literary work. Was the poison of Jessica too strong in his blood? Not that she blamed Jessica whose mere existence made people her slaves, but she often felt that Oliver was sacrificing his life to a useless dream and what was worse, enjoying it. Perhaps he found life at Marling too dull. And then her common sense told her that too dull or not it made an excellent background for him and was cheaper than racketing about at weekends and having to tip heavily at his friends' houses. For one of the only ways to return hospitality for anyone who has no home of his own is to overtip one's friends' servants if any, or their daily or weekend help or anything that is theirs.

After dinner Mr. Marling sat by Miss Dale and talked to her about Marling and his boyhood in the old home and the days when life was free and generous and the kitchen a centre of welcome for the whole estate and pigs were slaughtered and cured and there were two laundresses and a dairymaid and endless other workers or hangers on, and never less than four hunters in the stable. His wife had not heard him talk so freely and cheerfully for a long time and she wondered with a pang whether she had not done her best. Vain and foolish regret, for her life had become not her own under the stress of the war and the growing burden and menace of the peace, but some natures must always blame themselves. As for Oliver she had to admit to herself that he had not helped much. In fact he had been pretty selfish. An echo came back to her mind, something that old Mr. Leslie had said, many years ago, about his son David being bone selfish. She wondered if Oliver, David's cousin at a remove or two, had the same bone selfishness, and there was no answer to this, or at any rate no answer that she wished to hear.

The telephone rang. Oliver, who was nearest, answered it.

"For you, mother," he said and his mother noticed with concern that his face looked a nasty mixture of green and lead-colour.

"Mrs. Marling speaking," she said, expecting some village or county business.

"Good evening, Mrs. Marling," said a voice which she recognised but could not place, "it is Aubrey Clover. Jessica wants you to know that Sarah Siddons has made her first appearance on any stage. Eight pounds, a bright red face, straight black hair and lungs like Caruso. Can you hear her?" and indeed the sound of a very new baby celebrating its freedom by yelling itself red and purple in the face was distinctly to be heard. "Jessica wants to speak to you herself. Will you wait for a moment?"

It had to be faced. Mrs. Marling, one ear at the telephone, said to the room at large, "It's Aubrey. He says the baby is a girl, eight pounds, very healthy," but did not look at Oliver. Her husband said what the deuce was it all about.

"Darling Mrs. Marling," said Jessica's voice. "Sarah Siddons is too, too divine. Quite *revoltingly* hideous, just like something in a museum, and a voice like a siren, but quite Heaven and smells of baby in a perfectly divine way. I am frightfully well. Sarah has all the right toes and fingers I've counted them, and she has the most *adorable* flat ears. She sends love and kisses to you and Mr. Marling and says tell Oliver to come and see her soon. It is all absolute Heaven and Aubrey is going to write a play with a part for her. Nurse is making horrible faces at me to stop. Love to you all. Tell Oliver he must come and see her, because she changes every moment. Good-bye; blessings."

"What's all that about?" said Mr. Marling. "Nothing wrong with Lucy?"

"Of course not," said his wife, who had not realised how much he was thinking of his masterful daughter. "It was Aubrey Clover. Jessica has a little girl and they are delighted."

The news appeared to give Mr. Marling intense satisfaction and his pride in little Jessica's achievement—as he always called her—could not have been greater if he had been the father. Miss Dale was also pleased, though in quite a general way, as she had only seen Jessica at Lucy's wedding but had fallen, as everyone did, under the charm of that enchanting creature, and she rashly said to Oliver what delightful news it was.

Oliver remarked in a very conceited and artificial manner (so Miss Dale thought) that beauty was in the eye of the beholder and doubtless it was his tiresome eyes that were at fault, but he could see nothing in babies and really it was quite unnecessary for Aubrey to ring up at that time of night, with which he took a book from a shelf near him and retired into it. His father and mother soon went to bed and Oliver roused himself from his book to wish them a perfunctory good-night.

Presently, as Miss Dale was tidying the room and plumping up cushions, he sighed loudly, put a paper knife into his book to mark the place, shut it and put it on a table.

"Can I help you?" he said.

Miss Dale nearly said Yes, but not by sitting there sulking with your long legs stretched in front of you; but she had been well brought up, so she only thanked him and said that was all. Oliver said, to an unseen audience, that people were extraordinarily inconsiderate, which made Miss Dale say under her breath that he was perfectly right.

"I mean why ring us up so late?" said Oliver.

Miss Dale, hearing her own voice get almost out of control, said it wouldn't have been any good ringing up earlier if the baby wasn't born, which words appeared so to outrage Oliver's finer feelings that he got up and knocked his book onto the floor.

"Dr. Smith's Smaller Latin-English Dictionary," said Miss Dale, looking at it with interest as she picked it up, patted it as if to reassure it, and put it back in its place.

"Well, why not?" said Oliver. "And I admire Jessica tremendously," he added, for no obvious reason.

"So does everyone," said Miss Dale coldly.

"Exactly," said Oliver. "Everyone has a right to admire her and criticise her. When I think of her on the stage every night for everyone to gape at—it is unspeakable. And now the whole of England has to know about this baby. If you had ever cared for anyone you would know what I feel."

"I have cared," said Miss Dale, standing very straight and looking right through Oliver, as if there were, beyond him, something that would keep her steady.

"I am sorry," said Oliver, horrified by what he had done. "I am deeply sorry. I am ashamed of myself. I don't know what to say. I beg you to forgive me and on my word of honour such a thing shall never happen again."

"I shall not say anything to Mr. and Mrs. Marling about it if that is what you mean," said Miss Dale. "Good-night."

Oliver opened the door for her and stood aside to let her pass. To his horror tears that she could not control were brimming in her eyes.

"I must have been mad," he said.

"Only selfish," said Miss Dale and hurried up the stairs to reach her own bedroom and be alone.

After this Oliver did not have a good night and we think that it served him right.

CHAPTER 6

The christening of Anne Dale's twins (and Robin's too, if it comes to that) was an important event in the life of Southbridge School. For more than twenty years there had been a sad dearth of babies born on the premises. The half-witted but beautiful Rose Birkett and her uninteresting sister Geraldine had been born even before their parents came to the Prep. School. Assistant masters who had wives had always moved on elsewhere before having children; entirely by chance, we may add, for the School liked to have babies about. The only exception was the Everard Carters who now had three children, but Kate Carter, an angel of goodness and kindness, was so obviously a Mother from the very day of her marriage that her children hardly counted. And now we come to think of it the Carters' babies had been christened at their mother's old home at Northbridge. So everyone in the School was interested and the Chaplain, better known to several generations of boys as Holy Joe, wondered where the font had been put.

"It is an extraordinary thing," he said to the Headmaster Everard Carter during Sunday supper, a tradition which the Carters had taken over from the Birketts, "to lose a whole font. If it had been the lid—but it's the whole thing. I wonder when it was last used. Not in my time. The only christening I had was Matron's eldest nephew's child and that was at the parish church, because Crofts was away and asked me to do the job

for him. I remember it because they wanted to call the baby
Marconi Sparks."

"And what *did* they call it?" said Kate Carter, attracted from
her conversation with Leslie major, for the Birketts' custom of
having one or two senior boys on Sundays had also been carried
on.

"Marconi Sparks," said the Chaplain, surprised at his hostess's inattention.

"Excuse me, madam," said a voice from behind Kate's left
shoulder, "it's in the coal-hole."

"What is, Edward?" said Kate, who had never been known to
be ruffled, even when Master Bobbie Carter and Miss Angela
Carter had set out for Barchester with fivepence half-penny
between them and had been brought back six hours later by the
Northbridge policeman who was the cousin of Jessie, head
housemaid at Everard's old House.

"The font, madam," said Edward. "It was when the Men were
repairing the nineteen-fourteen-eighteen Old Boys' Memorial
Window in the chapel after the unexploded bombs went off in
the allotments. There wasn't room for their ladders, so Mr.
Birkett had it put in the coal-hole. It's all wrapped up in hessian,
madam, quite carefully, so no one wouldn't pinch it."

"But why would anyone want to pinch a font?" said Kate.

Mr. Feeder, who lived in Louisa Cottage in Wiple Terrace
down in the village, said They would pinch anything. They, he
said, had pretty well pinched the Empire.

Mr. Traill, who lived in Maria Cottage next door to Mr.
Feeder, said They were like the base Indian who threw a pearl
away richer than all his tribe.

"Pearls before swine," said Leslie major, addressing this remark to the circumambient air, but if he hoped that someone
would rise to this, no one did, and he then wondered if what he
had said really meant anything—a doubt by which we are all
assailed from time to time.

"One might write a book about how awful the government

are and call it *They*, sir," said Mr. Shergold, the ex-naval assistant master who was now in charge of what used to be Everard Carter's House, and was doing very well.

"One might," said the Headmaster. "So might Kipling."

"And if you tried to use anything old Kipling said, you would jolly well have some people down on you about copyright," said Mr. Traill, "as the B.B.C. too well know, don't they, Feeder?" which was an obvious bait for Mr. Feeder whose wireless blared through the thin party-walls of Maria and Louisa for every moment when he was at home. Mr. Feeder, choosing to take offence, said he only listened to its cultural programmes, to which Mr. Traill cheerfully replied that he didn't think there could be enough culture in the world to fill the working hours of Mr. Feeder's wireless.

Kind Mrs. Carter, who could not bear unpleasantness, said Mrs. Dale's babies were to be called Dora Maud and Roberta Fielding the first name in each case being after one of Anne's parents.

Leslie major asked if that was after Tom Jones.

"Don't try to confuse issues, Boy," said Everard, who had found this form of address distinctly quelling to the more uppish members of the Middle School. "And what had we better do about the font?" he said, appealing to the Chaplain.

The Chaplain, unexpectedly showing the same kind of commonsense as was shown by Mr. Dick when Miss Trotwood asked his advice about little David Copperfield, said Put it back where it was.

"Whenever I go into the chapel I think of Rose Fairweather's wedding," said the Headmaster. "That *was* a day! By the way, Kate, where is Rose now?"

His wife said she didn't know, as she hadn't seen Rose's people for some time, but she believed Captain Fairweather was at the Admiralty at present.

"Dreadful, dreadful girl," said her husband. "Still, she was gloriously rude to our Miss Banks who was trying to teach Latin to the Lower School without the most elementary idea of quantities."

"But, darling," said Kate Carter. "She didn't *mean* to be rude."

"I daresay Leslie major didn't mean to be rude or impertinent either," said Everard, "when he told Mr. Birkett that Miss Banks had taught them to say Uraynus. But it came to the same thing," at which Leslie major, that hardened masterbaiter, reddened to the roots of his hair.

The font, none the worse for its experiences, was replaced in the chapel. The day for the christening was set. There were to be a good many guests from Barchester, for Anne Dale's father Sir Robert Fielding was, as we know, the Chancellor of the Diocese and Anne had many friends there. Robin Dale also had friends among the higher clergy, and Dale cousins and army friends scattered in Barsetshire. Anne had made up her mind to do as many young mothers were doing and looking after the baby herself as she had an adequate domestic staff in her husband's House, but when Dora Maud turned out to be probably also Roberta Fielding, her mother and her husband had put their foot or feet down and said a nurse she should and must have. By great good luck Sister Chiffinch of the Harefield Cottage Hospital, who had been with Robin's father on the day of his peaceful death, was just about to retire and only take chosen private cases and hearing that Anne was expecting a baby had at once offered herself as monthly nurse, and as Anne very much wished to have her baby at home, and Dr. Ford saw no reason against it, Sister Chiffinch had come over to see her prospective patient and also to renew acquaintance with Matron who was, as she told Robin, an old pal of hers, though not fully trained.

"Now if this isn't exactly like old times," said Sister Chiffinch, who like so many of her noble profession looked distinctly less charming in ordinary clothes than she did in uniform, to which Robin had replied that as far as he knew Anne had never looked like this before and Sister Chiffinch had laughed and said the gentlemen would have their jokes.

"Dr. Ford says it is probably twins," said Anne, who looked, so her husband thought, more lovely and more peaceful every day. "Will that be too much for you, Sister?"

Sister Chiffinch assured her that it would not, bringing forward her own experience with one Mrs. Harris who had had premature triplets in a small cottage in Devonshire with great success under her, Sister Chiffinch's, guidance; also the case of Lady Tadpole of Tadpole Hall near Tadcaster, sister of that very smart Mrs. David Leslie, which Lady Tadpole had quite taken the wind out of their sails by popping out the dearest little mite of a girl at seven months, only four pounds and *such* an old-fashioned little expression, who had done splendidly owing to her, Sister Chiffinch's, fine work with a fountain pen filler and had never once looked back as the saying was.

Robin had looked anxiously at Anne, ready to take Sister Chiffinch by the scruff of her neck and throw her out of the window if she frightened his beloved wife, but Anne in the remote security, as near one kind of heaven as one may reach, which a happy woman can feel with her first and even with her other babies, had only smiled which, in the words of the Arabian Nights, had made Robin's heart contract.

"And now," said kind Sister Chiffinch, "it is quite time Mrs. Robin stopped talking and had a little shut-eye. And if I may, Mr. Dale, I will just pop in and see Dudley."

"Who?" said Robin.

"My old pal Poppy Dudley," said Sister Chiffinch. "I had an ever so sweet note from her when she heard I was coming. Of course we mustn't disturb House routine, and well do I remember the day Dudley and I—we were only probationers at Knights then, but she didn't go any further with her training— were doing the trays and took Matron's tea in to her at two minutes to four. 'Take it away,' she said, looking absolutely *through* me as the saying is. 'Two minutes too soon is as bad as two minutes too late, Chiffinch,' she said, for she remembered the name of every single doctor, nurse and probationer in Knights. I can assure you, Mr. Dale, that I went out of the room my face as red as a piece of burnt toast. And when Mrs. Robin wrote to me about this wee stranger-to-be for of course we did not know then it was twins, I hadn't any more idea than Mr. Attlee and goodness knows that is saying something that the Matron here was Dudley till Mrs. Robin happened to mention my name to her and of course she wrote me at once. I always say it's a small world."

Owing to Matron having been so long known and respected as Matron, very few people remembered her own name and even Robin had to think sometimes when he made out her monthly cheque. But during Sister Chiffinch's monologue he had time to pull himself together and offered to take his guest to Matron's quarters.

Exactly what happened when a Nation spoke to a Throne Robin never knew and told Anne he was glad he didn't because he would have been frightened out of his wits. Jessie, the hideous head housemaid whose only fault was that she *would* not wear her glasses, brought back work to the staff sitting-room that she had took the tea in and Matron and the other lady were laughing ever so and saying something about nights and Matron called the other lady Squiffy, which her fellow-servants rightly did not believe.

After this historic interview Sister Chiffinch had come back to the drawing-room to say good-bye.

"And there's just the one thing, Mr. Dale," she said before she left. "If it is twins Mrs. Robin *must* have a nannie. I've seen a lot of young wives doing the housework and the cooking and the baby and doing it very well. But Mrs. Robin isn't that sort. She was a delicate girl, Mr. Dale, and she has got over it but she mustn't run risks. If you don't know of a good nannie I shall do a bit of sleuthing and see what I can find. There's Mrs. Belton over at Harefield, I nursed her daughter Lady Hornby the

Admiral's wife with her last up in Scotland, and a sweet little boy he was and the Admiral gave me this lovely cairngorm brooch. I always think cairngorms are a bit different from other stones, and Mrs. Belton's maid Wheeler has a niece who has been in a quite nice family as under-nurse and wants to better herself. Ellen Humble her name is her auntie keeps the libery at Harefield. So I'll just make some enquiries like a real Sherlock Holmes. And now I must fly or I'll miss the train. I will send you my London address with my old pals Wardy and Heathy that I share a flat with. Au revoir and *not*," said Sister Chiffinch, "good-bye."

Robin went back to Anne, fearing that she would be worn out by this visit, but she seemed quite well and calm and said, quite truly, that she had enjoyed it. And she told her mother, who at once wrote to Sister Chiffinch who sent her Ellen Humble's present address, and everything was settled for her. And Anne in a contented peaceful dream waited so angelically that Robin felt perfectly certain that she would die; as did her mother, except that her saner self told her that she wouldn't. As for Sir Robert, the Dean who had a very wide personal experience of children and grandchildren said the Chancellor had less self-control than a beetle, which left his hearers delightfully vague about his mental processes though of his ultimate meaning there was no doubt.

The christening was to be on a Saturday afternoon, followed by a party at Robin Dale's House, which was still technically known as Carter's and would be till Everard died. Anne, who had shed all the more distressing manifestations of her shyness since her marriage two years ago, had seized this opportunity for asking a good many old friends of her own and her parents and the invitations were for the most part gratefully accepted. For though England was technically at peace such were the restrictions and difficulties of every kind in travel, food, drink and the amenities of a lost civilisation that people of goodwill were thankful for any gathering that enabled them to see a number of acquaintances in a place which could be reached by train and motor-bus, even though the National Railways had lost their personal pride and the motor-buses were always overflowing with Mixo-Lydian and other permanent refugees, who were all doing very well, and spoke English with a fluency and wealth of colloquialisms that no one wished to imitate.

To find four godmothers is not an easy task when one has to consider the varying claims of relations and friends. Anne and Robin had decided to invite Lady Fielding and Mrs. Francis Gresham for Miss Dora Maud by which proof of Anne's love and thoughtfulness Lady Fielding had been deeply moved. As for Miss Roberta Fielding Anne wanted Mrs. Martin Leslie, for Sylvia had been a great friend of hers at the golden moment when a young girl, sheltered by a delicate childhood and adolescence, began to love Robin Dale without knowing that she was in love. And who is to say whether bud or blossom is the lovelier. But they were still a godmother to the bad and were racking their brains among rival claims when Robin said what about his cousin Isabel Dale.

"Her mother's an awful lump of selfishness," he said. "She wouldn't let Isabel get married and then of course John was killed and Isabel had to go on being a daughter. The old lump wouldn't give Isabel more than pocket-money and when she wanted to take a job Cousin Priscilla threw heart attacks. Anyway she got some sort of companion to bully and that's why Isabel can be with the Marlings. She's a nice girl and I'd like to see more of her."

To this Anne agreed, as indeed she nearly always did agree with what her Robin said.

The godfathers were to be Everard Carter and—to his extreme delight—Bishop Joram, who had endeared himself to everyone since he came into the Close. The Dean was to perform the ceremony, with the School Chaplain and Colonel The Reverend F. E. Crofts, Vicar of Southbridge, in attendance.

"And short of a wicked fairy I think we have everything," said
Robin, at which Anne's eyes grew dark with anxiety, so that he
had to tell her very affectionately not to be a silly as the Dreadful
Dowager was the nearest approach to a Wicked Fairy that the
County could produce and she had not been asked. But no more
had the Wicked Fairy, said Anne, who appeared to find a
terrifying attraction in the idea.

Saturday afternoon appeared to be the most satisfactory day
for everyone. The first and second elevens were playing away
from home. Lord Pomfret had offered the freedom of Pomfret
Towers and the estate to the devotees of Victorian architecture,
Italian gardens and game-preserving. Glamora Tudor at the
Barchester Odeon in Honka-Tonka-Bodyline would be searing
the hearts of the film fans, and there was a display at the
aerodrome with five-shilling flights over the city and as Everard
knew that he could not stop his pupils breaking bounds he had
given permission for the Upper School and the two top forms of
the Lower School to go provided they were in for call-over, all of
which cleared the ground considerably, not to speak of the
rowing men who went silently and determinedly to the river on
all occasions.

The School Chapel is so well known to all lovers of Southbridge that we will merely remind our readers that it had been
designed by the same architect who had designed Pomfret
Towers, and combined darkness and inconvenience in an un-
paralleled degree, not to speak of the hideous east window
(Munich 1850 style) and the tiles on each side of the altar copied
from those used in the kitchen at the Towers. But long familiarity had bred toleration, and the memorial tables to former
masters and boys had covered much of the pitch-pine panelling,
while the Boer War, the 'fourteen war as it is convenient to
call it which had taken a heavy toll of old Southbridgians, the
last war—which name is indeed the triumph of hope over
experience—had all done their share. And any place in which

boys have grown in stature and learning and in the diabolical knowledge which boys acquire of their masters' weaknesses has its own atmosphere and become part of the living tradition of a school.

The guests had gradually drifted into the chapel and taken their seats. The organist had done his best with both hands and both feet though not loudly enough to interfere with the whispered talk which ran from pew to pew, for with the decay of civilisation and proper parties such semi-public functions were becoming the only way of seeing distant friends. Sister Chiffinch, who had come back for the occasion in a quite hideous suit of purple rayon with black spots had taken command near the font and was holding Miss Roberta Fielding, while Anne was holding Miss Dora Maud who was her sister's junior by a very short space of time, till the ceremony should begin. The Dean, supported by the School Chaplain and Colonel Crofts whom no one ever called anything else but Colonel, gave a short and moving address to the congregation clustered near the font, the babies were transferred each to a godmother, and then he took Miss Roberta Fielding, holding her as Matron afterwards said like an Old Master; and we think we understand what Matron meant. The baby gave one beady-eyed look at Dr. Crawley, smiled a divine vacant smile and began to talk to him, telling him in the softest of voices and quite unintelligibly to outsiders, how happy she was and how she felt complete confidence in the way he held her and the words he was saying, and so babbled herself through the short service of dedication. When she had been returned to Sister Chiffinch's arms her sister was handed to the Dean. Being slightly younger than Roberta Fielding she did not talk, but gazed intently from large wide-set eyes upon the Dean, uttering from time to time squeaks of ecstasy. When the brief service was over, the Dean with tremendous courage took a baby on each arm and walked with them to the altar, nor did they once cease their talking and squeaking, though subdued by the unseen presence, till they were returned to their guardians, from which point they slept ferociously.

"It was the most heavenly and touching service I have ever seen," said Lady Fielding (who was unashamedly wiping her eyes) to Dr. Crawley. "How do you do it?"

The Dean said that he had always liked babies and had christened eight of his own and all his grandchildren.

"I always feel," he said with a diffidence most unusual in him, "that I am nearer the altar with a baby in my arms than at any other time. One can't explain these things," at which words Lady Fielding had to wipe her eyes again, but it was a very happy kind of crying and did her no harm.

For the last few weeks Matron had concentrated upon a two-tiered christening cake, saving fats, rifling her hoarded American and Canadian and Australian parcels, not to speak of other parcels sent to her from different parts of the world by old boys. The result was a superb erection, crowned by two large silver paper hearts, with names and dates in pink icing, much admired by the guests who now poured into the large dining-room whose double doors were opened to include the drawing-room. And presiding in glory was Simnet, the ex-butler at the Headmaster's house, who had come with Dr. Joram and was presiding over the refreshments, for the Dales did not have a butler.

"A very nice christening, sir," he said to Robin. "We could have wished to see more champagne, sir, but doubtless Sir Stafford does not agree."

"I'll say he doesn't," said Robin feelingly. "But do not have any anxiety, sir," said Simnet. "I myself will see to the champagne, sir, for it takes a great deal of experience to make it go round."

At this moment Mr. Wickham, the Noel Mertons' agent, came into the room and buttonholed Robin.

"Sorry to miss the doings," he said, "but I had to drive carefully. If you look in my car, Simnet—it's got one mudguard tied on with string and the bumper bar aft is buckled—you'll find two dozen champagne in a laundry basket. I couldn't go fast with it on board. Perhaps I'd better come with you," and he went out with Simnet, leaving Robin face to face with Mrs. Morland, whose hat and hair were suffering a good deal from her emotions.

"A *perfect* christening," she said, pulling hairpens out of one part of her head to ram them into another, "but as for Sir Stafford Cripps, I can never, never forgive him. I heard you talking about him just now and my knees literally *quivered* with dislike."

Robin said he had an old aunt who said her leg always ached if there was a clergyman in the room, but quivering knees if a Chancellor of the Exchequer was mentioned were new to him.

"Not that I *know* him," said Mrs. Morland, "and people say he is quite human in private life, but after all I don't know him in private life. But what I cannot abide is rudeness to Kings."

"My dear Laura," said the Dean who had overheard the end of this conversation, "what on earth do you mean?"

"I mean the year of King George the Fifth's Jubilee and his talking about Jubilee Ballyhoo," said Mrs. Morland earnestly.

The Dean said there was always a great deal of loose talk about party ministers and it behoved us to prove all things and hold fast to that which was true.

"But it is true," said Mrs. Morland, "because I was in the Barchester public library looking up something in an old *Times* for George Knox and it was 1935 and he said quite *disloyal* things abut a hereditary monarchy and about only having to look at the pages of British Imperial History to hide your head in shame that you're British. Free speech may be all very well," said Mrs. Morland judicially, "but not about Kings, because they can never, never answer back."

Such was Mrs. Morland's loyalty that her voice was beginning to quaver and her hairpins to rain on the floor, when Mr. Wickham and Simnet came back carrying the washing basket which was then reverently unpacked. Simnet, who had a well-founded distrust of other people's arrangements, produced his own nippers, the joyful noise of a champagne bottle being opened was heard and everyone pretended not to look and feel excited.

"Hullo, Wicks," said a pleasant voice and Mrs. Crofts, the Vicar's wife, clove her way through the rapidly filling room to Mr. Wickham's side, "what's this I hear about a white pheasant at Gatherum? I didn't know there were any in the county."

Mr. Wickham said you never knew when a sport would turn up, even in the best regulated families, but he would make it his business to enquire and then he asked how the pictures were getting on, for Mrs. Crofts was doing a series of coloured pictures of birds for the well-known publisher Mr. Johns, who was Mr. Wickham's uncle. Mr. Wickham had described the undertaking as a whacking great series of books about natural history and also as awful rubbish, but Mrs. Crofts was a real artist and a bitter devotee of birds, and she and Mr. Johns found the venture to their common profit. And when we say a bitter devotee of birds, all our readers who have had close acquaintance with bird-lovers, those peculiar and almost inhuman fanatics, will know what we mean.

"I'll ask Peggy to find out," said Mrs. Crofts, alluding to her sister-in-law, formerly Mrs. Arbuthnot, now Mrs. Francis Brandon. "She and Francis are always over at Gatherum now. Theatricals," at which moment Mr. and Mrs. Francis Brandon came in.

"What have you done with Mrs. Brandon?" said Mrs. Crofts, who was fond of her sister-in-law's mother-in-law.

"Mamma ought to be here by now," said Francis. "Our car's a bit small and as a matter of fact I'm afraid we've used more than our share of petrol, so mamma isn't using her car for a bit. But the Millers are bringing her in theirs. They couldn't get here in time for the christening itself but they'll be along at any moment," and the Brandons passed on. Mrs. Crofts looked troubled but said nothing.

However before long the Vicar of Pomfret Madrigal and his

wife were seen with Mrs. Brandon, whose still lovely eyes and
becoming dress at once attracted a group of admirers.

"There's something wrong at the Brandons', Wicks," said
Mrs. Crofts, who was on much the same friendly and unemo-
tional terms with Mr. Wickham as Miss Sally Brass was with
Mr. Richard Swiveller, to which Mr. Wickham replied darkly
that marriage was good for some people and not so good for
others, that she, Mrs. Crofts, had done absolutely the right
thing by marrying, but it wasn't everyone who did and as
Colonel Crofts hadn't a mother living the question didn't raise.
He then went back to Simnet and worked very hard as voluntary
butler.

As both the babies' health had been drunk, and replied to in
their absence by their father, the party was free to enjoy itself, a
state of things of which it took every advantage, being nearly all
old friends or acquaintances. The only people missing were the
ex-Headmaster of Southbridge School and his wife, but as he was
well-known to fall into a kind of author's frenzy while working
on the Analects of Procrastinator and become unconscious of
time, meals and temperature, no one was anxious, though his
absence was regretted.

It is a well-known social phenomenon that when people go to
a party they will probably talk with the people they can talk with
every day. In vain are they introduced to a delightful professor
from Mixo-Lydia, or a brilliant female economist from Sweden,
or an art-lover from Omaha; on the first possible opportunity
seven-tenths of them will fall off and be found with Aunt
Fanny, or old George. So it was at the Dales' large, noisy and
successful party, and the noise and success came chiefly from
people talking in much louder voices than usual because of the
crowd to other people whom they could and did meet very often.
Men have perhaps in this respect even less social sense than
women and as iron is drawn to the lodestone (if it is) so were all
the clergy present drawn towards the large bay window in the
drawing-room where Dr. Crawley and the Archdeacon from

Plumstead were discussing infant baptism; not in its larger aspect, but with regard to the best method of handling the infants and getting a good grip on them so that they couldn't fall out of one's arms.

"I'll tell you something, Crawley," said the Archdeacon, "that isn't generally known. If you can once get them to hold your little finger, you're safe. Once a baby has got a good grip of a finger nothing short of personal violence can get it loose. I have noticed it again and again."

"I remember," said Colonel Crofts, "that on the day of my induction the Dean gave me some valuable hints on how to hold babies with the help of a sofa cushion, for which I have since had cause to be very grateful."

"Ah," said Dr. Crawley, interrupting the Vicar of Southbridge almost before he had finished, "that is when they double themselves up backwards and go red in the face. You grip them like this—excuse me, Archdeacon," and he reached across to a sofa and took a bolster-shaped cushion the better to demonstrate his tactics, while the inferior clergy looked on with interest.

"Most interesting," said Dr. Joram, "most interesting indeed. It would be a great privilege to christen a baby in the cathedral if ever anyone is kind enough to ask me, and I must give my mind to this question. In Mngangaland of course I always rubbed my hands in sand before beginning the ceremony."

Mr. Miller from Pomfret Madrigal said indeed, indeed he would not in any way wish to criticise Dr. Joram's methods, but were they not a little harsh for creatures so young and tender.

"Good gracious, Miller, you don't think I would do anything that could possibly offend a baby," said Dr. Joram. "Those babies are oiled all over every day for a fortnight before the christening. It keeps bad spirits away and is also quite a good skin food. But I would as soon christen an eel as a Mnganga baby without sand on my hands."

The School Chaplain, who had the morbid affection for animals peculiar to the English and one or two saints, said he had sometimes wondered how St. Francis would have treated an eel. To put sand on his hands would have seemed to that great-hearted animal-lover, he said, a denying of all he stood for.

Mr. Wickham, who though not in orders always said he liked being with parsons because you never knew what they'd say next, remarked that judging by what he had seen of the Eyties when he was out there in '42 or was it '43 St. Francis would have skinned an eel alive as soon as look at it, to which Mr. Miller, who had a kind and peaceful nature, replied that some Italians were really quite English in their outlook and doubtless St. Francis was one of them.

"Have you ever had triplets, Crawley?" said the Archdeacon, who disapproved of all foreigners and owing to having been taken to lectures by M. Paul Sabatier on St. Francis in his youth never wished to hear of St. Francis again.

Dr. Crawley said, with sincere regret, that he had never had the privilege, nor, it appeared, had any other of the reverend gentlemen present. It was perhaps, he said, spiritual pride that made him carry Mrs. Dale's twins to the altar one on each arm.

"That's all right, Dr. Crawley," said Mr. Wickham. "You haven't got three arms so you've only room for two," which echo of a pleasantly rowdy song from the Scottish Students' Song-book made some of the party smile. "But I've never seen a job better done," said Mr. Wickham, who was enjoying his company, "and I may say I felt uncommon like crying. Funny the way things get you."

Father Fewling, the ex-naval officer who was priest in charge of St. Sycorax at Northbridge and a very present help in trouble to Mr. Villars the vicar even if he did use incense, said he quite agreed with Mr. Wickham that to hold a very small baby at the font was one of the most moving experiences one could have. They had, he said, a most disconcerting way of looking at you and right through you without blinking; that was, if they weren't asleep all the time, which led to the beginning of what might have been a very interesting theological discussion upon a point new to all present, namely whether if you christened a baby while it was asleep the ceremony had the same validity as if it was awake.

"You mean it mightn't take," said Mr. Wickham, "and you'd have to do it again like vaccination," but the Dean, who felt that this conversation had perhaps gone on long enough, moved away to speak to other friends and the group broke up. Mr. Wickham was caught by Robin who said he wanted to introduce him to his cousin Isabel Dale, one of the godmothers.

"Hullo," said Mr. Wickham. "How's Lisa Bedale getting on?" at which Miss Dale crimsoned, then looked alarmed and asked Mr. Wickham what he meant.

"I say, don't be frightened," said Mr. Wickham. "It's all right. Old Johns is a sort of uncle of mine and he told me about it."

"But he promised it would be a secret," said Miss Dale, not angrily, but with a kind of despair that touched Mr. Wickham's heart; which was not difficult.

"It is," said Mr. Wickham. "Cross my heart and wish I die. He told me four or five years ago that he had a new best-seller coming on. All right, no one is listening. So I've read all your books and I may say they are winners. That's a jolly good one about the house where all the taps turn on and off the wrong way and I like your detective, what's his name, Gerry Marston. I never spotted Frank Mulliner as the villain till the very last page. Stupid of me. I ought to have noticed that he was left-handed but somehow I never put two and two together. How do you do it?"

"I don't know," said Miss Dale, half alarmed, half flattered.

"I knew your John, you know," said Mr. Wickham. "One of the very best. He talked to me about you a bit. It was in Italy. I was with the navy and the Barsetshires were on the coast. We got to like each other. Birds and country life and that sort of thing. Then we went into action and I never saw him alive again; nothing brings a good man back."

"I know," said Miss Dale.

"Look here, if I've said the wrong thing I'm more sorry than I can say," said Mr. Wickham.

"You haven't," said Miss Dale. "I'm beginning to forget him even. But sometimes I remember and then I find Gerry Marston a great help."

"Good girl," said Mr. Wickham, which expression of sympathy or approval she wasn't sure which, somehow didn't offend Miss Dale in the least. "And why are you Lisa Bedale?"

"Oh, it's an anagram of Isabel Dale," said that lady. "I didn't want my mother or any of John's people to know. They might have sympathised, or they might have taken offence and I didn't want either. And of course ever since I decided on that name I've been perfectly sure that someone would guess."

"Lord bless you, people would never guess that sort of thing," said Mr. Wickham. "Look at the chaps—and the chapesses—that do *The Times* Crossword Puzzle every day. Tubby Fewling—you know him don't you—the Padre at Northbridge, at least he's second-in-command but he has a church of his own and Villars lets him run it his own way and he's one of the best, an old naval man like me—does the Crossword every day. I've tried once or twice and I can't make head or tail of the clues, too brainy for me, but give me an anag. as they call it and I'll get it right in one. Rum thing the brain. And talking of rum, shall I get you some more champagne? Not a headache in a tumbler of it. Old Horrabin, you wouldn't know him, man with a big gap between his front teeth in Hull, always sends me six dozen about this time in memory of the night we had in Malta in '42. Lord! What a night! It gives me a headache to think of it. I hope I've not been a bore."

Miss Dale said of course he hadn't and no champagne thank you. She then added diffidently that she liked to know anyone who had known John, which made Mr. Wickham grasp her hand with almost painful violence and go back once more to Simnet and help him to finish the last bottle.

Hospitality had always been on a generous scale at Carter's

and it pleased Everard to see that though he and Kate were translated to the Headmaster's house the tradition was well kept up. The champagne was finished, but so many old friends were there and both host and hostess made the company so welcome, that no one wished to go. Some however had duties elsewhere and Mr. Miller came up to tell Mrs. Brandon that he really must get back for a meeting of the Pomfret Madrigal Fête Committee and was she ready to go, or would she wait for Francis and his wife, to which she replied, with many thanks for his kind thought of her, that she would really like to stay a little longer as there were so many old friends and it was such fun to see them all, so Mr. Miller went away with his nice wife.

"Well, Lavinia," said her old friend and trustee Sir Edmund Pridham, who so far had not had an opportunity of talking to her, "you're looking charming as usual. Who have you been making eyes at?"

Mrs. Brandon, at once becoming a Victorian, looked up at Sir Edmund from under her lashes in a most provocative way and said there was really no one to make eyes at now. Only one's *real* old friends, she murmured.

"Well, I'm old enough," said Sir Edmund. "Eighty-three last birthday and going strong. Let me see. You married Brandon just after the war ended: I mean the '14 War, and a dull stick he was."

"My dear Sir Edmund, you shouldn't say things like that," said Mrs. Brandon with great dignity. "I am fifty-five."

"You don't look it," said Sir Edmund gallantly. "Wouldn't give you a day more than fifty myself. Henry would have been close on seventy if he hadn't died when he did—well, well, we're all getting on," and then Mr. and Mrs. Francis Brandon came up with Dr. Joram.

"Are you going now?" asked Mrs. Brandon of her daughter-in-law, who looked slightly confused.

"Would you mind very much, mamma," she said, "if we ran away quietly? Lady Cora is so keen for us to do the Argentina

Tango song for her show—you know, the one I did with Aubrey Clover at the Red Cross entertainment. She wanted Aubrey to come but he can't, so we thought Francis and I. The Millers will take you back, I'm sure."

"But they went some time ago," said Mrs. Brandon. "I'm so sorry, Peggy. I thought you and Francis were driving me."

"Well, we can easily go round by Pomfret Madrigal," said Francis, "and drop mamma at the cross roads. Only we must hurry or Lady Cora will throw sixteen fits."

"Hadn't we better go straight to Gatherum?" said Mrs. Francis. "Lady Cora would adore to see you, mamma, and you could have a nice rest while we go through the Tango and we'll all go home together."

"Didn't Lady Cora say something about going to the Barchester Odeon afterwards?" said Francis. "It's a nuisance only having enough petrol for one car."

The words were not meant to be unkindly spoken, and Francis would have been horrified if he had realised how ill they sounded, but to Sir Edmund they sounded so unthinking, as indeed they were, and even callous, which again perhaps they were, that nothing kept him from telling Francis what he thought of him except the certainty that that dear silly little Lavinia would be the one to suffer, so he had to content himself by calling Francis a damned young puppy under his breath. Everyone felt extremely uncomfortable and Mrs. Brandon felt that a shattering of her world, a thing she had for some time tried not to think of, might be upon her and beyond her power to prevent. And what was worse, she wondered if she could get out of the room without crying.

"You two young people go off and amuse yourselves," said Sir Edmund with all his county authority. "I'll drive you home, Lavinia. My car's a bit of a rattle-trap, like myself, but you won't mind. When you want to go, just say the word, I'll be about."

It is possible that Mr. and Mrs. Francis, who were more thoughtless than really selfish and certainly did not mean to be unkind, might still have offered to take Mrs. Brandon home in her own car and with her own petrol, but a martial noise coming into the drawing-room proclaimed itself as Miss Hampton and Miss Bent from Adelina Cottage who greeted Mrs. Brandon and Sir Edmund warmly, under cover of which Mr. and Mrs. Francis slipped away, with the combination of shame and relief that we have all felt when we have been selfish and got away with it.

The host and hostess came up to greet the newcomers and the social waters closed over the heads of the young Brandons.

"I can't tell you how sorry Bent and I were to miss the doings," said Miss Hampton, whose well-tailored suit had a slight but dashing New Look which sat very well upon her, "but Bent and I took Amethyst to the Dog Show at Northbridge. He wasn't placed, but he liked it."

"Amethyst?" said Robin Dale.

"The dog," said Miss Hampton. "Must call him something," for the ladies' sad-faced dog with its large head and very short legs and black hearthrug hair had been given the name of one hero of the war after another and did not answer to any of them. "No gallant people to call him after now, except Churchill, and Bent and I feel that would not do. But the Amethyst's gallant. About the only thing that has been gallant since this lot began dismantling the Empire and making us laughed at all over the world. Besides, there's not one of this lot with a name I would give a dog."

"Call a dog Cripps and I will dislike him," said Miss Bent, which Johnsonian sentence deeply impressed her hearers, the more so owing to her appearance in a very full ankle-length skirt of printed cotton, a floppy Mixo-Lydian blouse embroidered in red and blue and a halo hat of shiny red straw, the whole embellished with six coral necklaces.

Most luckily politics were pushed into the background by the simultaneous appearance of the Misses Dale who had slept themselves awake again and were proudly brought in by Sister

Chiffinch and Matron with their own nurse, Ellen Humble, in the background.

"Bent!" said Miss Hampton, clutching her friend's arm, "look at them. To think we were like that once!"

On hearing these words Anne Dale became quite pale, in case her daughters might some day be like her two gifted friends. But her anxiety was dispersed by Miss Bent who said defiantly, "I wasn't. I was born with jaundice. Bright yellow for my first fortnight. And Hampton was born in Leeds."

At this point Mr. Wickham, who was not deficient in tact or courage, came forward to greet the ladies from Adelina.

"I knew you'd turn up," he said, "so I hid a bottle of champagne for you to drink their health. Here goes," and with a swift and skilful movement he released the champagne, poured out three large glasses and joined himself with the ladies in drinking to the babies, who, possibly remembering their success in the chapel earlier in the afternoon, began the one to talk melodious rubbish, the other to emit fluting squeaks of happiness.

"Well, here's to literature and lots of clean fun," said Mr. Wickham, finishing the bottle with a bow to Miss Hampton. "What's the latest?"

"*I'll* tell them, Hampton," said Miss Bent. "Hampton is prostrated with the effort," she continued. "She wrote the last words on Friday night. It is the Biggest Thing she has done yet."

"All right. I'll be the Mug," said Mr. Wickham. "What's it about this time?"

"It is an unfaltering exposure of Infidelity," said Miss Bent reverently.

Mr. Wickham was heard to say that Johnny Turk called us Infidels.

"No, no; not *that* kind," said Miss Bent sharply. "It goes deep, very deep, psychologically and ethically. We haven't decided on the title yet. Hampton thinks 'My Lesbia has a roving eye.'" She paused for the words to sink in.

"And what do *you* think?" said Mr. Wickham.

"It was difficult, difficult," said Miss Bent, raising her coral necklaces and letting them clash upon her Mixo-Lydian bosom. "At first I thought just simply "Sister Helen," but it was not courageous enough. So I said "My Sister, my Spouse," which I think gives the tone of Courage which runs through the book. One hundred and eighty thousand words," said Miss Bent in a low tone, as of one walking in sacred places.

By this time a good many of Miss Hampton's friends were on the verge of having the giggles, but were saved by Sister Chiffinch who said that was an ever so sweet book her pals Heathy and Wardy that she shared the flat with got from the Book Society, all about what hospitals used to be like in the olden days and no wonder they all died and how Florence Nightingale was quite a reformer and so dreadfully sad that she seemed to have been really quite mental at the last.

The party was now beginning to disperse.

"Anything wrong?" said Robin Dale to his wife. "You look as if someone might have broken a cup."

"Do you think the Birketts have forgotten?" said Anne.

"Lord! I hadn't noticed," said Robin. "I do hope they haven't. I'll ask Everard if he knows. Everard, one moment. You haven't heard anything of the Birketts, have you? Anne is wondering if they mistook the day, or had gone away and forgot to let her know."

Everard said someone must have been at home because he had tried to ring up three times and the line had been engaged. And then, just as in a novel, a noise of visitors was heard in the hall and in came the former Headmaster of Southbridge School and Mrs. Birkett.

"I'm sorry we are late," said Mrs. Birkett to Anne. "The fact is——"

But her sentence was never finished, for in the doorway, looking exactly like a page from the American Vogue, was the lovely and idiotic Rose Fairweather wearing a New York dress of such ravishing elegance and simplicity, her feet so exquisitely sandalled, her fair hair so exquisitely set, her complexion so skilfully aided by art, that everyone stared, speechless.

"You see," said Mrs. Birkett, "we were just starting when Rose and John came down unexpectedly and the time simply flew, so then John said they would come over with us and get the express back from Barchester. How do you think Rose is looking?"

"Lovely," said Anne on a long-drawn breath, with the free and generous appreciation of a beautiful woman—for we may by now almost use this word of Anne Dale—for another beautiful woman.

"Hullo, Anne," said Rose, "I wanted to come for the christening, but mummy said to have lunch and daddy would go on talking to John and it was too absolutely futile. Where are the twins? OH, aren't they pets! Which is which?"

"One is one," said Robin gravely, "and the other is the other."

"Oh, don't be so absolutely futile," said Rose. "Can't you tell them apart?"

Robin said they were identical twins.

"John," said Rose to her husband who was talking to Mr. Wickham whom he had at once recognised as an old acquaintance of Pantellaria days, "John, I want you!"

"Well?" said her husband, interrupting his conversation with Mr. Wickham just enough to show that he had every intention of going on with it.

"Oh, John," continued Rose, upon whose lovely face and form every eye in the room was now fixed, "have you got your camera. I want you to take me with the twins. They are pets!"

"Not on your life, my girl," said her ungallant husband. "You'd be bound to drop one while you were putting on the lipstick. So then Wicks, Number One said a few nasty words——" and the talk about old times went on.

Rose, whose buoyant nature was never depressed for long, said affectionately that John was too absolutely futile for words and made her way to the Crawleys whose youngest daughter Octavia had been a school friend. Bishop Joram, who was standing by them thought he had never seen anything so exquisite, with a mental reservation that he had never heard anyone so silly. Dr. Crawley introduced him to Mrs. John Fairweather, as Dr., or should we say Bishop Joram.

"Then where's his wife?" said Rose.

Dr. Joram, imagining that Rose might be confusing him with someone else, said he wasn't married.

"But I thought Bishops *had* to be married," said Rose. "I mean that was what the Reformation was about, wasn't it?" With which words she opened her bag and began to repair her perfect complexion.

"That's enough, my girl," said her husband, putting her powder compact and lipstick back into the bag. "Didn't I see you in East Africa before the war, sir?"

"Now I thought I remembered every face I had ever seen," said Dr. Joram, "but for the moment——"

"The row at Butler's Hotel and the stuffed jerboa," said Captain Fairweather.

"Of course!" said Dr. Joram. "And you are Lieutenant Fairweather."

"Captain now, sir," said Captain Fairweather. "And you seem to have turned into a doctor," at which everyone laughed except Rose, who said with a becoming pout that John was absolutely too futile.

"Well, Mrs. Fairweather," said Matron, who had dumped her twin upon Ellen Humble and joined the guests, "this is indeed like Old Times. I was only saying to Jessie this morning when we were putting the serviettes out for lunch, for believe it or not Mrs. Fairweather we actually have laundry now that can be relied upon to call every week, 'Jessie,' I said, 'today is quite an Event, and I don't remember feeling so really wrought up since the day Miss Rose Birkett was married,' you remember Jessie, our head housemaid, Mrs. Fairweather, just the same she is, and *will* not wear her glasses though if I have told her once I have told her a hundred times, 'Jessie!' I have said, 'if you don't wear your glasses you cannot,' I said, 'you simply *cannot* see to darn the gentlemen's socks and Mr. Sherlock who is our present Headmaster is a very particular gentleman as naval gentlemen are and if you darn his socks too tight, Jessie,' I said, 'the brunt will fall upon me, Jessie, for of course he wouldn't think of speaking to you.'"

"I remember," said Kate Carter who had stopped in her progress to listen to this conversation, "before I was engaged, Matron, Mr. Carter asked me to darn a pair of socks for him and they were black socks and one of them was darned with navy blue."

"There now," said Matron, "that was Jessie all over. Dear me, she will be quite pleased to think you remember a little thing like that. Now my eldest nephew's wife, Mrs. Carter, darns quite exquizzitly. Really quite artistic her work is. Well, I must be hieing me back to see about the boys' tea. And then Miss Chiffinch and I are having quite an Outing, going down after supper to the Vicarage to have coffee with Colonel and Mrs. Crofts. Ellen is quite to be trusted with Mrs. Dale's dear little girls now."

And then the remaining guests all began to exclaim on the lateness of the hour and apologise for having enjoyed themselves so much. Sir Edmund Pridham took Mrs. Brandon away and there was again an unspoken feeling that Francis and his wife had not behaved very well, which feeling was also possibly due to their new familiarity with Gatherum Castle. Ever since the days of the great Duke of Omnium the Gatherum connection had been on the whole disapproved by the county, for the castle looked to London while the rest of Barsetshire looked to the cathedral city and gradually the old landed gentry who were the aristocracy of Barsetshire had withdrawn from the Gatherum sphere and took but slight interest in their goings on. The Pomfrets it is true exchanged courtesy visits with the castle from time to time, but Lord Pomfret, Lord Lieutenant of the County, with an almost unbroken line of ancestry from the twelfth century could afford to do so. The leading commoners considered Gatherum as on the whole below them and alien to the county interests, but it was all the same galling to find the Francis Brandons so much at home there. For though Mrs. Brandon was a charming, a kind, and still a very good-looking woman she was not Barsetshire; and her husband though of Barsetshire stock had been nobody in particular, of a family with wealth but no connections. In fact, the county's feelings on the subject were distinctly muddled, though as it rarely stopped to analyse its feelings and would probably have had very little success if it had done so, this did not much matter: but that afternoon the county, in the person of Sir Edmund Pridham, had silently resented the defection of Mr. and Mrs. Francis and the slight to Mrs. Brandon. No particular show of indignation was made, but the undercurrent of feeling was strong and if anyone had asked for three cheers for Sir Edmund, they would probably have been forthcoming.

The Birketts went back to Worsted, having hoarded petrol for the purpose of this journey, while Captain and Mrs. Fairweather pursued their journey to London by the local train which connected at Barchester with the express. Mr. Wickham collected his empty champagne bottles in his rattling old car and went to dine at the Vicarage and discuss the white pheasant with Mrs. Crofts, the Everard Carters went back to the Headmaster's house and Simnet took his dignified way to the Vicarage kitchen to sup with his sister-in-law and her husband ex-corporal Jackson before catching the last motor-bus to Barchester.

Robin and Anne went up to the nursery to look at their daughters.

"They've been as good as gold, madam," said Ellen Humble proudly, "and not a mite of trouble," and she stood aside to let her employer look at the two cots. In the first Miss Roberta Fielding was lying on her back, the dark fluff on her head damp with the exertion of sleeping, her tiny fists thrown up above her head. In the other Miss Dora Maud had managed to hump herself into a kind of croquet hoop and her tiny hands were spread like starfish. Anne very softly laid her little finger in one of the starfish, and the so very tiny fingers closed about hers.

"What shall I do?" she whispered to Robin. "If I tried to get out I might wake her."

"Now let go, there's a lamb," said Ellen Humble and with gentle firmness she loosened the vice-like grip of those incredibly tiny fingers and softly covered the sleeping baby who with a little murmur sank down again in to the depths of sleep.

"I think we are very lucky," said Anne when they were safely out of the nursery.

"To have such satisfactory babies?" said Robin.

"They are angels," said Anne. "But I meant more Ellen. She is a *real* nurse."

And as Anne said these words Robin felt that in gaining these soft, warm-scented, mysterious, adorable babies he had in a way lost his Anne. She was far more to him than ever he had imagined she could be, but not only for him. From now onwards she would have allegiances to these little unknown spirits, as yet so entirely fearless, not conscious of their need for human help and protection. From now onwards. For a moment his heart felt desolate. Then Anne asked some question about Rose Fairweather, the moment of vision was over and perhaps forgotten: but not lost.

We need hardly say that the ladies of Adelina were not of the metal that follows a social afternoon by a quiet evening. They carried back to the cottage with them Mr. Shergold the housemaster of Everard's old house, Mr. Traill of Maria Cottage and Mr. Feeder of Louisa, co-opting on the way Mr. Feeder's widowed mother, who had taken Editha from Mrs. Arbuthnot when that lady married Colonel Crofts.

"Find seats for yourselves, everyone," said Miss Hampton, which was achieved with some squashing, for the Wiple Terrace cottages were on the small side. "A good show this afternoon. Almost made me cry. Can't think why though. There's Scotch, gin, rye, French vermouth, It, sherry, bitters, and some odds and ends. Get the ice, Bent. Mrs. Feeder?"

Mrs. Feeder, a spare elderly woman in black with a black ribbon round her bony throat, said straight rye and offered her large well-filled cigarette case.

"Stout woman," said Miss Hampton approvingly.

"My late husband," said Mrs. Feeder, "*his* father I mean," she added, poking her head towards her son, "had bad gastric ulcers for the last few years of his life, so I learnt to drink, to please him."

"I say, good show," said Mr. Traill who had just put down the larger part of one of Miss Hampton's generous cocktails. "How comes?"

"Comes this way," said Mrs. Feeder brightly, thus causing Mr. Traill to show signs of confusion. "His father was a great drinker. Not heavy, you understand, but great, and he often said he felt just like an artist who has lost his hands or a short-sighted man who has lost his glasses. So to cheer him up I used to have a drink at the same times he used to. He said to see me put it down was almost as good as drinking it himself. He had a very beautiful nature. So has *he*," she added, again poking her head towards her son. "Don't drown it," she added, with such assurance that Miss Hampton almost dropped the bottle of rye.

"That was a very good record you were playing last night," said Miss Hampton to Mr. Traill. "What was it?"

Mr. Traill said he wondered which one.

"I mean the one you played nine times running," said Miss Hampton.

"Oh I say, I'm most awfully sorry," said Mr. Traill. "I put the gramophone right up against Feeder's wall to deaden the sound."

Mr. Feeder was heard to confide to an unseen audience that he would say Traill did.

"No, dear man, not the walls, nor having all your windows open back and front," said Miss Hampton. "In My Work I have

to forget self, stiffen the sinews, and summon up the blood. Play
away, dear man, as long as you like. What was it?"

"It was only Cash Campo and His Symposium Boys," said
Mr. Traill. "They've got a new hot number,

> 'Oh, the boy from the ships, he sips from her lips,
> And boy! how he rips the zips on her hips!
> But who is it nips what he slips for her tips?
> It's the fellow that grips his Switzerland trips.
> It's good old, funny old, dear old, sweet old, holy old,
>   *kind* old——' "

and here we regret to say (not really), that the whole party joined
in the last line, repeating that unfortunate (for us) name five
times with crescendo and a loud shout on the last.

In the silence which followed Mrs. Feeder was heard to say,

> "A Lemon has pips,
> And a Yard has ships,
> And *I'll* have Cripps.

And I wish I were the Devil, with a rat that could speak on my
shoulder," she added.

There was a brief silence.

"Fill up," said Miss Hampton and raising her fifth glass of a
great deal of gin and very little vermouth she added, "To the
immortal memory of Charles Dickens."

The toast was drunk in respectful silence, after which the
party was a great success till Mr. Shergold had to tear himself
away and go back to his House, so everyone else went round to
Maria to hear Mr. Traill's gramophone and then to Louisa to
hear Mr. Feeder's wireless and then to Editha to sample some
very old brandy imported by the late Mr. Feeder senior.

"Eleven o'clock," said Miss Bent suddenly. "Hampton, what
about bed?"

"Bent is right," said Miss Hampton. "Good-night, all. Come on, Bent. We'll sleep tonight."

"Hampton does plunge so in bed when she is Writing," said Miss Bent with a kind of holy awe, "that it is quite uncomfortable. But now she will be as quiet as a bolster. Come on, Hampton. Where's Amethyst?"

The large-headed dog was dragged by the scruff of its neck from under the sofa and the party dispersed.

CHAPTER 7

Nineteen forty-eight had been, to all right-thinking people, a lucky year in some ways. Not because of everything being more and more uncomfortable and the name of England dimmed all over the world by those who were steering, if so devious and ill-omened a course can be called steering, the ship of state; but because (if we may as Virgil so beautifully says compare puppies with their dog fathers and kids with their goat mothers) owing to the discovery of a disused cesspool under the Palace kitchen the Bishop and his wife had been away and not given their annual garden party. Hopes had been expressed by most of Barsetshire that something of the sort would happen again, but even this small solace was denied to England in her dark hour, and all over the county people were angrily accepting invitations to the Palace for Friday, July 15th. A remark by the Dean that had his lordship made a more profound study of hagiology he would not so rashly have tempted the gods went down very well, for though St. Swithin has never had as far as we know any appreciable effect upon the weather, superstition dies hard and most people feel a slight sinking or tightening of the stomach when rain falls on that day. Of course the whole county prayed for rain and not just any kind of rain but a drizzle in the morning which would gradually increase in volume as the day went on, turn to a thunderstorm about three o'clock, deluge the lawn and if heaven were propitious flood the Palace drain, as had happened in the flood during the war when, so rumour had it in the Close, the Bishop's second-best gaiters were washed up on old Canon Thorne's front steps. But St. Swithin, who as Bishop of Winchester possibly felt that the episcopacy should stand shoulder to shoulder, was not favourable. The sun rose through a slight haze foretelling a scorching July day and in East Barsetshire, West Barsetshire and Barchester itself lunches were eaten with ingratitude for the perfect garden party weather.

Of the preparations in the Palace we shall not speak, but as the Palace had been famed ever since the days of Bishop and Mrs. Proudie for its cheese-paring and inhospitality, there probably would not be much to say.

"You know," said Mr. Tozer of Messrs. Scatcherd and Tozer the well-known Barchester caterers to Simnet, Dr. Joram's butler and handyman, with whom he was having on the evening before the garden party a friendly glass of beer at the Precincts Club, a very select society which met in a room behind the bar of the White Hart, admitting no outsiders except the proprietor, "if it wasn't for the prestige We wouldn't handle this job. My grandfather used to tell us lads when we were kids about the doings in Bishop Grantly's day. Ah, the Palace *was* a Palace then. Champagne as soon as look at you. Patties, jellies, good claret, lobster salads, and everything left over went to the Hospital. Not that the Barchester General would thank anyone for jellies nowadays. Too frightened of what Taffy would say."

"Taffy, Mr. Tozer?" said Simnet, raising his eyebrows in the celebrated manner which had quelled even the Master of Lazarus who had tried to drink port in a claret glass when staying at Southbridge School for a speech-day.

"Welshman," said Mr. Tozer briefly. "All alike they are. Taffy, that's the word. Mark my words, Mr. Simnet, there's Welshmen and Welshmen, and this one is one in the derogaroratory sense, if you take me."

"Derrygorratory, pardon me, Mr. Tozer," said Simnet.

"Giving that word a miss," said Mr. Tozer in a lordly way, "let me tell you, Mr. Simnet, that if it wasn't for supporting the Church of England We would give up the job. But as I was saying to old Mr. Scatcherd—he's bedridden you know been so for years but knows every single blessed thing that goes on in the firm—it looks well to do the Palace. There's no money in it, Mr. Simnet, but it's a good advert. The old man had the idea we might get permission to have Purveyors to the Bishop of Barchester and a bishop's mitre on our correspondence and over the catering establishment, same as By Royal Warrant, but when he did as it were glide over the subject to the Bishop his lordship was quite disagreeable. In fact, if he weren't a Bishop I'd have said he was no gentleman. And his good lady *certainly* isn't."

"We," said Simnet, who from long habit dating back to his Oxford days had always identified himself with his employer, "have nothing to do with the Bishop except *as* a Bishop. We did ask him to dinner, but Dr. Joram being a bachelor has bachelor parties."

He paused dramatically.

"And what did Her Nibs do?" said Mr. Tozer in a very common way.

"Her Nibs," said Mr. Simnet, torn between wishing to snub Mr. Tozer and feeling that by so doing he would lower himself, "her Nibs answered the invitation in her own writing and said the Bishop did not dine out alone as he was not a bachelor. I never see a man laugh so much," said Mr. Simnet rather forgetting his position, "as Dr. Joram. He said it beat the band," a statement which we may take as being quite unsubstantiated, for Dr. Joram would not have used such a phrase.

"Tea and lemonade," said Mr. Tozer dejectedly. "Sangwiches and gatto on our lowest tariff. Ah, when I think of what Our gattos used to be; petty fours and all sorts. Still, one must be fair and I dessay his lordship never saw good food where he was brought up, nor her neither."

"You could not be more right, Mr. Tozer," said Simnet, who

condescended occasionally to the use of everyday slang or what he considered such. "Anyway there'll be good sherry at the Vinery and open house from 5 o'clock onwards. If you feel like dropping in Mr. Tozer when you've packed up, Mrs. Simnet and me will take it as a compliment. Well, here's to Close and County," which fine sentiment was a kind of masonic sign between members of the Club and used as a greeting and a farewell.

"And here's to more and better Bishops," said Mr. Tozer and then they went each to his own home.

Not only did the County attend the Palace garden party unwillingly, but also uncomfortably. Petrol rationing had made life difficult enough already. The Palace, who were popularly but we regret to say incorrectly supposed to have at least a hundred gallons of petrol stored in what used to be the wine cellar in Bishop Grantly's days and who had always enough for what the Bishop's wife called pastoral visits, which included dining at Gatherum Castle, and never used motor-buses, had with lamentable want of tact arranged for the Garden Party to be Market Day, which meant that every motor-bus would be chockfull till Closing Time and that such permutations and combinations of transport had to be planned all over the county as would have puzzled Sir Isaac Newton and Descartes rolled into one. The horrid fact dawned upon the Bishop's wife two days before the party through old Lady Norton who not being quite county herself, did not suffer in dignified if useless silence, but attacked the Bishop's wife violently in Bostock and Plummer's where Barchester did its shopping for clothes and household furnishing. The Bishop's wife who was trying on a New Look beige afternoon dress with some aimless trimming was at a disadvantage as she had forgotten to put on her party corsets and was wearing a utility belt which gave her the appearance of being an aunt of the Michelin tyre gentleman. Lady Norton, who was as always corseted from neck to knee, or at least appeared to be so, put up the face-à-main with which she was accustomed to terrify her acquaintance, looked the Bishop's wife up and down and said that it was a pity about Friday being market day.

The Bishop's wife said Why.

"Keep still, if you please, moddom," said the elderly fitter who was down on her knees, a black velvet pincushion strapped to her left wrist as it had been ever since she was an apprentice, "It just dips here a little," and she put pins into the skirt with an unfaltering hand.

"I shall come in Norton's car of course," said Lady Norton, who was alluding not to her husband who had long been dead but to her son, "and so will my daughter-in-law, and I am bringing Mrs. Grant who is back from Italy. Every bus will be full and mad bulls all up and down Barley Street. The Palace Garden Party always used to be on Wednesdays. There's a wrinkle across the shoulder, Miss Brown. It needs lifting. You can't see it," she added to the Bishop's wife, "and if you twist it only makes it worse."

She snapped her face-à-main shut and went away to bully the haberdashery about a bill for seven and sixpence three farthings, leaving the Bishop's wife distinctly uncomfortable.

"Just stand still a moment, please, moddom," said the fitter, speaking through a kind of *chevaux-de-frise* of pins in her mouth. "We'll just lift it across the back of the hips and ease it on the shoulders and you'll find it quite different. That's one thing about beege, no one notices it. I always tell My Ladies when in doubt stick to beege, or a nice elephant."

The Bishop's wife who felt a mad desire to assert herself after being caught so to speak defenceless by Lady Norton said elephant spotted so easily. The fitter's glacial silence implied so clearly that Her Ladies never spotted anything that the Bishop's wife said no more. Presently the fitter had finished and the Bishop's wife began to get out of the beige dress.

"Gently, moddom," said the fitter. "Let me get the Zip

undone. That's it. You shall have it the day before the party, moddom, without fail."

The Bishop's wife then bought a crushed strawberry hat which was to be worn almost vertically on the right cheek and went home.

On Market Day afternoon Barchester gave a very fair representation of the approach to Rome when Lars Porsena was sighted, as described by Lord Macaulay. There were no gates to roar except the gate into the Close which would never have been guilty of such behaviour, but Barley Street was a very good second-best. What with the local motor-buses, the long distance motor-coaches, the parked cars and motor-bicycles, enough horse-drawn vehicles to add considerably to the confusion, several bulls which looked though they were not mad, crowds of sheep playing the endless and unprofitable game of trying to climb on each other's backs, cows and calves conversing in various tones, several pigs shrieking for mercy for no reason at all, a loudspeaker which said repeatedly Arshy, booshy, marmsy goggo, or so Mrs. Morland a devotee of Burnand insisted, and half Barsetshire queueing at the Odeon for Glamora Tudor and her new lead Crab Doker in the Greatest and Most Smashing World Hit of the Century *Too Close for Love*: a Mammoth Scenario of King David's court with a distant view of the Pyramids, a specially constructed model of the Temple five hundred feet high, a gate under which six African elephants passed abreast and a procession of priests carrying the Ark (which bore a remarkable resemblance to an empty black box with the lid tumbling off left over from Hamlet): while Glamora Tudor as Tamar and Crab Doker as Amnon with the muscles of his arms rippling ceaselessly, regretted the fact that marriage between them was impossible because of consanguinity till Zadok the high priest (with obbligato by Handel on the Mighty Wurlitzer) said it was all a mistake and Tamar had been changed at birth, which enabled the producers to make use of six high priests, ten fakirs, ten bonzes and a band of devil-worshippers, besides six peacocks and two performing seals left over from an educational film called Funny Flappers: which would appear to be the end of the sentence.

It was with considerable difficulty that the guests penetrated the crowd, but once through the gates of the Close the noise sank to no more than a big city's hum and peace lay upon the great open lawns and the great white stone cathedral with its heaven-pointing spire. Only the grass was not green, for no rain had fallen for months and though Tomkins and his assistants had done their best with the water that was syphoned from the river it was not the same thing as having the sprinklers, now officially forbidden, at work. Gone were the daisies. The motor mowers and old Tomkins's scythe were idle in the Close and in the cloisters for the grass was too short, too scanty, too brittle: and wicked little boys had even made a kind of slide on the side of a mound which marked where the underground Air Raid Shelter had been.

The Palace, and this the Dean had been heard to say was a crowning mercy, did not form part of the Close. To reach it one followed the carriage road through the arch into the Close, and went right past the cathedral to where, behind the West End a semicircular sweep led to the large red brick house, not of so good a period as the houses in the Close, for it had been extensively remodelled by the incumbent before Bishop Grantly, but not unhandsome in its heavy way. Behind to the south lay a large garden with a very fine cedar tree and a tulip tree reputed to be the highest in England except the one in the garden of the Great House at Woolbeding, and at the foot of the garden was the river which had come round a bend from the west or Deanery side. A more perfect setting for a garden party could not be conceived and had it not been for the unavoidable presence of the host and hostess, the afternoon would have been perfect.

For the last few days a rumour had been going about, no one could say whence, that some of the Gatherum people were coming. It was not a story that anyone would have thought of inventing and there was a good deal of speculation about it among the guests now assembling.

"Of course I don't know anything," said Sir Edmund Pridham, doyen of the county in age, knowledge and public service, "but there isn't any law against putting two and two together. Daresay there will be soon. It's just the sort of thing those people in the cabinet would do."

"And what are the results of your addition, Pridham?" said Noel Morton who was there with his wife Lydia.

"Liberal Party at its tricks again," said Sir Edmund. "They're all Liberals at Gatherum now. Used to be Whigs of course in the Great Duke's time," by which Sir Edmund did not mean the Duke of Wellington but the Duke of Omnium who was a great county autocrat in the fifties of the last century: nearly a hundred years ago, though it seems but a generation or two. Then Whiggism had watered itself down in his descendants to what we can only call Liberal-Unionism but the family were honest and did not try nor wish to be intellectuals and the liveliest member, Lady Cora, so named from the Lady Glencora MacCluskie who had brought her great wealth into the family when she married Mr. Plantaganet Palliser the Duke's heir, was far more interested in the theatre than in politics and had, as we know, drawn the Francis Brandons into her net for amateur theatricals.

"Lavinia Brandon's boy and his wife are always out there," Sir Edmund continued. "Well, well, nothing to do with me, but I don't care for the set. Never have."

"Do my eyes deceive me or do I see what I see?" said Noel Merton, partly to Sir Edmund, partly to his wife. "Over there. Shaking hands with the Bishopess."

"It's Lady Norton," said Sir Edmund. "Old Lady Norton I suppose I ought to say, though I'm a good deal older than she is. Don't see young Lady Norton though."

"Oh, she's in Holland," said Lydia, "at a ghastly kind of meeting of lots of people who write books. It must be *awful*."

"Pull yourself together, my precious Lydia," said Noel, "and use your eyes. Just behind the Dreadful Dowager."

All three looked in her direction as she majestically passed from the Bishop's presence with an air of having conferred rather than given an audience. With her, but slightly in the rear, quickening her steps to keep up with her ladyship's majestic stride, was a woman with a handsome but weather-beaten face and grey wavy bobbed hair, dressed in a combination of the New Look and the female chorus in the *Gondoliers*. On her head was a large floppy straw hat with a brightly striped scarf round it, on her arms an unusually large number of bracelets and on her feet a kind of rough sandals. A number of necklaces of amber, coral and other semi-precious stones, rattled upon her bosom as their wearer moved.

"By Jove," said Sir Edmund Pridham, "it's Felicia Grant. Thought she was in Italy. Her boy married Delia Brandon. I've not seen her since the year before the war."

"I know," said Lydia. "It was at the Pomfret Madrigal Flower Show the time Tony Morland and I went on the roundabout on the cock and the ostrich. We had fifteen rides for half-a-crown each. It was really threepence a time but Mr. Packer let us go on for twopence because we were friends of Delia's. I wish there was a roundabout here."

"If there was I would pay half-a-crown not to go on it," said Noel with feeling. "I had to go round in one of the boats with a swan's head like Lohengrin, sitting backwards, and I have never felt so sick, not even after Dunkirk. Lord! that little ship that took me off, God bless it, how it rocked."

Lydia looked at him and in her face he read, not for the first time, what she had silently endured while the sea before Dunkirk beaches was covered with little ships and boats and those at home could have no true word of good or ill. And as always happened his heart was pierced with love for his Lydia's quiet deep steadfastness; and also, as alas always happened now, hot self-reproach for the summer when he had, meaning no harm, so pierced that faithful heart by his foolish and passing flirtation with Mrs. Francis Brandon, then Mrs. Arbuthnot.

At this moment Mrs. Brandon accompanied by her son and his wife joined them. From afar Mrs. Grant caught sight of the group, waved at them with a clanking of bangles which, so Francis afterwards said, could be heard half across the county, and came speeding towards them like a kind of heavy-footed elderly Bacchante.

"Eccomi!" said Mrs. Grant, throwing both arms wide so that her necklaces and her bracelets clanked and clattered in sympathy. "Eccomi!" she said again, stretching her hands towards her friends as a shipwrecked sailor might stretch towards his rescuers. "Sir Edmund! You remember me. Felicia Grant."

Sir Edmund said with great truth that no one could ever forget Mrs. Grant.

"Ah, we were younger then," said Mrs. Grant. "We meet now nel mezzo del cammin di nostra vita. But in sunny Calabria age has no terrors. A crust, a clove of garlic, what more is needed? Brother Sun and Brother Sleep."

Noel said under his breath And Brother Mosquito Net, which made Lydia laugh.

"And Mrs. Brandon," said that lady. "And my son and his wife," who both greeted Mrs. Grant with polite want of interest.

"Ma!" said Mrs. Grant, looking about her. "Where is Vittoria?"

"Not Vittoria, Felicia, *Vick*-toria," said Sir Edmund. "You've been abroad too long. You're forgetting your English. How's your boy?"

"Hilary is very well," said Mrs. Grant in a quite English way. "He and Delia have such a delightful little house in Chelsea, and the babies! Che bambini! E dire che son io la nonna! I can never believe it."

"I can quite believe that I am a grandmother," said Mrs.

Brandon firmly, "because the lambkins live with me and Nurse won't do a thing for me while they are there, bless them."

"I have brought little charms for them both for luck," Mrs. Grant went on. "Sir Edmund, I shall get Victoria Norton to let her chauffeur run me over to see you. Ma! un uomo simpatico! who loves his car like his mistress."

"No accounting for tastes," said Sir Edmund. "Wouldn't love Victoria Norton myself, but you never know."

"Mrs. Grant doesn't mean *that*, Sir Edmund," said Lydia. "She only means he loves his car as much as he loves his mistress. Only I don't suppose he has one," she added in a lower voice so that Sir Edmund who was intermittently deaf would not hear.

"All right, young lady," said Sir Edmund, who still looked upon Lydia as a schoolgirl, or at the most newly married. "All I can say is, in that case he can't be very fond of the car. It's a cranky old thing. Victoria ought to have got another three years ago."

"Lydia meant," said Mrs. Francis Brandon, "that the chauffeur is as fond of his car as his mistress," and then Lydia took Noel away before he went mad.

"What I said," said Sir Edmund. "If Victoria Norton is fond of that car she's a fool. I've known it for twenty years. Uses more petrol than any car in the county."

"And when I come you shall give me lunch and we will have a long delightful talk," said Mrs. Grant, who had placidly ignored the foregoing conversation, probably thinking as her Calabrian friends thought that all Englishmen were mad. "I must return to Victoria. We are going to find refreshment and then go to Evensong. Of course in Calabria I go to Mass with my dear peasants and a wonderful chemist called Aurelio with whom I lodge who has killed five men——"

Sir Edmund broke in to say that in England the Pharmaceutical Society would have taken up a thing like that very strongly, but of course in Italy it was every man for himself.

"Not by medicine!" said Mrs. Grant indignantly. "Three with

his gun, his grandfather's gun who went as a boy with the Garibaldini; one with a knife and his rich uncle by mistake. The uncle had a chill so Aurelio who is so kind put charcoal—mi mancano le parole, come se dice scaldino? a brazier, a warming pan, under his bed and locked the door."

"What about the window?" said Sir Edmund, who by now was almost under the impression that he was on the bench.

"But there *was* no window," said Mrs. Grant. "In Calabria the sun shines all day and at night there is no sun so the bedrooms have no window. And next morning the uncle was dead. Che disgrazia!"

Sir Edmund asked if they hung the feller.

"Why?" said Mrs. Grant. "There was plenty of money and he paid for masses for his uncle's soul."

"The devil was sick, the devil a monk would be," said Mrs. Brandon unexpectedly.

"My dear mamma, you mustn't say things like that," said her son and Mrs. Brandon laughed and smiled and looked, or so Sir Edmund thought, as young as ever, for we do partly live by the kindness of our young and value it more than they know.

"How pretty mamma is looking," said Mrs. Francis, with the generous admiration that one good-looking woman so often has for another. And then Mrs. Grant clanked and rattled herself back to old Lady Norton.

"Peggy, my pet," said a voice behind the group, "and Francis," and Lady Cora Palliser in the most ravishingly simple frock with a wide black straw hat aslant her sleek dark head and the latest sandals on her nylon-clad and beautiful legs joined the group.

"Mamma, I don't think you know Lady Cora," said Francis. "Cora, my mamma."

Lady Cora who appeared to have practically no heart and exquisite manners, like so many of our darling young, clasped Mrs. Brandon's hand warmly and said she simply couldn't wait to meet Francis's mother.

"I have heard so much about you from Francis," said Mrs.

Brandon. "Ever since you had those garden theatricals last summer he and Peggy have talked about simply nothing else. I have told him at least thirty-six times to bring you to Stories."

This might have been considered an indirect snub but we must do Lady Cora the justice to say that she took it with great good humour and with the inherited worldly wisdom of her worldly-wise family realised that Mrs. Brandon meant not a pennyworth more than she said.

"You don't act, do you?" said Lady Cora. "You know I simply *see* you as Mrs. Holinshed in Aubrey Clover's *In for an Inch* simply *wiping* out the other woman."

"Oh no," said Mrs. Brandon. "I have never acted except at school when I was one of Queen Elizabeth's ladies in a kind of pageant we did. Where Francis gets his acting from I simply cannot think because my husband, who after all was Francis's father, simply hated Shakespeare."

Lady Cora suggested that it was just that Francis had inherited his father's dislike for the theatre only the wrong way up; like psycho-analysis and existentialism, she added vaguely.

"There's a man who wrote a book about something like that," said Mrs. Brandon. "I can't remember his name, but I know I had it from the library and sent it back next day because it was so dull."

"Library books! I couldn't agree more!" said Lady Cora. "We've got about a million books in the Old Library at Gatherum, quite ghastly affairs all bound in calf with both covers coming off and weighing about a ton. Father's tried to sell them again and again. I just simply read Proust, backwards, forwards, non-stop. I'm frightfully religious."

Mrs. Brandon's was one of those happy minds that accept everything outside the domestic circle just as it comes, but for once her placidity was disturbed and she said doubtfully that she had read some of Proust in a translation but it wasn't very religious, but of course she liked the proper service, not Low.

"But, my *sweet*!" said Lady Cora, "there's a whole section

about religion. I mean look at Sodome et Gomorrhe. It's taken straight, but *absolutely* straight from the Bible, only of course in modern dress."

"I haven't read that bit," said Mrs. Brandon. "At least I don't remember the name. Of course with Proust you never remember where you've got to."

"But how *swooningly* right your mother is," said Lady Cora, drawing Francis and his wife into the discussion rather against their will, for both of them felt and often did feel though they only spoke of it to each other with an amused laugh which was gradually becoming less amused, that Mamma got away with it rather too often. "That's the joy of Proust. You can open him anywhere and wherever it is you are *so* safe, because it's bound to be the same as the place you thought it was which seems to take all the nastiness away. Because he *is* a bit nasty, you know," said Lady Cora seriously. "I wouldn't *dream* of letting the parents read him, sweet lambs. But you *must* have read Sodome et Gomorrhe. I mean it comes quite early in the story, if story you can call it, though Here we go round the Mulberry Bush would be more like it."

Francis said, too impatiently, that the English version called it The Cities of the Plain and hadn't they better see if there was any tea left.

"Oh, if you call it that, of *course* I've read it," said Mrs. Brandon. "But what it was all about I could not make out, I must ask Mr. Miller. He is a clergyman and ought to know."

"My dear mamma, you simply mustn't say things like that," said Francis.

So had he spoken a hundred times before and his mother had always laughed at him. But this time it was not very kindly said. Aubrey Clover, that acute observer of unconsidered trifles, would have heard at once in his voice the acute exasperation of a son hearing his mother who is though illogical far quicker and cleverer than himself saying something which may somehow bring a little ridicule upon herself and hence—which is the really important part—on him.

Sir Edmund, who owing to deafness had not heard much of the foregoing conversation and had understood that little imperfectly, saw by Mrs. Brandon's face that something had ruffled her and that she was doing her best not to show it. Not that Sir Edmund was a very acute observer of social shades, but he had known Mrs. Brandon ever since her marriage and had a pretty shrewd guess what was going on behind that still very attractive face. He had thought from the very beginning that Lavinia was a fool to have her young couple living with her. Stories had enough rooms in it, but Francis was doing extremely well in business and what is more would come in for quite a nice little bit of money in spite of Them when his mother died, and he ought to be making a home of his own for his wife and babies. Francis had always been selfish, he considered, and that nice little wife of his was spoiling him as much as his mother. All of which thoughts caused him to utter, almost unconsciously, a sound rather like the heavy Puff of a stationary engine.

"Come and find some tea, Lavinia," he said. "I don't suppose it will be fit to drink. Pity we don't ever get a gentleman here. And talking of that," he continued as they walked across the dry, yellow lawn towards the Palace, "has Miller said anything to you?"

"Mr. Miller?" said Mrs. Brandon. "No, nothing particular except about Jimmy Thatcher. You know the Thatchers' boy from Grumper's End. He's got a University scholarship from the Grammar School."

"Good God!" said Sir Edmund. "What are we coming to? Not to Oxford?"

"Oh no, not to a *real* university," said Mrs. Brandon. "One of the other ones. I can't remember which because they don't *sound* like Oxford or Cambridge."

"Must be the Great Western University," said Sir Edmund. "Suppose They'll call it the British Western next. All this nationalising!" which reflection caused him to make a loud puffing noise again. "How old's the lad?"

Mrs. Brandon said she did not know, but she knew he was eight the year before the war, though why she knew that she could not imagine.

"Good God, Lavinia!" said Sir Edmund, "can't you add? Jimmy must be eighteen now. Oh well, he'll have to do his military service. No, I mean the news about Miller. He's coming to Barchester, St. Ewold's. Used to be a pretty little village when my father was a boy. The living's in Pomfret's gift and I think he has done very wisely. Mrs. Miller's a first-rate woman and she'll run the parish properly. It's a good income too as incomes go nowadays. Well, well, they'll be calling it the British Church next. British! We aren't painted blue. England and English are good enough for me."

While Sir Edmund was talking Mrs. Brandon had time to pull herself together. The Vicar of Pomfret Madrigal and his wife were old friends of hers, in fact she had almost made the marriage or thought she had. She was truly glad to hear of good promotion for them, but her heart sank to think of strangers in the Vicarage and perhaps a Low Churchman, which adjective seemed to Mrs. Brandon to describe very well the kind of clergyman she was thinking of. Her kind and tolerant mind would not let her add, even to herself, "And on top of Francis being not very kind" but it was what she felt.

"I'm so glad for the Millers," she said.

"You don't sound glad," said Sir Edmund, who had disconcerting flashes of shrewdness. "Anything wrong, Lavinia? Francis been a bit selfish, eh?"

"Oh no," said Mrs. Brandon, rapidly shutting several watertight doors. "Only I was thinking we are so used to the Millers."

"Come, come, Lavinia. They're used to you," said Sir Edmund. "Here's a nice corner. You sit down and I'll get you some tea."

He installed her on one of the wide window-seats in the

dining-room, and made his way into the crowd between himself and the long table where Mr. Tozer was presiding.

Meanwhile Mrs. Brandon sat alone which did not often happen to her, looking very charming in a tired way, thinking about things she did not want to think about. Francis. The Millers. Stories where she had so gladly welcomed her son's wife. Peggy was a darling but so easily led and whither was Francis leading her? That a daughter-in-law should lead her husband away from his mother seemed to Mrs. Brandon eminently reasonable and if her husband's parents had been living when she married him she would doubtless have done the same. Henry had been a good husband and a generous husband, but looking back on her own early married life as if it were a different woman she had more than once come to the conclusion that he was rather selfish. Perhaps Francis was rather selfish too. With all her silly but affectionate heart she hoped that Francis would never be selfish to Peggy. And now the Millers were going and they might have one of those earnest young men without a background, with an education as narrow as would just let them satisfy their examiners, with probably a worried draggled wife and several skinny children. Stories, which had been an island of safety all through the war and even since the war, was now an island among troubled waters, so it seemed to her, and for once even the thought of Rose and Nurse and her warm soft bed did not comfort her. Dr. Joram, carrying a tray of tea-cups and cakes, was struck by the pensive charm of her attitude and came up to her.

"Have you got some tea, Mrs. Brandon?" he said. "No? Then may I offer you some? I thought if I had a tray in front of me I should be safer and She couldn't order me about," he added, quite obviously alluding to his Bishop's helpmate.

"I believe Sir Edmund is fighting for some," said Mrs. Brandon, "but yours looks so good. Won't you rest for a moment and keep me company?"

"I remember so well the first time I met you," said Dr. Joram.

"It was the first winter of the war, at a dinner party at the Deanery. You were wearing such a charming dress. I cannot describe it, but it was like a bunch of sweet peas."

There is a very subtle flattery in the remembrance of a dress, a tribute not only to the looks but the taste of the wearer. Mrs. Brandon looked gratified.

"Oh, that rag," she said. "Do you know, I still have it. My old Nurse, or at least she was the children's nurse and stayed on with me and is a great help, won't let me give it away. I'm really too old for it now," she sighed, looked at Dr. Joram and cast her beautiful eyes down upon her still exquisite hands, as she had a trick of doing.

"I wanted to talk to you after dinner," said Dr. Joram, "but you were on a little settee and your dress took up so much room that I didn't dare to try."

"I remember," said Mrs. Brandon, with what her son Francis called her mysterious mischief face. "Noel Merton was in love with Lydia Keith and I felt he ought to propose to her as he might have to go abroad in the Secret Service or something of the kind at any moment, so I wanted him to come and sit by me so that I could egg him on. But somehow he didn't, which was most annoying. And to think that I might have been having a perfectly delightful conversation with you all the time."

"I'm rather frightened of ladies," said Bishop Joram, who still used this word in its true meaning, for though our daily helps, those pillars of society, and the bus conductresses who in trousers and crimson lake nails on penny-dirtied hands so admirably keep their temper with us are all called ladies and are ladies in many senses of the word, there is still the old meaning attached to the word by a dying civilisation and we hope this meaning may not die, "so I did not intrude on your sofa. But as you so kindly ask me to share your window-seat, I shall be proud to do so," and so saying he put his tray on the floor under the window-seat and sat down.

"By the way," he said, "I hear that your vicar is going to St.

Ewold's. We look forward so much to seeing more of him. A delightful fellow and so is his wife. I fear you will miss them at Pomfret Madrigal."

"Dreadfully," said Mrs. Brandon. "I practically pushed them into getting married and they are such good friends to me. I suppose you don't know who is coming to us?"

"I'm afraid I do," said Dr. Joram.

"Not one of the Palace lot?" said Mrs. Brandon, ruffling like an angry dove.

Dr. Joram said not exactly, but a young man called Parkinson, one of those young men who had only been to a theological college and though doubtless worthy in the sight of the Lord to labour in his vineyards would be so much better placed labouring somewhere else.

"Peggy," said Mrs. Brandon to her daughter-in-law who was passing with her sister Mrs. Crofts, wife of the Vicar of Southbridge, "do come here. Dr. Joram has just told me about the new vicar we are going to have. His name is Parkinson and he sounds *horrid*."

"Oh, *dear*," said Mrs. Francis sympathetically. "Is he very Low?"

"Not in that sense," said Dr. Joram. "But by the way, Mrs. Francis, he said he had met you at the Deanery."

"Me," said Mrs. Francis. "When? Effie, do I know a Mr. Parkinson, a clergyman? He is coming to Pomfret Madrigal."

"Oh dear, I'm afraid you do," said Mrs. Crofts. "That night we dined at the Deanery, before Lydia took us to see Editha Cottage. Lydia would remember. I'll ask her," and she moved a step towards Lydia who was penned into a corner having an unwilling conversation with the late Canon Thorne's widowed sister, who was inviting her to come to tea on any day within the next few weeks and see her little Life of her Brother, privately printed.

"I'm awfully sorry," said Lydia, "but I can't because of the children's holidays. Your house sounds lovely. What is it, Effie?"

she asked, moving a few steps to get the Precentor's burly form between herself and her Old Woman of the Sea.

"Dr. Joram says a Mr. Parkinson is to be the new Vicar of Pomfret Madrigal," said Mrs. Crofts. "Do you remember him at the Deanery when you took us to dinner there? Mrs. Brandon wants to know about him."

"He was Awful," said Lydia. "He had an Adam's apple and talked about people who went to posh schools. Oh and he was engaged to someone called Mavis Welk whose father was an undertaker and he quoted the Bible all wrong and Dr. Crawley glared at him."

"Oh *dear*," said Mrs. Brandon, her lovely tired eyes darkening at the thought.

"Edward tried to coach him in Latin, but it was pretty hopeless," said Mrs. Crofts and then the party melted away, leaving Mrs. Brandon and Dr. Joram on the window-seat.

"I am afraid this news has depressed you," said Dr. Joram. "I am extremely sorry that I mentioned it. There is a proverb in Mngangaland which runs roughly "The bearer of ill tidings is like the Mngpapawe—that is of course the hippopotamus— ugly before, behind, inside and outside."

"One might as well know the worst," said Mrs. Brandon though without conviction. "I daresay he is not so very dreadful, though I am sure he is and his wife too. But certainly you are not like a hippopotamus, Dr. Joram. More like a pelican, I think," she added thoughtfully.

"I would cheerfully be like a Tasmanian Devil if it would help you," said Dr. Joram. "But *why* a pelican?"

"I think you would pull all your feathers off to make people comfortable," said Mrs. Brandon. "I must go and speak to the Bishop's wife, I suppose," she added rising. "After all it is her party, and I avoided saying How do you do, so I really must say good-bye."

"From five o'clock onwards there will be sherry at the Vinery," said Dr. Joram. "If you would come in—and of course your son and his wife—I should be honoured."

Mrs. Brandon smiled a kind of yes smile and went to do her neglected duty, waiting till a great crowd of Grahams and Leslies and Beltons had gone out into the garden where, as usual, they all talked to the sisters, brothers, cousins, and near relations whom they saw as often as possible and in some cases nearly every day.

Acting on the suggestion of Leslie major, the party walked slowly over the brown parched lawn to where, on the far side of the Tulip tree, was a small pond with a flat stone parapet, fed most romantically from a spring, which though reputed to be one mass of typhus and other germs had been for centuries the sole supply of drinking water for the Palace and indeed had been, before the Reformation, celebrated as a kind of Means Test for witches, coiners and scolds, either by drinking or ducking. Sympathetic readers will doubtless be relieved to hear that so much strong ale was drunk on these occasions that the victim nearly always got away with his or her life, and with no particular ill effects from the water, for when the whole town drainage seeps into the wells the population acquires a high degree of immunity.

The only present connection with the pond had with these interesting old customs was that some immemorial fish lived there, popularly supposed to be carp, but distinguishable to any zoologist or ichthyologist as a rather unpleasant kind of jack or pike with diseased-looking scales. The carp tradition, however, died hard and it had been a custom dating from the seventeenth century for the Bishops and the other inhabitants of the Palace to feed them with bits of bread or cake. For his better entertainment a worthy prelate had towards the end of the eighteenth century caused a bell to be hung over the edge of the pond so arranged that whenever a fish swimming on its own concerns brushed or glided against it, its peal sounded through the garden. And if the peal happened to coincide with the end of breakfast, lunch, or tea in the warm weather, some one of the Palace inhabitants would come out with a plate of bread or cake and throw pieces in one by one. The goggle-eyed fish would then come in a silent rush-hour crowd and if the throwers were quiet they could hear the sound plop-plop of the fishes' mouths as they gulped the tasty morsels and licked their lips for more, a tradition handed on from father to son, if we may so speak of an order of creation, who, except for the male stickleback, are notoriously indifferent to the parentage, upbringing and ultimate fate of their million offspring. In his later days it had given pleasure to old Bishop Grantly to sit by the pond and hear the bell ring and scatter crumbs on the water and though Mrs. Proudie had deprecated such pleasures as partaking more of the nature of the savage than the man, besides the waste of good bread that might go into the Palace stockpot, she had so much meddling and intromitting of other sorts on her hands that the fish were left alone. Free Trade bread and Protection bread had been scattered by various visiting Prime Ministers, and Queen Victoria, herself looking in her old age not unlike a sunfish in mourning, had been graciously pleased to observe that she would write to the Princess of Hohenstiel-Schwangau about this modern miracle of loaves and fishes. The 1914 war, that little toy war as it now seems, left the fish unmoved, unchanged. But with the enthronement of the present Bishop the fish were conscious of a chill. Both he and his wife took an active pleasure in Rationing because it enabled them to do less entertaining and the Bishopess loudly disparaged the pampering of fish. No bread, no scraps except what the few servants scattered while their employers were not looking. When the bells of the cathedral were hushed the Palace seized the opportunity to remove the fishes' bell. The great tradition was broken. But the goggle-eyed fish still steered themselves under the lily pads and many a fly regretted his curiosity when two plopping lips seized and engulfed him.

The feeding of the fish had been a tradition in the Leslie

family. Lady Graham and her three brothers had been to the Palace as children, before the present incumbent's reign, and had lively memories of the fish-feeding which alas, their children had never known. As they all walked towards the pond, a handsome and well-disposed party as one would wish, old Tomkins came hobbling out of the shrubbery where the tool-shed lived, a romantic haunt beloved by all the children in the days before the present incumbents, where Agnes with her brothers had been Red Indians and Vikings and Crusaders.

"Hullo, Tomkins," said Leslie major. "Any luck with the Pools?"

Tomkins said he didn't hold with them Pools. Stood to reason, he said, if a man paid his last sixpence down, that man wanted to see it back bringing its sheaves with it same as like the Bible said. But for a man to put his sixpence down and not get nothing for it, a man would be a fool to do it. And so was the Government, he added, though more from habit than from any particular relevance to the subject in question.

Leslie minimus, producing from his blazer pockets two nasty-looking paper bags, said he had brought some food for the fish. He had, he added, kept it till it was nice and wormy for them.

Lady Graham meanwhile had taken a seat on a green garden bench with Mrs. Belton and from it dispensed gentle inanities in her soft attractive voice while the young of all ages disported round the stone edge of the pond.

"None of you young ladies and gentlemen knows what I've found," said old Tomkins. "Something rare it is."

Leslie major said a hoard of spade guineas, whatever they were. His cousins John and Robert Graham thought probably an atomic bomb, while James the eldest, now an extremely handsome young Guardsman, hoped it was Scotch whisky.

"All wrong, every one of you young gentlemen," said old Tomkins. "Down by the old compost heap it was. A mucky old corner and the man as calls himself gardener here doesn't know a pig's foot from a potato," which at the moment impressed his hearers a good deal, though reflection showed them that it meant very little. "I'm no gardener, I'm a sexton I am, but my old Dad he always said 'Turn your muck and earn your luck!' I turned the muck I did and what did I find?"

"Well, we've all guessed," said Charles Belton who was as usual in attendance on Clarissa Graham, though apparently more as a sparring partner than a suitor.

> "'Goodman Robin here I stand,
> Lifting up my either hand,
> Choose the best or choose the worst,
> Some are sained and some are curst.'"

said old Tomkins, which interesting quatrain when repeated in various quarters by his audience nearly drove the Barsetshire Archaeological Society mad, being obviously a pre-Reformation folk-rhyme of the utmost value which they had in vain endeavoured to get out of Tomkins for the last sixty years or so.

"Come on, Tomkins," said Leslie major.

"Aha!" said Tomkins, slowly drawing from what was obviously a poacher's pocket a peculiar rusty object. "It's Old Tinkler, that's what it is. Now keep off, you young ladies and gentlemen. I'll show it to her ladyship. *She* knows Old Tinkler."

Followed by a troop of Leslies and Grahams he carried his treasure trove to where Agnes was sitting and stood before her in a silent and rather threatening way which did not discompose her ladyship in the least.

"What is it, Tomkins?" said Lady Graham. "A fish?"

"That's a good 'un, your ladyship," said old Tomkins, shaking with a kind of subterranean laughter. "I'll tell that to my old woman. That'll make her laugh."

"It's one of those bells like the ones at Pomfret Towers," said Second Lieutenant James Graham. "You know, the ones in the kitchen passage that jiggle for hours after you've rung them with things like Small Foxglove Dressing Room and White Dimity Bedroom on labels. I say, it would be a good rag to go to the Chelsea Arts Ball with one of those on one's head. 'Belle of the Ball.'"

But his mother, though normally the most besotted of parents, was looking back into her childhood and the many great houses where as a child she had been free of the housekeeper's room and the still room and had known and adored all the footmen by their Christian names, and did not hear her gifted son.

"I remember," she said, "mamma telling me that when she was engaged to papa the butler at the Towers swept all the bells with the large kitchen broom and sent grandpapa into one of his rages. What is it, Tomkins?"

"It's Old Tinkler, my lady," said Tomkins. "Him as used to call the fish. Some people as think they're better than other people because they wear gaiters had Old Tinkler thrown away on the rubbish heap. Said the Germans would know it was the Palace grounds when they heard it. Shall I put him back where he belongs, my lady?"

It was only very rarely that Lady Graham was at a loss, but now instead of making up her mind at once and sticking to it with her usual placid obstinacy, she said perhaps they ought to ask the Bishop.

"My *good* aunt," said Leslie major, "not on your life."

"Too, too weak, darling," said Clarissa.

"Come on, Cousin Agnes," said Charles Belton. "Think of Guy Fawkes."

"I quite often do," said her ladyship, "though I really can't think why," she added with the mild surprise that her own mental processes often caused her. "But why just now?"

"Look here, mother," said Emmy Graham who had unwillingly left a heifer in an interesting condition at Rushwater and was not going to stand any nonsense. "You know what the Bishop did last Guy Fawkes Day. The choir school had a lovely

Guy and they'd collected all their pocket money for fireworks and the Bishop said they mustn't because it was un-Christian."

"I am really quite annoyed to hear that," said Lady Graham, her mild dove's eyes almost flashing with indignation. "If Guy Fawkes isn't Christian, what is? He is in the big Prayer Book in the Pomfret pew and grandpapa always made the clergyman pray for him at least it was against him. If only he could have lived till today," said her ladyship in a very historical voice, "only of course we would have to see that Mr. Churchill and Mr. Eden and all the rest didn't go to the House that day, he would have been *most* useful."

"That means it's O.K.," said James Graham, winking at his brothers and sisters and contemporaries. "If you've got some oil, or some metal polish, or something, Tomkins, we'll give it a bit of spit and polish."

With a cackle of malignant joy old Tomkins went away to the kitchen quarters and presently returned with rags and polish. Second Lieutenant Graham under the admiring eyes of all his juniors then took off his coat, washed the bell thoroughly in the pond and began to polish it with loving care while his elders talked comfortably about families and gardens.

"It needs a lot more," said James, "but that will do for the present. Where do we fix her, Tomkins?"

"Here, Mr. James. You hang she," said the old sexton, becoming more archaic with every word, "on that there hook," and kneeling down with creaks and groans he pointed a gnarled, earth-grimed finger at a hook driven in between the stones, just below the old stone wall. The curly spring of the bell was still in good condition, and when James had hooked it to its rightful place the bell dithered just above the water, and the boys sat on the edge and waited for the fish to come.

CHAPTER 8

While the cleaning was in progress Clarissa Graham, who suddenly felt grown-up and bored, had walked away towards the river, followed by Charles Belton who felt responsible for her without knowing why. Twice had Clarissa turned to him in her hour of need and twice had Charles told her in no uncertain terms how silly she was, but in a reliable, comforting kind of way. Two years ago she had been extremely rude, heartless and impertinent about her hard-working unselfish cousin Martin, and a few days later had completely lost her temper at the great combined Conservative Rally and Barsetshire Pig Breeders' Association and in so doing tripped over a tent rope and nearly fallen on her face. On each occasion Charles had spoken to her almost exactly as he would have spoken to any of the engaging young fiends under his charge at the Priory Preparatory School, and the pretty, wilful, spoilt Clarissa had kissed the rod and hung upon his arm more heavily than ever. Of her own wish she had gone with a scholarship to a woman's college to make a foundation for the training in engineering draughtsmanship which Mr. Adams had promised her, but she had not made any friends, looking always towards Barsetshire and to Holdings in particular. Her grandmother Lady Emily Leslie had been her dearest friend in spite of the years between them and Clarissa had been more shocked and wrenched by her death than anyone knew; even her mother. To

Charles she had turned as a large, comforting safety-valve, and from Charles some glimmerings of the necessity for self-control had found their way into her pert pretty head. Charles with unconscious horse-sense, inherited through his parents from a long line of country squires, had suggested as a helpful occupation for the vacations the new Pig Club which Philip Winter had allowed Charles to start at the Priory School, and the pretty, precocious, spoilt child had found pigs very soothing, and had also followed the hounds on foot and bicycle a good deal during the Christmas holidays, again with Charles. It was a mild disappointment to Lady Graham that neither her downright cow-minded Emmy nor her pretty graceful Clarissa had wished for the London dances and the Ascot week that their mother would willingly have given them, but with the good sense for which many of her acquaintances did not give her credit she realised that the young now will take their own way and had not insisted. Also Edith her youngest girl was growing up and Edith showed a pleasant aptitude for enjoying everything that life offered. True, Edith was only twelve, but in five years one could quite well take her to the Garden Party and a little season in Town and so her ladyship sat in a peaceful reverie watching in an absent-minded way the young barbarians at play.

To the east of the cathedral where the Palace stood the garden did not slope to the river as did the gardens of the south or Deanery side. The lawns lay level, most suitable for the tennis and croquet which were never played there, most suitable for garden parties of which the Palace gave its one grudging sample every year. At the far end where there was a drop of some ten or twelve feet to the river was an embanking wall of pleasant red brick which on the garden side was just low enough to lean on comfortably and here Clarissa was standing, her elbows on the stone coping warm from the sun.

Presently Clarissa said she wished she were dead.

"You should think before you speak, my girl," said Charles. "When people say they wish they were dead they only mean they are too lazy to go on fighting or working. What do you want to be dead about?"

"Oh—things," said Clarissa, tracing with her elegant tip-tilted forefinger the line of rusty moss between the stones. "I wish Gran hadn't died for one thing."

"Well, there are thirty or so fellows I wish hadn't died too," said Charles, "but there it is. You may be killed in a war, you may be killed in a motor-bus, you may die in your home like your grandmother. It's coming to you whichever way you look."

"And I'm so tired of Myself," said Clarissa.

"And well you may be, my girl," said Charles. "Going off the handle about nothing and showing off when all the others are enjoying themselves in an ordinary way. It's a pity girls aren't beaten at school. Do them a lot of good. It sweetens the blood as our old nurse Wheeler used to say. Any more complaints? Real complaints I mean?"

"The real ones aren't so bad as the other ones," said Clarissa. "I don't think I've got any real complaints."

"Ten marks for telling the truth, Miss Clarissa Graham," said Charles. "And now I'll tell you what as Lucy Adams is always saying. Try thinking a bit about other people's troubles. Try thinking about mine for a change."

"Yours, Charles? You haven't got any," said Clarissa, mildly interested.

"You wait, my girl," said Charles. "Younger son. Prep. school-master earning my living. No prospects when my people die so I hope they never will. And here I am, teaching little boys till I retire on a miserable pension and my best friend grumbling all the time."

"Do you mean me, best friend?" said Clarissa artlessly.

"Of course I do," said Charles. "Best girl friend anyway. There are some old friends I'd like to see more than anything in the world, but they are blown up, or drowned, or died in prison camps, or they're in hospital with no eyes and arms and legs, poor devils."

Clarissa raised her beautiful dark eyes, so like her mother's, but with Lady Emily's fire, to Charles.

"I know, I know, my dear," she said. "Gran died happily I know—if one really does know anything about how people die—but I do want her so *dreadfully*, Charles."

Tears brimmed and overflowed. There was no temper now, only a child bewildered by a loss she could not understand and ready to hurt anyone because of her own grief.

"Do you ever read Kipling?" said Charles. "Here's my handkerchief, it's bigger than yours."

Clarissa was heard to say through the muffling handkerchief Why.

"Well, I think he's a jolly good poet," said Charles. "He says exactly what you think only with a kick in it. He knew about people dying that you're fond of. I'm not much good at saying poetry and I daresay I won't get the words quite right, but I'm going to say it.

"'The dead they cannot rise, and you'd better dry your eyes,
    And you'd best take me for your new love.'"

Clarissa had stopped sniffing and looked away across the river, across the water-meadows and the tilled land and the new ugly suburbs to the eternal line of the downs, grey in the summer haze.

"What does it mean?" she said uncertainly.

"It means you are going to be engaged to me and then I can beat you if you are silly," said Charles, not feeling at all as calm as he sounded.

"Does it?" said Clarissa, interested.

"Not just yet. I've got to earn some more money and you've got to finish this college idea of yours. No use leaving a job half done. But after that. Is that all right?"

Clarissa looked away and began again to trace with her elegant tip-tilted finger the rusty moss between the stones while

Charles waited, his heart bumping rather rebelliously for one who was to be Clarissa's guide, philosopher and friend, not to speak of her future husband.

"Yes," she said presently. "And thank you very much. Had I better tell mother?"

Charles, his perceptions not so blunted by love that he did not notice how she said "I" not "we," said it would be quite a good thing and he would tell his mother. But nobody else. He wondered if he ought to kiss her, but as she made no sign of requiring this attention he didn't, reminding himself at the same time, for he was not without a sense of humour, that he had so often given her a friendly hug when she was feeling low that a kiss more or less would mean very little. Not the kind of kiss he would have liked to give her anyway, for he was not going to alarm this bird of paradise who was content to perch on his finger.

As they sauntered back the gentle tinkle of the bell could distinctly be heard. Leslie minor, who had an excellent head and had climbed all over the roof of Southbridge School chapel and up the hideous iron spire, had found a ladder near the rubbish heap, not unassisted by Tomkins, and was already almost at the top of the tulip tree. Leslie minimus was quietly feeding the gobbling fish from his packet of decaying food. John and Robert Graham were talking about cricket and James Graham with Leslie major had vanished to the dining-room to look, he said, for women and wine.

"Do you know," said Agnes to Mrs. Belton, "I have an idea that Clarissa is quite fond of Charles. He is such a dear boy and darling mamma liked him so much. But these young people manage their own affairs now. Did I ever tell you how I got engaged to Robert?"

"Yes, quite often," said Mrs. Belton calmly, "and it is a very good story."

"I only mentioned it," said Agnes, with gentle firmness, "because darling mamma was such a help. It was at a dance you

know, and a waiter spilt some coffee all down Robert's shirt
front, and I said, "Oh, Colonel Graham, that coffee will stain
your shirt." So he asked if he could have the next dance but two,
and he went straight back to his rooms and put on a clean shirt
and came back and proposed to me and I said it sounded very
nice, so I told mamma and we got engaged. I wonder if Clarissa
will say anything."

"I expect Charles will," said Mrs. Belton calmly. "I think it
would be a very good thing, don't you, Agnes?"

"A duke would have been nice," said Agnes, "but there aren't
any at the moment. I like dear Charles very much and so did
darling mamma. Oh dear, one does miss her. Not with sadness,
but thinking of all the things that would have amused her. I
ought to be going."

"So ought I," said Mrs. Belton. "Where are John and Mary?
Didn't they come with you?"

"Darling John," said Agnes, who was particularly fond of her
elder brother. "He and Mary wouldn't come out because they
wanted to corner the Bishop about amalgamating their parish
with the next one, at least I mean amalgamating the clergyman."

"What *do* you mean, Agnes?" said Mrs. Belton.

"I mean the bishop making the next-door clergyman whom
they *loathe* take the services in their village, because theirs got
very old and retired," said Agnes. "And he rushes breathlessly
backwards and forwards in a small car and John says it is a
scandal, besides doing the services all wrong, I mean that
peculiar service that has a thick black line down it in the new
prayer books and leaves out everything. So John and Mary are
determined to lodge a protest," said her ladyship, evidently
pleased with this phase, "as the Bishop only answers letters by
his chaplain who is evangelical."

Mrs. Belton asked if that would make any difference to
answering letters.

"Only that they don't seem to know about answering letters,"
said Agnes. "I think their parents cannot have been very well

educated or conscientious because I know darling papa said one should answer every letter the day it comes and do the dullest one first. But John wrote more than a fortnight ago and hasn't had any answer, so he is determined to get one, even if it means staying here all night."

Mrs. Belton said that certainly would not happen, as the Palace was notorious for its inhospitality and when the bishop's wife invited people to stay, which was hardly ever, she sent a list of the rations they were to bring. There had been a rumour, she said, that when the Archbishop came for a night, not only did the bishop's wife write to his chaplain and tell him to bring soap and face towels, but also put the unfortunate chaplain himself in a bedroom with a one-bar electric fire, and one glaring light in the middle of the ceiling which was quite useless for seeing one's face in the look-glass or reading in bed.

They were now joined by Agnes's brother John Leslie and his delightful dull wife Mary, who came to report that they had tanked right over the chaplain and frightened the bishop and had every hope of not being amalgamated with the neighbouring parish, though it was of course quite impossible to trust the bishop until they had it in writing, and now they must go home.

Leslie major who had been in the dining-room while the frightening took place said it was as good as a Cup Final and called his youngest brother Leslie minimus to stop feeding the fish and come along, but Leslie minor was not to be found.

"Be you a-looking for that young gentleman of yourn, Master John?" said old Tomkins, who had known John Leslie as a small boy and at once scented the possibility of a tip. "He's up the tulip tree, he be."

John Leslie walked to the front of the tulip tree. The thick trunk rose for some distance before the branches began, but against the far side was a ladder.

"I suppose that's your ladder, Tomkins?" he said.

"No ladder of mine," said Tomkins indignantly. "His Lordship's ladder that is, out of the shed. I never had no ladder in the

Palace grounds. You'll see my ladder in the shed behind the Cathedral, Master John. I wouldn't bring my ladder in the Palace grounds not if the Bishop was to pay me for it. Not if he was to give me half-a-crown I wouldn't."

"Well, here's half-a-crown," said John Leslie. "When that boy of mine comes down, tell him we have gone home. No, Mary. I am *not* going to wait. In fact the less I know about his being up the tree, the better pleased I shall be."

"Father," said Leslie minimus, rising from the edge of the pond as his parents approached, "we've put the bell back. The fish were a bit frightened at first, but they've got the hang of it now," and as he spoke a particularly hideous fish of leprous appearance rose to the surface and bumped the bell which tinkled across the water.

"All right, old fellow, and it's the end," said Leslie minimus, emptying the last of his crumbs upon the water. There was a plopping noise and then silence, while the ripples spread across the surface of the water and the bell tinkled, after which his parents thought it wiser to take him away.

At five minutes to five Dr. Joram had said good-bye to his host and hostess, expressed his gratitude for so delightful a party, and walked over to The Vinery, thinking as he did whenever he approached it that his house though not the largest was the most exquisite in the Close, which thought we may add occurred in that form, or with very slight alteration, to everyone who was lucky enough to live in the most beautiful Close in England.

"Several ladies and gentlemen have already arrived from the Palace, sir," said Simnet as he came into the hall. "I put them all upstairs, sir, where they couldn't do no harm," he added, as if the mere fact of having accepted the Bishop's so-called hospitality might drive his guests to carve their names in the window-seat or pocket small objects. So Dr. Joram went upstairs and there found Mrs. Morland and Miss Dale discussing thrillers.

"What is so *awful*," said Mrs. Morland, trying without much success to arrange her hair in front of a Chippendale mirror which though of beautiful design made the human face look green and distorted, not to speak of large black spots, "is *having* to write them. Every year I say to myself that I have worked long enough and I can live on my capital till I die. Only of course owing to the way They go on one's capital isn't worth what it says it is, not to speak of the income tax. Fine fun for Them, putting their incomes up to a thousand a year as soon as They got in, and then taking away the Nelson pension," with which words she grabbled fiercely in her bag, took out a handkerchief and blew her nose.

"I'm sorry," she said, "but whenever I think of Nelson it makes me cry. And whether it is worth while trying to save for one's children now I don't know. I wonder what They are doing for Their children."

"Have they any?" said Miss Dale.

"I took the trouble of looking Them up in Who's Who," said Mrs. Morland proudly, "and two of Them whose names I will not mention because They sound exactly alike don't seem to have any though of course if one hasn't a wife that is reasonable, and as for having one daughter I have absolutely no opinion of that at all," said Mrs. Morland, whose four sons seemed to her a far more valuable contribution to the world than her very successful novels about Madame Koska. "Or of one son and three daughters. And as for women being in the Government I am *extremely* sorry for their children, if they have any," said Mrs. Morland darkly. "What do you think, Dr. Joram?"

"As a bachelor I have no views at all," said Dr. Joram, "I became very fond of the black babies but to have one's own about the house might be disconcerting. I liked Mrs. Robin Dale's twins very much. They were such ladies. I have never seen better manners at a christening," and then friends began to fill the room and the shortcomings of the episcopal garden party were discussed in detail, with special reference to there being no ices.

"I do not myself eat ices," said the Dean, "but my grandchildren tell me that they are now extremely good."

"That," said Mrs. Morland, "is simply ignorance, Dr. Crawley. They have never tasted real ices, poor things, so they think they are nice," at which words a Babel of conversation burst out among the older members of the part about what ices were like before 1914.

"Real vanilla ices," said Mrs. Belton, "with specks of vanilla pod in them."

"And strawberries or raspberries all mushed up in a glorious *splodge*," said Lady Fielding whom no one had thought capable of such enthusiasm, "for fruit ices."

"And sponge fingers at thirteen for a shilling made with real eggs and sugar and real flour," said Mrs. Crawley, looking back to her Victorian childhood.

"None of you," said old Miss Thorne, sister of the late Canon Thorne, "remember sitting in a carriage outside Gunter's in Berkeley Square, with the footman bringing out the ices. I do, quite distinctly, with my old great-aunt Miss Monica Thorne," which utterance was of a nature to kill conversation. No one present had shared this experience and such is the depravity of human nature that everyone present felt that Miss Thorne was presuming, as indeed she always did, upon her great age. Mrs. Brandon said rebelliously that anyone could remember anything if they lived long enough.

"Yes, mamma," said Francis Brandon, "and if Aunt Sissie had lived till this summer she would have been ninety-one, but she didn't," which may have been meant for a joke, but made all those guests that heard it feel uncomfortable. Mrs. Brandon looked out of the window and said how beautiful the cathedral was. Everyone began to talk again rather disjointedly in sympathy and Mrs. Morland afterwards stated that she had distinctly heard herself say that it was very wet when it rained.

At this moment Lady Cora Palliser who had been talking to her host about her uncle the Honourable George Palliser who had been Governor of Mngangaland, said to Francis in a low voice but with extreme clarity, "Don't talk like that to your mother" and turning her handsome head again towards Dr. Joram asked if Uncle George had ever shown him his collection of Melanesian coral.

"Dear me, no," said Dr. Joram. "How very interesting."

"As a matter of fact it wasn't," said Lady Cora, "but he would show it to people when he had drunk too much whisky, and the more drunk he was the more he showed it. You can't have seen him at his best."

"I'm afraid I didn't," said Dr. Joram. "It was not so much spirits in his case as a native drink which makes people go into a kind of trance for three days with only the whites of their eyes showing. There was nothing that one could do for him unfortunately."

"Nobody could do anything for Uncle George," said Lady Cora, "and he wouldn't have thanked them if they had. But someone ought to do something for Mrs. Brandon, poor pet. Have you noticed anything?"

"If you mean that her son is a little thoughtless, I had noticed it," said Dr. Joram, looking cautiously round lest Francis or his wife, or even his mother who would feel it most, were within hearing distance.

"Good," said Lady Cora. "I like him you know, but he's a bit of a skunk to his mother. Not Peggy's fault. He is a great help with theatricals and as we have a little theatre at Gatherum it seems a pity not to use it. Not a real theatre. When the Americans were quartered at Gatherum they rigged up a sort of stage and some lighting. We are thinking of trying some Gilbert and Sullivan there. A bit lowbrow for you, I expect, but we'd love you to come."

"But my dear Lady Cora," said Dr. Joram, "I know Gilbert and Sullivan inside out. The head chief of Mngangaland had a new radio gramophone every year and about two thousand records. We used to go right through the operas at least three times a year."

"I say, you don't sing by any chance?" said Lady Cora.

"No," said Dr. Joram firmly. "I mean yes, but No, if you understand. As a locum I would have said yes, but now I am in the Close——"

"I know," said Lady Cora. "You really couldn't I suppose. But that's no reason why you shouldn't give us some tips at the rehearsals. It won't be till after Christmas anyway. Look here. About Francis. I don't think Peggy likes the way he is behaving to his mother, but she is not going to interfere. Mind you, I think she's wise. Mrs. Brandon would probably take his side. Mother love is much blinder than Love with a large L, because it sees everything and shuts its eyes all the same."

"You notice a great deal," said Dr. Joram admiringly.

"One has to," said Lady Cora, "in my job."

Dr. Joram asked what her job was.

Lady Cora said it was a charity called Hiram's Trust. There was some kind of row about it, she said, a long time ago and it was turned into a kind of company owning valuable land in Barchester and they gave money to deserving objects like the Barchester General Hospital.

"I'm really pretty intelligent," she said. "In fact I've got more brains than the rest of my family put together. But what's the use? One doesn't know. You must come to Gatherum and tell them about Uncle George and his native drink. The parents will adore it. Mother hates Uncle George like hell, sorry, because she says he is a bad influence though God knows none of us could afford to get drunk on whisky even if we wanted to. Now you really must go and be a good host," and so dismissing Dr. Joram as if he were at fault and not she, though quite kindly, she wandered into the back drawing-room to talk to Mrs. Freddy Belton, who had as good a brain as her own with the advantage of a husband and a most desirable baby.

So Dr. Joram did as he was told and more and more people

drifted in from the Palace. Simnet, entirely in his element, was handing drinks while Mrs. Simnet washed glasses in the first-floor bathroom and the people going on their lawful occasions through the Close stopped to listen to the roar of a sherry party of quite respectable and for the most part not very young people, all lashing each other to louder speaking.

"I wonder what the Palace is thinking of this delightful orgy," said Mr. Miller, the Vicar of Pomfret Madrigal, so soon, alas, to be translated. Not that we for a moment grudge him his preferment, but the thought of Mr. Parkinson in his place depresses us almost as much as it depressed Mrs. Brandon.

"I don't suppose they are listening," said Lady Graham who had just brought her contingent across. "How darling mamma would have loved your house, Dr. Joram. She adored looking at other people's houses. Old Canon Thorne and his sister were the only people who wouldn't let her in."

Dr. Joram was just about to offer her a personally conducted tour of the house from attic to cellar when Simnet came in and approached his employer with an air so full of importance and mystery that conversation near him was checked and the sound of a very successful sherry party died down to nothing as the roar of London dies on Armistice Day, until such times as They suppress that moving two minutes of quietness.

"Excuse me, sir," said Simnet, in a voice so fraught with importance that everyone wondered if he had come to say the Bishop was dead.

"What is it?" said Dr. Joram rather impatiently, for he was enjoying his talk with Lady Graham.

"I merely thought, sir, you might wish to know," said Simnet, deliberately speaking very slowly, the better to attract as much attention as possible, "that Mr. Tozer is in the kitchen. As you are aware, sir, he has been superintending the refreshments at the Palace."

"Well that's all right," said Dr. Joram, rather annoyed with his excellent butler. "Mrs. Simnet will look after him."

"It's very good of you, sir, I'm sure," said Simnet, "and if you hadn't got guests, sir, I would like you to allow Tozer to have a word with you."

"Afterwards," said Dr. Joram.

"It won't hardly keep, sir. According to Mr. Tozer, sir, there has been quite an unpleasant Scene at the Palace, owning to the 'igh spirits of some of the young gentlemen," said Simnet, who only omitted an H under very severe mental and moral stress.

"Oh Lord!" said Second Lieutenant James Graham, "It's those cousins of mine. I say, Dr. Joram, could we have Tozer up? I expect Minor and Minimus have got into trouble."

Such was also the opinion of his mother and of Mrs. Belton who had been sitting with her near the pond at the time, as Mr. Tozer appeared.

All were now silent and their countenances intent upon him. Then from the vantage-point of the doorway Mr. Tozer spoke thus.

"If you really wish me to tell the 'orrible story all over again, sir," said Mr. Tozer who only dropped his aitches when under great emotion, "it's this way, sir. I was in charge of the refreshments at the Palace. Tea, lemonade, sangwiches and gatto on our lowest tariff," at which point he paused to let his words sink in. "Well, sir, most people just took up a sangwich and put it down again, for at that price fish paste is the most you can expect, and the same with the gatto and I may say our baker nearly gave notice about the gattos, knowing what he can do even under present conditions if he is given his head. So there was all that stuff just went straight into the refuse bins, sir, shocking waste it was, till the young gentlemen came in and at that age well you know they've hollow legs as the saying is and the rest of the sangwiches and gattos were gone in a jiffy. And then young Master Leslie, the little one, sir——"

Second Lieutenant James Graham was heard to say that he knew Minimus was at the bottom of it.

"——the little one," Mr. Tozer repeated with a look that should have slain James Graham on the spot but didn't, "he took one of Our cake plates and he piled it with all the bits of sangwich and gatto and off he run into the garden shouting "It's the bell" and just as he was going out of the room he ran straight into his lordship's apron, sir, and all the sangwiches went on the floor, and his lordship said, "What's that, boy?" and the little one he said "It's for the fish, sir. They've just had word from Wells," he said "to stand up for their rights and not sit down under them the way the swans did, so they've rung the bell. We put it up again, sir," and what the young gentleman meant, sir, I couldn't say. But his lordship was most upset, sir. Dreadful it was. And the Reverend Poles, that's the chaplain, sir, he looked out of the window and he says, "There's a boy up the tulip-tree, my lord," and we thought he was barmy, sir, if you'll excuse me, knowing well tulips don't grow on trees. So the Reverend Poles he went out, sir, to look, but by the time he got across the lawn both the young gentlemen had gone off on their bicycles, sir. So his lordship was in a fine way and so they both was, sir, and me and Mr. Scatcherd who had just come down to see everything was cleared away proper, we cleared away and then I come over here, sir, just to see if I could help Mr. Simnet, thank *you*, sir."

There was a brief silence of a very holy and grateful nature, broken by Agnes who said John's boys were really too too naughty adding in a loving voice, "wicked ones, wicked ones," just as she used to say it to Clarissa when she was an adorable little girl.

"Well, that is all quite too dreadful," her ladyship added as no one seemed disposed to break the silence, "and we must be going. Thank you for this quite delightful treat, Dr. Joram. How darling mamma would have enjoyed it," and then she went away with her family.

There was very little comment upon Mr. Tozer's revelation. Some of the guests felt it would be perhaps out of place, however delightful, to discuss the bishop in the Close and were anxious to get home and discuss it there. Others were anxious to be the first to spread the good news to the remoter parts of Barsetshire where they lived, and so the party quickly dwindled to the Brandons, Dr. Joram and Lady Cora.

"It has been lovely," said Mrs. Brandon, "and we really must go, Dr. Joram."

"Why not all come back to Gatherum for dinner?" said Lady Cora. "The parents never mind anything and we can go through our dance again. You too, Dr. Joram, and we will have a good Gilbert and Sullivan talk."

"Well," said Dr. Joram, obviously flattered by the invitation and the lure of the Savoy operas, "it is a most handsome thought, Lady Cora, but I fear my petrol won't run to it."

"Oh, I'll manage that," said Lady Cora. "There always seems to be a bit in the garage somewhere. The whole family do county work and we all take each other's."

"Would you mind if I didn't?" said Mrs. Brandon. "It's so stupid, but I get so tired now. It's the Government of course which makes it worse. If it were His Majesty I wouldn't mind *how* tired I was."

"Really, mamma, you are talking nonsense," said Francis.

His wife looked at him, began to speak and checked herself. Lady Cora also looked at him, though so swiftly that he was hardly conscious of it.

"Of course you're tired," she said to Mrs. Brandon. "Anyone would be. Look here, let me drive you to Stories, and we'll take Dr. Joram with us and the I'll go on to Gatherum with him. You two go on your own," she added, addressing Francis rather as a nurse might address a tiresome though not actively naughty child, "and I'll drive you back to Barchester, Dr. Joram, whenever you like."

Mrs. Brandon looked rather than spoke her gratitude and within a few moments Dr. Joram was in the back seat, and she was in the front beside Lady Cora who appeared to do most of her driving with the tip of one finger.

"War," she said, when Mrs. Brandon commented on this. "I

drove generals and things all over the place. I really ought to be called Cara, not Cora," to which Dr. Joram gallantly said from the back seat that there was as much truth as humour in her remark.

When they got to Stories Lady Cora asked to be allowed to come in for a moment and see the house and was loud in her praises.

"It must be heaven to live in a house you can keep warm," she said. "Gatherum is just plain Ice Hell of Pitz Palu for nine months of the year. You must come and see it, Mrs. Brandon, while the weather's still warm," and to that lady's mild surprise she kissed her with a kind of affectionate carelessness and then took Dr. Joram to the Castle.

"Mr. and Mrs. Francis are dining at Gatherum Castle," said Mrs. Brandon to Rose, who had been hovering within earshot. "Will you tell cook that we won't have the chicken. I would like some of that soup we had yesterday if there's any left and I think I shall go to bed."

"Yes, madam," said Rose in a tone of deep disapproval, but so battered did Mrs. Brandon feel that she hardly noticed and did not care. Luckily Nurse was out that evening and could not fuss or ask questions, so she gave herself a cocktail and then had a bath and got into her dear comfortable bed.

To her own great surprise she woke up presently, saw that it was eight o'clock and felt quite mad, wondering if it was morning. There was a knock at the door and Rose came in with a tray which she set down on a table. She then silently brought her mistress a dressing-jacket, plumped up her pillows, put a bed-tray across her knees and on it a small and perfectly appointed supper of hot roast chicken, new potatoes, green peas, a little salad and a small carafe of Burgundy.

"Cook said it wasn't no use to keep the chicken back seeing she'd started it, madam," said Rose. "And there was just one of those nice little half bottles of red wine in the dining-room, so I opened it. Is there anything else, madam?"

Mrs. Brandon thanked her and said it was perfect.

"If you will ring, madam, cook has a little hot sweet for you when you are ready," said Rose and left the room, shutting the door with ostentatious softness.

As the Millennium appeared to have dawned, if one may use this expression when it is eight o'clock in the evening, Mrs. Brandon ate her chicken and drank her wine and read that very good thriller by Lisa Bedale called *Aconite at Night*. Presently she rang and Rose brought her a small chocolate soufflé and some coffee. And when Rose had taken away the remains she began to read again. It was a good kind of escape to have had such a delicious supper and some good wine and to wonder whether Gregory Hubbard or Frank Mulliner was the real villain and whether the super-detective Gerry Marston would marry the heroine; and if surges of unhappiness and even a little fear overcame her once or twice, she resolutely put them away and buried herself in that blissful dreamland of revolting crime which appears to be our best refuge against injustice and oppression and the shame we so bitterly and deeply feel for our country's name, till the dreams mingled with her own and the book, we regret to say, fell down as they far too often do between her bed and the wall and lay sprawled on the carpet, unable to shriek for help.

"Madam looked just like a ghost," said Rose to Cook over their supper, which we may say included some of the chicken. "Lady Cora's lovely. Just like her photo in the *Tatler* and ever such a sweet expression."

"I dessay," said Cook, who not having seen Lady Cora was not going to pander to Rose by showing any interest. "My mother's old auntie as was third housemaid at the Castle said they often sat down twenty to dinner and all the silver plate. Nasty stuff she said it was and scratched as easy as anything. It took the second footman hours to polish it. She was walking out with him but she didn't marry him—I'll trouble you for the bread sauce, Rose, and you might as well finish those peas—

because he got one of the kitchenmaids into trouble and she told him straight out if he thought he could get her into trouble he was welcome to try and see what he'd get for it."

"And did he?" said Rose, impressed against her better self by Cook's *chronique scandaleuse*.

"Not he," said Cook with deep contempt. "Didn't have no more sense than to marry the girl. So mother's auntie she took against men and rose to be head housemaid with six under her. And to think they've only some girls that come and go. Why, Madam is better waited on than Her Grace."

Rose said darkly that she needed it.

"You needn't tell me," said Cook. "What's the use of Madam having her car if there's no one to drive it? When that Curwen went into the garage business we all heard a lot about how Mr. Francis was going to do this and that. Now Mrs. Francis, she's a sweet lady but she can't drive a car, and as for Mr. Francis, well between you and I and the bedpost, Rose, I don't know what's come over him."

"Well, Cook, you never knew Mr. Brandon," said Rose pityingly. "Strong please and two lumps."

"All the lump there is, and that's not much with this Government," said Cook, "I need for My Preserving. There's plenty of saccharine, though they do say it Poisons the System. Hope old Strarkie takes it," with which unloving allusion to the Minister of Food she put two large spoonfuls of granulated sugar into her own cup and pushed the sugar basin to Rose.

If it appears to the reader that Cook was being unusually and unnecessarily self-assertive, we must explain that this was the result of what is loosely called an inferiority complex, for Rose had been with Mrs. Brandon ever since her marriage, whereas Cook had not come till after the death of the late and on the whole unlamented Mr. Brandon.

"They say you shouldn't speak ill of the dead," said Rose, "but Mr. Brandon's been dead a long time now and I don't see it can hurt. He was a nice gentleman and very fond of Madam, but as selfish as they make them. Things must be his way or not at all. What's bred in the bone comes out in the flesh, they say."

Cook said they might say it, but it wasn't a nice way to talk and Mr. Francis seemed to favour his father, at which moment Nurse came in.

"I've kept some chicken for you, Nurse," said Cook. "I'm glad you weren't in earlier. Me and Rose have been quite upset," and in strophe and antistrophe she and Rose related the events of the evening.

"So I told Mrs. Francis's Nannie she could fetch her supper and take it upstairs, Nurse," said Cook, "because there's some things she needn't stick her nose in, and me and Rose wanted to talk to you without interference."

Nurse, who was usually prepared to take offence at any action of Cook's or Rose's, felt that this was a moment to sink all differences in the common cause and while eating her chicken heard a highly coloured account of the evening's adventures and how Madam must have gone to sleep, quite wore out like, because Rose had knocked and she didn't answer. At any moment Nurse would have resented Rose's care for her mistress deeply, but for once all three ladies were in accord, and though the phrase *écrasez l'infâme* was unknown to them, the sentiment was the same where Francis Brandon was concerned, and at that moment, among chicken bones and strong cups of tea, a kind of Holy League was formed against Francis Brandon and Mrs. Francis's Nannie. As for Mrs. Francis, they all felt, as indeed we do, that she was so sweet and kind that no blame could be attached to her beyond that of being too submissive to her husband.

"Well, I daresay Mrs. Francis's Nannie will give in her notice now," said Cook, with the joy her class (and indeed all classes) take in prophesying woe. "It's time she learnt to come down and fetch her supper for herself, or have it in the kitchen. I'm sure *I* wouldn't mind," said Cook virtuously, who had done her best to make Nannie's life a floating hell as far as meals were concerned.

*   *   *

It was fairly late when the Francis Brandons got back but the evening was still light in the curious unreality of Summer Time. Mrs. Brandon heard their voices and half hoped Francis would come in and say good-night as he so often used to do; and half hoped he wouldn't in case he found something in her to disapprove, as he so often did now. There was a light tap and with great courage she said, "Come in," and in came Mrs. Francis, looking extremely pretty and yet anxious.

"A nice time?" said Mrs. Brandon, taking off her large owl spectacles.

"Very nice," said her daughter-in-law. "It was just us and Cora and Lord Silverbridge her elder brother, and she and Francis practised the Argentina Tango. Do you remember when he and I did it, mamma, for the Red Cross Fête? What fun it was."

"I hope it is still fun," said Mrs. Brandon.

"If you mean do I love Francis very much," said Mrs. Francis, industriously following with one finger the lines of quilting in her mother-in-law's bed-cover. "I do. Only——"

"Well?" said Mrs. Brandon, very kindly.

"Well, life is difficult sometimes," said Mrs. Francis. "It was difficult with Fred though I loved him very much. Not that Francis flirts as Fred did, but—oh, mamma, I can't *bear* to see him not be always quite loving to *you*, and if I said anything he might be a little annoyed. He *truly* doesn't mean it."

"What I ought to have done," said Mrs. Brandon, talking aloud to herself to clarify her idea, "was not all live together," which sentence appeared to be quite comprehensible to Mrs. Francis who said she loved being at Stories better than anything in the world, but if it was going to make Francis not be polite to his mother she would rather live in Hogglestock, after which she cried gently and without having swollen eyes or a red nose.

"We do look at houses," she said, "but Francis always says they aren't so comfortable as Stories," and then she did a little more crying in her own gentle unravaging way.

"Listen, Peggy," said Mrs. Brandon. "I don't quite know yet what I am going to do, but I am not going to have you made unhappy. Don't cry or Francis will wonder why. You and I will have a plan together, a secret, and I promise you I will make everything all right. Kiss the babies for me."

Much comforted, for her emotions were easy, Mrs. Francis looked at her pretty face, made it up a little, gave her mother-in-law a very loving hug and went away. Mrs. Brandon put on her owl spectacles again, rescued *Aconite by Night* from the ruelle and was quite unable to remember where she had got to, which is perhaps part of the great curative value of thrillers. Presently she shut the book and took off her spectacles.

"And what kind of plan I am to make I have not the very faintest idea," she said aloud to herself.

Earlier in the evening Lady Graham was doing some of her exquisite needlework in the large room called the Saloon at Holdings, while her daughter Clarissa amused herself by making pictures for that strange romantic phantasy, Henry Kingsley's *The Boy in Grey*. Just as Clarissa's grandmother, her own mother, the dearly beloved Lady Emily Leslie used to do, thought Agnes. The boys had all gone over to Rushwater to do what their Uncle David called bulldozing, that is to talk to their sister Emmy and their cousin Martin and his wife about cows and kindred subjects. Edith, the youngest, was at the far end of the room writing a very long poem about the fish in the Palace pond. Sad that she would soon be an ordinary schoolgirl, thought Lady Graham regretfully, but that was all one could do for one's daughters now, and Clarissa had remained herself in spite of communal life.

Presently Clarissa laid down her brush and brought her picture to show her mother. Like Lady Emily she composed straight onto the paper in water colours and the now unfashionable phrase water colour drawing described her work exactly. Her colouring was her grandmother's, her drawing her own.

"Lovely, darling," said her mother. "Gran would have loved it. Who is it for?"

"For you, if you'd like it," said Clarissa, at which her mother expressed gratitude and genuine pleasure.

"Mother," said Clarissa, tracing the pattern on the sofa cover with tip-tilted finger.

"Well, darling?" said Agnes.

"It was about Charles," said Clarissa, tracing the pattern as industriously as if her life depended on it. "He said he thought it would be a good thing if we were engaged, only he wasn't in the least frightening. He was *very* kind, because I told him about missing Gran so much. Only not yet, he said."

The busy finger moved and Clarissa's eyes were fixed upon it.

"So what did you say, darling?" said Agnes, almost afraid to speak above a whisper lest this rare confidence should take wing.

"I asked him if I had better tell you," said Clarissa, and with these words Agnes knew she and her child were already parted. In the future it was from Charles Belton that she would learn. Holdings would remain her home for a little, but Charles would be her lode-star and her spirit had already begun its journey, hardly knowing why or whither.

"I am so glad he did," said Agnes, pleased that Charles had thought of her. "I think it is a very good plan, darling, and I am very fond of Charles. How pleased Gran would be."

"She *is* pleased," said Clarissa, coming out of her dream. "Charles said he would tell his mother, but no one else yet. Are you pleased, mother?"

Agnes made no answer but drew Clarissa into an infinitely soft loving embrace to which the pretty, defiant creature gratefully yielded.

"And now we are both crying," said Agnes, though she laughed. "This will be our private secret for the present. I shall mention it to papa, but of course he will be pleased."

It was perhaps lucky that Edith who had just finished her

poem should have come rather noisily up the room at that moment.

"I've made the poem, mother," she said. "Shall I read it to you?"

Agnes composed herself to her work and Clarissa sat on a pouffe at her feet.

"It is called," said Edith in an important voice, "'Loaves and Fishes' and it is satirical."

"How lovely, darling," said her mother.

"I meant to make it very long, like Marmion," said Edith who'd just fallen into Scott's poetry, "but there wasn't enough to say, so I made it short. It says,

> "'Long long ago, all time beyond
> A bishop made a beauteous pond
> And it became a home for fish
> To come and go as they did wish.
> Beside the pond he hung a bell
> Which did give forth a solemn knell
> Whenever any carp or whale
> Touched it with head, or even tail.'

"I had to put whale," said the gifted authoress, "because of rhyming with tail."

"Quite right, darling," said her mother.

"It goes on," said Edith.

> "'And then the people all ran fast
> And bread into the pond they cast.
> But then there came a bishop foul
> Who nothing did but curse and growl,
> Because he did not want the fish
> To have a morsel from his dish.
> So he and his most odious spouse
> Said the bell made such awful rows

That never should it sound again,
And so they threw it down the drain.'

"That is not true, of course," said Edith, "it was the compost
heap but that wouldn't rhyme. It goes on,

"'But Heaven so kind to all below
Did pity all the fishes' woe
And sent the noble Graham clan
And Leslies too, each one a man,
Who found the bell and hung it too
So that the fishes quickly flew
To ring their old beloved bell.
And now the bishop is in hell.'

"I think it is very good," said Edith complacently. "Could I
get it published?"

"No," said her mother, with surprising firmness. "But it is a
lovely poem, darling. I know who would adore it, that is Uncle
David. If you write it out neatly Clarissa can do some pictures.
You must really go to bed now."

At Harefield Mrs. Belton had gone to bed and was peacefully
reading *Aconite by Night* by Lisa Bedale and had got to the really
nerve-shattering moment when the famous detective Gerry
Marston is waiting in the dark for He Does Not Know Whom,
when her son Charles knocked at the door, came in, and seated
himself on the end of his mother's bed.

"I say, mother," said Charles.

"Well, darling?" said Mrs. Belton.

"You know Clarissa," said Charles.

Mrs. Belton said she did and what a charming creature
she was.

"We're not in love, you know," said Charles.

Mrs. Belton said of course not.

"Some people get engaged right off," said Charles. "A friend of mine called Jimmy Butters met a girl at a dance and got engaged. But I don't think that's wise."

Mrs. Belton said she quite agreed.

"I had a few words with Clarissa this afternoon," said Charles in a manner which the words dégagé and insouciant do not at all adequately describe, "and we thought we might make a do of it. Sometime, I mean, not now," he added, lest his mother should have visions of a Fleet marriage with a curtain ring.

"I see," said his mother, artfully assuming an air of considering something deeply. "One might call it an understanding."

Charles said with evident relief that that was about it, a sentence which his mother appeared to comprehend perfectly. He then kicked the side of the bed in a way that made his mother want to kill him, kissed her with absent-minded affection and went out of the room, shutting the door so hard that it came open again, which annoyed his mother so much that she nearly called him back.

CHAPTER 9

When Sir Robert Graham came down that weekend his wife told him that there seemed to be a romantic attachment between their daughter Clarissa and Charles Belton, but she could not say if it was serious; to which Sir Robert replied with his usual commonsense that Clarissa was very young and Charles had as far as he knew little more than his pay as assistant master at the Priory School, so Agnes need not worry about it yet. As her ladyship had no intention of worrying she obeyed her husband and life went on much as before. When the school broke up Charles went abroad with the fifty pounds allowed by a government which had managed to spend millions with nothing particular to show for it except free hospitals and operations for the whole British Empire and all visiting foreigners and perpetually rising cost of living, and Mrs. Belton did not mention the matter to her husband, feeling with some justice that he would probably make a fuss. Nor did she say anything to her daughter, now Lady Hornby the Admiral's Lady, for Elsa though much improved by her marriage was now completely absorbed by her children and the place in Scotland. But she had a long delightful talk with her son Captain Frederick Belton, R.N., and his wife, formerly Susan Dean, during which talk the baby was understood to express his opinion that there was no hurry and it might be a very good thing.

The good news about the bell in the Palace fishpond spread

rapidly and so many people congratulated the Bishop and his wife that they came to think they had replaced it themselves and boasted a good deal. As for the tulip-tree old Tomkins when questioned became stone deaf and slightly senile and said he didn't know anything about the ladder. *His* ladder was in the shed behind the Cathedral he said and he wasn't such a gormed fool as to let no young gentlemen break their necks on it. So the Bishop and his wife went to Italy on their hundred pounds and stayed in Florence at the Casa Higginbottom where afternoon tea was included but decided, not without regret, that they would not go to Rome as it might cause the Pope to be unduly puffed up.

Meanwhile at Gatherum Castle the plans for Gilbert and Sullivan went on and Dr. Joram found it pleasant to be looked on as an authority by Lady Cora, while Francis sulked a little at being second fiddle and Mrs. Francis smoothed him down with great skill. Mrs. Brandon thought a great deal about her promise to Peggy and considered several solutions of the family problem, each more difficult or impossible than the last. When they were married she had privately decided that the joint household, though she loved their presence, should not be for ever, thinking that Francis would prefer to have his bride in a house of his own. But not for nothing had Francis been, except for the war years, a spoilt grown-up son at home. As his wife said, Stories remained the most comfortable house he knew, exactly the right size, with that modern miracle a good staff if getting older and occasionally bad-tempered. A house of her own was another of Mrs. Brandon's ideas, but that might make people think that Francis and his wife wanted to get rid of her. And then she simply must take Rose and Cook who were such old faithful friends, which again would be unkind to Francis and Peggy. As for Nurse, she had felt from time to time that her tyranny was becoming unbearable, but one could not suddenly turn off and pension a woman who had given all her best years to one's children and oneself. On the top of it all the dreadful day was at

hand when Mr. and Mrs. Miller were going to St. Ewold's and
Mr. Parkinson with his wife Mavis Welk and their two skinny
children would be in the Vicarage and the dear familiar church
and vicarage would no longer be her refuge. And so much did
she think and worry that even George Knox's new biography of
Cardinal Wolsey, *King's Bishop*, did not hold her attention and
Rose remarked darkly to Cook that Madam was fretting and it
was just the way her Auntie Poppy went into a decline.

She was writing letters in her sitting-room one morning not
long after the Palace garden party when her daughter-in-law
came in, almost in tears.

"Oh, mamma," she said. "Something *too* dreadful."

Now it had come. Francis was being unkind to Peggy and
that she could not and would not bear. Francis was her beloved
only son and for the peace of the family she would overlook his
changed ways and keep the peace. But if he were not kind to
Peggy she would for once assert herself. And as these thoughts
rushed at express-train speed through her head, she felt quite
courageous and Peggy, in her generous way, thought how pretty
mamma was looking.

"What is it?" said Mrs. Brandon, taking off her owl spectacles
which she still only used for reading and writing.

"It's Nannie," said Mrs. Francis. "She has given notice because Cook asked her to fetch her supper from the kitchen," and
she sank on to the sofa and buried her face in a cushion.

In Mrs. Brandon's experience people were always giving
notice and the world went on just the same. Her young married
life had been punctuated by notices which had always been
withdrawn and if in later years the crises had been rarer it was
simply because she refused to recognise them. Probably when
Peggy was married to Captain Arbuthnot in India she had
hundreds of black bearers, for so to herself did Mrs. Brandon
poetically put it. When she was for a short time at Southbridge
with her sister-in-law they had no resident maid, which made
life very easy: a statement which no man will understand. Now

at last, with three babies, doom ineluctable was descending on her and she was not standing up to it very well. Mrs. Brandon felt extremely sorry for her, but was not going to encourage self-pity and said how very annoying but probably she was already repenting and Peggy would hear no more of it and so sent her away comforted. From her long knowledge of her household it was to be expected that Nurse would not be far away and before long she appeared at the door.

"Yes, Nurse?" said Mrs. Brandon, laying down her pen again.

"Mrs. Francis seems quite upset, madam," said Nurse, "with Nannie giving notice. I can't understand these girls nowadays, Fancy wanting to leave those dear little babies. And as for having her supper upstairs it was her own wish, madam, and I'm sure we all did our best, but really as I was saying to Rose if we've got to have Mrs. Francis's Nannie in the kitchen every evening when Cook is the first to put a nice supper on a tray for her, well really she has no one but herself to blame."

Although Nurse's apologia if analysed impartially proved absolutely nothing, it was abundantly clear to Mrs. Brandon that this was a major domestic crisis and she would have to take command, though really Peggy ought to be able to manage her own affairs. But before she spoke she would try letting things simmer down for a bit. So she basely flattered Nurse by saying that she, Nurse, had always been one to make things pleasant in the house and we would wait a little and see how things went. Nurse went away, temporarily placated, and Mrs. Brandon tried to finish her letters as if nothing had happened, without much success.

Peggy's Nannie could not have chosen a worse day to upset the household as the Millers were giving a farewell sherry party at the Vicarage, a good many old friends were to be there, and Mrs. Brandon did not at all want to be a spoilsport. So she determined to put it out of her mind for the present and was fairly successful.

*   *   *

It was not without considerable heart-searching that Mr. Miller had accepted the living of St. Ewold's. He had come to love Pomfret Madrigal and it was in his own Vicarage that he had after twenty-five years at last been able to ask the woman whom he had loved as a girl to be his wife. Miss Morris had been companion and slave to Miss Brandon at Brandon Abbey and when her bullying old employer died it was Mrs. Brandon who had rescued her from the neglect of the pampered servants and brought her to Stories and so to the Vicarage. Their marriage had been quiet, continued happiness and a single mind and eye about parish matters. They loved the place and the people. But St. Ewold's was real preferment, with a larger income and, which perhaps attracted them even more, larger responsibilities. It was also, and no clergyman of good sense could put this lightly aside, in closer touch with Cathedral circles and generally looked upon as the prelude to a canonry. A former incumbent had gone straight from the parsonage to the Close and the name of Arabin was not altogether forgotten. So though they both grieved for what they would leave behind, they looked forward to working even harder and being nearer the Cathedral. The party would be only old personal friends and Mrs. Brandon meant to enjoy it very much.

By special invitation she went over to the Vicarage before the party began, bringing a large basket of flowers from her garden and some cakes made by Cook from American parcels.

"You won't mind flowers, will you?" said Mrs. Brandon to Mrs. Miller. "We have such a lot and they go bad if one doesn't use them."

Mrs. Miller, who was one of those rare women who do not notice there are flowers in a room, said flowers were exactly what she wanted and the Vicar said indeed, indeed Mrs. Brandon came like St. Elizabeth of Hungary with bread turned to roses.

"How nice of you, Mr. Miller," said Mrs. Brandon much gratified, "but I brought my bread as well. At least it is cakes, but

I really think they are nicer than bread because they are made with American flour and shortening and fruit. I said shortening," she added, "because that is what it is called on the tins, though I don't know what it really is."

"You are very kind," said Mrs. Miller. "I don't know what we shall do without you. We both have a dreadful guilt complex leaving Pomfret Madrigal."

"Some of my friends," said Mr. Miller, "have described my move to St. Ewold's as an answer to prayer, but I do assure you I never prayed for it or even thought of it."

"It is really *most* unsafe to pray for things," said Mrs. Brandon earnestly, "because you never know if They mightn't let you have them. And when I say They," she added, "I do not mean the present Government but Higher Powers," and in saying these words she looked as angelic as a Murillo Virgin only rather older.

Mr. Miller, who felt that this was his business, said there were things that were hidden from us and he was sure Mr. Parkinson would replace him admirably. And his wife too, he added. And it would be nice to think of children in the Vicarage, at which his wife smiled affectionately, for not having married till middle age she would have been excessively surprised if any of those little trials of clerical life had come upon the scene.

"No," said Mrs. Brandon, with unusual vigour. "From all I hear the Parkinsons will be entirely unsuitable. I shall of course go to morning service on Sundays for one must be polite and I shall ask them to lunch afterwards just once. But if I wish to enjoy myself I shall go to Barchester. I could easily go by the motor-bus."

"Are you short of petrol?" said Mr. Miller anxiously. "I am sure I could give you some of mine."

"How generous you are," said Mrs. Brandon. "I really have plenty, only you see not having a chauffeur makes it rather difficult now. You know I was very young when I married and my husband would never let me learn to drive."

As the late Mr. Brandon had been dead for some thirty-odd years it did just occur to Mr. Miller that his relict could during that time have learnt to drive if she had wished, but he stifled the thought as unworthy of him and said of course there was Francis. His wife, who from a long experience as companion to old ladies had a pretty good knowledge of the less friendly side of life, had noticed of late with disapproval Francis Brandon's increasing selfishness and had seen Mrs. Brandon trying to disguise it, so she quickly said perhaps Mrs. Brandon would come to them at the parsonage sometime for a weekend, which invitation was gratefully accepted. And then guests arrived and the party began to get under weigh, or way. It was not to be very large, but as most of them knew one another they would probably make a satisfactory amount of noise, for what people really like at sherry parties, not to speak of cocktail parties, is to talk to the people they meet every day about the things they always talk about, only much, much louder.

Colonel the Reverend F. E. Crofts, Vicar of Southbridge, with his wife, Mrs. Francis's sister-in-law, were the first to arrive, and the two clergymen at once got into a corner to discuss the parsonage at St. Ewold, for Colonel Crofts had about three years previously come to his first cure of souls at Southbridge and had made various changes in the Vicarage there generally considered to be a great improvement and Mr. Miller, the most modest of men, was anxious to learn.

"Here, you see," he said, "one knows everybody and whenever I want a job done about the house, there is always someone willing to oblige. In fact as my dear wife says, the kitchen is full of obligers from morning to night which makes it a little difficult with the rations. But Mrs. Brandon, of whom we shall often think, has kindly come to the rescue more than once with tea sent to her, I understand, by friends in America. Do you think, Crofts, from your experience, that it will be equally easy to find good workmen at St. Ewold? Anxious as I am to take up my new work and little as I would mind any inconveniences for myself, I do not like to think of my wife being uncomfortable."

Whether Colonel Crofts thought his brother priest was crying out before he was hurt, we do not know, but Mr. Miller's simplicity and shining goodness disarmed all his friends and Colonel Crofts only said that the person to ask would be Mr. Adams. A lot of the Hogglestock workers, the better class engineers and artisans, he said, now lived at St. Ewold, and doubtless among them some obligers might be found.

"But you had better ask Adams," he said. "Is he coming today?"

Mr. Miller said he hoped they were and also Mrs. Adams's parents the Marlings, and indeed indeed he must not delay Colonel Crofts any longer. But he looked so harried and wistful that Colonel Crofts said if he was in any real difficulty he would send his man Bateman over, who was an ex-gunner and could turn his hand to anything. Mr. Miller, much relieved by this suggestion, then went to do his duty as host.

> "Poor sleekit, cow'rin, tim'rous beastie
> Oh, what a panic's in thy breastie,"

said a voice beside Colonel Crofts. He turned and found Mr. Wickham the Mertons' agent who had come over with his employers, or rather brought them with him in his disreputable little car for which he always mysteriously had enough petrol.

"He'll be all right. St. Ewold is lousy, sorry padre, with men wanting to do a bit on the side. He'll be a godsend to them," said Mr. Wickham, who was carrying two bottles of gin, a bottle of vermouth and a bottle of Jamaica rum.

Colonel Crofts said, with a not unbecoming gravity, that he felt sure he would.

"Kamerad!" said Mr. Wickham. "Put my foot in it that time, didn't I?" at which Colonel Crofts laughed, for not only was Mr. Wickham Mrs. Crofts' valued associate in bird lore, but his uncle Mr. Johns the publisher was paying Mrs. Crofts a very handsome sum for her beautiful bird drawings the first volume of which had recently been published.

"And there's the Saucy Peggy," said Mr. Wickham sketching to Mrs. Francis across the room a salute which almost brought a whiff of brine into the room so nautical it was, for Mr. Wickham had been with the Royal Navy during the war and his heart was still with the ships. "What's wrong with Peggy, padre? She looks under the weather."

"Effie is worried about her," said Colonel Crofts. "Look here, Wickham, you know Peggy pretty well. If she tells you what's wrong let us know. I have an idea myself——" and he checked himself, not wishing to stir up trouble.

"So have I," said Mr. Wickham. "How two such charming women as Mrs. Brandon and Peggy can tolerate such a bounder as Francis beats me. I don't mean there's anything *wrong* with him, but he looks so damned pleased with himself. A Year before the Mast is what he wants."

"Come, come, Wickham," said Colonel Crofts. "He was all through the war," to which Mr. Wickham replied darkly that it took more than a war to get the bumptiousness out of some people and went away to put his gin among the Vicar's drinks.

By now the room was getting comfortably full. The roar of talk so grateful to a hostess's ear might have been heard from the churchyard beyond the garden and it was with a little difficulty that Mr. and Mrs. Marling with their son Oliver and their guest and friend Miss Dale could get near Mrs. Miller.

"Well, Mrs. Miller," said Mr. Marling, "so you're leavin' Pomfret Madrigal. Bad thing all this movin' about. My old uncle the Archdeacon had the same parish for fifty years and he's buried there. Must say for him though, he buried plenty of other people first. Well, I hope you'll like St. Ewold. The Thornes used to live there. Same family as old Lady Pomfret and Mrs. Belton. It's all council houses now. Good market garden land it was, best in the county. It's always the way. Now look at Middlesex," said Mr. Marling, well away upon one of his favourite topics. "Best market garden land in England. When I was a boy it was still gardens from Chiswick to Kew, and the market carts came rumbling in every night to Covent Garden. Now it's all nasty red-brick houses and airfields and you never see a vegetable in London less than three days old."

"I'll tell you what, father," said his daughter Mrs. Adams, better known to us and to all her friends as Lucy Marling, "there won't be a vegetable anywhere unless it rains. Hullo, Mrs. Miller, I'm most frightfully sorry my husband can't come and so's he, but he'll try to fetch me."

She then crushed her host's and hostess's right hand to a jelly, looked about her for more worlds to conquer and burst upon her brother Oliver who was talking about his book on Thomas Bohun the seventeenth century poet to Dr. Joram who was not much interested and welcomed the interruption. Nor did Oliver resent it, for next to himself and his projected book and the hopeless passion for Jessica Dean that he still nourished though with lucid intervals, he dearly loved his sister Lucy and was unselfish at least in rejoicing to see her so well and so obviously at peace with herself.

"Hullo, Isabel. I say, Oliver, do you like my turn-out?" said Lucy, who was looking very handsome and just so much tamed as to bring out her best points.

Oliver and Miss Dale expressed approval.

"You've done something to yourself," said Miss Dale. "What is it? Hair? Face? Clothes?"

"I went to London with Mrs. Belton," said Lucy proudly. "Sam said she looked tired and needed a change, and he's awfully fond of her because she was so nice to Heather, and would I do something about it. So I took her to the Bendor," said Lucy, naming a well-known, expensive and quiet London hotel, "and we did a lot of shopping and we went to a beauty shop and a hairdresser and three plays and a matinée," which distinction will, we hope, be clear to our theatre-going readers. "It was great fun and she said she felt much better. But I was glad to be back at the Old Bank House because I was afraid all the time Sam might be missing me."

"And was he?" said Oliver.

"*Awfully*," said Lucy. "And so was I. I thought I would die the first night at the Bendor, but after that I enjoyed it awfully. But home's best. I say, I must talk to Mr. Wickham about a pig. Oh, and Jessica sent you her love and Sarah Siddons is *divine*, with a sort of soft fur on her head and holds your finger till it really *hurts*. I saw Aubrey and Denis Stonor in their show and it was heavenly. You never knew if you would cry buckets or laugh till you nearly died. Hullo, Mr. Wickham, I want to know about that White Porkminster of yours."

"How clever Adams is," said Oliver to Miss Dale.

"So is Lucy," said Miss Dale. "It isn't every girl who would have the wits to let an older woman tell her where to have her hair done and get her clothes. Lucy is a very clever girl."

This view of the sister whom he had treated all his life with the condescension of an elder brother, though truly fond of her, took Oliver aback.

"Yes, I suppose she is," he said, wondering all the time why Jessica's name had not hurt him as it used to do. "By the way, Isabel, could you type a few pages for me? I have been to the British Museum and got a few useful bits about Bohun. Apparently Defoe might as a very little boy have seen him during the Plague and there is a reference in his *Journal of the Plague Year* which might apply to Bohun. It would be most kind of you. Writing a book when you have to get your facts right is no joke."

Miss Dale said she was sure it wasn't.

"It's all very well for people like Mrs. Morland and people who write thrillers," said Oliver. "They just have to turn out so many thousand words and it's done. But when it comes to facts and research and a sense of history, it is a very different pair of shoes."

"If you will let me have your stuff I'll type it for you over the weekend," said Miss Dale. "Duplicate?"

"Please," said Oliver. "Oh, would mind if it was triplicate. I should feel safer. I mean supposing two publishers wanted to look at it at once, I'd still have a copy for myself."

Miss Dale, refraining from comment upon Oliver's hopeful supposition, said she would certainly do it in triplicate and now she really must talk to some people and so melted from Oliver's side and inserted herself between the talkers till she reached the table where Mr. Wickham was dealing with the drinks.

"Anything I can do for you?" said Mr. Wickham. "Miller hasn't a ghost of an idea about drinks, bless him. And Gobbless the British Navy," he added as he put an empty gin bottle under the table and opened a fresh one. "How's old Uncle Johns treating you?"

"Very nicely," said Miss Dale. "We sold twenty thousand before publication and the repeat orders are coming in from the libraries."

"Good girl," said Mr. Wickham.

"Wicks," said Miss Dale, safely sheltered by the noise of a successful party, "I want to write something about John. Not a memorial of one of our gallant boys whose life was not given in vain," said Miss Dale rather bitterly. "Something for myself and his people and his friends like you. Would you help?"

"I would," said Mr. Wickham. "Like billyo I would."

"It's a secret," said Miss Dale.

"Top secret. Cross my heart and wish I'll die," said Mr. Wickham. "And what about Lisa Bedale's next thriller?"

"Oh, it will come," said Miss Dale. "Oliver Marling has just told me that anyone can write a thriller."

"That bit of cold fish," said Mr. Wickham with a kindly contempt. "Gosh! that's Cora Palliser. I haven't seen her since '44. I was in London on leave and she was driving some brass hat and there was a Godalmighty blitz. The poor old blighter was killed right out and I happened to come along to see the fun and we got about a dozen women and kids out of a bombed house and then I had to go back for a blasted dog and two canaries. We

got the whole lot into shelters and she never once batted an
eyelid, even when the kids were sick. Fine girl. You'd like her," to
which Miss Dale replied with every appearance of truth that she
was sure she would. The party which had been squashing itself
to death during the last half hour in order to be near the drinks
now began to ooze from the French windows onto the lawn and
Lady Cora with Mrs. Francis Brandon was carried on the flood
directly in front of Mr. Wickham. She paused, looked, and then
forced her way through the stream of guests.

"It's not Wicks?" she said.

"And with knobs on," said Mr. Wickham enthusiastically.
"What have you been doing all this time, Cora? This is Isabel
Dale. She was engaged to a pal of mine, one of the best John was
till he stopped one."

"I'm frightfully sorry," said Lady Cora. "I wasn't even engaged, but mind stopped one all the same. So did my young
brother. Some people have the hard luck."

"And some make a song about it," said Mr. Wickham, looking meaningly to where Oliver was making his way towards
them through the crowd. "Hullo, Marling. Cora, this is Oliver
Marling."

Lady Cora said she thought her father had sat on the War
Agricultural Committee with a Mr. Marling and was it any
relation of Oliver's. Oliver said his father.

"Look here, Cora," said Mr. Wickham. "I've got to look after
the drinks. Miller doesn't know the first thing about them and
he'll be mixing gin and sherry. Oliver is writing a book about an
Elizabethan Johnny who wrote pretty hot stuff. Get him to tell
you about it," with which words of counsel he went back to the
table where Mr. Miller was looking nervously at Mr. Wickham's
contribution to his party and in the kindest way in the world
suggested that if Mr. Miller went and made himself pleasant to
the ladies he, Mr. Wickham, would see to the doings, upon
which Mr. Miller, dimly grasping Mr. Wickham's meaning,
gratefully left him to deal with the drinks but preferred wander-
ing about the drawing-room to going into the garden.

"And who is the Elizabethan Johnny?" said Lady Cora to Oliver.

"He was really Caroline," said Oliver, not best pleased by Mr. Wickham's introduction which he felt was far from doing justice to him. Nor was he any more pleased when Lady Cora said it reminded her of Johnny Belinda, a film whose name had left such people as bothered to reflect upon it in a state of complete addlement. He said rather sulkily that he used the word Caroline as an adjective.

"I take you," said Lady Cora, "He was a Caroline Johnny. Is that what you mean?"

Words could not express Oliver's mortification. Not that he cared two hoots about Lady Cora, but to have the subject of one's valuable research made sport of, even by a Duke's daughter, made one think but poorly of such an one. With a dignity somewhat impaired by his inward rage he began to explain to Lady Cora that he was doing some research into the life and works of Thomas Bohun, M.A., Canon of Barchester.

"Oh, that one," said Lady Cora. "There's a memorial tablet to him in the Cathedral Cloisters. He wrote a sort of religious erotic stuff, didn't he, like Donne? Father's got a book of his at Gatherum, with a woodcut of him in a cap and bands looking like Judy."

"Not the 1668 edition?" said Oliver, suddenly realising how intelligent an audience Lady Cora was.

"Could be," said Lady Cora. "You must come over to Gatherum and see it. My brothers and I used to laugh a lot over some of the poems. Do you know that one that ends

'And so my soul, of thine the sole alloy,
Shall be the soul's sole solar soul of joy'?

"My brothers and I used to march round the dining-room reciting it, only we always said fowl instead of soul because of those long esses."

That was not the way to treat a Canon of Barchester, especially one whom Oliver Marling was editing, but even Oliver's absorption in his own affairs could not make him forget who Lady Cora was and how charming, so he said he would love to come, and then he and Lady Cora found a common subject of dislike in Geoffrey Harvey of the Red Tape and Sealing Wax Office and his sister Frances, of whom Lady Cora had no opinion at all.

After a few minutes Lady Cora, with cool and practised ease, shed Oliver as a chestnut tree drops its spiky ball and went over to Miss Dale to whom she had at once taken a liking and remained with her for some time while they compared war jobs.

"Well, Lavinia," said Sir Edmund Pridham to Mrs. Brandon, "I think it's time we made the presentation, eh, before everyone has gone," for he and Mrs. Brandon had secretly got contributions from Mr. Miller's personal friends for a farewell present to him and his wife.

"So do I," said Mrs. Brandon. "Oh, Mr. Wickham," she said to that gentleman, "excuse my interrupting, but do you think you could beat the gong?"

"Nothing I'd like better," said Mr. Wickham. "Why?"

Mrs. Brandon said just to make people be quiet.

Mr. Wickham without any enquiry as to the ulterior motive of this request went into the hall, detached from its stand a bronze Burmese gong with gongstick and beat upon it most skilfully, reminding Mrs. Morland, as that lady afterwards said, of Beethoven's Pastoral Symphony; the bit where he does the thunderstorm she meant and how clever it was of him considering he was deaf.

"Right, Wickham, that's enough," said Sir Edmund. "Well now," he continued, apparently under the impression that he was addressing the West Barsetshire County Council, "there's just one small matter of business. And pleasure," he added severely. "Our valued friend Mr. Miller and his wife, also much

valued, are leaving us—well, what is it?" he said rather crossly to
Mrs. Noel Merton who had touched his arm.

"It's Mr. Parkinson the new vicar and his wife," said Lydia in
a whisper. "They missed the bus or something," and in her
masterful way she cleared a path for the Parkinsons who looked
as if they would rather be anywhere else.

"I'm glad to meet you, Mr. Parkinson," said Sir Edmund, who
had a respect for the cloth almost unaffected by his opinion of
the man who was wearing it. "You're just in time. I am saying
good-bye to Mr. Miller on behalf of his friends here, who will I
am sure be your friends," he added with a conviction he was far
from feeling.

"Friends are a wonderful thing in life," said Mr. Parkinson.
"Pleased to met you, Sir Edmund. And this is Mrs. Parkinson,
and a real helpmeet, help*mate* I should say," he added nervously.

"We're ever so pleased to be here," said Mrs. Parkinson, the
ci-devant Mavis Welk, "and I'm sure we're going to be ever so
happy and we'd like to wish Mr. Miller and Mrs. Miller all the
best. And we're ever so sorry we're late, but I was pressing
Teddy's trousers and we missed the bus."

Every single guest was rent by his feelings. The first that if the
Parkinsons were all the Church of England could produce to
replace Mr. Miller, a scholar and a gentleman, and his wife
whose kindness and capability would have adorned the Palace,
or Bishopsthorpe, or even Lambeth, it was time something was
done about it; the second and perhaps the worthier that though
Mr. Parkinson was frankly no gentleman and Mrs. Parkinson
unplaceable socially, that they had a disarming confidence and
honesty and ought to be given every chance and encouragement
in this new, and probably to them terrifying adventure.

"Well," said Sir Edmund, who was an old soldier and used to
taking emergencies as they came, "I'm glad you are both here. I
shan't say much. On behalf of a number of old friends I am
asked to say how deeply we shall miss you, Miller, and your wife,
how sincerely our good wishes will follow you to St. Ewold, how

glad we shall be whenever you are able to come back and see us. We ask you to accept a parting gift from us with our heartfelt wishes for your future welfare. God bless you both. And welcome to your successors."

By this time most of the ladies were in tears, though of nice, comfortable sort and Mrs. Miller's face was unashamedly hidden in her handkerchief. A table which everyone, including the Millers, had studiously not seen was now brought forward covered with a large piece of silk. On the silk was a gold wrist-watch which Sir Edmund presented to Mrs. Miller, who was laughing and crying all at once.

"Here, Lavinia, you do this," said Sir Edmund.

Mrs. Brandon took the heavy piece of silk from the table, unfolded it and displayed to the Millers an altar cloth of her own exquisite embroidery sewn with pre-war silks from her hoard, upon which, everyone began to blow their nose or cough and Mrs. Brandon was quite dissolved in delightful tears.

"Let me offer you my handkerchief," said a deep, pleasant voice by her side and it was Noel Merton who had been her devout admirer and flirted with her as occasion offered ever since the summer, eleven years ago, when old Miss Brandon died and he had taken a small part in the temporary arrangements for her house and property.

"Oh dear, oh dear," said Mrs. Brandon, muffled in Noel's large handkerchief. "I *am* enjoying myself so much."

Mr. Miller then tried to thank his friends and broke down.

Mrs. Miller was heard to say what sounded like "Too much. Bless you all" and Mr. Wickham whose years with the Navy had not been wasted suddenly appeared with a fresh round of drinks for everyone. Dr. Joram in a quiet way said he thought they should not only speed the parting but welcome the coming guest and drank to Mr. and Mrs. Parkinson.

"I'm sure Mrs. Parkinson and I are much obliged," said the vicar elect, looking unaccountably nervous, which however was explained when he said he didn't hold with spirits. Not but what, he continued, he liked a glass of beer after, say, a day's hiking with the lads.

His wife said Teddy was funny like that and her father believed in them if one had a nasty winter cough.

"Quite right too, Mrs. Parkinson," said Mr. Wickham. "And this is real Navy rum, sent me by a pal at Portsmouth. Think of our gallant sailor lads."

Thus appealed to Mrs. Parkinson put hers down, as Mr. Wickham afterwards said, like a good 'un, and the guests began to disperse.

"There's just the one thing, Mrs. Miller," said Mrs. Parkinson. "Do you know anyone who could come in sometimes in the evening? We've the two kiddies, Harold that's after my father and Connie that's after Teddy's mother and I can manage the cooking and the housework all right, but it would be nice," said the Vicar-elect's wife wistfully, "if Teddy and I could get out together sometimes, if it's only to the Mothers' Meeting."

Mrs. Miller, touched by this echo of the Brave New World, said Mrs. Thatcher at Grumpers End would always come up to oblige, and sixpence an hour with liberty to make tea would be quite enough. "If you can spare the tea," she added, to which Mrs. Parkinson, much comforted, said her father got a lot from America as he had done the funeral work for an American hospital during the war and it seemed the Americans couldn't do enough for him, just because he'd laid their poor boys out nicely.

"Well, thanks ever so," said Mrs. Parkinson. "We must go now, because I had to ask the landlady to give the kids their suppers and I don't like to impose on her."

Touched by her frank simplicity Mrs. Miller kissed her and said she must ask her about any difficulties at the Vicarage.

"Thanks *ever* so," said Mrs. Parkinson in a trembling voice. "I know I'm not class enough for Teddy, but we can all learn, and he's one of the best," with which words she rescued her husband from Sir Edmund and took him away.

The company now began to disperse, Lady Cora, laying violent hands on Mr. Wickham and Oliver Marling, took them back to Gatherum, that she might talk with Mr. Wickham about the happy days of the blitz when England was free and united under the Great Commoner, and that Oliver might look at her father's edition of Bohun. Francis and Peggy were going to dine in Barchester and go to a film.

"I'll walk back with you, if I may," said Noel Merton to Mrs. Brandon. "Lydia went back with Colonel Crofts who will drop her at Northbridge and his wife is staying on to talk to Peggy, and I shall drive *her* back. Love's Cross-Currents," at which Mrs. Brandon laughed very pleasantly, though the reference meant nothing to her at all.

"I'll drop in sometime, Lavinia," said Sir Edmund. "All went very well. Pretty bit of needlework of yours, Lavinia. But you always had pretty things about you. Pretty hands too."

"They used to be," said Mrs. Brandon, spreading her still lovely hands despite the years of war work and far worse peace work, and gazing pensively on old Miss Brandon's diamond ring.

Then she and Noel walked back to Stories and sat on the lawn under the great Spanish chestnut.

"Do you remember the Flower Show the year that Miller married Miss Morris?" said Noel. "Lydia was very conspicuous on the roundabout with your Delia. I think they rode the cock and the ostrich. What a long time ago it seems."

"Well it is," said Mrs. Brandon, who had a sound bottom of commonsense. "Let me see it was the year Aunt Sissie died. Eleven years. One doesn't get any younger."

"You do," said Noel promptly.

"Deceiver!" said Mrs. Brandon and each remembered the afternoon of ridiculous deliberate flirtation in Mrs. Brandon's cool, flower-decked drawing-room and the pleasure which they, both artists in harmless love-making, had derived from their comedy.

"Noel," said Mrs. Brandon, who had never used his Christian name before, but now did so without thinking, "could I ask you something? Slightly professional."

"My briefs are marked a hundred guineas now," said Noel. "For you, to be allowed to kiss your lovely hand; I mean the one with the diamond on it of course."

"Foolish boy!" said Mrs. Brandon with intense enjoyment. "It is all rather stupid. Do you think I look much older?"

Noel recognised the seriousness in her voice.

"Yes," he said. "We all do, but you less than the rest. You do look—no, it isn't even a look. I'll say you do give me the impression that you are harassed. If I am wrong I shall be glad."

"I am," said Mrs. Brandon. "Do you think it's silly for people to live together? I don't mean in sin. But families."

Noel looked at her and her eyes moved away from his.

"I see what you mean," he said. "If you won't think it impertinent, and it is really only because we are very fond of you, Lydia and I have noticed it lately. I suppose the joint household isn't as easy as you all thought."

"No," said Mrs. Brandon, looking at her ring.

"If I am to talk to you professionally," said Noel, "which I may say is not in the least incompatible with speaking as a friend in this case, I should say it was a mistake. I know Peggy is good-nature itself." He paused.

"I know you do," said Mrs. Brandon.

"Touché," said Noel, for his brief and most innocent flirtation with pretty Mrs. Arbuthnot as she was then had made his Lydia unhappy for a few weeks of one summer. But all that was past history.

"Is Francis?" said Noel.

"No," said Mrs. Brandon.

"Well, there are two obvious solutions," said Noel. "One is that you should make it clear to Francis that he must find a home for himself and his wife and family. The other that you should leave them at Stories which I suppose Francis will in any case inherit at your death—forgive me—and find a new and possibly smaller home for yourself. You wouldn't think of living near Delia I suppose?" For Mrs. Brandon's daughter, now for a long time happily married to Mrs. Grant's son, lived near London, a place which Mrs. Brandon did not like.

"That is all the advice I can give you," said Noel. "It is the best I can do, for outsiders cannot settle anyone's life. But if there is anything practical, such as a house to be inspected, or a lease to be examined, please count on me," for Noel Merton's father was the head of an old and respected firm of solicitors in Barchester dealing largely with country properties, while the other firm of Keith and Keith, of which Lydia's eldest brother was now the senior partner, dealt almost exclusively with cathedral and town matters.

"Thank you very much," said Mrs. Brandon. "It isn't really a help—except that it *is* a help, if you can understand. You are so kind."

"Bless you, I'd be more than that for you," said Noel, sure of being taken at his exact value, and as their eyes met Mrs. Brandon gave him the same provoking glance that she had given him in her drawing-room eleven years ago and they both laughed.

"I wonder if Peggy and Effie have finished their talk?" said Noel. "I'll go and see. I don't want to be too late as I have to take her to Southbridge and it's out of my way. Have I your permission?"

He stood up, raised Mrs. Brandon's ringed hand to his lips, adumbrated a kiss and restored it to its owner who complacently received it. When he had gone into the house she sat in the pleasant glow that a gentle flirtation induces, till her attention was roused by a horrible noise which was Sir Edmund Pridham's clanking old car, well known throughout the county, which it was the owner's boast to have used ever since the end of the '14 War when he emerged from the army with a permanent lame leg. He stopped in the drive with a horrid scuttering of gravel and came across the grass to her.

"Dear Sir Edmund, how nice to see you," said Mrs. Brandon, for Sir Edmund was her trustee and her oldest friend in Barsetshire and though he had often and uselessly spoken to her for her good as she had never resented it and seldom paid the slightest attention.

"Well, Lavinia, you've seen me all afternoon," said Sir Edmund. "No, not that damfool chair," he said angrily looking at a deck-chair. "You know very well I can't sit down in it and when I have I can't get up."

"I'll get you a proper one," said Mrs. Brandon, "and a drink."

Sir Edmund gallantly protested, but most luckily Rose, who had heard the well-known noise of the car, came out with a tray of drinks and offered to get a wooden chair from the kitchen, such being the kind Sir Edmund preferred.

"Gin, Sir Edmund," said Mrs. Brandon, when he was seated. "Or I have a little of the brandy you gave me."

"You know I never touch gin," said Sir Edmund. "The brandy is all right. Thanks, my dear. Well, it all went off very nicely today and I dare say Parkinson will do. He'll go down well at Grumper's End. Shocking lot of foreigners they've got there in those new council houses. I fought those houses tooth and nail. Shoddy material, built in a hurry. And if the drains all flood back into the kitchens this winter it won't be for want of a warning. But you can't knock sense into anyone's head now."

"Are they Russians?" said Mrs. Brandon.

"Who?" said Sir Edmund.

"The foreigners," said Mrs. Brandon.

"Don't be silly, Lavinia," said Sir Edmund. "Foreigners, I said. From the other side of the county. Poor lot. Well now, Lavinia, I've come to talk sense and I want you to listen."

Mrs. Brandon looked as intelligent as possible and at once began to think of her sitting-room curtains and whether one could get any lining that wasn't quite hideous and outrageously expensive.

"Now. What about Francis?" said Sir. Edmund.

"Francis?" said his mother, coming to all at once.

"You heard what I said," said Sir Edmund. "Now listen, my dear. You've spoilt that boy all his life. You'd have spoilt little Delia only the child had the sense to get married young and make her own life. Are you using your drawing-room?"

Mrs. Brandon said that she had suggested that Francis and Peggy should use it as they liked friends and dancing and she was very happy in her own sitting-room.

"Are they paying you anything?" said Sir Edmund.

Mrs. Brandon said of course not. One could not, she said, indignantly, ask one's own flesh and blood to buy its food in one's house.

"Are they thinking of finding a house for themselves?" said Sir Edmund.

"Well," said Mrs. Brandon with desperate courage. "I have come to the conclusion they aren't. But you see," she added, "they *couldn't* find a house as comfortable as Stories, or a cook who wouldn't mind babies. And I do love the babies."

"H'm," said Sir Edmund. "That nurse of theirs. Is she civil to you?"

"Of course," said Mrs. Brandon.

"And does she let you go into the nursery when you like?" pursued Sir Edmund remorselessly.

"No," said Mrs. Brandon. Sir Edmund said nothing.

"I don't *really* mind," she said. "And when Nannie has her day off Nurse and I enjoy it frightfully. Oh! Peggy says Nannie has given notice. I'd forgotten. I promised her I'd make everything all right and I don't quite see how at the moment. You see, Sir Edmund, Francis naturally doesn't want me to interfere."

"Well, Lavinia, you are as silly as they make them," said her old friend, though not unkindly. "That boy of yours is bone selfish and his wife, nice little woman too, can't stand up to him, and you are the one that suffers for it all. I'm not blind, Lavinia."

"I know," she said and then there was a silence.

"Francis is so like his father," she said. "He can't help it, Sir Edmund."

"Well, *de mortuis*," said Sir Edmund, "though if you can't say what you think of a feller when he's dead, when can you? Listen, Lavinia. This can't go on. Francis is a damned fool, saving your presence, my dear, and if I were ten years younger and he weren't your son, I'd thrash him. He is making you extremely unhappy, Lavinia. I wouldn't say this if I could avoid it, but everyone has noticed it. Now, don't cry. There are two courses open to you and you must choose one. Either you tell Francis he must find a house for his family—increase his allowance if you like—or you must find one for yourself."

"That's what Noel said," said Mrs. Brandon.

"There you are," said Sir Edmund. "Counsel's opinion. He can see as well as I can."

"Francis doesn't need any more money," said Mrs. Brandon. "He is really doing extremely well and as a matter of fact I haven't given him an allowance for some years now."

"First sensible thing I've known you to do," said Sir Edmund. "But I expect their keep comes to twice as much."

"Oh, I never thought of that," said Mrs. Brandon. "Oh dear, Sir Edmund, I am so unhappy," and she began to cry, quite quietly, without making faces or having a red nose, a most rare gift.

"Poor little woman," said Sir Edmund, at which Victorian endearment she had to laugh in the middle of her crying and then cried more than ever, but always quietly.

"Now listen," said Sir Edmund. "This. Can't. Go. On. We've known each other getting on for forty years now, Lavinia—not that you look your age——"

"I was very young when I married Henry," said Mrs. Brandon.

"Never mind that," said Sir Edmund. "Just stop being silly,

Lavinia, and try to concentrate. You know me. I know you. Pridham Hall isn't a bad place. If you will come as its mistress, Lavinia, you shall never have cause to regret it. You can visit your young people as often as you like and as soon as you aren't living together everything will be like a house on fire. Think about it."

"Do you mean *marry* you, Sir Edmund?" said Mrs. Brandon.

"Good God, Lavinia, what do you think?" said Sir Edmund. "Think I want you as a permanent paying guest? If you will do me the honour and I might almost say the pleasure of becoming Lady Pridham, that will settle everything. I'll give you my old mother's bedroom. It's a modern bed but it's all her furniture, good Regency stuff. I'll keep my own room. Other end of the passage. Lock your door if you like. And in any case with my game leg it's not the sort of thing I'd think of. Well, my dear?"

"Thank you a million, million times, Sir Edmund," said Mrs. Brandon.

"That's all right, then, I suppose," said Sir Edmund.

"But I *couldn't*," said Mrs. Brandon.

"Well, my dear, you must please yourself," said Sir Edmund, "and I don't mind saying it's a relief in a way. You are the best-looking woman for her age that I know, but one gets used to one's own ways and living alone. One thing I will do, Lavinia. I'll tell one or two house agents to look out for good houses in the market and let you know. You can't go on being bullied by that boy of yours and your friends won't have it. Well, well, I must be getting along. When do the Millers go?"

"In two or three weeks," said Mrs. Brandon. "It depends on how soon they can get the parsonage at St. Ewold repaired. I daresay the Parkinsons are really very nice."

"I daresay they are," said Sir Edmund, "but not your sort. Well, good-bye, Lavinia. I'll let you know as soon as I hear of a house," and he limped back to his car and drove away.

Nurse then approached across the lawn.

"Excuse me, madam," she said, "but Mrs. Francis's Nannie is

off this evening, so I'm putting the children to bed. I suppose you wouldn't care to come and help?"

Thankful for this complete change from the cares that were oppressing her, Mrs. Brandon willingly followed Nurse to the house. Here, in the nursery where a fair-haired Francis in a green linen suit and a brown-haired Delia in a yellow muslin frock had been eating their tea on the day when old Miss Brandon paid her last terrifying visit, Francis's three divine babies who were as near the same age as makes no odds were the one playing on the floor the other two lying in the play pen wondering what on earth their hands were.

"Well, my precious silly-billys," said their grandmother, "are you going to have your bath now?" to which number one said "Habbarth" and laughed at its own wit, while numbers two and three continued to inspect with bewilderment the five-fingered things that they were waving in front of their faces. The twins were in the bath together, splashing and squeaking with joy when Rose came in, looked benignantly upon the scene and said "It's Bishop Joram, madam. He said was it too late to call on you."

"Oh, ask him to come up, please, Rose," said Mrs. Brandon. "I know he likes children. One must if one is a clergyman or one would never have the courage to christen them," she added to Nurse. "It must be terrifying the first time," and then Dr. Joram appeared in the doorway.

"I hope this isn't an intrusion," he said, "but I am on my way back to Barchester and looked in to tell you how much I admired your embroidery. I heard you were upstairs with your grandchildren and asked if I might see them. And what *beautiful* babies. May I hold one?"

To Nurse's pleasurable horror he took a bath towel from the stand, picked one of the twins out of the bath and began to dry it on his knees, while Mrs. Brandon took number two and Nurse cleared the bath things away. She then resumed possession of her temporary charges while Mrs. Brandon took Dr. Joram downstairs and in her sitting-room they talked about the babies and Dr. Joram's lovely house and the afternoon's proceedings.

"I'm sorry my young people aren't here," she said. "They have gone to the cinema. But if you aren't doing anything, why not stay to dinner? It is only a scratch meal as I'm alone. Unless you *must* catch a train," but Dr. Joram said he was bicycling as it made him so independent and would be honoured if he might stay. This news was favourably received by the kitchen who had already heard from Nurse how nicely the Bishop, as all the servants still preferred to call him, looking upon Doctor as a comedown, managed the babies.

"It'll do Madam good to have company for once," said Cook, "and I'll make a nice omelette and there's plenty of vegetables," to which Rose replied that there was still some of that burgundy and if Cook didn't mind she'd run down to the village on her bike and get an ice-cream block from the shop, for in Pomfret Madrigal closing hours meant nothing at all to those who knew the shopkeepers and shopping went on in a mild way far into the unreal late twilight.

Though Dr. Joram had an excellent cook and butler, to eat a meal alone with an elegant and still attractive woman was a rare pleasure. Mrs. Brandon felt that she was admired and responded to it and looked far younger and less tired than she had of late. After dinner Rose willed them to have their coffee under the Spanish chestnut in the late sunlight and they talked very comfortably about the afternoon ceremony and how much the Millers would be missed.

"And what is so dreadful," said Mrs. Brandon, "is that I know Mr. Parkinson is very low. Not that Mr. Miller is *very* high, but he has what I call just the right kind of highness and Peggy likes it too."

Dr. Joram said that his own tastes lay that way, though the Cathedral was not quite so inclined.

"But don't you think," said Mrs. Brandon, "that being a

Cathedral somehow makes things higher than they are?" which Dr. Joram said was a point worthy of consideration.

"I think I shall have to go to the Cathedral more often now," said Mrs. Brandon, "though I wish the buses were more convenient."

Dr. Joram said sympathetically that he supposed petrol was difficult.

"It's not only that," said Mrs. Brandon, "but I haven't a chauffeur now and I don't drive and Francis can't always be expected to drive me. Besides he often has the car on Sunday and takes Peggy out. But I shall manage. One can hire a car here, but he is usually engaged for long journeys on Sunday."

"Mrs. Brandon," said Dr. Joram. "May I say something which you may not like to hear?"

Mrs. Brandon said of course unless it was anything *very* awful like the nine o'clock news.

"It couldn't be as bad as that," said Dr. Joram. "It is only that your friends, and I hope I may count myself as one, do not like to see you in any way distressed. Forgive me if I say how deeply shocked I have been more than once by your son's attitude and how willingly I would help if I thought anything I could say would be of the slightest use."

"It wouldn't," said Mrs. Brandon. "I know what you mean and I am truly grateful to you, but it is really all my own fault. Do you mind if I talk to you?"

"That is what a clergyman is supposed to be there for," said Dr. Joram, "and I shall feel privileged."

"It is all so difficult," said Mrs. Brandon, emboldened by the gathering twilight. "I am afraid I have been very silly and let things go too far. Noel Merton says I must either find a house for Francis and Peggy, or find one for myself. Sir Edmund Pridham said much the same. In fact," said Mrs. Brandon, suppressing a tendency to laugh as she thought of it, "he offered me a home in his, if the worst came to the worst. He is so kind."

"I am thankful to hear that you have good friends who give

you good advice," said Dr. Joram. "And I hope you will count upon me as a real friend. I would do a great deal for you if I knew how, but the position is not easy. I have no right to interfere between you and your son."

"Well, I really sometimes wish somebody would," said Mrs. Brandon, and what with the excitement of the day and the burgundy and the twilight and the unhappiness and her own sense of humour which was greater than many of her friends realised, she began to cry again, quite silently; yet with a sense of relief.

"Don't cry," said Dr. Joram, taking her hand and holding it very kindly so that she felt she could easily withdraw it and therefore didn't. "I beg you not to cry."

"I won't," said Mrs. Brandon, who to do her justice had done her very best not to. "Thank you so much for being so kind. I think I can manage now."

"And I must be going home," said Dr. Joram. "Or at least to my house, for I have felt ever since I came to the Vinery that it had not quite accepted me. I think, with your help, I might get it to settle down as my real home. But we will not talk of that till you wish."

Mrs. Brandon was silent.

"Have I said too much? Or too little?" said Dr. Joram.

"Neither," said Mrs. Brandon. "May I talk to you again presently. Today has been a little too much for me."

"God bless you then, till we next meet," said Dr. Joram, and then he walked across the lawn, mounted his bicycle and rode down the drive without looking back.

Mrs. Brandon remained under the tree for a while till the air began to grow chill and then she went to bed with a book. Presently she heard her family coming in and there was a tap at the door.

"Good evening, mamma," said her son Francis coming in.

"Did you have a nice cinema?" said his mother.

"Quite good," said Francis. "Cora says we simply must bring you to Gatherum. Any news?"

"Only Noel Merton came for a drink and Sir Edmund," said Mrs. Brandon. "And Dr. Joram came in to discuss the Millers going and stayed to dinner."

"Very nice and dull," said Francis, though quite kindly. "Well, good-night, mamma."

"Good-night, darling," said his mother and retired into her book.

Francis went away and reported to his wife that mamma seemed to have had quite a happy evening with all the old gentlemen. But the Francis of old days would have noticed that his mamma had her mysterious mischief face.

CHAPTER 10

As all amateurs of Barsetshire must know, Gatherum Castle, built by the father of the Great Duke when the Omnium fortunes were at their highest, had probably cost, first and last, something like half a million. A huge stone palace, an entrance hall comparable with Euston Station furnished with marbles from Italy, armour from Wardour Street and old masters mostly genuine and corridors which one agent had computed to cover at least five miles, it had for many years been the bane and almost the ruin of its owners.

The northern seat Matching Priory in Yorkshire had long since been sold to a school. What was left of the Scotch property was let precariously from year to year for the shooting. The Horns, near Richmond, had been requisitioned during the war and was now so surrounded by red brick that the Duke was thankful to let the County Council take it as a Mental Hospital or Loony Bin as the younger Pallisers preferred to call it. As for the Castle it was so huge, so hideous, so inconvenient that to dispose of it was impossible. The National Trust did consider it, but it was impossible for the present Duke to make over the money needed for its upkeep. As for pulling it down it had been calculated by the surveyor and architect that the lead on the acres of roof might just pay for the demolition if any labour were forthcoming to demolish it; which it wasn't. The gardens were a limited company, supplying fruit, flowers and vegetables to the market. The stables had been taken as a warehouse by a large firm of furniture stores and removers. But the house, or mansion, or castle itself remained a nightmare to the family or rather to the Duke and Duchess and their very conscientious elder son, for the younger children including Lady Cora had deliberately or in unconscious self-defence so hardened their hearts that Lady Cora had suggested advertising in *The Times* for a descendant of Guy Fawkes. But the tide had turned, or at least had slackened in this work of erosion, when a few years previously the Ministry of General Interference, anxious to find safe quarters for themselves in the next World War to End War, had taken the Castle, and sent down an army of workmen who had turned it from what had been an extremely uncomfortable if impressive house into a kind of modern and also extremely uncomfortable hotel and office.

Every bedroom had been divided into three or four small rooms about ten feet square by twenty feet high with the vertical half of a window and running water; the wide corridors had been partitioned as offices in a way that made access to the bedrooms extremely difficult; the huge reception rooms had been converted to Social Recreation Rooms and offices for the Higher Officials, and the basement, which was really the ground floor, was now kitchens and canteens of different social grades, with a central heating plant in the cellars. Lord Silverbridge, a studious and conscientious M.P., said that the cost of these alterations would pay a year's interest on the National Debt, but no one believed him, as indeed he did not intend them to do.

In the old servants' quarters, as we have previously said, or think we have, the present Duke and Duchess lived, made a home for their hard-working family whenever it could get a holiday, and worked ceaselessly themselves for the County and for the Conservative Party.

"And what's really marvellous about my people," said Lady Cora to Oliver Marling, who had come to Gatherum Castle by Lady Cora's special invitation to see her ducal father's edition of

Bohun, an edition he had long wished to see and if possible to collate with the 1665 edition which he had rescued from salvage during the war, and what the people in charge of salvage thought it meant, we shall never know, "what is really marvellous about my people is that they know all this is over and done with, but they go on just the same."

"So does my father," said Oliver.

"Oh, but your father is a good half generation older than mine," said Lady Cora. "I do think it is so awkward that the generations overlap. I mean there are so many people that ought to be contemporaries but aren't."

"I think I know what you mean," said Oliver. "In generations I am on a level with my cousin Agnes Graham's children, but I am more like their uncle. I mean they are all under twenty and I'm middle thirties. In fact I might be your uncle."

"Quite easily," said Lady Cora. "Uncles can be younger than their nephews and nieces, like the man who was Vicar of Southbridge."

"But you aren't older than I am," said Oliver.

Lady Cora laughed.

"I'm as old as my tongue and a little older than my teeth, as our nurse used to say," she said. "Thirty to be exact," and why Oliver should have felt the fact of Lady Cora being thirty and he himself thirty-six to be in the nature of a coincidence, we cannot explain. Human nature is a rum affair.

"I don't look it though," said Lady Cora. "I think my American grandmother accounts for it," for Lady Cora's grandfather had married a Miss Isabel Boncassen of New York whose good looks and money had after some heart-searchings been welcomed by his father the Duke of Omnium, he who had been Plantagenet Palliser, and from her there had come into the family an alien strain. But a good strain, alive, untiring, eager for adventure, and with the sense of ancestry combined with an almost total absence of class-consciousness that is often found in old New England stock. "I have her elegant legs and feet," said Lady Cora. "My face is my own."

This was sheer impudence on Lady Cora's part, for no woman's face is her own now. Many of us would be thankful to relax and forget the daily maquillage, but after years of bludgeoning by Germans, by life and by Them, few of us over thirty have faces that stand the light of day, or of night either for that matter, without the assistance of art. And Oliver, who had so long and so often seen Jessica Dean make up her enchanting face for the theatre or for daily life, had few illusions about women's pink and white or sun tan.

"And what about your Caroline Johnny?" said Lady Cora, lightly putting by the question of ages and looks. "Come on, let's look at him." And she led the way along a stone passage to a large mahogany door with gilded handles. "It's frightful luck that we can get into the library from this end of the house," said Lady Cora, "otherwise we'd have to go round simply miles. It's pretty dismal, isn't it?"

And indeed the large room lined with massive mahogany bookcases with gilded grilles to keep the books from escaping, the blinds pulled down, was not very cheerful.

"This is father's Bohun," said Lady Cora, opening a grille and taking out a calf-bound volume. "They're all crumbling to death. We're always meaning to massage them with lanoline, but no one has time and when they have time they're too tired to bother. Is it a good one?"

"Very good as far as I can judge," said Oliver, regarding the calf-bound volume with affectionate admiration. "Do you think your father would allow me to collate it with my copy? There are one or two additional verses and at least one new poem here, as far as I can see at a first glance."

"Are they any good?" said Lady Cora.

"It depends of course whether one is interested in Bohun's metaphysics," said Oliver, in we must say a patronising way.

"Well, one isn't," said Lady Cora. "But one is quite willing to listen. Let's hear one of the new bits."

A heartless, nay an uneducated way of speaking Oliver felt. Yet to a charming woman and one who happens to be the daughter of a duke one may allow much. Much more certainly than one would put up with from that dreadful Frances Harvey who had for a short time tried to make him think he was in love with her and pretended to be interested in Bohun.

"Well, there is a couplet from the poem *To his Mistress on Seeing Sundrie Woorme-castes*, which is certainly not in the first edition, nor in the 1665 edition which I have," said Oliver.

"Let's have it," said Lady Cora, "and then I'll show you the Shepherd's Cottage. What's it about?"

"Well, the poem itself," said Oliver, "is a conceit, comparing the earthen worm casts with the result of the physical union of the Lover and the Beloved."

"God!" said Lady Cora. "Not Talks on Sex for Seventeeners at that date. I thought they were all coarse and Facts-of-Life-ish then."

Even a duke's daughter, Oliver felt, had no right to speak so flippantly, for coarsely he would not say, of a seventeenth-century metaphysical poet. He said coldly, or he meant it to be coldly though even as he said the words he felt his voice was more affected than cold, that the best way to explain Bohun's conceit—conceit he meant in the old sense, not the modern—would be to read her the two additional lines and before she could express her pleasure or displeasure at this offer he proceeded to do so.

"The last lines of the poem in the 1665 edition," he said, "run,

> 'So I, my *Body*'s race through thine b'ing runne,
>   Do void (nor can avoid) th' immortal *Seed*
>   Making (with thine) our true *Effigies.*'"

Lady Cora waited till he had finished and then said it didn't seem to rhyme. That Oliver said, restraining his annoyance as a gentleman should, was because the other words that rhymed with the words at the ends of the lines in the last part were in the first part; and then wondered if he had said what he meant to say.

Lady Cora said like sonnets. And what, she added, were the new lines.

> "'And like th' *Arabian Bird*, self-immolate,
>   So is thy Fowle,'

"I'm sorry," said Oliver, "it's those long esses."

> "'So is thy *Soule* by mine made procreate.'"

He paused, or rather stopped, having come to the end.

"Thank you so much," said Lady Cora in a voice, so he bitterly felt, that she might have used to a child who had recited Who Killed Cock Robin. "It's just like T. S. Eliot and those people, isn't it? Now come and see the Shepherd's Cottage. I asked Mr. Wickham to meet us there and I thought he could take you back part of the way as he always has petrol," for which considerate thought Oliver was genuinely grateful having come by relays of train and motor-bus and not looking forward much to going back the same way, especially as beyond Barchester he would be involved in the after-work rush hour.

Lady Cora took him to the stable yard where her car was standing and drove him, mostly on one wheel he felt with some terror, round the outbuildings to the Lime Avenue. This avenue, planted by the Great Duke's father, ran for a mile north and south from the castle. The noble limes which stood on each side were giants of their kind and up till the 1914 War had been well looked after and pruned and lopped. After 1918 they had been got into order again and by 1939 were the finest example of a lime avenue in England. But now they were alas past recovery. At a distance the effect was still magnificent except for one or two gaps, but at close quarters their decay was but too sadly evident. Dead wood abounded on their heads where no woodman had pruned or thinned. Here and there huge branches had fallen through decay or in a great storm and great jagged splintered boughs pierced the green leaves. The grass verges were wild and rough. Beyond them where the Great Duke's deer used to be seen on the grassland, their elegant dappled bodies almost at one with the sundappled leaves of the woods on the farther side, the land was being put to corn and potatoes, and tangles of rusty barbed wire round shapeless concrete heaps showed where the Home Guard strong points had been.

"It used to be nice," said Lady Cora. "In June one smelt the lime-blossom for miles and the bees hummed like a threshing machine," with which words she accelerated alarmingly and swerved to the left with a violence that terrified Oliver. The side-road which they were now following ran across the fields into the woods beyond and gradually mounted with the rising ground till they came out into an open space where Mr. Wickham's well-known disgraceful car was sitting by itself.

"I expect he's gone to the cottage," said Lady Cora. "We'll go and look."

She led the way up a green drive which gradually narrowed to a green path meandering among the trees. Suddenly the trees stopped, the ground in front of them fell rapidly away and below them lay a large dark pool, on the farther side of which two figures were standing. The hill behind, the trees all round, the precipitous rocks in front with the pool at their feet, the shadowy woods beyond, the two figures by the water, gave Oliver so astounding a shock of romance and hidden beauty that he was quite incapable of words.

"Grandfather made it, the one that married an American," said Lady Cora. "There is a spring in the pool. It never runs dry and is cold, cold, cold. There's Wicks," and she went down the narrow path where loosestrife grew shoulder high and brambles lay in wait to tear.

"Hullo, Cora," said Mr. Wickham. "I brought Miss Dale."

"But of course I know Isabel," said Lady Cora. "We meet on

more committees than I like to think of. What is Eleanor Norton doing with the Hospital Libraries?" and the two ladies fell into professional talk as they disappeared into a path among the trees.

"Women all over," said Mr. Wickham. "They'd sooner talk to each other than to a man now. Isabel's a fine girl. So is Cora. Croix de Guerre. Not that I think much of these French decorations myself. Those Johnnies always want to kiss you and that gets my goat. You know the man Isabel was engaged to was in the same regiment as Silverbridge, her brother that is. Have you seen the cottage? Come on then."

He led Oliver to the path by which the ladies had gone. It wound among bushes and trees and after fifty yards or so came out in a little clearing, through which a small cheerful streamlet ran towards a little cottage.

"This way," said Mr. Wickham and Oliver followed him to the cottage gate. The garden must once have been a pretty sight but was now overgrown. The door was open. In the one living-room Lady Cora and Isabel Dale were standing by the little window in talk.

"Look out," said Mr. Wickham. "You'll be in the water."

He laid a hand on Oliver's arm who, confused by the sudden gloom after the sunlight, was on the edge of the small cheerful streamlet which ran in its narrow channel right across the living-room and so away again into the forest.

"Carasoyn!" said Oliver. "I didn't know it could be true."

"We were all brought up on George Macdonald," said Lady Cora, "and my elder brother and I always wanted to be the shepherd's little boy with a stream running through the cottage. My father had this cottage built for us when we were small and sometimes for a great treat we were allowed to sleep here in the summer. It made Nurse livid because we didn't have sheets, only blankets, and she said it wasn't nice for young ladies and gentlemen. But we never saw the fairy fleet come past. *All* my children will be brought up on his fairy stories—if one can get them."

"We have some at home," said Oliver. "I didn't know anyone else read them now."

"I do," said Mr. Wickham. "I used to think the woods near my old home over Chaldicotes way were the woods in Phantastes and I frightened my mother into fits by saying the Ash was putting its hands through the window to catch me. I never knew what it all meant, but what the dickens does it matter what things mean?"

"How right you are, Wicks," said Lady Cora. "And anyway you can make them mean anything if you try hard enough."

"It's like that man at Oxford or somewhere who writes books about Fredonia—no that's the Marx Brothers—anyway Something-landia," said Mr. Wickham, "where the land goes up and down in waves all the time like the sea and somehow it's all very religious. If he'd ever been forty-eight hours in a high sea steaming round and round and the galley fires out and feeling as sick as a cat, he'd feel religious all right. Which reminds me, I've got a new gadget. Pocket flask for parties."

He took out of his pocket a kind of small size Thermos whose top when unscrewed turned out to be four small cups or beakers. Into each of these he poured something from the flask and handed a cup to each of his friends.

"Well, here's more and lousier governments," said Mr. Wickham, draining his cup. "Do you like the mixture?"

As his three friends were for the moment speechless, with a delightful sensation of hot lava flavoured with spirits, Mr. Wickham tilted the flask and drained it.

"Wicks's Number One," he said. "You won't get that once in a blue moon. An old pal of mine Pinky Smith, you wouldn't know him, man with a lump on the back of his neck, sends me some rum from the West Indies from time to time. One hundred per cent pure cane sugar. And now, what about a spot of tea, Cora, before we go home?"

They retraced their steps through the wood and up the hill and drove back to the Castle, where the Duke and Duchess and their son were having tea in what used to be the housekeeper's room.

"You know Wicks," said Lady Cora to her mother. "And this is Isabel Dale who was working with Sally Pomfret and this is Oliver Marling. You know his sister married Mr. Adams."

The Duke, a tall middle-aged man with a drooping mustache and a gentle bewildered manner, who seemed very kind but rather vague, asked Oliver if he was in Parliament and Oliver had to say he wasn't and wondered why he should feel slightly ashamed of the fact.

"I know, I know," said the Duke. "It's difficult to find a safe seat now. I think Silverbridge ought to fight Adams whenever we have a General Election, only it costs such a lot."

Lord Silverbridge said if his father would find an American heiress for him he would begin canvassing at once, and then he talked to Isabel Dale about the Barsetshires while Oliver listened to the Duchess's troubles with her Grade A dairy herd and her difficulties in getting proper canvas for her embroidery.

"My mother-in-law," she said not without pride, "embroidered seats for every chair in the big rooms, which of course are all shut up now, and I belong to the Friends of Barchester Cathedral Embroidery Guild. We are refurnishing all the choir stalls from special designs by Professor Lancelot, you know, the man who unearthed the mural paintings in Pomfret Madrigal church, though unearthed is not quite the word. Do I mean disinterred? I should like to show you the cushion I am doing and then the Duke would like to talk to you about a book that Cora said you were interested in. Have you ever played games with her?"

By this time Oliver was so overpowered by the Duchess's flow of talk that he had not the faintest idea what she meant and wondered in a bewildered way whether she suspected him of having tampered with her daughter's affections.

"She gets it from the Duke, not from me," said the Duchess. "She always guesses anything like charades at once. Do you act?"

Not at all, said Oliver, convinced that Her Grace would at once make him dress up and perform in a charade if she thought he could act and he rather wished he were at home again. But his fears were groundless and when she had shown him the portraits in stump stitch done by her husband's grandmother and the water-colour drawings of Alassio done by her husband's aunt Mary, she handed him back to the Duke.

"Cora tells me," said the Duke, "that there is a book in the library which interests you. Let us go and look at it."

They went back to the library. The Duke looked round and asked which book it was and when Oliver had shown him the bookcase he unlocked the elegant gilded grille.

"How annoying," said the Duke. "I had honey with my scone and I'm a bit sticky. I ought to have washed my hands first, but we haven't a cloakroom near the library. I'm always saying to the Duchess we ought to have a cloakroom at this end. It's useful you know, but we can't afford it. It might interest your father to know that there are two miles of copper piping in the Castle and we can't get hot water. All choked up or furred or something. The Ministry of General Interference are putting in a new hot-water system and they have promised to extend it to our quarters. I shall ask them if they can put a cloakroom in that little lobby outside. Would you like to see it?"

Oliver would far rather have examined Bohun again but common civility forced him to say he would.

"It's this way," said the Duke, opening a door masked with books. "Take care, it's rather dark. We were going to have Gatherum re-wired just before the war and now we can't run to it. I am going to ask the Ministry if they can put some lights here. This is the awkward corner. Do take care. Let me see, the light should be about here."

The click of a switch was heard and an unshaded bulb of about ten candle-power sprang into a depressing yellow light.

"There, you see what an awkward corner it is," said the Duke, as indeed it was, for the passage which was in any case almost pitch dark took a hidden turn to the left and then to the right again, giving anyone ignorant of its meanderings an excellent chance of stubbing their toes and cracking their forehead.

"This is a most curious thing," said the Duke, pointing to the large projecting piece of wall. "There's something inside there and no one knows what. In the original plans it is marked as The Duke's Bathroom, though why he wanted a bath on the ground floor next to the library I don't know. It must have been walled up at some time and none of the old people about the place know anything about it. Now I wonder if you will agree with me. I should like to have this wall taken down and a cloakroom put here. Of course I can't with things as they are, but it would be most convenient to have a cloakroom here, as then one could wash one's hands. It really wouldn't be difficult as the kitchen is just beyond. Would you like to see it?"

Oliver did not in the least want to see the kitchen, but from politeness to his kind harassed host he said he would love to. So the Duke went round one more corner and opened a door.

"Mind the steps," he said to Oliver, "I can't think why there are steps here, it's most awkward. Are you there, Lily? Lily, this is young Mr. Marling. His father sits on the Bench with me sometimes and his sister married Mr. Adams the Member for Barchester. Lily has been with the family since she was a girl, Marling, and I don't know how we'd get on without her."

"You wouldn't get on at all, your Grace," said Lily, an elderly woman in black with her gray hair strained off her forehead and steel-rimmed spectacles. "There's no one here but me understands the Begum cooker, your Grace. And I wish your Grace would speak about the coke. Dreadful stuff it is and if the Begum gets full of clinker it's more than I can do it get it out. Great lumps as big as a football."

"I'll speak about it, Lily," said the Duke. "How's the sciatica?"

"Dreadful, your Grace," said Lily. "I remember when I was lady's maid to Lady Mary Palliser, her ladyship went off in agony for days at a time. My mother said it was catching and I oughtn't to stay, but my poor lady depended on me so much. 'Lily,' she used often to say at three in the morning when I got her a fresh hot bottle and gave her her sleeping stuff, 'I don't know what I'd do without you.' Well, she's dead and I've got the sciatica. We've a brace of nice partridges for dinner, your Grace."

The Duke said that was good news and they said good-bye to Lily.

"Excuse me," said Oliver and then was stricken dumb, for he had never before met a duke at close quarters and though the present duke of Omnium was as gentle and unalarming as could be Oliver was not sure whether to say Duke would be too familiar or your Grace too pompous.

"I've let the shooting of course," said the Duke, "but they are a decent lot and often send in something. These are our first partridges. What were you saying?"

"Only—if you don't mind," said Oliver, "I think we are going the wrong way for the library," at which the Duke apologised.

"Do you know," he said, "I often forget and go up the passage as if I were going to our old rooms. Habit, I suppose, for we are really very comfortable where we are. I must apologise for being so absent-minded," and he anxiously hurried back to the library.

"I like those doors with books on them," said Oliver.

"Do you?" said the Duke. "So do I. I'll tell you what I did. The books on the door were terribly out-of-date. A lot of them were sermons and homilies and there was a History of the Manichees in fourteen volumes. They were in rather bad condition too—this door used to be used a great deal—so I took a very bold step. I had them all taken off the door and had new ones put on."

"What fun," said Oliver, to whom the Duke now seemed a very pleasant easy host and rather touching in his enthusiasm.

"Wait a minute. I'll pull up the blinds and you can see for yourself," said the Duke. He pulled the cords. Two blinds rushed up to the top and jerked themselves to a standstill and the afternoon light poured in.

"Dickens," said Oliver, examining the backs of the books. "Thackery, Trollope. How much nicer than homilies."

"Ah!" said the Duke, "But have you looked at them."

Oliver looked along a shelf at eye level.

"Oliver Twist, Our Mutual Friend, David Copperfield," he read. "Edwin Drood, Altered Circumstances; that doesn't belong in this shelf."

"It does though," said the Duke. "There's Dickens's name on it," and sure enough at the bottom of the spine was the magic word Dickens. "Just look at my Scotts."

Oliver, a little puzzled, looked at two fine rows of Scott's novels, mostly in two volumes.

"They look very nice," he said. "Flodden Field? I had never heard of that book."

"Nor had I," said his Grace, with the engaging candour of a schoolboy who has been caught cheating. "But I thought it would be nice to have a few new books by the authors one loves. I sometimes almost believe in them and think that if these books were real and not just gummed into the door, I would have the fun of reading them. I have a nice Thackeray called Hearts and Clubs and a Trollope called Why Did He Love Her. I assure you I almost believe in them. As you see the bottom shelf is not finished. I couldn't think of any more titles just then."

Oliver said quite truly that it was the nicest way of filling a shelf he had ever seen and he was quite sure that if one went into the library at midnight one would be able to take the books from the shelves and read them.

"I quite agree," said the Duke gravely. "But I do apologise, my dear boy, it was my Bohun that we came to look at. Here it is," and for the second time that day Oliver had the precious book in his hands.

"How did you come to be interested in him?" said the Duke and Oliver explained how a friend had saved his copy from being sent away with the so-called salvage to be pulped and how he had gradually become more and more interested in the Canon of Barchester.

"If you don't mind, I should like you to keep it," said the Duke. "I should never read it and as for selling you can't get much for books now. I did have a man down from London, but he had a poor opinion of my books. He said he admired them as part of a country gentleman's library but they were worth very little. He suggested another dealer which was very friendly of him so when I was in London I went to see him, but when I showed him the catalogue he said much the same. So I took the Duchess to the theatre to make up for the disappointment. You know, or you will know when you are older, that when you lose money or don't get the money you had hoped to get, the best way to comfort yourself is to spend some. We went to a very amusing play with Jessica Dean in it. Have you seen her?"

Oliver, hoping it didn't sound boastful, said he knew her very well and her husband.

"Do you?" said the Duke, evidently much impressed. "Well now, I have a suggestion. When next the Duchess and I are in town, will you come to the theatre with us and take us behind the scenes to visit Miss Dean? It would be most exciting for us both. And in return, as a very small return, will you accept the Bohun from me. I should like a scholar to have it."

A present so offered could not be refused. Oliver did not bandy words with his Grace and accepted at once with real gratitude, at which moment Lady Cora came in.

"Come along, Oliver," she said. "Wicks is waiting for you. He's taking Isabel Dale back too. Silverbridge is showing her the book he's writing about the Barsetshire and Wicks will be hopping mad in a minute. He always wants to do everything at once. Always did."

So they all went back to the room where they had had tea and the Duke told the Duchess that Oliver knew Jessica Dean quite well and was going to take them behind the scenes when next they were in London and Oliver told the Duchess about her husband's kindness.

"You must write Mr. Marling's name in it, my dear," said the Duchess, which the Duke willingly did.

"May I offer you something in return, Duke?" he said, almost stammering over the title but glad to have tackled it at last. "If I may I would like to add a book, or at least a book-back to the library door. May I give you one?"

The Duke appeared to be delighted and asked Oliver what author he would choose.

"Might I, if it isn't impertinent," said Oliver, "call it Rare and Curious Books by the Duke of Omnium?" At which suggestion the Duke was enchanted and the Duchess looked approving though she evidently did not quite understand.

"And now young feller-my-lad," said Mr. Wickham, "come along. Where's that girl?"

"I'll get her," said Lady Cora and so the two men made their good-byes and went out to Mr. Wickham's disgraceful car.

In a few moments Lady Cora was back with her brother and Miss Dale who were both rather quiet. Miss Dale got into the front beside Mr. Wickham, Oliver got into the back seat with some sacks, a good deal of loose iron, an empty wine crate, a brace of rather bloody partridges and a large tyre and wished he hadn't got his best grey flannel trousers on. The moment when a pleasant visit is over takes different people differently. Some will go on talking about it, remembering or laughing or criticising till midnight. Others, as if exhausted by the social effort, will fall as silent as they have hitherto been loquacious and entertaining. Oliver had enjoyed the visit but preferred to drive in silence. Mr. Wickham who had after tea looked up several old friends in cottages about the place and distributed one or two of his store of bottles was cheerfully talkative.

"Silverbridge is a good fellow," said Mr. Wickham. "His little lot were near us in Italy. What's his book going to be like?"

"I don't know," said Miss Dale. "I think a book about a

regiment is rather dull for people who aren't connected with it. But I liked it. The part about the fighting in Italy was exactly like some of John's letters. I'm lending them to him. And there's a nice bit about the Navy."

"I said he was a good fellow," said Mr. Wickham, much gratified. "I'll take him over a bottle of whiskey one day soon. Was he near John when he was killed?"

This conversation was, Oliver felt, quite intolerable. How could Wickham open old wounds in so heartless a way.

"The Duke was very kind," he said. "He gave me a book I hadn't got."

"Better than giving you one you had got anyway," said Mr. Wickham over his shoulder.

"Yes. He was with him when he died, which was quite quickly," said Miss Dale as if Oliver had never spoken. "It's a good thing to be sure of that. And he saw him buried. It was all rather comforting."

"John would have liked that," said Mr. Wickham. "Good girl," and he patted her hand in a fatherly way. Oliver, who could not help from the very uncomfortable back seat seeing and hearing all that went on in front was revolted by this display of indifference and thought very poorly of his companions, and directed waves of disapproval at their backs, but as they were entirely interested in their own conversation so were they entirely unruffled by his attitude.

At Marling Halt Mr. Wickham dropped them and they walked up to the Hall, Oliver to his annoyance having to carry a bottle of liqueur whisky, a respectful offering from Mr. Wickham to Mr. Marling whom he described as the old codger.

At dinner Mr. Marling, who was delighted by the present, made what his son considered an unnecessary fuss about the whisky and insisted on offering it to everyone. This was a time-honoured ritual. It was part of Mr. Marling's code that the best one had should be offered to guests and he got, as far as one can tell, equal pleasure whether they accepted or refused. What particularly annoyed his son Oliver was that on these occasions his father would sometimes treat him as a schoolboy and imply to the company that good drink would be wasted on him.

"You don't drink whisky, my dear," he said to his wife, "so I won't offer you any. Miss Dale?"

"Rather," said she. "Thank you very much," and she drank a sip of it with a bow towards him.

"To your bright eyes," said Mr. Marling with what his son considered senile lechery, but Miss Dale seemed pleased and bowed to him in return, at which Oliver's opinion of her went down several degrees. Mrs. Marling, observing them all in her usual aloof though kindly way, was pleased to see her husband enjoying himself with a good-looking girl and wondered if her difficult Oliver would ever grow up properly.

After dinner Miss Dale played picquet with Mr. Marling while Mrs. Marling wrote letters and Oliver made notes from the new Bohun rather ostentatiously.

"Nice time at Gatherum, my dear?" said Mr. Marling. "I've not been there for years, but I see the Duke on the Bench occasionally. What's Silverbridge like now?"

"Very nice," said Miss Dale. "He was in Italy with the regiment and is writing a history of it and I am lending him all John's letters. Lord Silverbridge was there when he was killed, and he says that he died very quickly. You can't think what a relief that was. I had very kind letters from other officers but one knows that sort of letter, just trying to be kind. Lord Silverbridge is the first one I have met personally who was with John and now I feel safe. Forgive me. I have misdealt."

"That's all right, my dear," said Mr. Marling. "You're a good girl and a plucky one. I miss my Lucy, but you are a great help to Amabel and me."

"And so are both of you," said Miss Dale. "To me I mean. Shall I deal now?"

As no one noticed that Oliver was making notes, or if they did saw no necessity to make any comment, he soon went to bed.

*   *   *

When Mr. Wickham's little car had clattered away Lady Cora took her brother's arm and they walked round their wing of the Castle to the formal gardens, now in a very poor state of repair, where Lady Cora had sown nasturtiums in the place of bedded out plants; and very pretty the golds and reds and oranges of the nasturtiums had looked, but now they were only straggling greenery. Beyond the formal garden was the Maze, copied from the well-known prehistoric labyrinth up on the downs at Maze-field, cut in the green turf probably more than two thousand years ago and still kept clear with its white chalk paths by the Barsetshire Archaeological Society supported by local enthusiasts. But at Gatherum the paths were green turf with walls of box: or had been, we should say, for the turf was now chiefly mossy earth and the box trees were thin with age and unchecked growth.

"Come on," said Lord Silverbridge. "First right, second left all the way and sixpence if you get to the middle."

"Do you remember when we acted Fair Rosamond and Queen Eleanor?" said Lady Cora, "and Gerry was Fair Rosamond with Grandmother's second best wig and how angry her old maid Parkin was."

"And old Parkin is still alive with a whacking pension and likely to remain so," said Lord Silverbridge and they both fell silent for a time. For Lord Gerald Palliser had been killed on D-Day, enjoying every moment till the very end.

They had now reached the centre where a rickety seat with the paint peeling off invited the explorer to a precarious repose, and here they paused.

"What a nice girl Isabel Dale is," said Lord Silverbridge. "I wouldn't risk that seat, Cora. I'll see if I can get it patched up. She is letting me look at her John's letters from Italy and I think she may give me a hand in other ways. Which Dales are they?"

Lady Cora said she thought the Allington lot. The ones that married one of the Thornes with pots of money, though we know she was wrong, for the money had come through the rich

Miss Dunstable who had left a considerable fortune to her niece Mrs. Bernard Dale, and though Miss Dunstable had become Mrs. Thorne in her middle age, the money was all hers. But these things are forgotten.

"Well, there won't be pots now," said Lord Silverbridge. "And what's more, if there's a General Election this year I don't see how I can afford to stand again. Why didn't you nobble that man Adams, Cora, the one that the Marling girl married?"

"I might have if I'd known him," said Lady Cora, not in the least meaning what she said. "Come on, Jeff, let's come and do some Gilbert and Sullivan before we go melancholy mad."

The so-called theatre at Gatherum was the old laundry, a large room built in the days when the Castle kept a Head Laundress and three underlings in full employ. The American troops had built a platform across one end, put in quite good lighting and rigged up a proper curtain, all of which they left behind when they went away. One wall was occupied by a row of washing tubs, but the huge coppers were luckily in the next room and the rest of the floor was available for an audience or for dancing, and here it was that Lady Cora proposed to perform one of Aubrey Clover's little one-act plays with Francis Brandon. That the performance was to be in aid of the local Conservative Association is neither here nor there. Lady Cora wished to appear on a stage, not for the first time, and that was that. Below the platform was an upright piano, exiled from the disused schoolroom in the Castle, and at this piano Lord Silverbridge seated himself, and began to play dance music with the velvet touch and impeccable rhythm which heaven so often sees fit to bestow on those who are entirely unmusical in the classical sense, and as he played he also sang with the kind of heart-rendering voice that two singing lessons infallibly ruin.

"Thank God you can't dance," said Lady Cora to her brother. "If you could I'd murder you," which words he took exactly as they were meant and slid into the intricacies of a rumba.

"I wish we could do one for the Conservative Association,"

said Lady Cora, not implying any disrespect for that respectable institution, "but I don't know if they'd stand for it. Hullo, Dr. Joram!" and in came the former Colonel Bishop.

"I was over this way on professional business," said Dr. Joram, "and thought I would call at the Castle and when I heard the piano I simply couldn't resist it. Please go on, Lord Silverbridge."

"Call him Jeff," said Lady Cora, while her brother, who had not stopped playing nor had the faintest intention of doing so, nodded to Dr. Joram and continued to make passionate his audience's sense of hearing. "It's his name, so he can't help it, Bishop," for it amused her ladyship to use from time to time the address to which he was still entitled. "Can you dance the rumba?"

Dr. Joram said he was very sorry he couldn't. He had, he said, learnt with some measure of success the Mnganka-mnganka but the rhythm of the rumba was beyond him, he feared.

"*Do* teach me the Whatsitsname-anka," said Lady Cora, "and then we could dance it for the Conservatives."

"I should be delighted to teach you," said the Bishop, "but it is I fear quite unsuitable I won't say for you, because you are above suspicion——"

"She can't scare and she can't soil," sang Lord Silverbridge in an abstracted way but very distinctly, using the romantic words of Richard Hannay (now and for ever, we believe, Brigadier-General Sir Richard Hannay with many letters after his name) about his future wife.

"I just couldn't bear to be like Calpurnia," said Lady Cora. "She must have had a ghastly time with Caesar."

"—but," continued Dr. Joram who being used to prolonged comments in Mnganganese from his ebony flock took not the slightest notice of this private outburst, "but for anyone."

"Why?" said Lady Cora.

"Prurient mind, Silly but kind," sang her brother to an unseen audience.

"Shut up, Jeff," said Lady Cora.

"To dance it correctly," said Dr. Joram, "requires at least twenty male dancers with horns and tails, stupefied with a native drink and carrying the body of a ritually sacrificed hippopotamus cub."

"And that, my girl, is that," sang Lord Silverbridge.

"I'm sorry," said Lady Cora, with a simplicity that touched Dr. Joram. "We ought to know better. In fact, we really do, but—oh well, things, and Them."

Dr. Joram, whose charity was deep, wide and understanding, felt compassionate admiration for these gallant supporters of a dying civilisation living so often behind a mask of flippancy, and had no wish to criticise.

"If I were the Bishop of Rum-ti-Foo," he said, "I would even land, My leg supported in my hand, to give you pleasure. But as a Canon of Barchester——"

"I'm sorry, Dr. Joram," said Lady Cora, and touched his coat sleeve lightly as a kind of token of apology. "Let's have some Gilbert and Sullivan, Jeff," and for the next half-hour they enjoyed themselves excessively. Lady Cora was willing to sing any female part, missing out the notes that were too high for her, Lord Silverbridge obliged after the manner of Mr. Frank Churchill with a slight second and the Bishop turned out to have a light baritone voice which didn't mind singing tenor though, like Lady Cora, ignoring the high notes. And while they were all thus a-merry-making the Cat and her Kittens came tumbling in, in the shape of Mr. and Mrs. Francis Brandon.

"Cora darling, I'm so sorry we're late," said Mrs. Francis. "Difficulties with Nannie, as usual. You know she gave notice."

"But I thought she'd taken it back," said Lady Cora.

"She had. But then she gave it again," said Mrs. Francis, "and I'd forgotten this was her afternoon out, so it was all rather awkward."

"Poor lamb," said Lady Cora. "Never mind, you're here now.

Sit down and relax with Dr. Joram while Francis and I do our number."

So Mrs. Francis sat on a hard wooden chair against the wall and Dr. Joram on another and he made sympathetic enquiries about her domestic troubles. For though the Church of England does not hold with confession (except for the amiable eccentrics whom She in Her wisdom keeps within Her fold) any good clergyman knows, just as all intelligent people know, that the one thing your friends want to do is to talk about themselves and that when they say "Now darling," or "old fellow," as the case may be, "I want to hear all you've been doing since I last saw you," what they mean is "Just wait while I put on a bit of lipstick" or "light a cigarette" as the case may be, "and then I'll get going about myself."

"I wouldn't really mind looking after babies myself a bit," said Mrs. Francis, "only Nannie won't let me except on her times out and then she *has* to."

Dr. Joram said wasn't Mrs. Brandon's old Nurse a help.

"Oh Nurse is very kind and *adores* the babies," said Mrs. Francis, "but lately Nannie has taken to being jealous of Nurse and behaves as if Nurse would poison their food or drown them in the bath, and then Nurse is Offended and you can't think how awful that is. And Francis doesn't quite understand and it annoys him rather if I'm not free when he gets back from work."

With most women any criticism of a husband to another man, even to a clergyman or perhaps even more to a clergyman, is a danger light and Dr. Joram was quite aware of this fact. But he understood a good deal about human nature and he thought Mrs. Francis's complaints were not so much to gain sympathy for herself as a kind of fluttering effort to make her own mind clear to herself and he could not help feeling a certain compassion for this pretty creature whom life had evidently got between its fingers at the moment and was pinching severely. But he could not say this, so he quite wisely suggested that Mrs. Brandon was the proper person to deal with these difficulties.

"Oh, mamma is *always* kind," said Mrs. Francis, "and we talk about it and she says she will make it all right and I'm sure she will, but——" and then she paused.

Dr. Joram knew as well as if she had spoken the words that Francis was the difficulty. Francis who was very well off, who found the comfort of his mother's house more attractive than a house of his own, who could use his mother's car but did not think of her need of it, who enjoyed gallivanting about the country and doing theatricals with Lady Cora (for so he put it not very kindly to himself) and at the same time demanded his wife's presence who was not taking part, though a few years earlier it was she who was the theatrical star. Who—and then Dr. Joram checked his thoughts, for not only were they uncharitable but they were true, which was a horrid thing to contemplate.

"So," said Dr. Joram, very kindly, "I expect Mrs. Brandon is doing nursery maid at this moment."

"Yes," said Mrs. Francis. "And she said not to bother about supper if Lady Cora asked us to stay, because it was Cook's evening out and mostly cold. I expect Francis would like to stay."

And so, thought Dr. Joram, must the late Captain Arbuthnot often have liked to stay when the society was attractive to him if not to his charming wife, for he had heard a good deal about Mrs. Francis's first marriage from her sister-in-law Mrs. Crofts, wife of the Vicar of Southbridge. He felt compassion for this pretty affectionate woman who seemed almost damned in attractive husbands.

Francis and Lady Cora were now doing Aubrey Clover's Argentina Tango on the rough stage, dipping and swaying in effortless ease, as he and Mrs. Arbuthnot had dipped and swayed three years ago, at the Barchester Red Cross Cabaret and fête while Lord Silverbridge sang the foolish words as he played, drawing rhythmical ecstasy from the old schoolroom piano.

"I remember with pleasure how charmingly you danced that at the Red Cross Fête in Barchester," said Dr. Joram.

"But I wasn't married then," said Mrs. Francis with great

simplicity, which words pierced the kind Bishop's heart and made him feel in a most un-Christian spirit that he would much like to deliver Francis to his local witch-doctors, whose methods with neglectful husbands were alarming and ninety-nine per cent successful.

"What delightful babies you have," he said, at which Mrs. Francis bloomed again visibly. "I am so sorry about those domestic troubles. But I am perfectly sure Mrs. Brandon will manage something. I have a great respect for her and her kind heart and her abilities," at which promises, vague though they sounded, Mrs. Francis looked much comforted and her own pretty affectionate self.

"Well, I must be off," he said. "I only looked in because I heard the piano. Good-bye and God bless you." He then went over to the piano and asked Lord Silverbridge to make his excuses to Lady Cora which his lordship, never ceasing the intricate measure of the Tango, promised to do.

"Lovely!" said Lady Cora when the music came to an end. "But I wish I'd see you do it, Peggy. You wouldn't give me a lesson, would you?"

"Oh, but you do it beautifully," said Mrs. Francis, who was almost speaking the truth.

"Come on, Peggy," said Francis, slightly over-excited by the dance though Lady Cora had not always been quite rhythm-perfect, for the rhythm that runs from head to feet and must remain rigid yet supple through each swoop and bend of the Tango is not within everyone's power.

So Mrs. Francis went onto the platform, thinking how lucky it was that she was wearing her one New Look summer dress, for in her old ones she would have found the dance less easy. Lord Silverbridge after marking the rhythm with his left hand only while he smoked part of a cigarette began to play very softly the haunting tune and the dancers moved into its spell. Lady Cora had few illusions about herself. She could dance as well as most, but Mrs. Francis's Tango was of professional level. Not for a moment she knew could she move as Mrs. Francis was moving. She recognised at once that Francis was dancing better with his wife than he had with her and with quick generosity she acknowledged that hers was but amateur's work.

"Look here, Francis," she said when the dancers, after keeping their last attitude delicate porcelain for a moment, came to life as ordinary people, "You'll have to do that Tango with Peggy. She knocks me into a cocked hat and what's more she shows you up far better than I can," at which words Lord Silverbridge, still at the piano, gently played the theme-tune of Glamora Tudor's very successful film *Renunciation*, in which she had as La Gioconda told a Pope (unspecified) that now he was Pope she would for his sake never again know Love and after having her portrait painted by Leonardo da Vinky, or sometimes Vinsy, had gone into a convent and taken eternal vows, supported by twenty glamour-nuns and the Mighty Wurlitzer playing Schubert's *Ave Maria*.

"Shut up, Jeff," said Lady Cora. "I really mean it."

"If you really think so," said Mrs. Francis, "of course, I'd simply love it. What do you think, Francis? Of course, there are the babies and what with Nannie giving notice——"

"Oh, mother will see about all that," said Francis. "It's a thing I'd never have thought of, Cora, but if you really say so and it's most charming of you, I'd love to have Peggy."

"Of course I think so," said Lady Cora firmly. "Peggy is ninety-nine per cent professional and I'm only gifted amateur daughter of Duke. Never mind. I've got my lovely legs," and she exhibited one of those perfect and elegant objects.

"Never mind," said her brother mockingly. "We'll have a leg contest at the Conservatives Do and you shall win. I'm delighted, Peggy. You'll make twice as much effect, Francis," with which flattering words he glanced at his sister who glanced back at him and slightly contracted her right eye.

"I'm afraid we really ought to be going, or mamma will be quite sick of the babies," said Mrs. Francis and so much impressed was her husband by her success that he agreed without a murmur and they went away.

"I must be off too," said Dr. Joram. "I left my bicycle against the big copper."

"Oh, stop to supper," said Lady Cora. "It's only cold partridge but we've heaps of garden veg and they manage some sort of ice with our Jersey milk."

The Bishop was persuaded and came back with them to the Castle where the Duke talked to him at some length about his experiences with Oliver Marling. Dr. Joram was enchanted by his Graces's description of the door with sham books in the library and asked if he might contribute a volume.

"How very kind of you, Bishop," said the Duke. "I do value your encouragement. I think it would be a delightful plan to ask one's friends if they would name a book. Of course I should not expect them to give it, as Mr. Marling is so kindly doing, but a suggestion of a name would be a great help. Now, what for instance do you think your book would be called?"

"I haven't really considered," said Dr. Joram. "It should, I suppose, be something connected with my work, but nothing comes to me at the moment."

"I might suggest," said the Duke diffidently, "though I know my ignorance of such matters, a title which might be taken as an allusion to your change from a Colonial Bishopric to a Canonry in the Close. Do you think that The Bishop's Move would be a good name?"

The whole company, though all with a vague feeling that someone else had used this title or something exactly like it before, agreed that this was an excellent idea and Dr. Joram looked gratified.

"And if you will allow me," he said to his host, "it would be a real pleasure to present it to you for your collection," and the Duke said he could only accept with gratitude so kind an offer, and after supper he took Dr. Joram away to see the masked door and discuss the size of the new book, while the Duchess used the late daylight to do some weeding and Lady Cora and her brother watered the vegetables, for the long dry summer was becoming a menace to gardeners.

"I can't help feeling sorry for Peggy Brandon," said Lord Silverbridge.

"Try," said his sister. "The one I'm sorry for is Isabel Dale. She is so reserved that one feels it must hurt her, and she never talks about herself."

"Doesn't she?" said Lord Silverbridge. "She talked to me quite a good deal this afternoon when we were going over the regimental records. Really, Cora, I sometimes wish I hadn't taken on the job. I see no end to it."

"Of course you don't at the moment," said Lady Cora, "but you will. Why don't you get Isabel to help you? I'm sure Mrs. Marling wouldn't mind."

"I might," said Lord Silverbridge. "John was an extraordinarily good fellow. I'm glad old Gerald wasn't in the Barsetshires. I couldn't have written about him."

"How he would have laughed if you had," said Lady Cora.

CHAPTER II

A few days later Isabel Dale was helping Mrs. Marling with her letters as usual. When all the county and parish and Women's Institute and other business had been cleared away, Mrs. Marling looked with relief at the pile of neatly typed envelopes.

"Thank you, my dear," she said. "I wonder how much a year I spend on postage. I have sometimes thought that if I could do something for the King like saving him from a mad bull and he were kind enough to ask me what I would like for a reward, I would ask to have all my letters franked. But I don't suppose They would allow even His Majesty to do that."

Miss Dale said she was sure They wouldn't and she would very much like to know whether They paid for Their letters.

"It is extraordinary how little one knows about Them, or indeed about anything now," said Mrs. Marling and we are inclined to agree with her.

"I'm sorry to bother you," said Isabel Dale, "but I'm afraid it looks as if mother were going to be ill again."

"I am very sorry," said Mrs. Marling, not thinking of herself as much as of Isabel. "Is it something serious?"

"It is one of those illnesses that doctors won't give an opinion about because they haven't really the faintest idea what it is," said Miss Dale. "Something inside and it flares up and goes away and is very painful. And short of keeping her doped the whole time which they won't do, they can't do anything. One wouldn't mind so much if they would *say* they don't know. In fact," said Isabel, who not usually very expressive seemed to be finding comfort in letting herself go for once, "they behave exactly like the Government, though of course," she added hastily, "mother employs her doctor privately otherwise he'd be able to do even less for her than he does."

"My dear, I am so very sorry," said Mrs. Marling.

"You see I am the only one," said Isabel, "so I'll have to go. It's pretty depressing at Allington now. The Great House needs young people and fun and poor mother sits being gloomy and ill and lonely and complaining that I neglect her though when one does go she bites one's head off all the time."

It was rare for Isabel to express herself so unreservedly and Mrs. Marling felt she was suddenly seeing a new person. Not the competent matter-of-fact secretary-friend, but a woman, for girl one could not say though heaven knew unmarried women went on being girls till they were more than middle-aged nowadays, who had known unhappiness and had resolved to bear it without demanding sympathy.

"You're like an old lady in the village, my dear," she said, "who was fond of saying that you had to be happy without happiness because there wasn't any."

"I don't know," said Isabel, which brought that particular bit of the conversation to an end. "And about Oliver's book," she continued, "I said I would type it and it's rather fun, but it is not a life's work."

"What do you mean, my dear?" said Mrs. Marling.

"Well, he seems to have been working on it for several years," said Isabel, "and there still isn't enough of it to make even a small book, not by twenty thousand words at the very least."

"I never thought he would get even as far as that," said his mother, not unkindly, but with the complete disillusionment that a loving parent can feel without loving her child the less. "In fact I really don't know *where* he will get."

"He seems to do very well in London," said Isabel. "I mean I hear that from other people, not from him."

"Yes, I believe he does," said his mother, "and he has never come upon us for a penny apart from living here, which of course we love him to do. And all the more since Lucy was married."

"Is it partly Jessica Dean?" said Isabel, to whom at different times Oliver had confided or may we unsympathetically say rather boasted about his hopeless passion, a passion which seemed to her to be deliberately nourished when it was really a sinking flame.

"A few years ago I would have said yes," said Mrs. Marling. "Now I'd say no. Of course he never talked to me about it, and I must say I wouldn't have known quite what to say if he had. One's children are so awkward."

"So my mother says," said Isabel. "And I'm afraid she's right. I was just getting not awkward when John was killed and there I was back in my mud hovel like the fisherman's wife."

"But not shut up in your private, personal hovel, like my poor Oliver," said Mrs. Marling. "You have been very good for him, my dear. Without Lucy there is no one to laugh at him. I don't mean laugh," she added, thinking that her dear Lucy had not any great sense of humour, "but to make him fell less important. It's all very well for him now with Marling for weekends, but when my husband dies his elder brother will have the property and though they are great friends it isn't the same thing."

"Poor Oliver," said Isabel, not unkindly. "I'm sorry for him. If you don't need me this afternoon I'm going over to see Mr. Wickham. Saturday is his best day and Lord Silverbridge is coming over. He's writing the War History of the Barsetshire Yeomanry and Wicks was near them in Italy. Where John was killed," she added. "We are doing a sort of collaboration."

Mrs. Marling, lucky in a soldier son who had come through the war unscathed and her difficult Oliver who had been turned down on account of his eyes and his general physique at once, could all the same feel real sympathy for those whose menfolk had not returned. Many, too many of her contemporaries, had lost sons or beloved young grandsons and she knew more than one girl who would probably never marry now. It might be that Isabel Dale was one. It was inevitable that she should think of every not so young girl as a possible wife for Oliver and she had wondered about Isabel. But it was now abundantly clear that Oliver looked upon her as a nice useful girl who would type for him in her spare moments and as for Isabel's view of Oliver and his great work on Bohun it was but too plain. Well, at least Oliver was not always running after girls which men of his age were sadly apt to do and heaven, she had noticed, always looked after bachelors even when they were getting rather high in the forehead and rather thin on top, for maternal love had never managed to overcome her detached attitude to her children.

In a car one could get to Mr. Wickham's house in about half an hour. By railway with one change to a train that did not always connect, or by two motor-buses with a wait of nearly half an hour for the second, one could get there in an hour and a half with luck and if it wasn't market day. Miss Dale preferred the train from Marling Halt, for the railways though now British, a word forced on them to destroy as far as possible their individualism, still have a fine solid English flavour in the provinces and the older men, like Mr. Beedle so long the stationmaster at Winter Overcotes, still speak of The Line, counting all other lines as naught. At Northbridge Station she found Lord Silverbridge.

"Wicks told me you were coming," said Lord Silverbridge, opening his car door, "so I thought I'd tell the Government I had to fetch some guano from Barchester for the bailiff, which was perfectly true, and then I could come on to Northbridge, so that I could use my petrol. And while I was in Barchester I bought a card index. You know, a kind of what-not with very long drawers and you put A to C and X to Z on them and write things on cards and then don't know where you've put them."

Isabel said she had had exactly the same experience at the Barchester Hospital Libraries.

"But I really got the better of them in the end," she said, as St. Paul may have mentioned Ephesus. "If it would be any help I could easily show you how they work."

Lord Silverbridge thanked her with what she felt to be disproportionate gratitude.

"You know," he said, "no of course you don't know, why should you, that I'm in a publisher's office from Monday to Friday turning a fairly honest penny and all the card index stuff is done by a secretary. The other day she was out and I wasted hours looking for one of our authors called Spenderton-Cook because she had put him under E."

Isabel said it must have been a mistake.

"As a matter of fact it wasn't," said Lord Silverbridge. "At least not exactly. His name is Evan-Spenderton-Cook and sometimes he hyphens them all and sometimes he doesn't. But I thought the secretary could have done a kind of cross-indexing if that's the right word and put them in under everything. She's one of those educated young women that are obviously going to bully their employers all their lives till they marry one of them. Only it isn't going to be me, because it would annoy my parents and I should find it perfectly revolting."

"Would your people mind who you married?" said Isabel.

"I never asked them," said Lord Silverbridge, "but I don't think so. I mean they would like a lady if possible and of course a little money would not be unacceptable. When father dies pretty well everything will go I'm afraid, but one would like to be able to live near Gatherum because one knows all the people and one could give them a hand sometimes when they can't understand all these Government forms. Not that I understand them myself, but I could find someone who does, which they don't know how to do, poor devils."

Isabel asked which publisher he was with.

Lord Silverbridge said with Johns, Mr. Wickham's uncle. Johns had quite a good list, he said, and was specialising in good novels including thrillers.

"He has some of the plums," said his lordship. "He has that man that wrote *Crackajack and When You Are Dead, Little Finger.* And he does Mrs. River's divine books about Middle-Aged Women Inspires Passion in Pink Undergraduate. They sell like hot cakes. Her husband is a cousin of Pomfret's and some kind of relation of my mother's. And of course Lisa Bedale. I believe she's a man in disguise. She's got a brain and she's extremely funny."

"But why couldn't a woman be like that?" said Isabel.

"I really don't know," said Lord Silverbridge. "I suppose what I mean is I haven't met one."

"John knew her," said Isabel, half wishing, half reluctant to disclose herself as the ordinary person she was.

"Did he?" said Lord Silverbridge, interested and a little curious. "No one at the office has seen her except Johns himself. We wonder at the office if she is Mrs. Morland under another name. Authors do that sometimes, don't they? Only I don't quite think she can be, because her books are more educated than Mrs. Morland's, at least I don't mean that."

"You mean what the lower orders have now learnt to call sophisticated," said Isabel.

"Not quite that either," said Lord Silverbridge. "I mean all her people have characters of their own. One could quite well meet them in real life if one were lucky enough and though I'd love to meet Mrs. Morland's I don't think I'm likely to," and then they had arrived at Mr. Wickham's house and the conversation came to an end as their host came out to meet them.

"Now mind, nothing to drink till we've finished whatever it is we are supposed to be doing," said Mr. Wickham, leading the way into his extremely comfortable bachelor sitting-room.

"Tea, yes, if Bell would like it, but that's the limit," he added, as if his guests had already been clamouring for alcohol.

"You said Bell," said Miss Isabel Dale.

"I've blotted my copy-book again," said Mr. Wickham. "I'm sorry, Miss Dale. John always spoke of you as Bell."

"Oh, I didn't mean to sound annoyed," said Isabel. "It was only that no one calls me Bell now and it reminded me. It was after an old great-aunt or something who was always called Bell, short for Isabel, and John liked the name."

"Isabel. Bell," said Lord Silverbridge, aloud to himself. "I do beg your pardon, Miss Dale," he added, suddenly coming to with a jump. "I was just wondering which name suited you better."

"Please use whichever you like," said Isabel. "I rather like Bell from real friends because of John, and you both knew him."

Mr. Wickham said everyone called him Wicks, which was true in the larger sense though not perfectly accurate.

"Then will you please say Jeff," said Lord Silverbridge. "It's a silly name, not even Gee-off, but we've always had a Jeffrey about the family. I've really forgotten how this conversation began. Shall we look at your notes, Wicks?"

Mr. Wickham, whose methodical ways of business always surprised people who had thought of him only as a kind of superior bailiff with a talent for drink, had arranged all his material on a table by the window. His war diary, kept somehow from day to day, some photographs that he had no business to have taken, various scribbled notes and printed orders and in his surprisingly neat writing a précis of the whole landing operation from the naval end.

"You'll find that covers the landing more or less," said Mr. Wickham. "Our chaps threw in the heavy stuff on the Eyeties good and proper for an hour and then your chaps went in with planes in support. Casualties pretty high but they got the beach-head and kept it. Half of us were thanking our stars we weren't on the beach and the other half were cursing the Captain's head off because he wouldn't let us land too. Of course the Old Man was right."

"We were terrified," said Lord Silverbridge. "I don't think I've ever felt so frightened in my life and at the same time I didn't care. If I had been killed then, there was still Gerry to carry on. Then we ran up the beach to get some shelter among the bushes and a lot of our fellows dropped some bombs about a hundred yards ahead of us and while the Italians were picking up the pieces we made a dash for them. Just there," he said, pointing to one of Mr. Wickham's illegal snapshots, "where that bush is. That's where John was. He couldn't speak and he died almost at once, but he didn't look unhappy. That's all I can tell you, because we had to go on."

"Thank you very much," said Isabel. "And you too, Wicks. And now," she continued, "if you get your card index, Jeff, I'll give you a lesson. It isn't really difficult," and Lord Silverbridge went out to the car to fetch it.

"Lisa Bedale had a narrow escape just now," said Isabel and she told Mr. Wickham about her conversation with Lord Silverbridge in the car.

"Why don't you tell him?" said Mr. Wickham. "He'd be as pleased as Punch," but Isabel could not see, nor we admit can we, any valid reason to believe that Lord Silverbridge would be any the happier for knowing that she wrote detective stories and in any case he was back with the card index cabinet almost at once. Isabel found, as she rather expected, that his ignorance or incapacity was much less than he made out and very soon her pupil had in Mr. Wickham's words got the hang of the thing quite nicely.

"Now we'll have some tea," said Mr. Wickham, putting all his notes and photographs into a large envelope which he handed to Lord Silverbridge. "You'd better have these, Jeff. Let me have them back when you've finished with them. I shan't be long," and he went into the kitchen, whence the sound of a cork being drawn afforded an indication that tea would soon be ready.

"Wickham has some nice books," said Lord Silverbridge, looking at his host's bookshelves which filled almost the whole of one wall. "I see he has all his uncle's publications. Here's a complete set of Hermione Rivers, and old Lord Pomfret's book, and those dreadfully historical books of Mrs. Barton's. And Lisa Bedale! He's got one I haven't read. *Hot Cross Roads*. Have you read it?"

Without waiting for an answer he took the book from the shelf and opened it. Mr. Wickham coming in about five minutes later with a large tray on which were a teapot, several bottles and the rest of the paraphernalia of tea, found one of his guests standing by the bookcase absorbed in a book and the other with a look of mingled pride and nervousness on her face.

"That's all, I think," said Mr. Wickham, putting the tray on the table where the plans had been. "Will you pour out, Bell? Come on, Jeff, tea!"

Lord Silverbridge turned and came to the table, the book still in his hand.

"Not on your life," said Mr. Wickham, taking it away from him. "I may be a beggarly agent, but I was brought up properly. Never take a book in your hands when there's butter about. Your father wouldn't stand for that kind of behaviour. Crumbs are nasty things to find in a book. So's a long hair. But butter is permanent. What will everyone drink? There's beer and gin and bitters and a nice Marsala I got the other day from old Joe Hodgkins, you'd remember him, Jeff, he was with the Barset-shires in '43 and played a very pretty hand of bridge. If there were five aces in the pack he always had the fifth, that kind of fellow, but a good sort once you knew his ways. Well, here's his health," and he drank the greater part of a glass of beer in apparently one gulp, while Isabel poured out tea for herself and Lord Silverbridge and presently Mr. Wickham's employers the Noel Mertons looked in. Noel and Lord Silverbridge were acquainted in London but Lydia had never met him and made an unconscious and immediate conquest of him by her interest in his work on the Barsetshire Yeomanry in which her beloved younger brother Colin had served during the war. And as Mr. Wickham and Noel had to say a few words about a cattle sale, Isabel found herself with no one to talk to and told herself, not for the first time, that it was, and would always be, her lot to be an onlooker. Her heart had not broken when John was killed. She was well, she could say without vanity that she was not bad-looking, she was a successful writer in secret, but she was terrifyingly conscious of the nothingness of being alive, well, and almost famous though under another name. This was not patent to her friends with whom she was just Isabel Dale (there had been a time which she tried to forget when she was "Poor Isabel—too sad about John, you know," but this had passed, with other and greater troubles in the world). A certain number of people said Why didn't that nice woman Isabel Dale get married, which was really almost as bad as living with her mother. And then she blamed herself for not being able to get on with her mother and her thoughts went squirrelling round in her head as they had done a thousand thousand times till they were interrupted by the entrance of a clergyman of the peculiarly firm and unbending stoutness which so often goes with the quarter deck, wearing a cassock.

"Hullo, Tubby," said Mr. Wickham. "You are the chap I wanted. I've got some Marsala I'd like you to try. You know everyone."

"Not quite," said the clergyman addressed as Tubby, smiling at Isabel, upon which Mr. Wickham hastened to introduce to Miss Dale Father Fewling; priest-in-charge at St. Sycorax in Northbridge, who had been in the Navy during the first war and risen to the rank of Commander before he entered the church. "And one of the best," said Mr. Wickham enthusiastically. "What he doesn't know about rum would go into a thimble."

Father Fewling declined for the moment anything stronger than tea, so Mr. Wickham suggested that they should look at his garden and then come back for a spot. Isabel said she would love to see the garden only she must keep an eye on the clock because of her train. Lord Silverbridge said he might as well be hung for a sheep as a lamb and as he had the petrol he would drive Isabel home with pleasure. Mr. Wickham said that was a nice way to talk about a girl at which Lord Silverbridge looked rather uncomfortable, which made Isabel feel uncomfortable too, and Lord Silverbridge picked up the book that Mr. Wickham had taken away from him and was so absorbed by it that he did not follow the others into the garden.

Mr. Wickham's garden had no special features of interest, being a lawn with a flower bed on one side and a gravel path on the other, but his vegetables were famous and it was these that his visitors were requested to admire. Noel and Lydia Merton were enthusiastic about the beautifully kept borders and the exquisite regularity of the rows. Even the green vegetables in spite of the long drought were fresher than other people's, which Mr. Wickham ascribed to his old gardener's patience in loosening the soil and watering by hand.

"We can't last much longer," he said, referring to two gigantic rain-water barrels which stood against the back of the house, "but we've not done too badly. Would you like some figs?" and while he picked the figs, the purple and the white, Miss Dale and Father Fewling, not great garden enthusiasts, strolled down the garden path.

"There is one thing I really covet here," said Father Fewling. "If you will come round this corner——" and he led her past the kitchen garden to the far angle of the little estate. And here, built against the mellow red brick wall, was a brick garden-house of two stories. The lower was a tool-shed. The upper was approached by a flight of brick steps built against the wall and a brick balustrade and at the top of it was a small room with a door in one wall and a window in each of the other three. Two of the windows overlooked the garden but the third looked over the world outside, across a field away to the distant downs. Below was a well-trodden path leading to the village allotments.

"It makes me think of Elisha and the little chamber on the

wall," said Father Fewling. "And a crow's nest too," he added rather wistfully, for the Navy still held so large a place in his heart that he sometimes blamed himself for it; we think unnecessarily.

"You were a sailor, weren't you?" said Isabel.

Father Fewling said yes, in the last war; he meant the first war.

"I expect you miss it," said Isabel.

"Well, I sometimes do," said Father Fewling, "though I try not to. But now and then, do you know, I can't help wishing that I had waited till I was a Captain and had read the Service on my own quarter-deck. Not even the Archbishop has done that."

Isabel said sympathetically that it must be almost like being the Archbishop and the King in one.

"It is," said Father Fewling, pleased with her enthusiasm. "Is yours a Service family? Wickham told me you were helping Lord Silverbridge with his account of our Yeomanry."

"Oh, no," said Isabel. "My people are just Barsetshire with a little land. But the man I was going to marry was in the Yeomanry. He was killed in Italy, in a landing."

"I am very sorry," said Father Fewling, who was used to these sudden confidences and sometimes said with a kind of rueful self-depreciation that he supposed it was because he wore petticoats.

"So was I," said Isabel. "I wondered so much about him. But I have been lucky. Lord Silverbridge was there and he saw John and told me that he died quickly and didn't look unhappy, which is all that really matters. He would tell me the truth, wouldn't he?"

Father Fewling assured her that he would.

"And Wicks was there in his ship," said Isabel. "And somehow—I know it's ridiculous—I feel that John was safer with the British Navy there, even if they couldn't save him. I can't explain what I mean. It seems worse to be killed inland, though I know it's silly to think that."

"Not silly at all," said Father Fewling. "I think I can truthfully say that all through the last war, or first war or whatever you like to call it, I was never afraid when I was at sea. But once or twice—there was a landing-party I remember and an air raid while we were in dock—I was terrified out of my wits. One knows that God's hand is everywhere but I am sure it is nearer at sea than on land, although I am a priest. And I am certain that it was better for your John that the Royal Navy was at hand even if it could not protect everyone. I almost think," said Father Fewling, "that one could die more happily among the ships than in any other way, or near them with the waters that no human power can alter or control in sight. It is the sort of thing one feels but can't explain. I am talking too much. Shall we go back to our friends?"

"You have saved my life," said Isabel with great simplicity, and they went down the mellow red brick stair with a hollow in each step where the feet of generations had passed. "I wish I could thank you."

"You have," said Father Fewling.

At the bottom of the stairs they met Mr. Wickham and the Mertons and returned together to the house where Lord Silverbridge was standing by the sitting-room window reading.

"What's the book?" said Mr. Wickham.

"*Aconite at Night*," said Lord Silverbridge, "by somebody called Lisa Bedale. There's a delightful detective called Gerry Marston. I've just got to where he goes to see the old lady at Platt Farm and when he turns round she has gone out of the room and the door has closed of itself and looks exactly like the rest of the panelling and then he thinks he'll get out of the window but two panels come sliding out of the wall and lock and there he is. And I'm pretty sure," he continued, looking hurriedly through the next few pages, "that there's a furnace in the cellar below and that's where Paul Stone's body is and they are trying to cremate him too."

"I've read that one," said Father Fewling, "and I shan't," he added with a manner far from Christian, "tell you what the clue to the villain is because you ought to have spotted it."

"Well, *I* didn't spot it," said Noel, "and I'm a lawyer."

Father Fewling, again with a sad want of charity, said reading Blackstone didn't solve thrillers and probably the more law you knew the worse detective you'd make and doing *The Times* Crossword Puzzle was a far better sharpener for the intellect and he would bet Noel sixpence that Lord Silverbridge wouldn't guess the villain.

"I'm your man," said Noel, bringing some coins out of his pocket. "Here's the sixpence. My sixpence I think."

"It's Claud Masker," said Lord Silverbridge. "That bit about the table with the pretence drawer should have told you."

"Well, if it had it would have told me wrong," said Noel. "Look at the end. It's Frank Mulliner."

Lord Silverbridge turned the pages rapidly.

"You're quite right," he said. "But then the bit about the table is wrong," to which Noel, who could now afford to be generous said it didn't do to examine thrillers too closely.

"But the bit about the table *isn't* wrong," said Isabel. "The pretence drawer had a keyhole and a key, only there wasn't a lock so no one could open it. The real drawer had a key and a keyhole and no lock too but you could open it by turning the handle like a screw only the wrong way round. I know it's all right because our old carpenter——"

She stopped. Mr. Wickham was looking at her in amused sympathy. The other disputants, neglecting the question of the sixpence, were looking at her too.

"Then you," said Noel, whose reputation as a lawyer seemed to the audience to be at stake though he had never touched criminal law, "knew the secret all the time."

"Well, yes," said Isabel. "You see——" but before she could say whatever it was she was going to say, Father Fewling said, "I know. I don't do *The Times* Crossword Puzzle for nothing. Anag. Lisa Bedale. Isabel Dale. But I hope you don't mind."

"I couldn't, after what you said," said Isabel, who did not mean his exposure of her but the comfort he had given her in the upper chamber upon the wall. "It doesn't really matter much. I only thought it would be fun to pretend to be somebody else. Mrs. Morland knows and Wicks knows and you all know now. Only please don't tell people unless you happen to forget which it is so easy to do." And what with excitement and a kind of triumph in suddenly appearing as a best-selling thriller to friends she liked, her eyes began to prickle and for twopence she might have cried had not five o'clock sounded from the tower of Northbridge Church across the fields.

"Is it only five?" she said.

"It's six all right," said Mr. Wickham. "Mr. Villars won't have the church clock altered for summer time because the works are old and the man who looks after it says it might do it harm."

"But it couldn't hurt to put the hands *on*," said Lydia.

"O.K.," said Mr. Wickham. "But come winter time or ordinary time or whatever you like to call it, you'd have to put them back or else let the clock run down till the proper time caught it up again, which would make the Golden Number and Easter get out of gear wouldn't it, Tubby?" to which Father Fewling said rather wistfully that as St. Sycorax hadn't got a clock he hadn't much considered the subject, and then the party dispersed.

As Lord Silverbridge drove back to Marling he said he hoped she had not minded the discussion about her book for no one had had the faintest idea that it was hers, and speaking for himself he would like her books just as much whether they were hers or not; at least, he added, he didn't really know, now that he knew her.

"I really don't know yet what I *do* think," said Isabel, who had just tasted her first draught of personal fame and found it unexpectedly pleasant. "I suppose it was what people call escapism. I must say it has been extremely nice to earn extra money because a hundred a year doesn't go far."

Although the Pallisers were all very badly off in comparison with what they had been, no one of the family had yet had to think of life in those terms and Lord Silverbridge was horrified.

"But that's less than two pounds a week," he said. "How do you manage? Forgive me, I don't mean to be inquisitive, but I can't understand."

"If your mother were like mine, you would," said Isabel. "I believe she is really rather well off but she doesn't like giving me an allowance. I lived on my pay in the war and now I am earning more money in royalties every year, not much, but steadily. Mrs. Marling is giving me three pounds a week for living at Marling and helping her and she is as kind as she can be. If mother is really ill again I must go back to Allington which I shall loathe. And that's really that."

Lord Silverbridge said something sympathetic, but his whole mind was occupied by the speaker, not by what she was saying. Something had happened to her. She was a different woman from the Isabel Dale he had picked up at Northbridge Halt. What he did not know was the effect on Isabel of suddenly finding herself a slightly romantic heroine instead of that nice, steady Miss Dale. To hear real people whom she liked discussing her thrillers and talking about the characters and the action as if they were real was an intoxication not known to those whose success has been easy and seen by the eyes of the world. It had been her own wish to be anonymous, fearing a failure and the inevitable criticism of her family. If John had been alive— but John was lying in Italy and her heart was numb. Now quite suddenly it was alive again. People whom she liked and trusted had given her the last mortal news of John. The same people had talked about her books as if they were real and she had felt the happiness of a little fame. And perhaps the talk she had with Father Fewling about the Royal Navy had helped as much as anything, for somehow the Royal Navy stands for a great many other eternal values, some of which she had doubted or forgotten in the long twilight of her unhappiness.

"Do come in for a moment and see Mrs. Marling," she said, so Lord Silverbridge came in with her. They found Mrs. Marling at her writing table as usual, fighting the ever-rising tide of her letters.

"May I bring Lord Silverbridge in?" said Isabel. "He kindly drove me back from Northbridge."

The Marlings had never been acquainted with the Omniums except when the men met on the Bench from time to time, and Mrs. Marling was pleased to see the future Duke. For though she had not a daughter to marry she was quite ready to be interested in the family who had once almost ruled West Barsetshire, though there were lesser families, Thornes, Pomfrets, and even perhaps Marlings, who had deeper roots, some, if the Thornes were to be believed, going back to the Heptarchy. She saw the heir of the once magnificent dukedom and felt that England was not in so bad a plight. And then, for she had been brought up to try to speak to people about their interests rather than her own, she asked Lord Silverbridge how his book about the Barsetshires was going, to which his lordship replied that it was going pretty well and Miss Dale was showing him how to use a card index and Mrs. Marling who knew her county very well was able to supply one or two bits of information, after which, in pursuance of her instinct to talk to people about their own interests she asked him if he was thinking of standing for Parliament, for it had been a tradition in the old days that the heir should represent either West Barsetshire or the borough of Silverbridge.

"I would like to," said Lord Silverbridge, "but we can't afford it. When the Silverbridge of that time was put up everyone voted for him because he was who he was. In fact I believe that when one of them changed his politics and became Conservative the borough put him in just the same. Now it means a nasty contested election and lots of money. I wouldn't mind the fight but my father couldn't put up the money, nor could I."

Mrs. Marling said it was a great pity and she hoped some day it might be possible, but this though a true hope was they all knew a vain one.

"As They raised Their own wages and are talking of raising them again," said Isabel, "perhaps They will pay all election expenses," which Lord Silverbridge said was quite probable only They wouldn't do it for him. And then Oliver came in, down from London for the weekend as usual and Lord Silverbridge asked after Jessica Dean whom he had met more than once in Oliver's company.

"She and Aubrey are going to America for the autumn," said Oliver. "They are taking Sarah Siddons and her nurse and the faithful Miss M. and letting their flat at an exorbitant rent to the Mixo-Lydian ambassador. Jessica says she will use it as an Abode of Love, but Miss M. says she will come back a week before they do and see that everything is nice and clean. And if the Mixo-Lydian ambassador so much as leaves a lip-stick mark on a teacup I wouldn't be in her shoes for something," said Oliver, who always felt that the qualified approval which was all Miss M. gave him was on the whole more valuable than the Order of Merit.

"Her?" said Lord Silverbridge.

"Yes, it's a woman," said Oliver. "I thought only the Americans had women ambassadors, but I was wrong. By the way I haven't forgotten the book I promised the Duke for his bookcase door. I'm having it specially tooled with a ducal coronet and the Palliser arms. I hope he won't think it a liberty," to which Lord Silverbridge replied that he felt sure his father would like it of all things because he loved crests and armorial bearings and was too shy or too proud, or both, to make much use of them.

"I sometimes wish," said Lord Silverbridge, "that he could have a pair of golden boots and silver underclothing," but only Isabel took his allusion and if the Marlings thought he was eccentric he really didn't mind and asked Oliver how he was getting on with the Bohun poems, on which interesting subject Oliver talked for several minutes.

"Of course," he said, "it isn't the sort of work that will attract much attention, but it will be a small contribution to English literature. The Duke's edition has a variant of the *Sonnet on his Mistress's Pox* which no one else has noticed."

Lord Silverbridge who had caught Isabel's eye and knew he might have a fit of the giggles if he were not careful asked what it was.

"Oh only a minutia," said Oliver carelessly and before he could continue Isabel said how funny minutia sounded.

"Why?" said Oliver rather coldly.

"I don't know," said Isabel, with perfect truth. "I just don't happen to have heard it in the singular before. I know minutiae."

Lord Silverbridge, interested in this question from the point of view of words, said he rather agreed though, he added, seeing a look of grave displeasure on Oliver's face, if there was a word called minutiae it stood to reason there must be one called minutia, or where was the Latin Grammar?

"It's here all right," said Isabel who had been looking in the Concise Oxford Dictionary.

"So are lots of other words," said Lord Silverbridge, suddenly bitten by an unreasonable desire to score off Oliver. He gently took the book from Isabel and opened it at random. "There's naker."

"It sounds like a person who nakes, whatever that is," said Mrs. Marling who was not altogether sorry to see her son being teased, for much as she loved him she had watched with a maternal mixture of love and irritation his growing disposition to take himself seriously, and thought that perhaps his family, rather tired of what his elder brother Bill had unsympathetically called "Oliver's faithful dog act" with regard to Jessica Dean, ought to stand up to him more.

"Or," said Isabel, "it might just be somebody saying 'an acre'," to which Lord Silverbridge said that was exactly what he had said and after a second of hesitation saw what she meant and couldn't help laughing at himself, which laughter Oliver chose to take as directed against him personally and said Oh well, it didn't matter.

"Well, what is the variant, darling?" said Mrs. Marling, skilfully avoiding the disputed word. "Will you put it into your book?"

"Oh, something very slight," said Oliver, already a little ashamed of his manners. "My edition has 'Who mounts on Venus' mount sore plagued may be,' whilst the Duke's edition has 'more shotten he'."

"They both sound very unpleasant," said Mrs. Marling. "Of course shotten is in Shakespeare. Falstaff calls himself a shotten herring. I never knew what it meant and I really don't suppose there is any need to. Oliver dear, give Lord Silverbridge some more sherry," but Lord Silverbridge said he must really be going as Cora had a rehearsal for her Conservative do and he was washing-up so that she could get away directly after supper.

"You see," he said, with engaging candour, "our woman who cooks is really very good but she has her husband and children to look after as well, so we usually wash up after supper to make it easier for her."

Everyone understood this state of things and said of course he must go. So he thanked Mrs. Marling for letting him come in and hoped she and her husband would come over to Gatherum some day. "And thank you again for showing me that card-index business," he said to Isabel. "Could you come over again next week?"

An arrangement was made and he went away. Mrs. Marling returned to her everlasting letters while Oliver and Isabel went out and like almost the whole of Barsetshire weeded and watered in the long border to supplement the labours of the old gardener and Ed Pollett the useful man. Oliver was still rather sulky and knew he was, which did not make it easier to stop.

Isabel felt sorry for him and asked if the Duke's Bohun would mean much extra work on his book.

"Not very much," said Oliver. "I had really broken the back of it, but of course these last-minute discoveries mean one has to rearrange a good deal. In fact I think I shall have to rewrite Chapter Three."

Isabel rashly said What a pity as she had just typed it in triplicate for him.

"Is that three times as difficult?" said Oliver, in the easy voice of a grown-up who is laying a snare for a child, but Isabel who saw trouble looming said it only took a little longer to arrange three pieces of paper and two carbons and make the typewriter bite without letting them slip, and she could easily put in his corrections as an extra page, numbering it something *a* or even something *b* if it was longer.

"I don't want to be a nuisance," said Oliver, implying that he was determined to be one, "but don't you think an intercalated page or two would rather spoil the effect, from the publisher's point of view I mean? He might find it easier to read if the pages ran straight on."

"Not a bit," said Isabel. "They don't worry about that sort of thing. I always do it myself," and that, said to herself the Isabel who since the teaparty at Northbridge felt such blessedly re-newed confidence that life was still worth living and risks worth taking, may make you think. But it takes more than that to make selfishness open its eyes and Oliver merely repeated, with an exasperation that he half tried to conceal in an almost offensive way, that in so small a work as his one had to be most meticulous about such minutiae, at which reappearance of the disputed word Isabel could not help a very friendly amused laugh and Oliver suddenly had to laugh too.

"I apologise," he said. "I believe I have been rude and selfish. I really won't do it again. Will you forgive me?"

"Of course," said Isabel, disarmed as any generous nature

always must be by an apology. "And I'll do the whole chapter again. It won't take long."

Oliver offered her an earthy hand with nails blackened by weeding to which she responded with a wet and almost equally dirty hand.

"And now," he said, determined to make up by every means in his power for his previous sulkiness, not to say downright rudeness, "I would like to tell you my idea—only an idea, an adumbration, of course, for my final chapter. A kind of knitting together of all the strands which so strangely started him—what revolting alliteration. Sorry. I mean to try to show the essential trend of his genius from first to last. And when I say genius I don't mean genius. I mean———"

"I know," said Isabel in perfect good faith, "you mean genius. Only not that kind of genius."

"I had better stop talking altogether," said Oliver ruefully. "I mean the last chapter will be a bit like the end of Proust; Le temps retrouvé," to which Isabel, who was on the verge of having the giggles, said weakly that would be very nice.

"So," said Oliver returning with the perseverance of an ant to the road from which he had been deflected, "could you really re-type that chapter for me?"

"Of course I will," said Isabel. "Though I do assure you publishers don't mind an intercalated page or two. I give mine lots and he never minds in the least."

"Your what?" said Oliver. "I mean who do you give lots of to?"

"Why did you bring that book I don't like to be read aloud to out of from up for," said Isabel, at which Oliver stared. "Redundant prepositions," she explained kindly. "I mean my publisher doesn't mind if I stick in an extra page here and there so long as they are numbered or lettered so that they can be followed."

"But why do you have a publisher?" said Oliver.

"To publish my books," said Isabel, always in the grip of the unaccountable unwonted happiness that had been with her since tea with Mr. Wickham.

"But what books?" said Oliver. "I'm afraid I don't understand."

"Oh, I don't suppose *you* would have read them," said Isabel,
meaning we are afraid rather basely to flatter Oliver, "they're
only thrillers."

"That is *very* interesting," said Oliver, "because" and Isabel
wondered what further admiration might be waiting for her,
"because," he continued, "now you can help me with my book
about Bohun, tell me what publishers want and all that sort of
thing."

Isabel was but human. She had done a good deal for Oliver
and stood a good deal from Oliver, because she liked his father
and mother and indeed liked him too in many ways. That he
should not have read her books was reasonable, nor did she
expect his parents to have read them, but that because she
had told him she wrote books he should at once make even
larger demands on her time and her typewriter seemed to her
unreasonable.

"I can tell you one thing," she said, "your book will have to be
at least twenty thousand words longer if it is to be a book at all,"
but no sooner had the words passed her lips than she wished
them unsaid, so completely taken aback did Oliver look.

"But I couldn't. I mean there's nothing more to say," said
Oliver. "Are you *sure*, Isabel? I've been working on it for ages—
though of course that doesn't make it any longer," he added
thoughtfully. "I'm afraid I've been rather a fool. And a bit
selfish," he added. "And now I'm being a masochist," he said
angrily, to which Isabel replied that she had often read the word
but never heard anyone say it.

"But I'll tell you what," she said, unconsciously using the
words that Oliver's dear Lucy would have used, "couldn't it be an
opuscule? You could get it printed by the *Barchester Chronicle*
and publish it privately and give copies to people you liked. You
don't *need* the money do you?" she added anxiously, for she knew

that often people who look well dressed and have an atmosphere of ease have not much loose cash.

"Luckily I don't," said Oliver. "I mean one would always *like* more money but I earn quite a satisfactory amount. How much do you think the *Barchester Chronicle* would charge?" but Isabel said she hadn't the faintest idea and really he must do some work for himself.

"I might give a copy to the Duke of Omnium," said Oliver. "And one to the Dean, and the Barsetshire Archaeological. I'll go to the *Chronicle* offices next weekend. It may really be the best solution," and he went on talking about it while Isabel thought, with her usual withdrawn contemplative amusement, that by next weekend he would think the idea was his. And as for any further thanks for herself she did not expect them for she knew Oliver pretty well. But in her curious new-found happiness she was able to be amused by it all and by the fact that Oliver had not shown the faintest interest in what she wrote. In any case she supposed thrillers weren't in his line. But luckily they were in other people's line and her heart beat faster as she remembered the kind excitement at Northbridge and the first realisation of a little fame.

Presently Mrs. Marling came out of the house and down the long walk towards them.

"It's the telephone for you, Isabel," she said, "from Allington. I'm afraid your mother isn't well."

"I knew it would happen," said Isabel, looking up from her weeding. "Thank you, Mrs. Marling. I expect I'll have to go home," and she went into the house, while Mrs. Marling and Oliver followed her slowly, hoping that the news was not bad. As they came into the hall she had just finished her conversation.

"I am very sorry," she said, "but mother is ill and the doctor says I'd better come. Quite honestly," she said, with that freedom from conventional feelings that sometimes comes under great stress, "I would much rather not. But I'm the only one and

I must. He says she might live for weeks or even months or might die almost at once. If there's a train to Barchester I could get a bus out to Allington. There's a late one on Saturdays."

"I can drive you," said Oliver. "We're well in hand with petrol at the moment."

Mrs. Marling looked her approval. Isabel went upstairs and packed a suitcase while Mrs. Marling and Oliver waited in the hall.

"Poor Isabel," said Mrs. Marling. "I never met Mrs. Dale, but I have always heard she was very difficult and very stingy in little things. I believe she could be generous when it suited her. I think she gave a lot of money to the Red Cross during the war. I shall miss Isabel very much."

"So shall I," said Oliver, in so heartfelt a tone that his mother, as a rule the least suspicious or match-making of women, suddenly wondered if propinquity had been at work and her difficult Oliver had at last got over Jessica and found the wife she would love him to have. "She was going to type a chapter again for me with some important corrections," he added. "It's a frightful nuisance," from which words his mother realised that his sympathy in this matter was entirely for himself and no feelings of affection were involved.

Then Isabel came down and said good-bye with a clinging hug of affection, promising to ring up and to come over presently if possible. The car went down the drive, out of sight, and Mrs. Marling returned to her letters.

CHAPTER 12

The Conservative do, as Lady Cora so unsympathetically called it, was a kind of garden-party and bazaar combined which the Duchess felt it her duty to give once a year. There was usually some special attraction and this year it was to be the Aubrey Clover play *Out Goes She* in which the Francis Brandons were to dance and sing the haunting Argentina Tango. Lady Cora, who had the splendid lack of petty inhibitions which we are thankful to say is still a feature of many of our aristocracy, had nobbled, to use her own phrase Mr. and Mrs. Aubrey Clover on the platform at Barchester whence they were returning to London by train, for once, after a visit to Jessica's family, and had asked Aubrey Clover straight out if she could act it without paying the performing rights.

"God knows what my agents will say," said Aubrey Clover, "and I don't care. For a Duke's daughter I would do anything. When I think that a Duke's daughter is born into the rank of a Marchioness it makes me want to break the Union Jack at the masthead and burst into tears. No, Cora. I will *not* produce it for you. Peggy Brandon is perfectly capable of doing that."

Lady Cora said Peggy was also acting in it.

"I made her," she said. "She's twenty times the dancer I am, though I *have* got the loveliest legs in Barsetshire."

"In all England," said Aubrey Clover, "bar none except Jessica's. How is that insufferable husband of hers behaving?"

Lady Cora said quite well to his wife, but not very nicely to his mother.

"How too, too wrong," said Jessica. "Now Aubrey, who though plainness itself is quite clever, is absolutely devoted to his mother and so am I and she is perfectly devoted to us. And what is so too divine is that she doesn't like theatres and never comes to London, so we all send each other telegrams of affection and Sarah Siddons and Nannie go down there whenever they want a breath of country air. You know we're taking her to America for the winter."

Then a great hideous unintelligible voice began to blare out of a loud-speaker and half the people on the platform couldn't hear it and didn't want to, and the other half tried to hear it through the noise of engines letting off steam, or getting up steam, or whistling and the clank of trucks being shunted, and misheard what they did hear and rushed into porters to ask them if this was the right train and deeply offended an official of the St. John Ambulance by taking him for a ticket collector. All of which made conversation impossible, so the Clovers got into their first-class carriage with first-class tickets and Lady Cora went off to whatever duty she was doing. And we are glad to say that Aubrey Clover summoning his agent to the flat told him not to ask for performing rights of *Out Goes She* at Gatherum Castle and when the agent said rather huffily that he was paid to protect Aubrey Clover's interests, Aubrey said another word like that and he could consider himself unpaid, after which Miss M. brought in the drinks and there was no ill-feeling. And if anyone thinks that Lady Cora took an unfair advantage we must state our firm opinion that she did not, for Aubrey Clover was not a person of whom anyone could take advantage fairly or unfairly unless he wished it. Also we must allow our Dukes to be privileged. They are, we sadly believe, a dying caste. Those that are dukes already shall live; the rest we hope shall keep as they are, as Hamlet says. We firmly believe that English dukes, even if eccentric almost beyond reason, are something so English, so

rooted in our traditions, our prejudices, our inherited conglom-
eration of ritual and caste, that we must cherish them till the last
Duke dies with no heir. But may no more Dukes be made; for
what kind of Duke They would make is a terrifying thought.

Meanwhile preparations for the do and entertainment went
on at the Castle. Lord Silverbridge was in town at his office
during the week and had rung Isabel up several times to enquire
about her mother, who was alternatively sinking and rallying in
the sad way invalids do. Isabel had come over to Gatherum
occasionally to help with the Barsetshire Yeomanry book, leaving her mother in the care of the excellent Sister Chiffinch who
had now arrived at a height in her profession where she only
took a job if she wished and was able to exercise a kind but lofty
toleration of the night nurse which made that worthy creature
determine to do exactly the same when she had risen to that
eminence.

Lord Silverbridge had mastered the card index and now
begged Isabel to help him with the contributions, good, bad,
relevant and irrelevant that were coming in from the relations of
dead men, besides trying to extract from the usually far too
modest survivors what they had really done. The work was
interesting, sometimes heartbreaking, always hard, but both
workers enjoyed it, Isabel as escape from the suspended life at
Allington, Lord Silverbridge because he said it made him feel
really useful for once, and both of them perhaps because each
was happy with the other. The work was going to take time and
would probably not be ready for another year at the very least
and might not be published for two or three years, but progress
had been made. Lady Cora came and went on her county affairs,
drove the rehearsals for the entertainment with unflagging zeal
and sometimes came and sat in her brother's room while he and
Isabel checked and counter-checked and tried to reconcile the
account of Captain Colin Keith who had been Adjutant and had
a trained legal mind with that of Lance-Corporal Thatcher
from Grumper's End who had been mostly under arrest for

pinching stores but had the poacher's eye for the lie of the land and the uses of camouflage.

"Well, Jeff," said Lady Cora to her brother while he was waiting for Isabel's coming, "when are you going to propose?"

Lord Silverbridge looked up from his papers and asked his sister what she meant.

"What I say, my sweet," said Lady Cora. "You can't go on having a girl here and not make an honest woman of her. I like her."

"Well, so do I," said Lord Silverbridge, ignoring his sister's first remark, or rather taking it as it was meant, as nonsense. "But even if I were in love with her this isn't the moment to talk about it when her mother is dying."

"Awful old woman," said Lady Cora dispassionately. "It must be plain hell for Isabel from all I've heard of her. But why not cheer the girl up? I don't suppose the parents would mind. And if they did they'd soon come round, bless them. I'm sure mother thinks grandchildren are more than coronets. Anyway you've got to marry, Jeff. We don't want the title to go to the Jeffrey Pallisers. They nearly got it when great-grandmamma Glencora didn't have a baby for ages."

"I know," said her brother. "If only Gerry hadn't been killed. He would have loved getting married and having a family. I don't think I'm really the sort that ought to. I'm terrified of babies," to which his sister's inelegant answer was to call with vehemence upon her Maker to testify how stupid men were.

"She is lucky in some ways," said Lady Cora, looking depressed in a way most unlike her, at which her brother besought her to cheer up, for he was very fond of her, and to remember that the man Isabel was engaged to was killed.

"That's what I mean," said Lady Cora. "He was killed, but she had one person who cared for her more than anything in the world. I had *dozens* of friends. None of them wanted to marry me, or if they did they never mentioned it, and they are nearly all dead. I sometimes wish I had let myself get engaged to Froggy, just to be able to boast about it. Not that Isabel boasts. But I've missed something, Jeff, and don't you go and miss it too."

"Poor Froggy," said Lord Silverbridge, thinking of the delightful but most ineligible young man, the poor younger son of an earl, who had a love in every night club and had died at Arnhem.

"Poor Cora, I think," said her ladyship. "Oh, well. And if you won't propose to Isabel you might see if you could marry a spot of money, Jeff. It would do the parents no end of good and you could stand for Parliament," and then the pony-cart which had gone to fetch Isabel from the station came rattling up to the side door and Isabel came in.

"Well, my lamb, you *do* look a hag," said Lady Cora, but with considerable affection. "Jeff, you mustn't work her too hard. She is not Ambitious Secretary Marries Boss, she's just a nice girl who comes all the way here to help you for nothing. Bring her in to tea in Mother's room and I'll drive her back. I've lashings of petrol never ask why. Mostly Red Cross," and she went away.

"If anyone says I look tired again I shall skin them alive," said Isabel with a vehemence unusual to her. "I know *exactly* what I look like, and I don't like it," and she sat down rather fiercely at the big table where they worked and began to deal with papers. Lord Silverbridge thought it better not to argue and for a couple of hours they only spoke of business and Isabel's manner gradually softened. Then Lady Cora came back to say tea was ready and they all went to the duchess's sitting-room which had once been the still-room and looked out onto a paved courtyard open at the further end to a lawn and trees.

The duchess, who had seen a good deal of Isabel during the last weeks and liked her, said a few words of sympathy about her mother but did not press her enquiry for everyone knew there was not much hope of improvement.

"I don't think she is any better, thank you," said Isabel, "but having Sister Chiffinch makes all the difference."

The duchess said she had heard of Sister Chiffinch from Lady

Hartletop who said she was the only person who could deal with the Marquis when he had shingles and Lady Cora said she had met her during the war in the Barchester General and simply adored her and conversation continued on these lines in a manner very soothing to Isabel and after tea the Duke took her to see the book on Seats of the Nobility and Gentry in the Vicinity of Barchester that he had picked up in Charing Cross Road for twelve and sixpence, with a map of that part of the county before Gatherum Castle was built by the Great Duke's father.

"Nice little place they had then," said the Duke, turning to a hand-coloured engraving of Gatherum Park, the residence of His Grace the Duke of Omnium, a harmless and very plain-faced square stuccoed house of three stories and a parapet all round the top behind which the servants very suitably slept three and four in a room with low windows which only opened about six inches and had no view except of the brick wall of the parapet. "Why my ancestor had to spend all that money in making this dreadful monument I cannot conceive. There isn't a fortune in England that could keep it up now. And here's Hartletop Priory, not a bad place but they've had to let it as a girls' school."

"I wonder if mother's house counts as gentry," said Isabel, turning the pages. "Here it is. The Great House at Allington. Almost exactly like what it is now, only the gardens are different."

"I remember being over there with the hounds once or twice," said the Duke, "but that would have been in your grandfather's time. It was a very nice house, early seventeenth century I think with some woods at the back, nicely preserved too. Now wait a moment. His father married a niece of that woman whose father made his money in pills or something of the sort. Dunstable, that was her name, who married one of the Thornes. I believe the niece had a pretty big fortune too."

Isabel said she had heard her grandfather speak of it and she believed the Dales had been good managers.

"My father died just before the war," she said, "and left everything to my mother for her life but she has never told me anything. And I haven't the faintest idea what she has. Her grandfather was one of the Greshams and they had all the Scatcherd fortune. I expect you know more about it than I do, duke. It was all ages ago. The lawyers told me it was to come to me after her death, but one can't count on things like that and I've tried to be independent. Of course in the war I could earn my living quite easily."

"And now Silverbridge tells me you are a real author," said the Duke who was obviously impressed by this peculiarity in a member of a good county family. "The duchess was most interested and wrote to the County Library for one of your books at once and they said they didn't know the name and then Silverbridge explained that you write under another name and he bought one for us."

"Yes. Lisa Bedale," said Isabel. "It's an anagram of my own name Isabel Dale. Which book was it?"

"The last one *Aconite by Night*," said the Duke. "My wife has explained the mistake to the County Library and they are going to send her the others. I wonder if you would autograph the one that my son gave her, Miss Dale. It would give her such pleasure."

"But of course," said Isabel, touched and flattered. "Only if you wouldn't mind calling me Isabel, I should like it so much."

"By all means, my dear," said the Duke, "or Lisa," which joke appeared to them both very witty.

So the Seats of the Nobility and Gentry were put away and they went back to the sitting-room where the duchess was mending some linen quite beautifully.

"I told the famous authoress that you were reading her book," said the Duke, "and she is going to autograph it," which appeared to impress the duchess so much that Isabel felt quite ashamed of being the centre of such attraction.

"What shall I write?" she said when the duke had refilled the duchess's fountain pen.

"Anything you like," said her grace. "Will you put your nom-de-plume or your real name? They are both very pretty."

Isabel thought for a moment and then wrote.

"I hope that will do," she said handing it to the duchess.

"Lisa Bedale's book with love and gratitude to the Duke and Duchess of Omnium from Isabel Dale," the duchess read aloud. "Thank you very much, my dear. Isn't it clever, Plantagenet?"

"Most ingenious," said the duke. "My father knew Lord Tennyson as a young man, I mean when he was a young man, my father I mean, and Tennyson autographed a copy of *In Memoriam* for him. This must go beside it. We must order all Isabel's books from the library, my dear," and Isabel who knew that a great many people really feel they are conferring a benefit upon a writer when they borrow a book from someone else was touched by the duke's thoughtfulness. Lady Cora who had come in during this scene slightly contracted her right eye in Isabel's direction.

"You ought to have a book of Isabel's on the library door, father," she said. "One of your sham books."

"Would you let me give you one," said Isabel, "if I could think of a good name for it?" which offer was very well received and several very poor suggestions made.

"Where is Jeff?" said the duchess. "I am sure he could help us."

"Someone rang up," said Lady Cora. "He'll be here in a minute," and as she spoke her brother came in.

"I'm afraid it's for you," he said to Isabel. "Sister Chiffinch asked me to tell you some rather bad news."

"Mother is dead," said Isabel. "And I wasn't there."

"My dear child," said the duchess. "You couldn't possibly tell. No one could. You mustn't blame yourself. We are all so very sorry. You will want to get home."

"I'll take you back at once," said Lady Cora. "The car's outside."

"I'll take her," said Lord Silverbridge.

"Yes, do," said the duchess. "A man is so useful. Don't wait, my dear. We all feel for you very much and you must let us know if we can help you. I will telephone and say you have started."

With kindly haste they accompanied her to the stable yard and bade her farewell most affectionately. Lady Cora got into the back seat saying firmly that she would be just as useful as a man. "You go in front with Jeff," she said to Isabel who in a confused dream did as she was told. There was little or no talk on the way to Allington, for there was really nothing to say. In the late afternoon sunlight the lovely yellow-grey stone of The Great House was pure gold, but the crystal of the windows was obscured by drawn blinds.

"Perfect!" said Lady Cora aloud to herself as she got out of the car. "Chiffinch does know Etiquette."

It was evident that Sister Chiffinch was on the watch, for the door was opened by that delightful woman before they could ring.

"Sister, I am so *dreadfully* sorry," said Isabel.

"Now that's all right, Miss Dale," said Sister Chiffinch. "Your mother just slipped away in her sleep and even if you had been in the house I couldn't have got you in time. It was all very peaceful. Now, you need a cup of tea, and your friends too."

"Oh, this is Lady Cora Palliser, Sister," said Isabel, remembering her manners, "and this is Lord Silverbridge who drove me back."

"Hullo, Sister," said Lady Cora. "Do you remember the entertainment at the Barchester General the Christmas before the war stopped when we did a skit on Ward Seven and that nice man with no legs came in as a mental patient and Dr. Ford pretended to give him Shock Treatment? This is my brother."

"Well, we do indeed meet in different surroundings, Lady Cora," said Sister Chiffinch. "Come into the dining-room and

I'll have tea ready in a jiffy," and the kind creature bustled them in. "Nurse Poulter is upstairs, Miss Dale. You must have a cup of tea first and then I am sure you'd like to Go Up."

As everything was by now entirely unreal, Isabel was content to do as she was told. Lady Cora gallantly kept the conversation going and when Sister Chiffinch found that Lord Silverbridge and Miss Dale were collaborating on the Barsetshire Yeomanry she said Now wasn't that nice and how pleased her nephew would be. Lord Silverbridge, also doing his best, asked where her nephew had served and said he would write to him and ask for particulars of the quartermaster's office at Falmouth in which he had spent the entire war, which of course won good Sister Chiffinch's heart completely.

"And now," said Sister Chiffinch, "perhaps you would like to Come Up, Miss Dale," upon which Lady Cora said they would go now.

"You couldn't just stay till I come back, could you?" said Isabel, so they remained in the drawing-room while Isabel went up and performed, under Nurse Poulter's guard, the ritual duty which even the most unwilling are compelled to do by some force beyond their apprehension, of looking down on the stranger who had been her mother for more than a quarter of a century. The still figure, composed, white-shrouded, was her mother no longer. She had not loved her greatly, not altogether through her own fault, but the sense that nothing could now ever be explained or bettered made her feel almost guilty.

While she was upstairs Sister Chiffinch had what she afterwards described to her friends Heathy and Wardy that she shared the flat with as a comfortable little chat with the guests, who bore it with patience well knowing that every moment spent in Sister Chiffinch's company would give so much more value to Isabel in Sister's eyes.

Then she came down again, thanked them warmly for coming and said good-bye. She was stunned, confused, desperately tired and without thinking she kissed Lady Cora and then kissed her brother whose feelings were deeply touched by this confidence, though he gave it no more value than a friend thanking a friend. And then they drove away.

"You'll have to marry her now, Jeff," said Lady Cora.

"I don't suppose she'd have me," said her brother.

Mrs. Dale's funeral took place two days later. Although the Dales had a good many connections in the County she had never been much loved, largely through her own fault it must be said, and those who were at the service only came because of family ties. Lady Cora came over with regrets from her brother who was in town, and a standing invitation from her parents for Isabel to come and stay whenever she wished. Isabel thanked her very much and said that for the moment she must be at home to see lawyers and try to understand her mother's affairs about which she knew nothing. The old established firm of Merton and Merton in Barchester were the family solicitors and with them she would, she thought, have to do a good deal of business.

"But when mother's will has been read and I know what I've got to do," said Isabel, "I would love to come and please thank them very very much," and for a week or so they heard nothing of her, except when Lady Cora rang her up which she only did when her brother was at Gatherum and could say a word.

A few days later Mrs. Marling rang up Lord Silverbridge and asked him if he could come to lunch on Sunday as her daughter Lucy Adams and her husband were coming. Lord Silverbridge had often met and liked the wealthy ironmaster in the House of Commons but not in Barchester and was glad to have this further opportunity of talking with him. He was also rather curious to see what the Marling girl was like who had married so completely out of her own class and how Mr. Adams fitted in with his territorial in-laws. Both impressions were satisfactory. Mrs. Adams was what one would expect from her parents' child, tall, quite good-looking, with tweeds that Lord Silverbridge recognised as of good cut and quality. Her hands were a worker's hands, large and with rather roughened skin and obviously competent to do anything and do it well. Mr. Adams he had only seen in town clothes and wished without envy that he had a country suit as good. Oliver, his mother said, had gone to lunch with the Deans at Winter Overcotes and left his regrets.

It was natural that Isabel Dale's name should come up. News was exchanged. Lord Silverbridge had been the last to see her, but Mr. Marling had later news through one of the Merton partners whom he had met at the Club.

"It seems she's coming in for something quite handsome," said Mr. Marling, "or it would be if this lot that call themselves a Government didn't want it all. They're talking of raising their own salaries again," and by the way in which her husband spoke, remembering deliberately not to drop his g's, Mrs. Marling knew that he was on his real country gentleman behaviour, not what his irreverent children called his Olde Englishe Squire lay.

"Well, money's still money to a certain extent if you know what to do with it," said Mr. Adams and began to talk to his father-in-law about certain changes in his industrial holdings and schemes for more agricultural investments, while his Lucy put Lord Silverbridge through a searching enquiry as to the livestock at Gatherum and the amount of land under cultivation, out of which he came very badly and had to explain to Lucy that he was really a Londoner for five days in the week like her brother Oliver and then he asked about Oliver's book.

"Oh, he'll go on writing it for years," said Mrs. Adams. "Like that story about the man that was going to paint a picture and he went on painting it all his life and when he was dead it didn't look like a picture at all. Isabel did all his typing and now of course she can't. I'm awfully sorry about her mother."

"So am I," said Lord Silverbridge, his heart warming to Mrs. Adams.

"I believe she was pretty ghastly," said Mrs. Adams, "but Noel Merton, you know, the one that his father is Merton and

Merton, says she ought to have left Isabel quite a lot. I'll tell you what. Why don't *you* write a book, Lord Silverbridge?"

"Partly because I publish them," said Lord Silverbridge, "at least I'm in a publishing office. But I am trying to write a sort of book about the Barsetshire Yeomanry," which piece of intelligence was very well received and they talked about the Yeomanry till Mrs. Marling took her daughter away, when the men talked county and then politics.

"Well, you can say what you like, you young fellers," said Mr. Marling. "I'll vote for Churchill."

"Not unless you live in Woodford, sir," said Lord Silverbridge which made Mr. Adams laugh and his host look like Highland Cattle at bay. "I'd vote for him like a shot if I lived there, but down here one doesn't quite know. If it were East Barsetshire I'd support Gresham. Who are the Conservative Committee putting up, Adams?"

"I couldn't tell you, nor I fancy could they," said Mr. Adams. "Fielding won't stand again and I don't know who will. But the Labour people are in a hole too. I shan't stand this time. I'd give my right hand to help England," said Mr. Adams, laying on the table a powerful and we must say hairy hand with capable workman's fingers, "but I don't see that the set I helped to get in have done anything but walk backwards over their own tails and muck everything up. I shan't leave the Labour Party, not just yet anyway, because I belong to that party and Sam Adams's word is as good as his bond. But my subscription to the Labour Association here runs out in November and after that I shall hold myself free to do as I like; for think as I like I always have," said Mr. Adams looking round for a possible contradictor.

"I'd stand like a shot if I could afford it," said Lord Silverbridge, "but I can't. Surely there are one or two good men who have the time and the money."

"Bring them here and I'll tell you," said Mr. Adams. "What we need is a policy and a man. We've got a leader but that leader is old. He's finest stainless steel and then something. But one man can't make a party or support it. It looks to me as if we'd have to put up with my lot, and a pretty scaly lot they are," said Mr. Adams reflectively, "for want of a better. Well, well," which comment seemed to Lord Silverbridge inadequate and the two men talked and argued with considerable earnestness across their host who was longing for a little nap but too polite to say so, till Mr. Adams seeing Mr. Marling drowsing in his chair motioned to Lord Silverbridge to come into the garden which the two men quietly did and walked up and down the flagged path talking of the fate of a beloved country and how we might avert ruin and set her again where she had been in 1945. This talk might have gone on till tea-time had not Mrs. Adams summoned her husband and reminded him that old Miss Sowerby was coming to tea.

"Right, my girl," said Mr. Adams, adding for Lord Silverbridge's benefit that she had a better head on her shoulders than the whole Government put together. "Let's meet again, Silverbridge. Come and lunch with me at the County Club," to which Lord Silverbridge agreed with pleasure for he liked the ironmaster and felt as a good many people did that if the Adamses and the Marlings and the Omniums could join hands, England would be the safer. And then he found Mrs. Marling, said good-bye to her and went away.

A week or so later Isabel rang up Gatherum Castle and asked Lady Cora who happened to answer the telephone whether she might come over and do some work on the Barsetshire Yeomanry and see the family. Lady Cora said that Jeff was lunching with Mr. Adams but would be back later and Isabel must come to lunch, which she accordingly did, by two buses, in a black and white printed silk dress.

"I thought not real mourning," she said to the Duchess who had said how pretty it was. "I did wear black for John because it protects one. People leave you alone if you are in black. But I can't feel like that about mother and she hated mourning anyway," to which the Duchess replied that everything had changed since her young days and though she would always herself go into black for her relatives, she saw no reason to expect it of other people. "Silverbridge is lunching with Mr. Adams," she said, "so we can have a nice talk all by ourselves," which included the Duke. And a nice lunch it was, if kindness, intelligence and good food off one's own land make for niceness: which we think they do.

"And now," said the Duchess, "Cora is going to rehearse all afternoon, so you had better come to my room, my dear, and rest and tell me about yourself and what your plans are. You must stop to tea and then Silverbridge will see you. I know he wants to ask you some questions about his book."

"As for plans," said Isabel, when they were safely in her grace's room and the duke had gone to talk to his bailiff, "I haven't any just yet. The house goes to a cousin, Robin Dale. He is a master at Southbridge School and married a very nice girl, Anne Fielding."

The duchess said it seemed rather hard on Isabel.

"Oh no, I always knew the house would have to go to Robin because he's a man," said Isabel, "and of course he gets the rents from the estate. He is very nice I believe, though I hardly know him. The Dales aren't very clannish."

"But what about you, my dear?" said the duchess. "Don't tell me you get nothing."

"Well, I don't get the place," said Isabel, "because it had to go to a man, but—I really don't know how to tell you."

"Do," said the duchess impelled partly by the curiosity we all feel about wills and partly by real anxiety that Isabel should not be left penniless.

"It's rather complicated," said Isabel, "and I'm not quite sure if I understand it myself, but you see when father married mother, Miss Gresham she was, there was the Dunstable money on his side and the Gresham money on hers. It all sounds frightfully rich on paper, but of course the Government are taking the lion's share. At least an elephant's share I'd call it and a hippopotamus's into the bargain. But what the lawyers tell me is," and she mentioned a sum of money which even under the present iniquitous system of forced levies and taxation directed against all wealth, public and private, depriving everyone of the old incentive to work and save for their children, squandering countless millions in ignorance and ostentation, made such a fortune as was not to be sneezed at.

"My dear Isabel, I can't tell you how glad I am," said the duchess. "I could not have borne to think of you having to work for your living. Plantagenet will be as pleased as I am. And what are you going to do with it?"

"I haven't the faintest idea," said Isabel and worn out by the shock of her mother's death and the subsequent interviews with lawyers she began to cry.

"My poor girl," said the duchess. "Never mind, it will do you good. I will get you one of Plantagenet's large handkerchiefs," for Isabel's would evidently not meet the case, and she went away to the duke's dressing-room.

As he went back to Gatherum in the bus, Lord Silverbridge thought a good deal about his talk with Mr. Adams and thought his father would be interested too, though he might not show it. As often happens in families whose birth, houses, possessions and duties make an extremely busy life for everyone, the younger members do not expect the immediate attention from their parents that is given to the children of people less bound by public ties. Before the war (and how much more before the 1914 war) while the son of the house of, say, Keith or Merton or Marling would come back from Switzerland or a weekend and find his parents slavishly pleased to see him and quite boring in the number of questions they asked about if he had enjoyed himself and who his friends had been, the son of the house of Omnium or Pomfret or Hartletop would probably come home to a house full of guests important by position or relationship

and not be noticed until his father said "Oh, you're back are
you," or his mother with a woman's greater delicacy and percep-
tion greeted him with, "Well, darling? Most annoying. We shall
be a man too many. Never mind it can't be helped and I'll put
you between Aunt Dodo and the vicar as we *had* to ask him."
There may be and doubtless is a perfect medium between these
two forms of welcome, but in its default we think the second is
possibly a better training for the young.

When he got back Lord Silverbridge went to the room where
his papers were and sat down to the Barsetshire Yeomanry, and
was soon absorbed in the unfortunate life story of Sergeant Alf
Thatcher who after incredible bravery and devotion had been
awarded the rare distinction of the George Cross and was
now serving a term of seven years for a peculiarly brutal attack
with several of his friends upon an elderly pawn-broker in
Limehouse suspected (on no grounds at all) of having thousands
of golden sovereigns in a box under his bed. Sergeant Alf
Thatcher's name could not be omitted from the Barsetshire
Yeomanry's annals, but the question was where to stop. So
puzzling and absorbing did Lord Silverbridge find this question
that he almost jumped when he saw his father in the room.

"Not disturbing you, am I?" said the duke, who was holding a
sheaf of papers in one hand.

"Of course not," said Lord Silverbridge. "I'm trying to fit Alf
Thatcher in—you know, the man from Grumper's End who
got seven years for beating up an old man. What have you got
there?"

"Letters," said the duke, sitting down. "I've been going through
some boxes in the estate room and found these. I'd never seen
them before. My grandfather must have kept every letter he ever
got. These are some that his father, the duke they used to call
Planty Pal, wrote to him when he was going to stand for
Silverbridge. They always returned one of us in those days and
didn't mind what his politics were. One of them struck me so
much that I think you ought to see it. I'd have shown it to your

mother but she is talking to Isabel, poor child. I'll just read you the passage that I thought so good."

"Thanks, father," said Lord Silverbridge, composing himself to listen though he would far rather have been allowed to read the letter to himself, for other people's reading aloud is often calculated to drive one mad and those who read by eye and in chunks rather than line by line with consideration are not very good in following the slow tempo of the spoken word.

"No, I'll leave the letters with you," said the duke, much to his son's relief. "But I'll just read you the bit that I think you'll like. 'And then I would always have you remember the purpose for which there is a parliament elected in this happy and free country. It is not that some men may shine there, that some may acquire power, or that all may plume themselves on being the elect of the nation. You are there as the guardian of your fellow-countrymen, that they may be safe, that they may be prosperous, that they may be well governed and lightly burdened, above all that they may be free. If you cannot feel this to be your duty, you should not be there at all. Gradually, if you will give your thoughts to it and above all your time, you will find that there will come upon you the ineffable delight of having served your country to the best of your ability. It is the only pleasure in life which has been enjoyed without alloy by your affectionate father Omnium.'"

"Above all that they may be free," said Lord Silverbridge.

"I know," said his father. "It's pretty bitter. The least free country in the world and all within four years. But it's a good letter. If you were going into politics and I wanted to give you advice, that is the best I could give, but you aren't and that's that. I wish Silverbridge were still a pocket borough."

"So do I," said Lord Silverbridge, "and then I'd get them to put me in. But if I could stand it would be for Barchester."

"I wish you could," said his father sadly. "I sometimes feel it is my fault, though I don't think it really is. Two wars and death duties and now this government. It would give me more pleasure than I have felt since Gerald was killed if I saw you in Parliament. We *could* manage it perhaps, and if you were returned it would be worth it. I've sometimes thought of making over most of the property to you and then going to bed to keep myself alive till the time limit. Old Lord Nutfield did it. It used to be three years and now it's five and soon They will make it illegal. One feels like a bull in a ring, only there is no one to fight. If there were I would fight to the death, but you can't fight men who are frogs trying to look like oxes."

Lord Silverbridge, more touched than he would have liked to admit, said it didn't matter a bit.

"We'll talk it over later," said the duke, very kindly. "Come and see Isabel," so they went to the duchess's sitting-room where the two ladies had been peacefully talking about embroidery, and Isabel had offered the duchess a whole drawer of silks and several rolls of pre-war embroidery canvas, relics of the late Mrs. Dale which the duchess accepted with enthusiasm for as all good needlewomen know the best materials for embroidery are very hard to come by. A girl brought in tea with more zeal than discretion, put the tray on a table with such good will that the milk slopped over and went away leaving the door ajar.

"Just shut the door, Jeff, dear," said the duchess. "Isabel and I have had such an interesting talk, Plantagenet. Just fancy, her mother had a lot of that Gresham money."

The duke asked which Gresham money.

"Don't be silly, duke," said his wife. "You know, the fortune that was left to one of the Greshams by an uncle in Australia," in which her grace was not quite correct for the money, as all lovers of Barsetshire know, was left to Mary Thorne the niece of Dr. Thorne by a very rich uncle who did not know that the doctor's niece, with no right to the name she bore, was also his sister's child, and as for the uncle in Australia he did not exist at all. Mary Thorne's mother had married a Barchester tradesman and they had gone to Australia and doubtless had a family, but of them nothing was now known. Meanwhile Mary Thorne had given her hand and her large fortune to Frank Gresham and it was a part of this fortune, well husbanded and increased in earlier years, that had come into the Dale family with Isabel's mother. And now Isabel would have, in spite of Them, a very large sum of money, though the house and what was left of the land passed to a male.

The duke had got to like Isabel very much and the news of her fortune was not of a nature to diminish his regard. The duchess felt, we really cannot say why, that heaven was but behaving as it should by arranging for this nice girl who was so helpful to Silverbridge with his book to be comfortably off. Lord Silverbridge also congratulated her in a very friendly way, but he felt an unaccountable chill on his spirits, which communicated itself to Lady Cora when she came back from the rehearsal and though she was as delighted as her parents by the news, she felt that something was wrong.

"I asked Mr. Wickham to come to tea, mother," she said. "Is that all right?" and luckily it was, for the duchess had a regard for Mr. Wickham not only as a war friend of her daughter's, but also because his people were still yeoman farmers over Chaldicotes way and in their own line of as good blood as the Pallisers and probably of an even older family.

Then Mr. Wickham made his appearance and heard the news and was loud in his congratulations to Isabel.

"But you mustn't stop writing, must she, duchess," said he, appealing to his hostess, who said of course not and instanced the case of old Lord Pomfret's mother whose three-volume novel *A Step Too Far* had shocked Mr. Gladstone, though where the analogy came in no one could quite make out. Isabel said she didn't suppose she would have any real money for ages as lawyers were so slow, and meanwhile she would certainly go on with the next book as her publisher Mr. Johns would be expecting it and she was afraid she ought to be getting back, as if she missed this bus she had to wait so long in Barchester.

"My dear!" said the duchess, rather shocked. "You can't go by bus now."

"I did think of taking a taxi," said Isabel apologetically, "but it seemed so terribly extravagant when the buses are there."

"Listen to me, my sweet," said Lady Cora. "You ought to learn what is extravagant and what isn't. Not to take a taxi when you can afford one is just plumb silly. You'll only get haggard and your books will be dull. Never economise on luxuries, my pet. I don't and God knows I'm poor enough. If I did I might as well be Gathered. You run her home, Jeff."

"*I* will," said Mr. Wickham. "I've got to go over Allington way about some brandy I've heard of. Ready, Isabel?"

Isabel said good-bye affectionately to the duke and duchess and Lady Cora and looked round for Lord Silverbridge, but he had gone. Just as Mr. Wickham was starting his dreadful little car Lord Silverbridge looked in at the window on her side.

"Oh, Jeff," she said. "Where were you?"

Lord Silverbridge said he didn't think he was really wanted.

"But you *are*," said Isabel. "When shall we begin work again? I could come quite often now."

"Whenever you like. To-morrow, the next day, always," said Lord Silverbridge, laying his hand on the open window, at which moment the little car growled hideously and gathered itself for a spring. Isabel laid her hand on his and then the little car leapt forward and rushed away in a stench of blue smoke. Lord Silverbridge looked at his own hand, considered the possibility of wearing a glove for ever that no other touch might profane it, rejected the idea as impracticable, called himself a fool and went to his own room where the case of Sergeant Alf Thatcher was still waiting his attention. Here he found his sister Cora who said "Well?"

"What do you mean?" said her brother. "If you mean did I ask Isabel to marry me how the deuce can I now, the very moment she has come into money?" to which Lady Cora replied that he could have it his own way and looked out of the window.

"You're not going, are you?" said Lord Silverbridge, who was really an affectionate brother.

"Oh no," said Lady Cora. "Only thinking that Froggy might have asked me to marry him if he hadn't been so poor. Never mind. He's dead and I'm alive," and she went on looking out of the window while her brother tried to concentrate on Sergeant Alf Thatcher with no success at all.

When they got to Allington Isabel asked Mr. Wickham if he would come in and have some sherry.

"Not on your life, my girl," said Mr. Wickham. "Is that all your respected mother let you drink?"

Isabel said she didn't know what there might be in the house, but they could look in the cellar if Mr. Wickham liked, for the longer she put off the moment of being alone the better pleased she would be, though this she did not say. We need hardly say that Mr. Wickham was delighted with the suggestion and they went down to the cellars where Isabel, an only child with no brother or boy cousins to inspire her to mischief, a lonely girl with no young men friends who might have thought it a lark to explore old Mrs. Dale's cellars, had never thought of going. Mr. Wickham, true to the naval traditions of general handiness, had brought a torch and an oil can with him from his car and after some difficulty they opened the heavy cellar door. A little light came in through dirty windows looking onto brick areas below ground level. Strong shelves and tier upon tier of racks stretched away into the dark.

"No light, I suppose," said Mr. Wickham. "Lucky I brought a torch. I thought so. Candles," and he pointed the torch at two or three flat candlesticks on a slate shelf covered with grease droppings. He lighted a candle for Isabel and took the torch himself, turning it full onto the wine racks.

"Holy jumping frogs!" said Mr. Wickham as the beam of his torch passed over one revered historic vintage after another. "Some of these will want re-bottling, my girl, but *what* a cellar.

I expect some have turned a bit. You ought to have a man down
to look through them. I'd do it myself if I had time. Now there's
a Pommard that ought to have been drunk ten years ago. What
the devil was your mother thinking about?"

"Mother only drank barley water," said Isabel. "And a glass of
port at eleven in the morning."

"I know those ladies," said Mr. Wickham. "They think they
aren't alcoholics if it's before lunch. And to think of all this stuff
sitting here. I'll put you onto a good man in London to come
down and go over the lot. My aunt! What a cellar. Well, I must
be going. Man's waiting to see me about some brandy."

He locked the heavy door and returned the key to its owner.

"Well, good-bye and good luck," he said at the hall door.
"Nothing wrong is there? You look a bit queer."

"Nothing, Wicks," said Isabel. "It's only that all this wine and
all mother's money and the lawyers and everything make me feel
so alone."

"Poor old girl," said Mr. Wickham putting an arm round her
in what we may call a naval uncle's manner. "Look here. You
wouldn't like to marry me, would you? I never drink alone and
I'd reorganise the whole cellar. Don't say yes if you don't feel
like it."

"Thank you *very* much, Wicks, but I don't in the least," said
Isabel.

"Good," said Mr. Wickham. "Dam' fool thing to say, but
when I saw you looking so blue I couldn't help it. I expect it's
Silverbridge, isn't it? No need to say yes. Well, God bless and all
that. What I'd do with a wife at Northbridge I can't think. I had
one lucky escape when Effie Crofts turned me down. And now
I've had another. Let me know if I can help," and he got into his
little car and went away.

CHAPTER 13

The great day of the Conservative do at Gatherum dawned bright and fair though no one noticed it as every day in that warm endless summer was the same and some ungrateful people were beginning to mention the word drought. By kind permission of the Ministry of General Interference the great hall was turned into a huge bazaar run by the Ladies' Conservative Association. Tea supplied by Messrs. Scatcherd and Tozer was in the garden, the maze was to be viewed price sixpence, there were sports for the children, two performances were to take place in the theatre and we are glad to say that Packer's Universal Royal Derby had also been secured. The sun shone and it was obvious that by the end of the day every dry, brown blade of grass would have been trampled out of existence.

To many of those present it was an echo of old days and perhaps Mr. Packer's steam roundabout or Universal Royal Derby was the most nostalgic centre. The older people remembered it when Mr. Packer's father was the owner and it was run by an oil engine whose smell alone was a romantic delight, with a kind of barrel organ which ground out popular melodies of the moment, or rather of ten years ago for it was steadily behind the times. Mr. Marling, in whose father's field it had often been pitched, had thought *Tommy Make Room for Your Uncle* and *Ta-ra-ra-boom-de-aye* the most beautiful tunes in the world. His elder son had fallen in love with the vicar's little girl for a whole hour, entirely owing to the influence of *Tommy Atkins* and *Sweet Marie*. The younger Marlings had almost swooned at *The Honeysuckle and the Bee*, just as now the youth of Barsetshire were pushing and jostling to be the first to career madly yet safely round and round to the strains of *Over There* and *Hand Hold in the Twilight*.

"It's one of the great mortifications of my life," said Aubrey Clover to Oliver Marling, "that I'll never write a song that will be played at the Universal Royal Derby. Denis Stonor will, but I am too refined. We shall be seeing him in New York where I understand his "Sweetest Sorrow" is still playing to packed houses. I apologise for the cliché. Where's that nice girl who was being quietly efficient at Lucy's wedding? Isabel Dale. I could make a one-act play about her. She's one of those women that you never know the value of till you've lost her."

"How do you know that?" said Oliver, interested.

"We players know," said Aubrey Clover. "And that, my boy, is a parody of Browning, but you wouldn't know it."

"I miss her very much at weekends," said Oliver. "She did my typing for me. But her mother died and she had to go home."

"No wonder, my sweet," said Jessica. "If Aubrey used the weekends to get me to do his typing, I'd go home at once, whether my mother was dead or not."

"Oliver!" said a voice somehow familiar. Oliver looked round and saw a tall striking woman not so young as she was and recognised with a mingling of amusement and horror and even a little fear Miss Frances Harvey who with her brother had spent a winter in Marling village during the war and nearly succeeded in making Oliver propose to her.

"Frances! my *dear*!" said Oliver, his voice sounding uncommonly false to himself. "Are you here?" by which we conclude that he meant not so much was she bodily present before him, but was she one of the officials at Gatherum Castle.

"Only temporary," said Miss Harvey. "I am down here from the Ministry to see what cuts we can make. So necessary now."

Oliver introduced Miss Harvey to Aubrey Clover and his wife and observed that they both appeared to find her singularly attractive.

"It is rather wonderful," said Miss Harvey, "to feel that one can help Our Government. I am getting rid of at least twenty girls and shall probably decrease the kitchen staff considerably. And then we can direct married women and children into the domestic work and I shall have a crêche and day-nursery for them."

"So will they oll grow up state-minded," said a large woman with an earnest face dressed in what we can only describe as a very expensive style of unbecomingness.

"Miss Bonescu, a friend of mine from Mixo-Lydia," said Miss Harvey. "She is at present the Mixo-Lydian Ambassadress. This is Oliver Marling, Gradka."

"Bog! Which pleasure, which joy!" said the ambassadress. "Now shall you tell me about Prodshkina Bunting of which I am coached in English so passing my exams and putting my first foot oponn the first rang of the ladder."

"We say rung, not rang," said Miss Harvey.

"So. I thank you," said Miss Bonescu. "And she spoke of Marling Hall and her pupil Oliver which is in Mixo-Lydian Hròj. We shall gossip together of her, yes?"

By this time it was perfectly clear to Oliver that the Clovers were imbibing every word and gesture not only of Miss Harvey, but also of the Mixo-Lydian Ambassadress, and that with any luck a little sketch of those ladies would be added to their repertoire both in America and in England.

"You and your delightful friends must have tea with me and Her Excellency," said Miss Harvey. "I have reserved a table. And your parents of course. They are still alive, I hope. One never knows now, alas."

"I am terribly sorry," said Oliver, "but I think my people and I are having tea with the duchess and I can't very well get out of it. But we *must* meet again."

Miss Harvey would doubtless have made a struggle against this defection and probably won, had not the Ambassadress interrupted her.

"Which coincidence!" she exclaimed. "See! these lady and man which you coll Clover are the landlords which in Mixo-Lydian we say Stryczks of my charming flat. So, by analogy, am I their tenant, or as we say Stryczksvicz, which I will translate for you that the former means the Cheat-devil and the unformer——"

"Latter, Miss Bonescu," said Miss Harvey.

"—latter, so, I thank you," said Miss Bonescu, "the Cheat-devil-cheat. So is oll happy."

"Well, we must go and spend our shillings for the good of the Conservatives," said Miss Harvey with a gracious smile, "though as a good Socialist I should not of course be here. But we are all friends in these lovely surroundings."

"Czy, prôvka, prôvka, prôvka," said the Ambassadress, her eyes flashing. "If you are Sozialiste it is to me as were you a swine. Schwenk, I name you, which is in English a vermin which is died and becomm eaten by maggots. I laugh till I burst of you!"

With which, much to Oliver's relief, the Ambassadress walked rapidly away towards the Universal Derby on which she spent the rest of her visit.

"These foreigners," said Miss Harvey. "Well, we shall meet again—Oliver," with which beautiful farewell she left them. And after this the Clovers were absorbed in the Dean family and Oliver was left to reflect upon life in general and look for his family. He did not see his family but he saw Isabel looking, he thought, somehow different. The perfect oval of her face, an unusual beauty; the gold in her brown hair; her wide-set eyes which when she raised them were so blue; a nose, if one must allude to that so often unsatisfactory feature, which showed a long line of good breeding, her elegant form and her good hands; all these, though Oliver had noticed them before, struck him afresh, and the black and white dress she was wearing set off her fair skin. How different from that dreadful Frances Harvey who had nearly frightened him into proposing to her some years ago: but that would not happen again.

If anyone had told Oliver Marling during the past few years that he could stop loving Jessica Dean and thinking her the most delightful and perfect of women he would have been deeply outraged. His passion had certainly lasted for more than three whole days together and he was distinctly conceited about his romantic adoration of another man's wife. But the romance had to be kept inside him only known to his sister Lucy, the whole county if it bothered to think of it, and latterly to Isabel Dale, who had listened very kindly to his maunderings when she was not listening to his lectures on Bohun or typing and re-typing his book. Now he felt (we regret to say) that he might reward her for her sympathy by offering her his hand, his now quite good income and the privilege of hearing him talk about himself for ever. She saw him and smiled, so he went across to her where she was talking to Sir Robert and Lady Fielding and the Robin Dales, who were apologising for having become the owners of the Great House at Allington.

"What we shall do with it I can't imagine," said Robin. "I have always loathed the place because once when I was small your mother found me talking to a frog who lived in one of those damp little areas outside the wine cellar and she said I was being cruel to it. As a matter of fact I was asking it if it would like to go and live in a nice pond and it said it was a bachelor and quite comfortable where it was, and it didn't mind my holding it a bit."

"I'm thankful it is yours," said Isabel. "I've always loathed it. Couldn't you let it?"

"It's just possible Southbridge School might take it as a pre-prep," said Robin. "As none of the parents have any servants they would be thankful to send them there. But it's all quite vague. And anyway we hope you will go on living there as long as you like," to which Isabel replied by thanking him warmly and saying she would like to remain there while the lawyers were tidying up, but she should sooner spend her life in a tube train in the rush hour than live in the Great House permanently.

"Well, Oliver," said Lady Fielding, Mrs. Robin Dale's mother, "how is your book getting on? The Dean is anxious to know whether you wish to make use of his Latin epitaph in Bohun's monument. I don't think he wants any royalties on it."

"Alas," said Oliver, and heard even as he said the word how silly it sounded, "it is rather held up. Isabel was doing my typing and it isn't everyone's work," which words he felt might wound Isabel to the quick, but unfortunately she did not hear.

Lady Fielding, ignoring these fine shades, said there was a very good woman typist in Barley Street who had done some work for Sir Robert and the Dean and could make almost anything look nice. And cheap too, she added. One and six-pence a thousand words and carbons threepence extra, which sordid details rather revolted Oliver and had no idea what typing cost as Isabel had done his among her other friendly duties at Marling Hall.

"Let's go and see the maze," said Mrs. Robin Dale. "I've never been in one," so she and her husband with Oliver and Isabel went away across the formal garden and Oliver treated the whole party at sixpence a head.

"First right, second left as you are friends of the family," said Lady Cora who was taking the sixpences between her theatrical performances while the old gardener had his tea. "Don't sit on the end of the seat or it tips up. Enjoy yourselves," and the two couples entered upon the adventure of the labyrinth, an adventure always dear to the human heart even if the way is quite simple. But, as we all know, it is humanly impossible to listen with real attention to anyone who is telling you how to get to a place and with the best will in the world you will start in the wrong direction and have to ask again in a few moments. And so it was with Oliver and Isabel, for she with the perfectly ground-less confidence that we often have in the stronger sex had not listened to what Lady Cora said, confident that Oliver would have grasped it, and so it was that they took the wrong turning at once and within a minute were back at the entrance.

"Sixpence more if you want to go round again," said Lady Cora.

"But we haven't been round," said Oliver. "We got out again at once."

"Sixpence each and try again," said Lady Cora, determined that no money should be lost on this entertainment, so Oliver gave her a florin.

"Nothing smaller?" said Lady Cora.

"Well, I have got one shilling, but I rather like them," said Oliver unwillingly.

"So do I," said her ladyship and taking the shilling she let them go on their journey once more.

By this time Oliver was rather cross. He had failed to take Isabel to the middle and he had been, unfairly as he considered, mulcted of a shilling by Lady Cora.

"If we had gone right outside it would have been fair," he said to Isabel, "but after all we only got back to the entrance and we were inside all the time."

"I'm sure Bohun had something to say about labyrinths," said Isabel, amicably desirous to pacify her escort, in which she was completely successful, for Oliver rather pompously said there were two references. One, he said, he would not repeat as it was of a highly embarrassing nature. The other——

"Did we go second left?" said Isabel. "I'm sure we were here only a second ago."

"If I had bits of coloured ribbon I'd tie them on the hedges to warn us," said Oliver, to which Isabel replied that even if they saw them it wouldn't tell them where they were, because they would just be in the wrong place again. Suppressing a strong desire to burst right through the hedges to the centre, which would not have been very difficult so thin they were in places, Oliver pulled himself together and in less than half a minute was back at the entrance. Luckily Lady Cora was collecting six-pences and threepences (children under twelve) from Edna and Doris Thatcher who had come over from Edgewood with all their children of shame and had already collected several male admirers, so Oliver and his companion in misfortune were able to retrace their steps unnoticed and by following Lady Cora's instructions were almost at once in the centre. As there was no sign nor sound of the Dales they had evidently found their way and gone back as they came, quietly and efficiently.

"Not that end," said Isabel, as Oliver was about to sit on the bench. "Lady Cora said it tipped up."

Oliver asked in a dissatisfied way whether she had said which end and it would be safer if they both sat in the middle, which they did and Oliver felt acutely how silly they would look if anyone came, though we suppose he did not think they would look silly if they were alone, as he did not attempt to alter his position.

"We have all missed you at Marling," said Oliver.

"I've missed you too, very much," said Isabel. "It's rather lonely at the Great House. But as soon as the lawyers have tidied up I shall go. It belongs to Robin Dale now, you know."

Oliver asked where she was going, to which she replied that she hadn't at the moment the faintest idea, but it would be near Gatherum she hoped as there was work to do on the Barsetshire Yeomanry for some time to come. The duchess, she said, had held out hopes of a cottage.

"Alas, poor Bohun!" said Oliver.

"But I thought he was finished," said Isabel. "I did that bit again for you. Have you made it any longer?"

"No," said Oliver in a lofty way. "No—it will just have to be an opuscule—your word you may remember. You were asking me about labyrinths in Bohun. I was just going to tell you the couplet when we got back to the entrance for the first time."

Isabel said exactly like Through The Looking Glass when the path gives itself a little shake and Alice is back where she started.

"The lines," said Oliver, disregarding her remark with slightly obtrusive patience, "run,

> 'As through the Body th' amorous Spirit strays,
> So do we in the Labyrinthine Maze,
> Seeking the Centre where the wanton Boy
> Holds us, made one, in his sweet Dam's employ.'"

"Not among his best," he added.

"Do you think not?" said Isabel in a voice shaken by trying not to have the giggles.

"Of course I didn't mean you to think," Oliver began, who had suddenly realised how silly he was.

"I didn't think," said Isabel, very kindly. "And there is something I want to tell you, Oliver. Only the lawyers and Wicks know, and the Omniums of course. To my own great surprise I am rather rich. I'd like you to know before it gets about."

Oliver said nothing. Not that his pride forbade him to press his suit, but when he realised that Isabel was rich he knew quite well that his reason for proposing to her was gone. If he could have descended, a Jupiter in a shower of typewriters upon the forlorn Danae, it might have been a fine gesture. But to have proposed to a girl who admitted she was rich would have filled him with shame. And the more he thought of riches the more he knew that he did not really love Isabel, and selfish though he was he felt that she certainly did not love him. He also found her reference to the Omniums unnecessary.

"I'm very glad," he said, and quite truly. "But I hope it doesn't mean that we have lost you for good. My father and mother will want to congratulate you and you must come to Marling again when you feel like it."

"Of course I will," said Isabel. "And if you have any special work that needs typing, do let me know. It wouldn't take long," which words she spoke without any arrière pensée about the extreme brevity of Oliver's book.

"I know it wouldn't," said Oliver. "Fack is, as my brother-in-law *will* say, that I am a failure. All this talk about Bohun and only an opuscule to show for it. And I don't think I would even have got that done without you. I owe you everything," and even as he spoke he had a curious empty feeling as if he had lost something that he never really had.

Isabel said nothing, for most of what he said was true.

"If I thought I could be of any use to you," said Oliver, urged against his better self by the demon of self-dramatisation, "I would offer you all I have," and he moved nearer to her.

"Don't do that," said Isabel. "Cora said it would tip up," at which they both laughed.

"That's better," said Isabel. "Two proposals in a week would be too much."

"I have *not* proposed to you," said Oliver with a mock dignity that reassured her as to his heart being unwounded. "Who did?"

"Only Wicks," said Isabel. "It was so kind of him, because he thought I was lonely. He seems to have proposed to Effie Crofts too."

"Lord! yes," said Oliver. "It means nothing," and then the Thatchers with their male admirers and all the children of shame came into the centre. The male admirers whistled loudly, Edna and Doris giggled, and the children of shame who were eating ices from cones began to fight, so Oliver and Isabel left the seat and the heart of the labyrinth to the strayed revellers and went out into the garden and over to the ducal quarters for tea.

Between the first and second performances in the theatre Lord Silverbridge would have liked to talk to Isabel about Sergeant Alf Thatcher but as the son of the house he felt he ought to make himself useful and if possible pleasant, both of which he did so successfully that Miss Pemberton who had come over from Northbridge with her friend and lodger Mr. Downing the Provençal scholar said later to Mr. Downing that

Lord Silverbridge reminded her of Guibert le Biau who was de cortez tout confaict.

"Do you think we could go once on the roundabout, Ianthe?" said Mr. Downing.

"Not at my age, Harold," said his Egeria. "If you wish to go I will stand here and wait for you. You know you have not yet answered M. Bontemps' invitation to Lille," for the maire of a small commune in that depressing district, an ardent Félibriste known in literary circles as Numa Garagou, had invited them to celebrate the publication of the volume Féau-Filhz of the great Biographical Dictionary of Provence, financed by Mr. Walden Concord Porter of Porterville, Texas, to which dictionary Miss Pemberton and Mr. Downing devoted most of their time. But sooner than be patiently waited for by Miss Pemberton her lodger went home with her and thought privately of the glory of riding on a cock or even in a swan gondola till she pulled him up sharply for want of concentration.

Lord Silverbridge continued his self-appointed task of looking after people and presently came across Mr. Adams and asked him if his wife was there.

"She's here all right," said Mr. Adams. "She's gone to the Home Farm with her cousin Emmy Graham to see the Duke's shorthorns and I'll probably have to get those girls out with a monkey-wrench. They're having tea with the bailiff's wife I believe."

"Why not come over to us for tea as Mrs. Adams has deserted you," said Lord Silverbridge, who had seen from the tail of his eye Oliver and Isabel going towards his parents' house, and the two men walked across the lawns and round to the back of the servants' quarters, where an old groom was scornfully cleaning the duke's shabby little car. Lord Silverbridge asked if he knew where his father was.

"His Grace is in the old harness-room, my lord," said the old groom, "cussing and swearing like old Staylin. It's that tap, my lord, again. That fellow as came from Barchester doesn't know his right hand from a pig's foot and the tap's leaking worse than ever."

"It's my revered governor being a handy man," said Lord Silverbridge. "If you will excuse me I think I had better see what he is up to," and they wend round to the old harness-room where they found the Duke of Omnium in his shirt sleeves fighting a tap that did not know when it was beaten and was spitting ferocious jets of water at him.

"Here's Mr. Adams, father," said Lord Silverbridge.

"I wish I could shake hands, but I can't," said the duke rather querulously. "That Barchester plumber is a perfect fool. When we had old Balder we never had this trouble. And I can't find where the mains tap is."

"Many's the time I've done a job of that sort when I was a kid," said Mr. Adams, "and though I don't believe in blowing my own trumpet I've not yet met the tap that could down me. May I have a look round, your grace?"

"Do," said the duke. "I can't control this thing much longer."

"No good spoiling my best jacket," said Mr. Adams, "and if you'll excuse me I'll work better in shirt sleeves like you," with which words he took off his coat, folded it neatly, laid it on a mounting block and after a stern look at the tap and the water pipe ran the mains tap to earth about twenty yards away and turned the water off.

"Splendid," said the duke. "How on earth did you find it?"

"Commonsense," said Mr. Adams, "and habit. When I was a youngster I got the stick for pretty well everything I did and didn't do and it sharpens the wits wonderfully. Stood to reason the main water supply being from the reservoir it must come from that side and stands to reason if there's a lot of taps about, as there always is in these old stables, there'd be a mains stopcock somewhere near, so I took a lucky guess and there it was. Have you got the plunger, your grace? You'd better let me have it," and with his apparently clumsy but none the less deft fingers he had reassembled the tap and screwed everything into place in a couple of minutes.

"Now if you'll turn the main tap on again, Silverbridge, we're set," said Mr. Adams.

So Lord Silverbridge, rather frightened of the tap but determined to be brave, successfully turned the water on and when he came back found his father and Mr. Adams in their coats again.

"You'd like a wash now, Adams," said the duke, "and then come and have a cup of tea. The duchess will be glad to meet you. Where's your wife? Silverbridge will find her."

"She's having tea with your bailiff and his wife, your grace," said Mr. Adams. "She and her cousin Emmy Graham. They want to talk about cows."

"Well, that's all right," said the duke, who appeared to think it reasonable that the wife of the M.P. for Barchester and a granddaughter of Lady Emily Leslie should prefer his bailiff and cows to his wife's drawing-room. "Cobbold's a good man on cows. I'll send word over that you are here. And I know what we'll do, Adams. I've got all the maps and plans in the estate room and I'd like you to see them. We'll have a look at the plans of the water supply. I ought to know where those mains taps are. We had a burst pipe last winter and couldn't get a plumber for six hours. It was different when we had our own plumber."

"It was much better," said Mr. Adams firmly. "I'd like very much to see those plans."

"Come along then," said the duke. "My wife shall give you some tea and then we'll go along to the estate office."

The tea party was almost over, for the second performance in the theatre was due to begin in half an hour and as seats were not reserved people were already going into the hall.

The duchess who had heard from her son about his lunch with Mr. Adams had some curiosity to see the Member for Barchester in the flesh and when she heard about his conquest of the tap her heart was completely won.

"I suppose, Mr. Adams, you couldn't find an estate carpenter who undertakes plumbing, could you?" she said, having the instinct of her class always to apply at the top; to ask the Archbishop of Canterbury, for example, when Easter Sunday was, or to write to the Prime Minister—in the days when they were people one could write to—to ask when Parliament was rising, or as in this case to apply to the Member for Barchester, a self-made man of great wealth, employing several thousand people, where to find a plumber.

"Well, your grace, it's not exackly in my line," said Mr. Adams, "but I daresay I could hear of someone."

"Yes, *do*," said the duchess. "And Mr. Adams, don't think it interfering of me if I say that duke and duchess will do very well."

"I take you, duchess," said Mr. Adams, not a whit disconcerted, "and I'm much obliged. I did once buy a book on Etiquette, but it didn't get me anywhere. All the etiquette I know I learnt from Mrs. Belton. She's been a wonderful friend to me."

"The Beltons of Harefield?" said the duchess. "The Beltons are fairly new," her grace continued, as one to whom a couple of hundred years are as nought, "but of course Lacy was a Thorne. You couldn't have a better friend, Mr. Adams. And do tell me about your wife. Her brother Oliver Marling has just been here with Isabel Dale who is a great friend of Silverbridge's and so helpful with his war book. They have all gone down to the theatre. You must come with us, we have a few reserved seats. What is it, Plantagenet?"

"We ought to be going to the theatre, my dear," said the duke. "I want to see that pretty little friend of Cora's who dances so well. I did want to show Adams my sham door, but that can wait."

"Don't be more than five minutes," said the duchess. "You can join us in our seats." And with the remaining members of the party she went over to the theatre.

*   *   *

Lady Cora, Lord Silverbridge, with Mr. and Mrs. Francis Brandon as stars and a few select friends as make-weights were now ready to give the second performance of "Omnium Gatherum" a medley of song, dance and the Aubrey Clover one-act play, *Out Goes She*, with a Palliser cousin as Henley Marlowe (Aubrey Clover's own part), Mrs. Francis Brandon as Mrs. Calliper and her husband as Phil Parradene. Looking through the curtain Lady Cora could see her mother's party in front though her father had not yet come, Mrs. Brandon, with Bishop Joram on one side of her and the Millers from St. Ewold's on the other, Aubrey Clover and Jessica Dean both looking like county people who knew nothing about the stage, the Dean and Mrs. Crawley with the air of people determined to enjoy what they had paid for, Oliver Marling with a woman Lady Cora didn't know; in fact an audience of friends and people from the estate, for the Barchester visitors had mostly gone home by now owing to the badness of the bus service.

"Jeff," said the duchess to her son who was at the piano, doing what in some kinds of song is called an Ad Lib Till Ready.

"Yes, mother?" said Lord Silverbridge, putting the soft pedal down.

"Tell Cora not to wait for your father. He is showing Mr. Adams the library."

Lord Silverbridge nodded, went behind the curtain and almost at once reappeared and began playing again. The curtain went up and the performance began.

We do not propose to give a full account of the entertainment which was, like most of these affairs, on the whole more fun for the actors than the audience, but the second audience was a more intimate one than the first and loyally laughed at its own friends and relations who were thereby spurred to greater efforts.

The first part was a variety entertainment with a good many local jokes and several songs and went down very well. There was an interval while the scene was set for *Out Goes She* and from the noise in the hall it was evident that the audience was enjoying itself very much talking to its own friends whom it could just as well have talked to anywhere else. The duke with Mr. Adams came in and found seats near the duchess.

"Sorry I missed the first part, my dear," said he to his wife. "I took Adams over to the estate office and he got the hang of the water systems in no time. He has put a red mark against all the stop-cocks and things and I want to ask him over one day next week and we'll go over them all together. I really must know these things myself."

"I wish you wouldn't, Plantagenet," said his duchess. "You ruin a suit every time you do other people's work. You remember when you said you would show the new sweep where the kitchen flues were. Thank goodness we've got Wheeler now," for Wheeler the hereditary sweep at Pomfret Towers was famed throughout that part of the world for his knowledge of crooked chimneys and how to dislodge nesting birds with the minimum of inconvenience to all parties concerned and occasionally condescended to oblige outside his own grounds.

"I know, my dear, I know," said the duke. "Adams is a remarkably intelligent man. I showed him my masked door in the old library and he actually asked if he might give me a book for it. He suggested *The Ironmaster*, by Samuel Adams."

"It sounds rather dull," said the duchess, with schoolroom memories of M. Ohnet's *Maître des Forges*. "But most kind of him. Your shelf must be nearly full. Do talk to Mrs. Crawley," which the duke accordingly did.

"What a delightful performance," said Mrs. Brandon to Mr. Miller. "I do think Lady Cora is so clever and her brother plays so delightfully. They are really as good as Francis and Peggy."

Mr. Miller said Indeed, indeed, these young people were very gifted and inquired after the Parkinsons, now firmly established in the Pomfret Madrigal Vicarage.

"People like them," said Mrs. Brandon, turning her lovely eyes on Mr. Miller as if to defy him to disbelieve her. "Mr. Parkinson has such peculiar services, though. I can really only describe them as Free Love," said Mrs. Brandon, "though that isn't exactly what I mean. He walks about the church and lets all sorts of odd people read the lessons and last Sunday he interrupted the service to bring all the Sunday School children in and they stood on the pews with their backs to the altar and sang 'There's a Friend for little children.' And he uses the wrong service. I mean, the one where they try to make the words more refined. I can't tell you how sad it makes me, Mr. Miller. I feel lost all the time."

Mr. Miller, really unhappy for Mrs. Brandon, said Indeed, indeed these innovations were deplorable, but he believed, or rather he tried to believe that God fulfilled himself in many ways.

"But it isn't *God*, Mr. Miller," said Mrs. Brandon, "it's Mr. *Parkinson*. And there aren't any more people in the church than when you were there. I sometimes think I shall have to be an Agnostic because they don't go to church but always tell you they are deeply religious," at which addled statement Mr. Miller could only smile, though very kindly, and say that Mr. Parkinson was young and must be allowed to sow his wild oats.

"But not in *your* church, Mr. Miller," said Mrs. Brandon, and so overcome was Mr. Miller by this fine partisan attitude that he had not the heart to correct Mrs. Brandon. She was then claimed by Bishop Joram who asked her if he could drive her home.

"It would be most kind," said Mrs. Brandon. "I must tell you, Dr. Joram, that I have done a very dashing thing. I am buying a new car for myself. Noel Merton who isn't my lawyer because he is a barrister but his father who is a solicitor is, at least his father's firm, for old Mr. Merton hardly ever comes to the office now but the other partner is very nice, says now is the time to spend money if you have it, because either you won't have it or even if you do there won't be anything to buy. I am going to let Francis have my old one which is still in very good order, because he never remembers to buy one for himself. For though I do *love* the children to enjoy themselves," she continued thoughtfully, "I never seem to be able to have my own car. And as they mostly want to go on somewhere after things or to outstay their welcome, I feel Henry would have liked me to do this."

"Henry?" said Bishop Joram.

"My husband," said Mrs. Brandon with dignity. "He died when Delia was only a baby, but I feel *certain* he would have wished me to have a car of my own. As a matter of fact I never think of him at all," said Mrs. Brandon with great candour, "but I'm sure he would not object to my using his name, wher*ever* he is."

Lord Silverbridge now returned to the piano, the curtain went up, or rather the curtains were drawn jerkily apart, and the audience discovered the Palliser cousin as Henley Marlowe in his service flat with Lady Cora as the very smart maid.

To Bishop Joram and Mrs. Brandon and the Noel Mertons and various other old friends it was like an echo of the Red Cross Fête at the Barchester Town Hall three years ago, when Aubrey Clover had played Henley Marlowe and Jessica Dean had brought the house down with an original and outrageous reading of the smart maid. While Francis Brandon and his wife swayed and dipped in Argentina Tango, Mrs. Brandon thought of that day and how in the evening, at Stories, they had most charmingly become engaged. And now there were three babies and Peggy was prettier than ever and always sweet-tempered. As for Francis, so long as he was kind to Peggy his mother felt it did not really matter if he was not always quite a kind and considerate son. But her mind was made up. The new car was her first move and presently she would perhaps make another move, always thinking of her children's happiness, but also now thinking of her own.

The curtain came down on enthusiastic applause and there

were repeated calls to which Francis and Peggy responded with graceful charm. Then another Palliser cousin began to shout We Want Cora and the whole respectable audience, by now rather above itself, joined in the cry. The curtains were once more drawn aside and Lady Cora came forward in her own clothes but still with her theatrical make-up.

"Good old Cora," shouted the youngest Palliser cousin, by now rather above himself. "Song! Song!" which cry was of course taken up by the audience who were rapidly approaching mass hysteria.

"All right," said Lady Cora. "I don't know anything new, so I'll sing an old one. Ready, Jeff?"

Lord Silverbridge played a chord. Lady Cora said, "Keep the Home Fires Burning," and a kind of polite gasp went up from the audience for this song from that old war which had alas produced little but a bad peace, a feverish flight of years between and another war to end all war; all in vain, all in vain. Lady Cora as we know had no particular voice, but she could please an audience and sang with no kind of self-consciousness as if singing to herself. Half-way through more than one of her hearers felt the sting of unshed tears, the tightening of the throat, the hysterica passio of Lear rising. Cheap sentiment one may say, but tearing the heart-strings. Though it was for an old unhappy far-off war it made many of her hearers think of the war they knew. Lydia Merton sitting by her husband thought of Dunkirk and the dark days of waiting in the brilliant summer weather. Leslie Winter who had come with her husband from the Priory School remembered the cold dark morning when she had plighted her troth to Philip Winter on the low-level plat-form at Winter Overcotes, not to know for weeks and months whether she would ever see him again. The duchess, thinking of this war, remembered the younger son who had been killed on D-Day enjoying every moment of it till the last and looked at her husband whose eyes met hers for an instant. And so in the hall there was hardly one of the audience whose old wounds did not bleed anew; not with that first searing pain, not with the aching misery of the later days, not with the hard brightness that had hidden the scars, but a little because those deaths were now a memory; because beauty vanishes, beauty passes. Martin Leslie sitting safely beside his golden Sylvia, his leg not hurting more than usual, remembered his grandmother and how Lady Emily, speaking of her eldest son Martin's father whom he could hardly remember, had said, "The Flowers of the Forest" and her brilliant hawk's eyes had been misty. Then Lady Cora had finished. For a moment there was complete silence and then another storm of applause. But she did not come back, the applause died down and everyone went out into the garden and most of them went away.

A few friends and the Palliser cousins went back to the castle to drink sherry in the duchess's sitting-room. The duke had asked Mr. Adams who, with his usual good sense, realised that in his own words you might spoil the ship by a ha'porth too much tar and said he must go and find his wife.

"If she's talking with your bailiff, duke," he said, "she'll be there till the cows come home and I've got to keep an eye on her now," so the duke asked him to come again, look at the plumbing and bring his wife, which he promised to do. The duchess reminded him that he was going to find a plumber for her and then he went away. As he came round to the front of the castle where he had left his car, he met Oliver Marling with a tall quite good-looking woman, no longer very young.

"Can I give you a lift?" said Mr. Adams to his brother-in-law.

Oliver thanked him very much and said he was going back with Miss Harvey—Mr. Adams, Miss Harvey—to the Castle for dinner.

"Pleased to meet you," said Mr. Adams. "Any relation of a man called Geoffrey Harvey?"

Miss Harvey said he was her brother.

"Him and I had Words," said Mr. Adams. "About 1944 it was. Tape and Sealing Wax Office."

Miss Harvey said she was sure Geoffrey would be quite devastated if he thought Mr. Adams had been badly treated.

"Don't worry yourself," said Mr. Adams good-humouredly. "If anyone was badly treated it was your brother and I did the treating. The Tape and Sealing Wax Office haven't forgotten it yet. That's one of the things made me decide to leave the Labour Party when I thought it over."

"What a coincidence," said Miss Harvey. "Geoffrey was always a Liberal, but he joined the Labour Party last year. How things do change."

"I suppose he saw more of a future in it," said Mr. Adams, so innocently that Oliver was quite taken in.

Miss Harvey said yes and then thought it was not the best thing she could have said, and looked cross.

Mr. Adams winked at his unfortunate brother-in-law and getting into his car drove away in the direction of the bailiff's house.

"My dear, I hope Lucy is happy," said Miss Harvey looking at Oliver with a sympathy that fascinated and horrified him. "We must hurry, for our evening meal at the Ministry, we do not call it dinner, is at half-past six so that all the staff can get away. Alas, we do not have drinks, but I will give you a glass of sherry in my own quarters and I daresay Her Excellency will come. She is temperamental like all these Slavs, but I jolly her along and she is really delightful au fond. And now, my dear, I must hear *all* about Bohun."

And with this we must leave Oliver for the present. He has not made a very good showing of late and we regret it, for there is so much good in him. If anything can bring him to his senses it will be a course of Frances Harvey, but more we do not at present know.

Lord Silverbridge with great skill cut Isabel out from among the guests and took her off to see what he had been doing with the Case of Sergeant Thatcher.

"Lovely to have a little rest," said Isabel. "I hope I did my duty as a guest. I took Oliver Marling to the Maze and we both got lost. Cora made us pay twice which I still think most unfair."

"So do I," said Lord Silverbridge, and put his hand into his pocket. "May I refund the sixpences? I'll get them out of Cora later on."

"How nice of you, Jeff," said Isabel, "but you mustn't dream of it. After all it's a shilling more for the Conservatives. What fun it would be if you could get into Parliament."

"It would," said Lord Silverbridge, "but we can't afford it and that's that. I met Mr. Miller the Vicar of St. Ewold's this afternoon, who used to be at Pomfret Madrigal and knew Thatcher quite well. He says he was always a difficult fellow but didn't have much chance as his mother ran away with a commercial traveller and his father took to drink and he was brought up by an uncle and aunt who seem to have been blood relations of Mrs. Squeers. They're a queer lot at Grumper's End, all Thatchers and all intermarried with a good deal of gypsy blood."

"Now the Conservative do is over we can really get to work again," said Isabel.

"What did you think of our entertainment?" said Lord Silverbridge.

"I loved it," said Isabel. "How good the Brandons were in the Aubrey Clover play. And Cora too."

"She is a clever girl," said her brother. "What did you think of the Home Fires?"

"I don't exactly know," said Isabel, looking out of the window across to the field where Packer's Royal Universal Derby was being dismantled.

"I couldn't bear to think that it might hurt you," said Lord Silverbridge.

"Hurt me?" said Isabel. "But how?"

"I mean because of John," said Lord Silverbridge. "When they wanted an encore we didn't know what to do and Cora picked that up among a lot of music. We had an idea of getting up a concert of old war songs for the Hospital Libraries and Cora had found a lot of old stuff. I never thought of you till she began to sing."

"And how beautifully she sang," said Isabel. "She *is* a dear creature."

"Then you didn't mind?" said Lord Silverbridge.

"I have never minded since you told me that you had seen John die," said Isabel. "You said he died quickly and didn't look unhappy. That was true, wasn't it?"

"Quite true," said Lord Silverbridge. "He looked a little surprised and then tired and then it was all over. My poor darling."

Isabel looked at him. Their souls were in their names. In an instant Isabel was crying on his shoulder from pure happiness and he was struggling to get his handkerchief out of his pocket to dry her tears.

"Not poor, Jeff," said Isabel.

"Lord! I had forgotten that," said Lord Silverbridge.

"Forgotten what?" said Isabel.

"Your money," said Lord Silverbridge, not however releasing her from an embrace in which she appeared quite content to remain.

"I didn't mean *that* kind of poor," said Isabel. "I meant I wasn't a person who you need be sorry for, because I simply *adore* you. And now you can go in for politics. How pleased your father will be."

Lord Silverbridge did not answer. Partly because he was kissing her hair and uttering words of pure folly. But also because his inner self recognised with approval that he had found exactly the wife that his traditions needed. Rich as riches go now, of as good blood as his family if not better, though not ennobled, one who would recognise the family claims that are now too often neglected or despised and, which is not to be despised either, a beautiful woman.

"And now," said Lord Silverbridge, "let's go and tell the

parents. They will be enchanted. Adams has helped father to put a new washer on the harness-room tap, and this will absolutely make his day."

So they went back to the duchess's room where she and the duke were exchanging the county gossip that they had heard during the day. The Palliser cousins were gradually removing themselves and while they were there the lovers behaved as usual, or at any rate thought they did though the cousin who had played the part of Henley Marlowe afterwards said he knew something was up, but nobody believed him.

"A very pleasant day," said the duke when the last cousin had gone. "I don't know when I've enjoyed a Conservative day more. We must have Adams here again, my dear, and his wife. She was down with Cobbold. He rang me up and said she wants to buy one of our shorthorns and he wouldn't let anyone make him an offer unless he thought they knew their job. Well, Jeff, that was a very amusing play. And now I suppose you and Isabel will be getting on with your Barsetshire book."

"I hope so, father," said Lord Silverbridge. "I want to get on with it, because I have an idea I ought to try for Barchester when we have the next General Election and then I wouldn't have much time."

"I'd like to see you do it, my boy," said his father, "but I don't see how we can manage it."

"What do you think, duchess?" said Isabel.

"I agree with my husband that we can't manage it. On the other hand," said the duchess who though not particularly intellectual had a great deal of worldly wisdom and common-sense, "I think there may be ways and means," and she looked piercingly at her son and his companion.

"If I could help——" said Isabel. "Dear duchess, *may* I help?" Upon which a great noise of everyone talking at once began and everyone became slightly demented and kissed everyone else and the duke blew his nose ferociously, just as if he were an ordinary person.

The duchess, who was eminently practical, then put searching questions to Isabel about the wedding and where she should live until that ceremony, as she said it was quite out of the question for Isabel to go on living alone at the Great House now, but Isabel though very sweet and loving said she would have to stay there till she had dealt with her mother's private affairs and found out from the lawyers exactly where she stood.

"You'd better let the young people settle it their own way, my dear," said the duke and then his son suggested that perhaps the Marlings would act as parents for Isabel, which idea was on the whole pleasing to everyone, though the duchess would have dearly loved to have the wedding at the Castle, as affording more opportunity for fuss.

Isabel had dinner with them and then Lord Silverbridge drove her back to Allington. What they said and how long they took over their parting does not concern us, but it was nearer eleven than ten when Lord Silverbridge set out for Gatherum.

When Isabel was alone she knew she was in a dream. A happy dream, but one that could not endure. Wishing to be reassured she thought of kind Father Fewling who had so helped her when she was struggling with her burden alone. On an impulse she asked for his number. Almost at once she heard his voice.

"Oh, Father Fewling, it's Isabel Duke," she said. "I want to tell you something. I am going to marry Lord Silverbridge."

Father Fewling's voice expressed delight though not much surprise.

"I only wanted to thank you," said Isabel, "because I was in dark despair till I met you and Jeff. And when Jeff told me about John and when you said those things about God and the British Navy, I knew how untrusting I had been. And now I am so happy that I feel I must thank you."

"Not me," said Father Fewling's voice. "But if under God I helped you at all I am profoundly grateful. It was good of you to ring me up. God bless you and keep you and let the light of His countenance shine upon you."

Then Isabel went to bed in a dream and slept dreamlessly all the night.

As Lord Silverbridge drove home he was assailed by doubts as to whether all these things had really happened, or if he had invented them and would find himself back in his mud hovel, but when he saw his parents who had been watering and weeding in the late daylight he knew that everything was real.

"Where's Cora?" he asked his mother. "I haven't seen her since the play."

The duchess said she had gone to dinner with neighbours and said she wouldn't be late and she thought she had heard her car come back. Her brother wanted to tell her his good fortune and went in search of her to the kitchen garden where he thought she might be watering, but it was empty. Thinking of what other occupation she might have he went across the lawn to the maze and there he found her picking up the paper and rubbish with which the public had obligingly littered the ground.

"Beasts!" said Cora, showing her brother two dustbinfuls of revolting refuse.

"Why not let the men do it?" said he, for there were still a few elderly men about the place, a kind of skeleton gardeners. "I've been looking for you everywhere. I wanted to tell you first, except the parents of course. It's about Isabel."

"Darling Jeff, how heavenly," said his sister and hugged him violently.

"It's all too extraordinary," he said. "She loves me. And she wants me to stand for Barchester. It's like a hundred miracles rolled into one. In a way I wish she weren't rich, but it would be silly to go on like that. What's wrong, Cora?" For his sister, sitting down on an upturned wheelbarrow was sobbing with a lack of control he had never before witnessed.

"I'm only so happy about you," said Cora in a muffled voice. "And when we did the Home Fires this afternoon I thought of all my friends. They are all dead. If only I had married Froggy.

He didn't ask me, but I could have made him ask easily. Now one just goes on till one dies. And then I daresay one goes on again."

"Poor old girl," said her brother, not knowing what else to say. "Isabel sent you her love and wants to see you soon."

"Tomorrow, when I've washed my face and forgotten what a fool I've been," said Lady Cora.

"Did you really care for Froggy?" said her brother. "Or don't tell me if you don't want to."

"I could have," she said. "I could have loved all of them. I did love them all. And not one of them is left. And Gerry was killed. I was a fool to sing that song. One never ought to remember anything. Sorry. Let's put the wheelbarrow away. Those men get worse and worse."

In silence they put the wheelbarrow into its shed and went indoors. Lady Cora kissed her brother, asked him to say good-night to her father and mother and went away to her room, to a night of memories and of sighs. But next morning she was so much herself again that her brother did not dare to ask her any more.

After the entertainment it gave Mrs. Brandon considerable pleasure to say that Bishop Joram was going to take her home, by which Francis chose to feel slightly aggrieved, the more so as he was not yet sufficiently without a sense of humour not to have noticed that his mother had her mysterious mischief face as he used to call it.

"How nice this is and quite like old times," said Mrs. Brandon as Bishop Joram's useful little car sped towards Pomfret Madrigal, though what old times she meant we do not quite know and doubt whether she did, but it seemed to please the Bishop.

"I am not driving too fast, am I?" he said, for he was a kind-hearted creature and felt chivalrous towards nearly all women as creatures who needed protection: in which he was the more deceived.

"How kind of you, and indeed not," said Mrs. Brandon, who had practically no nerves and would have been equally composed at twenty miles an hour or eighty. "I suppose in Africa you drove frightfully fast?"

Dr. Joram said on the contrary he rarely did more than twelve to fifteen miles an hour except in the town, owing to the nature of the country, the badness of the roads, and the way the natives would persist in lying in the road to get run over. Mrs. Brandon asked rather vaguely, if it was a suicide pact, or just being religious like Juggernaut. Not at all, the Bishop said. It was merely a form of blackmail. If you ran over them they claimed compensation and if you didn't they pretended to try to kill themselves in front of your door to make you lose face.

"And did you?" said Mrs. Brandon, looking with warm interest at the Bishop's strong face, pleasantly lined by years of work and browner from the years in his sub-equatorial diocese than most of the faces she met.

Certainly not, said the Bishop. No good churchman would allow himself to lose faith, face he meant.

"If they were troublesome I got the head witch-doctor onto them," said Dr. Joram. "He had been at Keble for a year, but gave it up to look after his father's business—it was an old witch-doctor family affair—and I said if I had any nonsense I would report him to the warden. I did once and he flew to Oxford to apologise. After that he ate out of my hand."

Mrs. Brandon thought of saying words to the effect that it was a hand anyone might be pleased to eat out of, but decided not to, and then they talked about the entertainment and how beautifully Francis and Peggy danced and how Lady Cora's song had made them cry and soon got to Stories.

"Will you put drinks in my sitting-room, Rose," said Mrs. Brandon to her faithful and trying old parlourmaid. "And Bishop Joram is staying to dinner with me. Mr. and Mrs. Francis have gone to Northbridge."

"Very well, madam," said Rose, "and Nurse wishes to speak to you but not if it's inconvenient."

"Then she had better come now," said Mrs. Brandon, and Rose sped away to tell the kitchen what a lovely man the Bishop was, and get the drinks.

"Not that it ever is convenient," said Mrs. Brandon, sinking gracefully onto a little sofa, "but it's simpler to get it over. Something quite dreadful must have happened if Rose is on Nurse's side. I often wish they would really quarrel and then one of them would go. Nurse is rather conceited now because Peggy's Nannie is what she calls college-trained and Nurse doesn't hold with it and since the babies had summer colds last week she has done nothing but go about saying it isn't her place to speak. Thank you, Rose. Now, Dr. Joram, will you help yourself. Just a little sherry for me, please." And as she cast her eye over the tray she noticed that Rose had exhumed from the glass cupboard a tumbler of gigantic size and had provided a mountain of ice-cubes. The Bishop gave her the sherry and was putting soda-water into a quite moderate helping of gin when Nurse came in unannounced as was her privilege.

"You know Dr. Joram, Nurse," said Mrs. Brandon. "Have the babies been good?"

Nurse said Mr. Francis's babies were always good. That was, she said, unless anyone upset them. She then paused and the Colonial ex-Bishop was curiously reminded of the dead lull in the middle of a tropical storm, prelude to a fiercer outburst than before.

"What is it now, Nurse?" said Mrs. Brandon, with a calm that her guest found little less than saintly.

"Well, madam," said Nurse, "we all know Mrs. Francis's Nannie gave her notice and then she took it back again and today she's given it again. And she says she is going to young Lady Bond, madam, where men are kept. So I said If you will call foreigners men you can please yourself, Nannie, but take it from me you'll have to look out for yourself and she said she could look after herself quite well and thank goodness she was going to a place where there wouldn't be two mistresses, let alone three. So I thought you'd like to know, madam."

"Who was the third," said Mrs. Brandon, with lively interest.

"Her ladyship was hinting at me, madam," said Nurse, "that's done everything in my power to help and letting her have extra days off and helping with the trays when they had those nasty summer colds and lending her my copy of the *Nursery World* every week. So I was sure you would prefer to know what was going on, madam."

Bishop Joram looked anxiously at his hostess. Had it been a fully armed warrior with his teeth filed to a point and a tommy-gun (for civilisation had spread its beneficent wings over Mngangaland), or even the rival witch-doctor, he would have known at once how to deal with them. But before Nurse he felt like a little boy of five and knew that she probably looked upon him as one.

"Well, we must talk it over, Nurse," said Mrs. Brandon placidly. "I sometimes think I shall give up Stories and take a cottage and then you and Nannie wouldn't see each other so much and she wouldn't trouble you."

Nurse's face grew pale and the Bishop, who had always regarded her as armed in triple bronze saw to his horror that she was preparing to cry.

"Would you expect me to come with you, madam?" said Nurse.

Mrs. Brandon said she supposed so.

"I'm really very sorry," said Nurse desperately, "but I couldn't. It's not that I wouldn't work my fingers to the bone for you, madam, and do the cooking or anything, but if Nannie is going I *can't* leave the dear babies to a stranger. It says in the *Nursery World* only this week any sudden change in the persons around a young child may have serious consequences to its mental stability even producing traumatic conditions and——"

"What are those?" said Mrs. Brandon.

"I'm sure I don't know, madam," said Nurse, "—and other undesirable conditions such as nail biting and bed——"

"Yes, Nurse, I quite see," said Mrs. Brandon, thus earning her guest's undying admiration of her generalship. "Well, we'll talk about it tomorrow. I should miss you dreadfully, of course, but we must consider the babies first. And Mrs. Francis really wouldn't know how to manage them with a new Nannie who might not be all we would wish. May I bring the Bishop up to look at them?"

Nurse, although with swollen eyes and a choked voice, was flattered that a Bishop even if he wasn't a real one (which is her way of putting it, not ours) should visit her young charges and led the way to the night nursery where the three children with little more than a year between them were sleeping the abandoned sleep of infancy, past the plunge of plummet, in seas we cannot sound.

"The lambs," said Dr. Joram in a low voice.

"Heaven," said Mrs. Brandon, gently removing from the eldest baby's rose-petal grasp a rather nasty tooth-brush with a few grey bristles.

"She found it outside the Post Office," said Nurse proudly, "and I couldn't get her to go to sleep without it. She called it Bigabig."

"Clever girl!" said Mrs. Brandon. "I wonder why."

"I'm sure I couldn't say, madam," said Nurse, and then the visitors went back to the sitting-room.

"How *do* you do it?" said Bishop Joram.

"I really don't," said Mrs. Brandon. "It mostly does itself. Well, that's that. I think Nurse will stay with Peggy and then I shall feel quite happy about them."

"But what about you?" said the Bishop.

"I expect I'll find a cottage," said Mrs. Brandon, "and take Rose with me. I can't leave them everything. And I shall be rather glad not to have Nurse, because she is getting a little bullying and that I cannot bear."

"Nor should you have to bear it," said Dr. Joram. "May I speak again about a subject which we agreed a little while ago should not for the present be discussed?"

Mrs. Brandon raised her still lovely eyes to him and dropped them again.

"If your own home is no longer a real home, no matter whose the blame," said Dr. Joram, "will you do me the honour of letting me offer you mine?"

"Nothing else?" said Mrs. Brandon.

"My heart you have had for a very long time," he said. "Ever since I first saw you at the Deanery during the war and you were wearing the dress that looks like a cloud of sweet peas, sitting on the little sofa that only held one."

"But I could have made it hold two," said Mrs. Brandon and as she spoke she moved into the corner of her own little sofa and looked up.

"Thank you, my dearest," said Bishop Joram settling himself beside her. They sat in complete quiet for a while, till Mrs. Brandon suddenly said, "Does it matter my being a widow?"

"Why, dearest?" said the Bishop.

"I don't quite know," said Mrs. Brandon, "but I feel as if St. Paul said something about widows, or it may have been about something else of course, only if he could be disagreeable he always was."

"Well, he can't be disagreeable here," said Bishop Joram. "You must decide everything, dearest. I am ready to do whatever you want and whenever you want it."

"Soon would be best," said Mrs. Brandon, which made her admirer's heart beat furiously. "Oh, will your servants mind?"

The Bishop said they were always complaining that if there were a lady at the Vinery they could have proper dinner parties. "I think," he said, "there is a kind of silent rivalry in the Close Kitchens about who gives the most, or the best dinner parties."

"Then we'll do both," said Mrs. Brandon firmly. "And what shall I call you?"

The Bishop, suppressing an insane professional desire to say N. or M., said as his name was William, perhaps she would use it.

"William," said Mrs. Brandon, her head a little on one side like a bird pecking at something sweet.

"When I first signed my name William Mngangaland I thought it was the proudest moment of my life," said he, "but this is even prouder."

"I think," said Mrs. Brandon cautiously, "that I like it better than Henry. Henry is a sort of name that people you can't remember have. Yes, Rose?"

"Oh please, madam," said Rose, at once scenting romance, "it's Sir Edmund Pridham. Shall I say you're not at home, madam?"

"Of course not," said her mistress. "Ask him to come in."

"Well, Lavinia. How are you, Joram?" said Sir Edmund.

"And some brandy, please, Rose," said Mrs. Brandon.

"Good girl," said Sir Edmund approvingly. "Well, I was passing and thought I'd look in. Where are Francis and his wife?"

Mrs. Brandon said they had gone straight to Northbridge and Bishop Joram had brought her home and Nannie had given notice again and was going to young Lady Bond.

"More fool she," said Sir Edmund.

"And I'm going to let Francis and Peggy have Stories," said Mrs. Brandon.

"More fool you, Lavinia," said Sir Edmund. "Where are you going? You won't find a house like this in a hurry."

"But I might find a different one," said Mrs. Brandon in a dignified way, casting her eyes downwards as she spoke.

Sir Edmund stared for a moment.

"So that's it, is it?" he said. "I wouldn't have thought you had so much sense, my dear. I hope you have considered it seriously though, Lavinia. I'm your trustee, you know."

"You know, Sir Edmund," said Mrs. Brandon with great

dignity, "that I am past child-bearing and Henry's money is all tied up for Francis and Delia after my death," at which Sir Edmund could not help bursting into a rather Restoration laugh, in which Dr. Joram was compelled to join him, though if one can laugh affectionately, at a beloved foolish woman, he did it.

"Well, in that case I'll have another drink," said Sir Edmund pouring an inordinate amount of brandy into his glass, "and be going home. God bless you both."

If Bishop Joram felt that a layman had unfairly got in first he gave no sign of it and Mrs. Brandon got up and kissed her old friend.

"Humph!" said Sir Edmund. "Sort of kiss you'd expect from an aunt. Never mind. Well, good-bye and good luck. And of course I'll give you away, Lavinia. No, Francis doesn't deserve it. His wife does, but that's neither here nor there."

He shook hands warmly with the Bishop and went away.

"I can hear him talking to Rose in the hall. I suppose she's telling him everything," she said resignedly. "What is it, Rose?"

"Excuse me, madam," said Rose, "but Sir Edmund did pass the remark you were going to marry the Bishop and may I say we're all ever so pleased. It's only right, I was saying to Cook, that a lady like you should have a house of her own and a gentleman to look after her. And I'd like to say, madam, that if you aren't suited I'd be glad to come with you. If Nurse is going to stay as Mrs. Francis's Nannie I really couldn't do justice to the silver, madam, nor the glass, and trays for the nursery on days out is what I cannot be expected to do."

"If for once in your life you can hold your tongue in the kitchen, Rose," said Mrs. Brandon very firmly, "and not mention anything to Cook or Nurse or Nannie till I tell you, I expect Dr. Joram will be good enough to have you at the Vinery."

"Thank you, I'm sure, madam, and the Bishop too," said Rose. "Mrs. Simnet, she's my auntie's cousin, says she could do with a nice lady at the Vinery and if there's a good parlour-maid, she said, as can work in with Simnet, she could give her mind to the dinner. Twelve you could manage in the dining-room there, madam. And there's a nice room on the top floor where I could do your ironing and little things."

"Thank you very much, Rose," said her mistress. "And let us know as soon as dinner is ready."

Mrs. Brandon's friends may remember her guardian angel who assisted, in the French sense, with such interest at her mild flirtation with Noel Merton in the hot summer eleven years earlier. So hard-working had her life been in the years between that her angel had rather neglected her, finding little amusement in war-work, or nursery school and no more parties. But some hidden sympathy must have told him that he was needed again, for he was sitting on the ceiling with Dr. Joram's guardian angel, taking in every word of the foregoing conversation.

"I hope yours is good enough for mine," said Dr. Joram's angel. "I've never had a better fellow in my care. Absolutely no trouble at all."

"I'd hardly care for that," said Mrs. Brandon's angel loftily. "Give an angel someone who is a whole-time job, that's what I say. Now I like to have someone who gives me plenty of variety."

"Yours certainly does that," said Dr. Joram's angel so disagreeably that Mrs. Brandon's angel moved away a little.

"Don't push like that," said Dr. Joram's angel. "You'll make me fall down off the ceiling. Now be quiet, there's an angel, I want to hear what they say."

"Only one thing, dearest," the Bishop was saying. "At least two things. First, when shall we tell people?"

"But we have," said Mrs. Brandon. "Sir Edmund knows and will have it all over the county in two day and Rose knows which means that even if she doesn't say anything everyone will know, just by the way she isn't saying it. I shall tell Mrs. Crawley myself. And as for the Palace I cannot think it would interest them any more than they interest me," which for so good-natured a woman as Mrs. Brandon was almost bitter. "What was the other thing, William?"

"I never knew my name could sound so delightful," said the Bishop. "What or when will you tell Francis?"

"I had thought of that too," said Mrs. Brandon, "and just at the moment I don't know. The moment will come. One just someone *knows* things sometimes if one waits, almost like direct inspiration if that is what I mean."

"Sensible woman," said Mrs. Brandon's angel.

"She didn't mean *you*," said the Bishop's angel loftily.

"Whatever you do will be perfect," said the Bishop.

And then Rose announced dinner with such an air of bedding and wedding that Mrs. Brandon caught the Bishop's eye and they both went out of the room laughing.

"È finita la commedia," said the Bishop's angel.

"Affectation. And Conceit," said Mrs. Brandon's angel. "And as well you know there is no end to anything, anywhere. Are you coming?"

And as the room was now empty they rose on strong wings towards their infinite eternal dwelling and were soon lost in the golden mist of the setting sun.

COLOPHON

This book is being reissued as part of Moyer
Bell's Angela Thirkell Series. Readers may join
the Thirkell Circle for free to receive notices
of new titles in the series as well as a newsletter,
bookmarks, posters, and more. Simply send in
the enclosed card or write to the address below.

The text of this book was set in Caslon, a typeface
designed by William Caslon I (1692-1766). This
face designed in 1725 has gone through many
incarnations. It was the mainstay of British
printers for over one hundred years and
remains very popular today. The version used
here is Adobe Caslon. The display faces are
Adobe Caslon Outline, Calligraphic 421,
and Adobe Caslon.

Composed by Alabama Book Composition,
Deatsville, Alabama.

County Chronicle was printed by RR Donnelley,
Bloomsburg, Pennsylvania on acid-free paper.

Moyer Bell
Kymbolde Way
Wakefield, RI 02879